"No one has ever died or been seriously injured on my watch."

Jesse wasn't sure why Abby was telling him this. "I can appreciate that."

"Eighty percent of the people I guide up here are men, and every single time, I have to prove myself and be questioned in a way that my brothers never are."

Now he knew why she was so upset with him. "I'm sorry I questioned your choice."

"It's just that it gets old after a while. What I did back there probably kept us alive."

"I never should have dragged you into all this. It's just that I couldn't get up here on my own. I would have died."

"Well, whether I like it or not, we're in this together. I can't in good conscience just walk away from you, and I kind of think those men would kill me just as fast as they'd kill you."

He felt a rush of gratitude toward her. "Thank you, Abigail."

"I will get you off this mountain alive."

DANGEROUS MOUNTAIN MISSION

USA TODAY BESTSELLING AUTHOR

SHARON DUNN

&

KELLIE VANHORN

Previously published as *Wilderness Secrets* and *Fatal Flashback*

LOVE INSPIRED
INSPIRATIONAL ROMANCE

LOVE INSPIRED®

INSPIRATIONAL ROMANCE

Recycling programs for this product may not exist in your area.

ISBN-13: 978-1-335-46917-5

Dangerous Mountain Mission

Copyright © 2021 by Harlequin Books S.A.

Wilderness Secrets
First published in 2018. This edition published in 2021.
Copyright © 2018 by Sharon Dunn

Fatal Flashback
First published in 2019. This edition published in 2021.
Copyright © 2019 by Kellie VanHorn

This edition published by arrangement with Harlequin Books S.A.

For questions and comments about the quality of this book, please contact us at CustomerService@Harlequin.com.

Love Inspired
22 Adelaide St. West, 40th Floor
Toronto, Ontario M5H 4E3, Canada
www.Harlequin.com

Printed in U.S.A.

CONTENTS

Ever since she found the Nancy Drew books with the pink covers in her country school library, **Sharon Dunn** has loved mystery and suspense. Most of her books take place in Montana, where she lives with three nearly grown children and a hyper border collie. She lost her beloved husband of twenty-seven years to cancer in 2014. When she isn't writing, she loves to hike surrounded by God's beauty.

Books by Sharon Dunn

Love Inspired Suspense

Montana Standoff
Top Secret Identity
Wilderness Target
Cold Case Justice
Mistaken Target
Fatal Vendetta
Big Sky Showdown
Hidden Away
In Too Deep
Wilderness Secrets
Undercover Threat

True Blue K-9 Unit

Courage Under Fire

Texas Ranger Holidays

Thanksgiving Protector

Visit the Author Profile page at Harlequin.com for more titles.

WILDERNESS SECRETS

Sharon Dunn

Trust in the Lord with all thine heart; and lean not unto thine own understanding. In all thy ways acknowledge him, and he shall direct thy paths.
—*Proverbs* 3:5–6

To my Lord and Savior, counselor and king, who makes all things new and is a God of second chances.

ONE

Fit to be tied.

That was the phrase Abigail Murphy's grandmother had used, and it was how she felt right now as she stalked toward the trees that would lead her back to civilization. The weight of her backpack seemed to increase as she hiked. Abigail adjusted the shoulder straps, lifted her chin and tried not to obsess over the notion that her client—Jesse Santorum—had not been completely forthright with her. As a wilderness guide, she worked with all kinds of people. But Jesse had gotten under her skin.

It had taken three days to hike up to the remote area where Jesse said he wanted to fish. He'd been tense the whole time, insisting that they put in long days to get to the destination. But once they stood on the shores of shimmering Crystal Lake, fishing seemed to be the last thing on his mind.

Four days ago, when Jesse had walked into the office of Big Sky Outfitters, his request had seemed strange from the get-go. He needed to be guided into the lake, but he didn't require her services to be guided out. He'd been up-front with her about not needing her to get him back out, but usually when a client wanted to improve their skills, they asked that the guide stay close in case they got lost.

She would have refused his request if it hadn't been the off-season, if this hadn't been the first time she was left alone to run the business while the owners, Heather and Zane, had gone on their honeymoon. She wanted to prove to her new employers she was worth her salt. Though she'd worked as a guide since she was a teenager in Idaho, she was new to this part of Montana.

Being a female guide meant she was always in a perpetual state of having to prove herself, anyway. She'd taken the crisp hundred-dollar bills Jesse had fanned out on the desk and made him sign a waiver that Big Sky Outfitters was not responsible if he got lost on his way back into town. She'd taken all the precautions. She'd left him with the satellite phone in case he did need help.

Then she prayed her bosses would be happy with her decision and nothing disastrous would come of it.

Abby pulled herself from her negative thoughts and took in her surroundings. She was only a few yards from the edge of the forest.

Five crows fluttered up from the edge of the trees. Their wings flapped in the breeze. Something had scared them.

Abby stopped as the hairs on the back of her neck stood at attention. She listened. Maybe an animal had alarmed the birds. Her heartbeat revved up a notch. This high up in the mountains, it could be something as benign as a deer, or as dangerous as a mama bear with cubs. Because it was spring, the bears would be coming out of hibernation, hungry and looking for food. She didn't want to be a bear appetizer today.

She turned back to look up at the mountain peak, where Jesse said he was going to hike to get the *lay of the land*. Those were his actual words: *lay of the land*. What did that have to do with fishing?

She clenched her jaw. She was no longer responsible for him. Why, then, did she feel like he wasn't telling her the whole truth? Why did it make her so mad? Maybe it was just because her trust in men had been broken to pieces in the last month.

She was still raw from her breakup with Brent. After three years and an engagement ring, he had started dating another girl in the church choir behind her back. When Brent got the job with the US Forest Service, she'd followed him out here to Fort Madison with the promise that they would be married within six months. She'd left her family and the small town in Idaho where they'd both grown up for a shattered dream.

Abigail stomped closer to the tree line, unable to shake off the tightening in her chest. Stupid Brent. How could she have been so naive? *Just because a man holds a girl's hand in church every Sunday doesn't mean he'll be faithful.* At least she'd dodged a bullet and found out before they were married. Tears warmed her eyes and she sniffled. That didn't make the heartache go away.

She glanced one more time up the mountain where Jesse had gone. She couldn't see him anymore. She had half a mind to go up there and demand an explanation. She turned and took several more steps toward the trees.

Let it go, Abby.

This was just about the pain of the breakup. Pain too easily turned to anger, and she was considering taking it out on the person in closest proximity, namely Jesse. She stomped forward. Getting into an argument with a client was never a good plan.

If he wanted to navigate himself down the mountain, fine. If he had never intended to go fishing, fine.

The truth was, she had never experienced betrayal at the level of Brent's. Her father had been a good man, a faithful man who had taught her everything about wilderness survival, just like he'd taught her three older brothers. Her throat tightened, and she swallowed to push down the heartbreak that kept nagging at her.

Would she ever be able to trust a man again?

She stopped abruptly when she heard a noise coming from the trees. A sort of rustling and moving around, almost indistinguishable from the other forest sounds. Animals were usually stealthier as they moved through the forest.

And then a sound that resembled a grunt reached her ears.

Her breath caught. Her heart pounded.

That didn't sound like a bear or a deer. The noise was human.

DEA agent Jesse Santorum perched on the mountain peak and drew the binoculars up to his face. At this high point, he had a view of the landscape down below to the west and to the east. To the west, he saw the woman who had guided him up here headed toward the trees. Abigail Murphy walked with a determined stride despite the weight of the pack she carried. Even at this distance, he could see her long blond braid flopped over the backpack. She walked with such intensity, almost like she was mad.

Though he'd been up-front with her, she'd seemed agitated that he only required her services to get him to this point. In fact, she had been a little huffy toward him for the three days they'd been together. She seemed distracted, as well. At one point, she'd led him down the wrong trail, and they had to backtrack several miles.

He hated not being totally honest with her about why he'd come up here, but he had no choice. For her own safety, it was better that she didn't know the real reason he was in these mountains. He'd needed her expertise to get to this remote location. He told her only part of the story to keep her out of danger.

The truth was, he had a different way to get out other than hiking. He turned and stared through the binoculars to the east. Camouflaged with tree branches, the downed drug plane was right where Lee Bronson, another DEA agent, had said it would be. If he had told Abigail about the plane, it would have made her a target. The cartel would stop at nothing to get information out of people.

He had a pilot's license. His plan was to fly the plane out. It was Lee's fingerprints all over the drugs, not his. The hard drive that contained the original photographs and audio tape that Lee had doctored and given to the DEA was in there, too.

While they'd been running an operation down in Mexico, Lee had been hit with a fatal bullet. His dying confession was that he had framed Jesse for the drugs he'd stolen. Now the DEA thought Jesse was the turncoat, and the cartel was after him for the drugs Lee had taken for personal gain. He'd gone rogue, not knowing who would believe him at the agency and who would turn him in. Agents in the field who worked with Jesse knew his character, but he was uncertain how much Lee had poisoned the higher-ups in the organization against him. If he had evidence, he might be able to clear his name.

He glanced back down to where Abigail was about to disappear into the trees. She stopped and lifted her head, as though she'd heard something.

Two men emerged from the forest and grabbed her, dragging her back into the evergreens.

His heart squeezed tight as he bolted up from his hiding place. He grabbed his handgun from the back-pack where he sat it on the ground, and raced down the mountain. He'd sent her away to protect her, to en-sure her safety.

Maybe those men who'd gone after Abigail lived up in these mountains and would be aggressive toward anyone because they weren't used to people.

As he sprinted around the rocks, navigating the steep incline with ease, he realized that a showdown with crazy mountain men would be a best-case sce-nario. At the back of his mind, he wondered if the car-tel had tracked him to Montana because they desired revenge and wanted their product back.

Oh, God, let that not be the case.

He slowed down as the terrain leveled off, seeking cover behind rocks and bushes. He entered the forest. With his weapon drawn, he pressed his back against a tree and listened for any sound that might be out of place.

He took in several ragged breaths and then moved

deeper into the forest. His heart drummed in his ears and his muscles tensed, ready for a fight.

He swiped any images of violent things happening to Abigail from his mind. He was no good to her if he let himself be distracted by his own fear. He needed to use the fear to focus, to stay strong, to keep any harm from coming to an innocent woman like Abigail.

With his gun raised, he took one careful step forward. A sort of crashing sound to his right caught his attention. He eased toward where the noise had come from. Through the trees, he saw a flash of movement and color.

He stopped when he heard voices.

A male voice said, "You two are in this together."

"I don't know what you're talking about." Abigail's words were filled with anguish. "I was hired to guide him up here."

Jesse pressed his back against a tree and closed his eyes. This was the exact opposite of what he wanted to happen. He had to get Abigail away from these men.

The same male voice responded, "You're protecting him."

"No, I was hired to do a job. That's all I know," she said.

"You will take us to him," the other man shouted.

Why hadn't Abigail said that she'd last seen him going up the ridge? Was she trying to protect him at the expense of her own safety?

"Please, let me go. I don't know anything. I dropped him off by the lake. He was going to do some fishing. I don't know anything. Who are you, anyway?"

"We ask the questions."

The second male voice piped up. "I bet we can use her to lure him out."

Jesse squeezed his eyes shut and gripped his gun even tighter. How dare they use her as bait?

"How do we know he's not sitting in the cockpit of that plane?" asked the first voice.

"Nothing's shown up in the sky yet. Besides, he's not going to leave his partner behind."

"I'm not his partner. I told you that. Please, just let me go. I won't say I saw you."

Jesse stepped a little closer to assess exactly what he was dealing with. He crouched and moved toward the voices, one careful step at a time. When he was close enough, he hid behind a tree and peered around it.

There were three men. One of them held a rifle and wore a backpack. His job appeared to be guarding and watching. He walked the perimeter around Abigail and the other two men.

Jesse's heart squeezed tight when he saw Abigail on her knees, her head down. They must have dumped her backpack somewhere. At least she wasn't tied up.

Both of the men standing over her were muscular and probably in their twenties. One of them had pulled a handgun from a holster and paced back and forth in front of Abigail. His hair was dark and slicked back, and he had a tattoo on his neck.

The other had bleached blond hair and a deep tan. He reminded Jesse of one of those men who appear on the cover of romance books at the checkout counter, kind of a pretty boy. He, too, had a gun, but it was not drawn, and their two backpacks were propped against a tree.

How was he going to get in there and rescue her?

"We would have been able to track him to the plane

if Eddy here hadn't gotten lost." Pretty Boy pointed at the guard.

The guard—Eddy—spoke up. "You wouldn't have gotten anywhere without my skills." Eddy had a low, deep voice, and every word he spoke seemed to contain a threat.

Jesse assessed that Eddy was probably the most dangerous of the three men. He saw murder in his eyes. But the dark-haired man appeared to be the one in charge. The neck tattoo, a scorpion, meant that these men were connected to the drug trade.

A plan sparked inside Jesse's head. He stepped back from the unfolding scene, then ran as fast as he could. When he got some distance away, he shouted, "Abigail, where are you?"

He bolted from the clearing where he'd made himself known, running in a wide arc back toward the men holding Abigail. Hopefully, at least one of them would run to find him. Then he'd have only two men to deal with.

He heard one man shout something at the other, their voices getting farther away. He came toward the area where Abigail was being held. Sure enough, only Pretty Boy had been left to watch her.

He waited until Pretty Boy's back was turned, leaped into the clearing and hit the back of his head with the butt of his gun. The man crumpled to the ground.

The voices of the other two men drew nearer. From their angry chatter, it was clear they realized they'd been tricked.

Jesse grabbed Abigail's hand. Fear was etched across her features.

"You're coming with me." He pulled her to her feet and sprinted away.

As he pushed through the trees, he let go of her hand. The steady pounding of her footsteps told him she was keeping up.

The voices of the men grew louder, filled with rage. One of them barked orders at the other two. Abigail and Jesse neared the base of the mountain peak that would lead them to the plane.

Jesse glanced over his shoulder. The man with the rifle, the one they called Eddy, had ditched his backpack and was taking aim with the rifle.

The rifle shot pummeled the silence.

Abigail did not even stutter in her steps. She only increased her pace, so she was now running beside him.

There was a cluster of evergreens at the base of the mountain that provided them with a degree of protection. He slowed, tiring from the intensity of the run and needing oxygen. Then he stopped altogether to take in a deep breath.

She quit running, as well. Sucking in air between each word, she asked, "Where are we going?"

"I have a plan. Trust me."

Her face blanched, and a curtain seemed to fall over her eyes. "*Trust* is the biggest word in the English language."

Pain seemed to undergird her words. There was no time to consider what was going on with her emotionally. "Those guys are out to kill us. I can get us out of here." He touched her elbow. "We need to keep moving."

He pushed himself off the tree he'd been leaning against and sprinted through the evergreens.

She followed behind him. He stayed in the trees, trying to get a little more distance between them and their pursuers, before they could veer back out in the open and head up the mountain.

They had to get to that plane and get it off the ground before the thugs caught up with them. It was their only way out.

He burst out into the open, where the incline grew steeper. At first, they were able to keep up a solid pace. But rocks and the cliff-like slant of the mountain slowed them, so they were climbing more than running and had to reach out for handholds as well as stable places to put their feet.

Rocks rolled down the incline, crashing into each other. This was much tougher going than how he had initially climbed the mountain. The peak was not even visible yet. He craned his neck, scanning the tree line below, half expecting to see Eddy with his rifle.

It appeared that Eddy had not followed them into the trees. That fact was troubling. It meant Eddy and the others might be headed up the mountain on a different route. Maybe one that would get them to the peak faster. They risked being ambushed.

The plane was camouflaged enough that it was not easily spotted from a distance. He doubted that even if the men got to the plane first, they would leave him and Abigail alive. They were witnesses. If Lee had set things up to make Jesse look guilty to the DEA, he might have been feeding lies to the cartel, as well.

As he was dying, Lee confessed that his plan had been to sell the drugs slowly, so as not to draw attention. It made sense that if he didn't want to be looking over his shoulder wondering if the cartel was after him, he would have Jesse take the fall for him. Lee had started to explain more, but he'd died before he could finish.

No, these three thugs would not leave until they knew he and Abigail couldn't talk. This wasn't just about getting their product back. It was about revenge for being crossed.

TWO

Abigail's leg and arm muscles burned as she reached up toward a rock that looked like it was stable. "This is getting too steep. We can't climb much farther without gear. We need to move that way." She pointed south.

Off in the distance, she saw the forest where Jesse had helped her get away from the three men bent on violence. Though she didn't see the men anywhere now, the memory of what she'd just been through made her shudder.

"Is there some other way?" asked Jesse. "Those men are probably going to be coming from that direction."

Even though her heart was already pounding from the adrenaline and exertion, it sped up even more from uncertainty. What was going on here? She could not process what had just happened.

Who was Jesse, anyway, and why were those men after him? Why did they think she was somehow involved in whatever had really brought him up here?

"We'll be stuck here if we don't move laterally. It only gets steeper if we head north." She didn't wait for his reply before she stepped sideways, seeking less treacherous ground. "I assume we're moving up this mountain to get to the plane those men mentioned?" Her voice was filled with accusation.

She didn't trust Jesse. She didn't know what he was up to. The only thing she knew for sure was those three men wouldn't flinch at killing her. And Jesse had risked his own safety to get her away from them. Getting to that plane seemed like the only way she would make it out alive.

Jesse didn't respond to her question about the plane.

All of this felt so wrong. How had she gotten into such an ugly mess? Why hadn't she trusted her gut feeling about Jesse, that he was up to something? Because the person she trusted the least right now was herself.

After Brent's grand deception, the new rule she operated under was that nothing was as it appeared. She wasn't a good judge of character.

Even though Jesse had risked his own life to get her away from those violent men, it didn't mean he wasn't a criminal, as well.

She walked carefully on the rocky, steep terrain until it leveled off a little bit, allowing her to climb upward. There were fewer rocks and jagged cliff faces and more grass on this part of the mountain. Even a few struggling junipers, trees that were more like bushes, dotted the landscape. Their tangled trunks and branches grew low to the ground. The breeze ruffled her hair as she focused on moving up the mountain. Silence surrounded her.

Then Jesse dived to the earth, taking her with him. Her stomach collided with the hard ground. She felt the weight of his hand on her back. "What's the big idea?"

"They're down there," he whispered. He rolled away

from her and crawled toward a juniper tree, peering through its branches.

She slipped in beside him. Two of the three men, Eddy and the blond man, huffed up the mountain at a steady pace. Eddy still held his rifle. She didn't see the dark-haired man.

Her heart squeezed tight. Growing up and in her line of work, she'd stared down a grizzly bear and an angry moose. But the terror that invaded every molecule of her body right now was more intense than anything she'd ever experienced. Fear threatened to paralyze her. She couldn't take a deep breath or think of what their next move should be.

They'd be spotted as soon as they left the cover of the juniper tree.

Jesse glanced one way and then the other, then looked up toward the mountain peak. He grabbed her hand and squeezed it. "Let's go for it." He locked her in his gaze for a moment.

She saw courage in those brown eyes. He gave her a half nod and then patted her shoulder as if to say "you can do this."

He burst to his feet. She did the same. He ran in a zigzag pattern, making his way toward a rock outcropping that might provide a degree of protection.

Abby pumped her legs as her lungs filled with air.

It took several minutes before the first rifle shot shattered the mountain silence. Judging from the sound, the bullet had come from pretty close to her left.

Inwardly she cringed, but she kept running, pushing up the mountain.

The sound of a bullet propelled out of the barrel of a rifle and moving through space, which she had heard a thousand times in her life, sent an unfamiliar wave of terror through her. She had never been shot at. She had never been the prey. She had been with her brothers when they went hunting and had witnessed the terror an animal felt when it thought it would die. A deer wounded by a bullet, normally a passive animal, would charge you to save its life.

Now she understood what it meant to battle against a death that seemed imminent. How intensely she felt the need to survive, to stay alive.

She lifted her head as she headed up the mountain. She could see the peak, twenty steep yards above her.

Jesse maneuvered so he was between her and Eddy. Was he doing that to protect her from the incoming bullets?

Another shot zinged through the air.

She kept running, praying that the bullets would not find their target. Once they were down on the other side of the mountain, they'd have a measure of safety until Eddy got to the top of the peak.

When she glanced over her shoulder, Eddy and the blond man were closing the distance between them. Both men seemed to be in good shape and weren't tiring at all.

The peak drew closer. They might make it after all. She willed herself to run even faster.

She darted out, separating from Jesse as she scrambled up the mountainside.

Another shot broke the silence around them. This one seemed to have gone wild.

She reached the peak. Jesse was right at her heels.

"There." He pointed down at the other side of the

peak, at the tree line where the forest butted up against a flat meadow.

She wasn't sure what he was indicating. She didn't see anything that looked like an airplane. They made their way down the mountainside and sprinted across the meadow. As they got closer, she saw now that there was a small plane camouflaged by evergreen branches.

Jesse arrived at the airplane first. He pulled away enough branches to open the cockpit door. She continued to yank away the branches to allow visibility through the front windshield. The plane was a small bush model designed to land in less-than-perfect conditions and terrain.

Movement at the top of the mountain peak drew her attention. Eddy had made it to the top and was lining up another shot, while the blond man jogged down the mountain toward them.

Jesse climbed into the plane.

She ripped away several more branches before yanking open the copilot door and slipping into the seat.

Jesse had flipped several switches. Lights on the control panel blinked on, but she did not hear the rumble and whir of an engine firing up.

Abigail was out of breath from running so hard. "Do you know what you're doing?"

Jesse continued to flip switches on the control panel. "I have a pilot's license. This thing hasn't been fired up for a long time. It's gonna take a minute."

Through the windshield, she could see that the blond man had made it to the base of the mountain and was now running across the meadow. He'd have to get within feet of them to make a shot with a handgun count. Eddy, who was halfway down the mountain, lifted the rifle and peered through the scope.

Her heartbeat drummed in her ears and she gripped the armrest a little tighter.

The engine roared to life and Jesse taxied forward. The plane wobbled a bit on the uneven ground.

Eddy gave up on making the shot from where he was perched and jogged toward a rock, where he propped his rifle to steady it.

The blond man was less than ten yards from them.

Jesse pulled a handgun from inside his jacket. "You know how to shoot, right?"

"Of course." Perhaps it was the severe tension of the moment, but she almost laughed out loud. "My dad taught me."

He handed her the gun. "Pretty Boy is coming up on your side."

"Is that what you call him?" She looked again to see that the blond man, Pretty Boy, had drawn even closer. As the plane gained speed, Pretty Boy took aim at her window. The plane bumped along. She opened the copilot door and fired off a shot that sent Pretty Boy to the ground. He got right back up. He must not have been hit.

The plane lifted off. When they were about forty feet off the ground, they flew right over Eddy, who was scrambling to line up a shot.

The plane was slow in gaining altitude. Jesse eased the throttle on the pedestal. When she peered out the front windshield, it looked like they wouldn't clear the tops of the trees.

Jesse stared straight ahead. "Come on, baby. You can do this for me."

As they flew over the tops of trees, she thought she heard branches brushing the underside of the airplane.

Abby let up on the death grip she had on the armrest of the seat and released the breath she didn't realize she'd been holding. "We made it."

He turned to her. She liked the way a spark came into his brown eyes when he smiled. "Yes, we made it."

She unclicked her seat belt and turned around to see what kind of cargo was in the plane. A tarp had come off what looked like neatly stacked rectangles of something. She leaned over the seat to get a better look.

Jesse's face blanched. "It's not what you think."

Her breath caught in her throat. The tarp had been covering what looked like bricks of some kind of drug. A mixture of fear and anger swirled through her. "And what am I supposed to think?" Men couldn't be trusted on any level. She was in an airplane with a criminal.

"Abigail, I can explain," he said.

She slammed a hand on her hip. "I just bet you can explain." All the anger she felt over Brent's betrayal flooded back through her. What Jesse had done was even worse. Why was this happening? Did she have a sign on her forehead that said she was okay with being deceived by men?

The plane began to wobble.

"Face forward in your seat, put your seat belt on." Jesse said in a raised voice.

One wing dropped lower than the other. She secured herself in the seat. "What's wrong with the plane?"

Jesse clicked some switches on the instrument panel. "Either we're having engine trouble or Eddy was able to hit the plane, and we just didn't hear it over the sound of the motor." He stared through the windshield. "Either way, I'm going to have to crash-land this baby."

Abigail's heart seized with terror as she stared through the windshield, watching the treetops grow ever closer.

Jesse stared out at the ground below as the plane lost altitude. He searched the landscape for a flat spot that could serve as a landing strip. What he saw was mostly forest and mountains.

"You know this area. Is there any place close by that would be flat enough to land on?"

Abigail stared through the front windshield. It took her a moment to respond. "Everything looks different from up here. Veer off to the west. I think there's a grassy patch on the other side of that cluster of trees." Her voice trembled as she spoke, a sign that revealed the level of fear she was battling.

The plane continued to sputter and lurch up and down as though traveling on waves. Jesse changed course. He dropped altitude as they drew near to the trees. He could see the flat spot Abigail had referred to. When he checked the gauges, he saw that they had lost substantial fuel since takeoff. The gas tank might have been hit. But some other damage was making it hard to keep the wings level.

The plane drew even closer to the ground, skimming the treetops. The strip of land was not very long. He'd be pushing it to try to get the plane stopped before they ran into the trees on the other side.

He nose-dived the plane, then leveled it off and dropped the landing gear. The wheels touched the ground, and the plane bumped along. The landing was so rough his body felt like he was being shaken from the inside and the outside at the same time.

The aircraft remained on the ground, but continued to rumble toward the trees. The entire cockpit vibrated as the trees drew closer. The nose of the plane shot through them. They rolled along, cutting through the trees that were far apart. Branches snapped until the larger trees served as a sort of net that stopped them. The body of the plane thundered and shook.

Both of them sat, clinging to their chairs while the dust settled, and the plane stopped creaking and groaning.

"If there's a fuel leak, there could be a fire," Jesse said. "You need to get out." He had to find that hard drive, or all of this would be in vain. Lee had died before he could tell Jesse where in the plane he'd hidden it.

Abigail leaned to push on her door. "My door won't open. There's a tree in the way." Her voice was filled with anguish. She slumped back in her seat and stared at the ceiling. Her lower lip quivered.

Jesse reached over and stroked her shoulder. "It's all right. We're on the ground now." He tried to sound reassuring, but they were far from being, literally or figuratively, out of the woods. He stood up from his seat and took a step toward the cargo area. "You can get out from my side."

"And what are you going to do?"

Her accusatory tone got under his skin. He was an honest man. "There's something I need to locate."

"You said yourself this plane could catch on fire."

He had no time to argue with her. "I'll explain later. Get outside and tell me if you can assess why we went down." He didn't mean to sound harsh, but time was of the essence.

She scowled but shifted over to his seat and pushed open the door.

Jesse scanned the cargo area. He flung open several storage drawers, not finding anything that looked like a hard drive. Maybe Lee had taped it underneath the control panel. He hurried toward the nose of the plane and ran his hands underneath the control panel. Nothing. He flung open a storage box behind the co-pilot seat and rifled through the contents. Not there.

The pilot-side door screeched open and Abigail stuck her head in. "There are flames shooting out."

He stopped his mad search long enough to register what she had said. A thunderous noise that sounded as though it was contained within a bubble surrounded him. A small explosion from the fire. More, bigger explosions might follow.

He needed to find that hard drive.

Smoke filled the interior of the plane. He coughed. His vision blurred.

He felt Abigail grab his hand and drag him out of the plane.

When his vision cleared, he saw a wall of flames by the plane's engine. Smoke began to rise in the air. He coughed, feeling a sense of defeat.

He hadn't found the hard drive. The cartel would be set on revenge even more because of their loss of product. He wasn't sure they had fired shots at the airplane. It didn't seem like they would risk the drugs burning up, but then again, if he got away in the plane they'd lose the drugs for sure and he could identify the three men.

Abigail rose to her feet. "It looks like it's too wet for the trees to catch on fire. The fact that it's been a wet spring will keep the fire from spreading." She still sounded shaken and upset.

Already the fire was dying down. That single burst of flame must have consumed all the oxygen and fuel. Part of the plane would still be intact when the flames died down, though the interior had filled with smoke.

Smoke rose up in the air. Probably not enough to be noticed by anyone in Fort Madison, the little town they'd hiked in from. The three men who had been after them would see it and know where they were located. They hadn't flown that far before landing.

Still trying to clear his mind, he placed his hands on his hips. What now? They needed to get off this mountain before the thugs found them. "Can you guide me back down to Fort Madison?"

She crossed her arms and glared at him, then angled her body so she had a view of the smoldering plane.

"Look, I understand your suspicions, and I'm sorry I wasn't up-front with you." The less she knew the better, for her own safety. "I'm a drug enforcement agent. I was set up by another agent so it looks like I was working with drug dealers. I needed to get this plane back. It has evidence that could clear me."

"And you came up here all by yourself? Don't you people usually work as a team? Even if you are a DEA agent, I'm sure they end up on the wrong side of the law all the time."

Without the evidence, he had no idea who in the home office would even believe that he'd been framed. As far as the agency was concerned, he'd gone rogue. Though DEA work involved a level of deception with undercover work, he knew it was for the cause of justice. He was a man who always tried to do the right thing. It bothered him that his character had been so smeared by Lee's frame-up. The only thing that bothered him more right now was the way Abigail was looking at him with suspicion.

"Look, we both need to get out of here and back to civilization as fast as possible." He took a step toward her.

Her mouth twitched, and she narrowed her eyes at him.

"Please trust me. I'm one of the good guys."

"*Trust* you?" The word seemed to upset her, when he had hoped that it would build a bridge between them.

"Abigail, what are you going to do? Those men are armed and they still have gear and food."

Again, she studied him for a long moment, probably considering her options.

He took a step toward her. "I need your expertise to get out of these mountains as fast as possible, and you need my protection in case those guys do catch up with us."

She stared at him, her mouth drawn into a tight line. "I wish I had my backpack." She turned sideways in the direction from which they had come.

He let out a breath. At least now she seemed to be in problem-solving mode. Maybe she was starting to come around, regardless of what she might think of him. "Going back for your gear is not an option. The fire is dying out in that plane. I'll go back in there and see if there's anything we can use."

A raindrop hit his nose. Good for drowning the fire, not so good for staying dry.

Abigail jogged toward the forest. "We can stay drier in the trees."

He liked the use of the word *we*. She seemed to understand the need for them to stay together. Really, he needed her more than she needed him. She was an experienced guide. She probably knew how to defend herself against man and animal. He was a city boy and could not navigate his way out of a paper bag in an environment like this.

By the time he reached the edge of the forest, the drizzle had turned into a downpour. The fire would be put out that much faster. Unless other people were close by, the chance of the smoke alerting someone other than the criminals that a plane had crash-landed was close to zero. The fire hadn't burned long enough and the smoke hadn't risen high enough for it to be seen in town.

It was possible that there were other hikers in these mountains who might alert authorities once they returned to Fort Madison. But Fort Madison was a three-day hike away. Help from the outside was not something they could count on.

Abigail found shelter underneath the long branches of an older evergreen. She crouched down and pulled her knees toward her chest. He sat down beside her. The rain pelted against the higher branches, but he and Abigail remained relatively dry.

"We need to assess what we have to work with. I have a Swiss Army knife I always carry with me, an energy bar in my jacket pocket and waterproof matches," Abigail said matter-of-factly.

He liked that she was thinking about how they were going to get off this mountain. "I have a gun with eight bullets left in it." He rifled through the pockets of his jacket. "And a metro pass, a very old piece of hard candy, a couple of paper clips, a pocket Bible and a tire gauge I forgot to put back in my toolbox the last time I checked my tire pressure."

She tilted her head and raised her eyebrows. "That is not very helpful. Even MacGyver would say that's not much to work with."

He laughed. "You watch that show, too?"

The faintest hint of a smile, a spasm almost, lit up Abigail's face. "I might have caught a rerun a time or two. That show's been around forever."

He liked her smile, however brief it had been.

Her expression turned serious once again, eyebrows drawn close together. "You didn't follow my instructions. When I told you how to pack, I said there were some essential things you needed to have on your person at all times."

"I know. I didn't think I'd be hiking out," he said.

"Rule number one about being in the mountains— you always hope for the best but plan for the worst."

"Yes, I remember you said that." He leaned a little closer to her. "Sorry I'm such a bad student."

She pulled away. She was still a little prickly. Maybe her coldness was about something more than just him.

"By landing where we did, we have gotten quite a ways from the main trail, which is the most direct route back into town," she said.

"But you can get us back into Fort Madison?"

She rolled her eyes. "Of course I can. It's what I do for a living."

"We can't wait here much longer. Hopefully, that fire will die out."

He listened for a moment to the rain falling on the higher branches, creating a sort of melody.

"Yes, I suppose we need to get moving as quickly as possible."

He imagined that she was thinking the same thing he was. Though they had a head start on the three men, waiting for the plane to stop burning would cost them valuable time, but hiking with no supplies could be costly, too. It was just a matter of time before the men tracked them to this spot.

THREE

With the rain still falling, Abigail ventured out of the trees to look at the plane wreckage. She was grateful for the baseball hat she wore and the waterproof jacket. Though it was spring, the mountain temperatures could still dip into the teens. She had dressed in layers. She was grateful to be warm and mostly dry.

Jesse followed behind her as they stepped out into the open. The plane was smoldering, and the stench of smoke and melting plastic was still heavy in the air. Her eyes watered.

She removed the bandanna from around her neck and placed it over her mouth.

Jesse coughed. "You think of everything, don't you?"

"It's called being prepared." There was a slight edge to her voice that caught her by surprise. Searching a drug plane for something that might help them survive with a man who might be a criminal was not her idea of a good time. "Sorry, I didn't mean to sound snippy."

"It's all right." He touched her shoulder. "I should have listened better when you gave me instructions before we left town for this trek."

Again, that stab to her heart sent waves of anger and

sadness through her. Brent had destroyed her ability to trust her own judgment. She had no idea if Jesse was being honest with her or not about being framed. He seemed apologetic and almost…nice. She clenched her jaw. *Nothing is as it appears.*

She was certain of only one thing—they needed to work as a team if they were going to get back to town. When she stepped into the plane, the toxic smell of burnt plastic was even stronger.

Jesse drew up his jacket collar over his nose and mouth. "Whoa, we better get this over with as quickly as possible. I'm sure breathing this stuff isn't good for our lungs. I'll look toward the back. You search the front."

She opened a box behind the copilot's seat and the storage pouches beside each of the seats. After searching for several minutes, she came up with a water bottle, several packages of candy and a hat. She tossed the hat toward Jesse. "Put that on. It will help keep the rain and sun out. What did you come up with?"

He caught the hat and placed it on his head. He pointed at the tarp that covered the drugs. "We could use that for shelter if we had to."

The drugs looked like they had been only partially damaged. The fire had consumed some of the plastic the bricks were packaged in. She shivered but not from the cold. How had she gotten connected to drugs and drug dealers? She had lived a really sheltered life and hadn't even rebelled as a teenager like her brothers had. All of this was so out of her frame of reference. Maybe if she hadn't been so naive, she would have realized what a player Brent was. And maybe she wouldn't be in this mess with Jesse. "Yes," she said, "bring the tarp."

She grabbed a lined jacket that was hanging over

the back of the copilot seat. She could fashion a make-shift backpack out of it.

"Also, I found this." He held up an unopened energy drink and a bowie knife. He put the energy drink in his pocket and zipped it shut.

The knife gave her the shivers all over again. "Let's get out of here." She pushed open the pilot's door and jumped out.

Jesse didn't follow her. He must have still been searching for something—what, she didn't know. A cold wave of fear washed over her. Was he looking for drug money?

She tilted her head toward the sky. Dark clouds all around, no sign of blue sky. The storm was probably going to last awhile.

Abigail retreated toward the trees. She pulled out her Swiss Army knife and slit the lining of the jacket she'd grabbed at the bottom hem. She cut holes at the ends of the sleeves and in the shoulders.

Jesse finally joined her.

"Find what you were looking for?"

"No," he said.

So, he wasn't going to be forthcoming about what he was searching for. "Turns out those paper clips you had in your pocket might come in handy."

He dug through his pockets. "Well, what do you know." He handed them to her. His fingers brushed over her palm. "Maybe I'll earn my MacGyver certificate after all."

She straightened the paper clips and then drew them through the holes she'd cut in the jacket, so the ends of the sleeves were attached to the shoulders. She put the candy and the water bottle in the backpack she'd just made. "Toss that knife in here, too."

Admiration spread across his face. "Wow, I'm impressed." He stepped toward her and placed the knife and drink in her pack. "What about the tarp?"

She handed him her knife. "Cut a hole in it and use it for a rain poncho. This storm is going to last for a bit."

As if to confirm her prediction, lightning flashed in the sky, followed by thunder a few seconds later.

He slit an opening into the center of the tarp. "What about you? Won't you get wet?"

She was touched by his concern for her. "My coat is waterproof."

"We better get moving." A wave of fear passed through her. "Those other men will catch up with us sooner or later, right?"

He nodded and tipped the brim of his hat to her.

They stepped out of the forest into the downpour. Abigail assessed where they were based on the mountain peaks. She didn't doubt her ability to get them back on the trail, but it would take some doing. She wasn't familiar with this part of the forest, but she knew if they moved in the general direction of the mountain peak referred to as Angel's Peak, they would intersect with the trail. When they got closer and the immediate landscape became familiar, she would pinpoint the trail's location with more accuracy and then figure out the best way to avoid the men. Maybe by staying close to the trail but not on it.

For now, all they had to do was keep Angel's Peak in front of them.

They stepped out into the downpour, hiked across

the wide-open strip of land where the plane had gone down and entered the forest on the other side.

They walked side by side without speaking, their footsteps pounding out a rhythm. Fear and doubt played at the corners of her mind. Heading back to the trail was the quickest way to get back to town, but it was also the most obvious. Those three men had followed her and Jesse up the mountain without being spotted, so it was clear they had some tracking skills and were in good shape.

In her mind, she saw the different topographical maps she'd studied of the various areas she'd camped and all the places she'd taken clients in these mountains over the few months she'd worked for Big Sky Outfitters. She still wasn't sure what the best strategy for avoiding the men was. Trying to come up with a less obvious way down the mountain could get them lost. They did not have the food or gear for that.

The forest thinned as the rain pelted her hat and drizzled from the trees. They stepped out into a flat area, where it looked like a forest fire had passed through. The grass had not grown back in yet. The ground was muddy, causing her hiking boots to make a suctioning sound with every step.

Jesse slid, his legs going into a split before he righted himself. "Kind of slippery out here."

"Yes, watch your step."

They trudged on through the slick mud. Jesse's tarp poncho made swishing noises as he moved. The rain tapped out a rhythm.

He did a double step to catch up with her. "Look, I'm an extrovert. This silence is killing me."

He'd been plenty talkative on his way up here,

mostly about the sports he played and music he liked. Nothing in his conversation had hinted that he was in law enforcement.

She had spent most of her time trying to teach him how to read the landscape. Since she had thought he would be hiking out alone, she'd tried to explain possible scenarios he might encounter and what to do.

She didn't really see the point of getting to know him better. "I'm an introvert. I like the silence."

"Suit yourself." He shrugged and kept pace with her. A moment later, he started to hum what sounded like the annoying theme song from a children's program her niece watched.

"Okay," she said. "You win. If it will stop you from humming that song, we can talk."

He smiled. "Good." He glanced over his shoulder. His smile turned grim and his voice dropped half an octave. "Never mind."

She spun around. Behind them, at the other end of the muddy field, two of their three pursuers barreled toward them.

Jesse scanned the landscape around them.

Nowhere to run. Nowhere to hide.

They were out in the open, exposed. Some rocks at the edge of the field looked to be their only option.

"Get over there as fast as you can," he said, directing Abigail toward the rocks.

The mud bogged them down. And now the hillside slanted up.

Abigail glanced over her shoulder. "Those trees are closer. It's easier to go across than up in this sticky gumbo." Abigail had already redirected her steps.

Where the wilderness was concerned, he'd trust her choices over his. He slipped a few paces behind her. "We shouldn't bunch together." Better to have two targets than one.

Abigail jogged through the mud in a sure-footed way. He stumbled behind, running in a zigzag pattern so it would be harder to shoot him. The tarp he wore as a rain poncho slowed him down.

The men had changed course, as well. Eddy had stopped to line up a shot, while Pretty Boy sprinted toward them. He wondered what had become of the third man, the one with the dark, slicked-back hair. Cell phones didn't work in the high mountains. But what if the men had some other way to communicate to bring in even more men to the hunt?

The special phone Abigail had given him in case he got lost on his way down was in his backpack. Lost forever, or maybe the men had found it and used it.

Abigail drew nearer to the trees.

The percussive bang of the rifle shot leaving the barrel of the gun pummeled his eardrums, but he did not hear the bullet hit, which meant it must have sunk into the mud. Abigail disappeared into the trees with a backward glance at him. His feet felt weighted down by the amount of mud on them. He lifted his legs, pumping fast and hard even as the mud suctioned around his boots. Pretty Boy had closed the distance between them and Eddy had run a dozen yards in order to line up another shot.

The trees were ten yards away. He saw no sign of Abigail—she must have kept running. He sprinted, fixing his gaze on the edge of the forest. The trees grew larger in his field of vision. Another bullet from the rifle traveled through the air. This one split the bark of the tree inches in front of him just as he entered the forest.

His heart beat a little faster, knowing how close he'd come to taking a bullet. A vibrating branch indicated the direction in which Abigail had run. There was no trail to follow in this part of the forest. The ground cover of pine needles, leaves and broken branches was thick. Some of the mud came off his boots, but he still felt like he was running with weights on his feet.

He caught sight of Abigail's blond braid flying as she ran. He hurried to catch up with her. He could hear the thugs yelling at each other as they entered the forest.

Abigail traveled steadily uphill. She must have had some kind of plan or route in mind that would throw off the pursuers. As the trees thinned, the terrain grew drier, populated with tiny pebbles and then rocks. He caught up with Abigail.

His words came out between gasping breaths. "Do you know where you're going?"

"Just getting away," she said, out of breath, as well.

Somehow, he'd hoped she had a better plan than haphazardly running away. He spotted some brush up ahead that was tall enough to hide behind. "Keep going," he said. "I'll try to stop them."

He crouched behind the brush, peering out to see if he could spot the two other men. Pretty Boy was the first to emerge from the trees. Eddy was probably slowed down by having to carry the rifle. Pretty Boy glanced in one direction, darted a few paces in the other and then ran up the mountain. Abigail was in plain sight. But she was too far away for Pretty Boy to get a decent shot with just a handgun.

Jesse waited with his gun drawn. Pretty Boy's attention was on Abigail as he ran toward her. At best, Jesse would get one shot before Pretty Boy had time to react. He had to make it count. The blond man continued to fix his gaze on Abigail as she made her way up the mountain.

Eddy emerged from the trees and took the same path as Pretty Boy, though he moved slower, bracing the rifle on his shoulder.

Pretty Boy drew closer to the brush where Jesse was hiding. Jesse waited, gripping his gun and listening to his own heartbeat drumming in his ears. Pretty Boy's footsteps grew louder, more intense. Jesse peered through the brush, which was just starting to leaf out.

He jumped up, located his target and fired off a shot. Knowing that Pretty Boy could just as easily shoot him, he took off running before assessing if he'd hit his target.

He heard a yelp behind him. Either Pretty Boy was injured or angry or both.

Abigail had reached the top of the hill and disappeared over the other side. Jesse willed his legs to move faster. His ears detected another rifle shot just as he edged toward the top of the hill. His heart pounded from the effort of running uphill and from the threat of death that pressed ever closer.

The other side of the hill was a boulder field that led to a river bottom, and beyond that a forest. He caught up with Abigail just as another rifle shot shattered the silence around them. The men had made it to the top of the hill. He grabbed her sleeve and pulled her toward a larger rock.

Both of them gasped for air, taking only a moment to rest before running again. He could hear the men's footfalls on the rocks as they closed in. Abigail headed toward the river. He couldn't see a bridge anywhere.

She approached the river's edge, glanced over her shoulder as the two men gained on them, then turned back and dived into the rushing waters. He watched her as she was carried downstream. That didn't seem like much of an escape plan.

What choice did he have? He jumped in, as well. The freezing water shocked his system. He drifted downstream, still stunned by the cold that enveloped him. Behind him he could hear rifle shots.

Abigail dived underwater. The tarp he was using as a rain poncho weighed him down and made it hard to maneuver against the current. He dived underwater and slipped out of it but held on to it as the river carried him farther along.

When he resurfaced, the river had taken him around a bend. He could no longer see the pursuers. Only one of the men had been hauling a smaller backpack. Would they jump in after them or try to find another way across the river?

He watched as Abigail swam toward the opposite shore. As the water grew shallower, she stood up and dragged herself onto the bank, flopping down in the grass on her stomach.

The current pulled him farther downstream as he struggled to get to shore. He grabbed hold of a tree limb that hung over the water and strained to pull himself up the steep embankment. He clawed the ground and reached out to grab onto any vegetation that grew close to the shore.

He shivered, and his body seemed to be vibrating from the exertion of the run and plunge into the cold water. He pushed himself to his feet and headed back upriver, where Abigail had come ashore.

As he moved through the forest, the cold seemed to seep down to the marrow of his bones. It was early evening and springtime, but the water in the mountain stream had been freezing.

Jesse heard Abigail before he saw her. It sounded like she was banging sticks together. When he found her in a clearing, she was gathering logs and twigs. Water dripped off her wet clothes. "We need to get a fire started."

"Was there no other option besides jumping in a freezing river?" His teeth chattered from the cold.

"Yes, there was another option, Jesse—dying from a bullet wound." She glared at him. "I made the best choice I could in a tough situation."

It was the first time she'd used his first name. All the way up the mountain before they had encountered the three men, she'd called him Mr. Santorum.

"I would appreciate some help gathering some tinder." She held up a trembling hand. "I'm freezing, too."

"They might see the smoke rising up." He was still concerned about their safety.

"Or they can find our frozen corpses." Maybe it was just because she was cold and exhausted, but she didn't seem to like being questioned about her decision. Her voice softened. "We'll keep the fire small and build it in an area that can't be seen from far away. A lot of this wood is wet from all the spring rain, but stuff in sheltered areas is likely to be drier." With the handful of sticks she'd gathered, she moved deeper into the trees.

He searched the area, finding some twigs and a couple of smaller logs that seemed pretty dry. He found her in a clearing where the trees created a sort of canopy that shielded the fire from view.

She had gathered moss and a few twigs. She blew on the flickering flames before putting a few bigger twigs on the fire. He sat down beside her as she put some bigger logs on the fire. It smoked a bit from the dampness of the logs.

He laid down the logs he'd found and sat beside her.

The fire began to throw some heat. He put his palms up to it.

She picked up the tarp from where he'd dropped it, then peeled off her coat and the vest underneath. She threw them on a nearby log, where the heat from the fire would dry them out. Then she turned toward him. "Hand me your coat. You'll dry out faster this way."

He took off his coat and tossed it toward her.

Still dripping wet, she perched close to the fire on her knees and crossed her arms over her body. "You know, I've been part of a team that found lost hunters in the most impossible places, and I've guided people to safety under extreme weather conditions. No one has ever died or been seriously injured on my watch."

He wasn't sure why she was telling him this. "I can appreciate that."

"I have worked as a guide since I was a teenager. I come from a family of guides. Eighty percent of the people who want to come up to these remote regions are men, and every single time, I have to prove myself and be questioned in a way that I've never seen happen to male guides."

The fire crackled with a rhythm that was harmonious and comforting. As it grew, the heat surrounded him.

He stared at the flames. Now he knew why she was so upset with him. "I'm sorry I questioned your choice."

"I don't have a chip on my shoulder. It's just that it gets old after a while. What I did back there probably kept us alive."

This wasn't even her fight. It was his mess to untangle, and yet she felt a responsibility to get him out of the mountains at the risk of her own life. "I never should have dragged you into all this. It's just that I couldn't get up here on my own. I would have died."

In that moment, he felt how alone he was in the world. Lee had so thoroughly smeared his name that he didn't know if anyone at the DEA would believe his innocence. He'd worked with those men and women for close to seven years, but there was no way to discern who would turn him in and who would rely on what they knew about his character.

She stared at the fire. Her voice grew softer. "Well, whether I like it or not, we are in this together. I can't in good conscience just walk away from you, and I kind of think those men would kill me just as fast as they would kill you, given what I know and what I've seen."

He felt a rush of gratitude toward her. "Thank you, Abigail."

"I will get you off this mountain alive," she said.

He felt a new appreciation for her and how she had taken on such a responsibility in the face of so much danger.

He hated that he'd put her at risk. That had not been his intention. Everything was so tenuous and uncertain. Abigail could identify the men who had come after them. Would she even be safe once they got back to Fort Madison…if they got back to Fort Madison?

FOUR

As she warmed up, Abigail repositioned herself, crossing her legs beneath her. The heat from the fire intensified. She'd stopped shivering at least, though her clothes were still damp. She tore open her makeshift backpack, grateful to see that she hadn't lost anything from her plunge into the river.

She pulled out a candy bar with the wrapper adhered to it from being exposed to the heat. It was now soggy. Once she peeled off the wrapper, she broke the candy bar in half and handed one section to Jesse. "You'll need this to keep up your strength."

She rose to her feet and took the protein bar out of her jacket pocket. She broke that in half as well, offering him a portion. "The carbs from the candy bar will burn off pretty fast. The protein will sustain you."

Jesse studied her with those rich brown eyes. "Thanks." He chewed the protein bar and spoke between bites. "So, what's the plan now?"

She still didn't know what to think of Jesse Santorum. He didn't act like a drug dealer. He seemed almost decent.

It would be nightfall soon. They'd gotten seriously

off course by jumping in the river. "Those men will probably track down the river several miles and find the bridge. If they jumped in after us, we should hear them coming in less than an hour. But if they go down-river to the bridge, we have several hours or more before they can pick up our trail."

Jesse wrapped his arms around his chest and scooted a little closer to the fire. "I suppose it would take them a while to figure out where we came to shore, anyway."

"I think the best thing for us to do is to rest and get dry," she said. "We'll head out at twilight."

Jesse pulled his gun from his waistband and sat it on a log. "But sooner if the men show up."

Navigating at night was never easy, but they could follow the river back up to where they'd been. The darkness would shield them from view. She felt a little flutter of fear. "Yes, of course. It's hard to predict what the men will do exactly."

He looked directly at her. "The only sure thing is that they will come after us sooner or later."

His words sent a new surge of terror through her. She took in a breath to clear her mind. "Why don't you try to get some rest? That's what I'm going to do."

She stretched out on the mossy ground, using her arm as a pillow. She closed her eyes and listened to the crackle of the fire. She heard Jesse shuffling around.

"I think one of us should stand watch," he said.

"Or sit watch." She spoke without opening her eyes. "We have a limited food supply. Food is energy. You need to conserve what energy you do have."

"Gotcha," he said, sitting down.

"Go ahead and keep watch for now, but you will need to get some sleep, too." Dragging his sorry, tired self upriver was not her idea of a good time. They both needed all the energy they could muster.

The fog of sleep invaded her brain, and she drifted off into a deep sleep, where she dreamed she was running on a trail pursued by a dark figure. She awoke with a start, bursting into a sitting position.

Jesse sat on the other side of the fire. He must have added wood to it to keep it going. "Bad dreams?"

"Yes, one where I'm running but can't seem to make any progress."

There was something comforting knowing that Jesse was watching and listening for any sign of danger.

She closed her eyes and took in another deep breath. She was accustomed to sleeping on the hard ground. Sleep came easily to her.

When she awoke again, the sky had turned charcoal and the birds had stopped singing. She sat up and stretched. Jesse was still sitting with his back to the log. He must have put his gun back in his waistband.

"Did you sleep at all?"

"I rested my eyes some," he said. "You must have fallen into a deep sleep. You snore a little."

"I don't snore," she said.

He laughed. "Just a little. A very ladylike kind of snore."

She hadn't meant to sound so offended. She appreciated that he was able to see the humor of the moment.

She rose to her feet and slipped into her coat, which was completely dry. "Why don't we have that energy drink you found?" she said.

He pulled it from his pocket, opened it and offered her the first sip. She took several gulps before handing it back to him.

"I already folded the tarp and put it in the pack. I'll carry it for a while. Lead the way," he said.

They stepped out into the evening light. She wove through the trees, following the sound of the rushing river. "They must be tracking us up from the bridge or they would have been on our tail by now."

"How would they know there was a bridge downriver? They don't know this country like you do," he said.

"There are maps of the area. I'm sure they had one to follow us up here and not be noticed. And if you walk beside a river long enough, you usually come to a bridge. To stay on us the way they did, we have to assume that at least one of them has some tracking skills."

"Yes," he said, coming alongside her.

Though it was hard to see in the dim light, she picked the path that was more level to walk on.

"Are we going back to where we got derailed?"

"It's the easiest way to navigate back to the trail," she said.

"They could be watching, waiting for us to return."

Once again, it felt like he was questioning her judgment. "Do you have a better plan? I said I would get you back to the trail and down the mountain."

His response was gentle. "I trust your expertise, Abigail. I don't know what their next move will be. That's what I'm worried about. The only thing we can assume is that they are still looking for us."

Something inside her softened when he didn't respond in a hostile way to her oversensitivity. Her reaction wasn't about Jesse; it was about Brent. Her anger at Brent simmered just beneath the surface and she'd projected it onto Jesse. His betrayal had caused her whole life to be turned inside out. Every assumption she'd made was no longer true. Since their engagement, every plan she'd made had revolved around thinking she and Brent would be married. The truth was, once she got down this mountain, she didn't know what her life would look like anymore.

They came out into the open, where a large sandbar bordered the river. On the other side of the shore, the deer had come to the river's edge to drink. They lifted their heads and stared with curiosity at Abigail and Jesse.

In the distance, the sun sank low on the horizon and then slipped behind a mountain peak. She hiked, letting the sound of the river determine their path, even when they had to slip back into the trees or thick brush. She took the lead as they walked in silence. The landscape became more shadow and outlined as night fell.

Jesse was probably right about one of the men watching the trail where it intersected with the place they had been headed. The three men could split up, each searching a different area. She had no idea if they had walkie-talkies or a way of communicating. They could just as easily have searched Jesse's backpack and taken the satellite phone. "I wonder what happened to the dark-haired guy? Why wasn't he with those other two?"

Jesse took a moment to answer, probably jolted from whatever he'd been thinking about in the long silence. She listened to his feet pad on the ground behind her. "I don't know. Maybe he stayed with the plane. Some part of that product might be salvageable, but they've got to figure out a way to get it out."

"There are only two ways to get this high up the mountain. On foot and by air." She tilted her head toward the sky, half expecting to see another bush plane. Certainly, they wouldn't be able to mobilize that fast. That satellite phone would be the only thing that would allow them to communicate with anyone not on the mountain.

When it got darker, they slowed their pace. Abigail stopped to fill her bottle with water from the river. They both drank several gulps. She refilled it and they continued on through the darkness. Stars sprinkled across the night sky, and the temperature dropped several degrees.

The forest opened up. They walked out onto a wide sandbar. Across the rushing river, partway up the mountain, a light flashed.

Jesse stopped and stared out across the river. The light blinked in and out as it moved down the mountain. "I suppose there are other people up here. Hikers and such."

"Some," said Abigail. "Most people would have set up camp for the night by now, though. They wouldn't be on the move like this."

The night breeze seemed to carry even more of a chill with it. She struggled to take in a deep breath. As she watched the light blink in and out of visibility, she was pretty sure at least one of their pursuers was making his way down the mountain toward the river.

As they traversed along the river, Jesse wrestled with all the unknowns. Would the men meet them on the trail? Would they track them by crossing the river and coming at them from behind? The only thing he was sure of was that the men would not just give up and head down the mountain.

As the sandbar narrowed, Abigail guided him back into the trees.

The silence made him crazy. It was too much of an opportunity for his thoughts to send him in a direction that messed with his composure. The whole trip up here was, at this point, an act of futility. The plane was still stuck in the trees, was probably not flyable, and he had no idea where the hard drive that would prove his innocence was.

His thoughts raced faster than a hamster on a wheel. Was all of this for nothing? And now he had gotten Abigail involved. He had to talk or his negative thoughts would derail him into a place of despair. "So did you always want to be a guide?"

She walked for several paces before answering. "It was sort of inevitable. My whole family is into hiking, camping and fishing, anything to do with the outdoors."

"Ever want to do anything else?" He stumbled over something in the dark.

She whirled around to face him, reaching out for his arm. "You all right?"

"It's getting hard to see."

"Test your step before you take it by putting your toe down first," she said.

The forest opened up, and they had a view of the river and the mountain on the other side. The light was still blinking in and out of view, moving ever closer to the river. Abigail slowed her step. He sensed her fear.

He tried to lighten the moment by returning to his

question. "If you did something other than be a wilderness guide, what would it be?"

"My turn," she said. "You already asked me a question."

"Fair enough." He was glad she had decided to play along. The conversation served as a distraction from speculating when the three men would catch up with them. "Ask away."

"Did you always want to be a DEA agent?"

"No, I was a pretty good musician in college, but you know how that goes."

"I never would have guessed that. What instrument did you play?"

"Guitar—" Something rustled in the brush and both of them fell silent. He stepped a little closer to her. She pulled him back toward a tree with a wide trunk. She tugged on his elbow, indicating they needed to crouch down.

Then he saw the flash of a light and heard footsteps. His heartbeat revved up ten notches.

It appeared the men had tracked them by crossing the bridge and coming up behind them. Maybe the light they saw coming toward the river was one of the other men, or someone not connected to them at all.

No voices. No exchange of instructions. Maybe it was just one man after them. The fire they'd built would be a clear indication of where they'd been.

The footsteps drew closer. This wasn't much of a hiding place. If the man shone the flashlight in this direction, they'd be spotted.

Abigail tapped his arm. She was already moving, probably toward a better hiding place. He could barely make out her silhouette; she was a shadow among shadows. She moved so quietly, he couldn't hear her. He had to guess at where she was going. He reached out a hand, touching the fabric of her coat.

She tugged on his sleeve again. He moved closer to her. In the darkness, he touched the roughness of a log and then the silky smoothness of her hair right before she slipped down low. He patted the log to get a feel for it before crawling over it.

Behind them, the flashlight spanned an area like a searchlight moving back and forth. He sank down even more behind the log. He could hear Abigail's gentle breathing. Their heads were close together. Pine needles on the forest floor poked his hand where it rested.

In the darkness, his heartbeat drummed in his ears.

The light swept over the top of the log.

Though slow and soft, the footsteps became more distinct. A boot broke some twigs on the ground. It sounded like the man was less than five feet away from them.

Somewhere in the distance, an owl hooted.

Jesse held his breath, waiting for the footsteps to resume. He counted the seconds. Silence.

Then he heard the sound of the man letting out a breath. Why wasn't he moving on? The man took a step and swept the light over the area around the log once again.

Jesse remained as still as a statue.

More footsteps and then silence.

A second before the light landed on their faces, Abigail sprang to her feet. Jesse jumped up, as well.

She was running through the trees. Branches creaked where she had pushed them out of the way. He followed the sound of her footsteps, stumbling in the darkness. Behind them, the light bobbed up and down, headed directly toward them.

The footsteps were loud and intensified as the pursuer drew closer, like the drumbeat before a firing squad.

Though he could only make out moving shadows and vague outlines, Jesse homed in on the noises that Abigail made as she retreated deeper into the forest. He felt as though he was a blind man running, and reached out his arms to feel when low-hanging branches were in front of him. One tree branch conked him in the head. He stopped for a moment to get his bearings. He'd lost track of Abigail in the dark.

The man with the flashlight remained close behind, but was unable to close the distance between them.

He took off running, guessing at where Abigail might have gone. She was much more sure-footed and certain of herself in the dark than he was. Suddenly, her hand touched his back at the shoulder.

"This way," she whispered, tugging his jacket at the elbow. She had to have doubled back to find him. He sprinted, staying right at her heels so as not to lose her again.

Footsteps of the pursuer approached at a rapid pace. He wasn't putting any effort into being quiet.

Jesse glanced over his shoulder. The bright light nearly blinded him.

He followed Abigail deeper into the forest and then up a wooded hillside. The hill grew steeper and the climb was more treacherous.

Abigail stopped and climbed up on a big, flat boulder. She held out a hand and helped him onto the rock.

"There." She pointed down the hill, where the flashlight of the pursuer could be seen as he ran parallel to where they'd gone. "People always take the path of least resistance. He'll figure out soon enough that we ditched him and backtrack." She rose to her feet. "But we'll be long gone by then."

Jesse barely had time to catch his breath. He pushed himself to his feet and fell in beside Abigail. They moved at a slower pace, pushing on through until morning light bathed the mountains and trees with a warm glow that was the color of marmalade.

They stopped to have some gulps of water and eat a handful of candy. They were at a high spot, where Jesse could see most of the landscape below. He saw the trail that disappeared into the mountains. Though he could no longer see the downed airplane, he recognized the grove of trees with the mountain peak behind it. The plane was on the other side of the trees. That was where they had seen the first light coming down the mountain toward the river.

"We've got to get some protein in us." Abigail placed her hands on her hips and turned from side to side. "Critters will be coming out to eat. I'll see if I can trap one. You rest."

She disappeared into the trees. He slumped down, using a tree trunk as a back rest. He closed his eyes and slept until he heard the sound of her footsteps.

"Nothing?"

"There's not a fast-food joint in there." She pointed back at the trees. She sat down beside him. "It takes a while to trap an animal. Let's rest, and I'll check the trap in a few."

Using her hands as a pillow, Abigail rested on her side and drew her legs up toward her chest. He was beginning to think her ability to fall asleep so fast in any condition was a real talent.

He closed his eyes, keeping his ears tuned to the noises around him. He slipped into a deeper sleep. Suddenly his head jerked. An out-of-place clanging reached his ears. It took him a moment to discern if the mechanical noise was part of his dreams or real.

His eyes shot open.

Abigail was still curled up, asleep.

The noise was not part of his dreams. Though he could not see it, he heard a helicopter.

He shook Abigail awake. "Would someone be coming to rescue us in a helicopter?"

She sat up. "No, it takes three days to hike in and three to hike out. No one would be alarmed until either day six or I send out a call for help, which I can't do without the satellite phone. Why?"

"Listen," he said.

The sound of the helicopter had faded.

"I don't hear anything," she said.

"I heard a helicopter." Above him, branches creaked. A crow cawed in the distance. He hadn't imagined it.

Abigail rose to her feet. "I don't hear anything. I'm going to check the trap." She took three steps and then paused, tilting her head toward the empty sky as all the color drained from her face. "Okay, now I hear it, too."

They gazed down the hillside to an open area where a chopper had landed. Jesse peered out from behind a tree, squinting to see better. The dark-haired man they'd seen earlier got out of the chopper, followed by another man, holding the leashes of three bloodhounds.

Abigail's voice was barely above a whisper. "They brought in dogs to hunt us down."

FIVE

Abigail's throat grew so tight it felt like someone was squeezing her neck. Her heart pounded as she watched the dark-haired man get out of the helicopter. "They must have found our backpacks. Our scent will be all over them." A fourth man, a man she hadn't seen before, held the leashes of three tracking dogs.

The helicopter lifted off as soon as the men got out. She recognized the logo on the helicopter. It was from a local business that transported hunters and hikers to the high mountains. No doubt the pilot had no idea what these men were up to. He'd probably been fed some story about what they needed the hounds for.

Jesse tugged on her sleeve. "We better get out of here."

There was not time to check the trap she'd set. She could hear the dogs baying in the distance, getting excited. The dark-haired man spoke into a walkie-talkie. They still had no idea where the two other men were. But the men were clearly in communication with each other.

She took in a breath. "We can't go back to the trail. It will be too easy to track us."

"What do you suggest?"

The dogs continued to bark as they worked their way up the hillside.

Mental pictures of the maps of these mountains flashed through her head again. She started to run up the mountain, still trying to come up with a plan.

The dogs' baying grew louder.

Her mind cleared. She knew what direction they needed to go. Little Spring Creek was not far from where they were. If they ran through it, the dogs would be thrown off the scent.

They sprinted through the trees until she heard the gurgling of the water. The creek was dry most of the year, but with the spring runoff, there would be at least a few inches of water flowing.

The barking of the dogs intensified still. If the pursuers spotted them at the creek, the plan would not work.

Water splashed as she ran through the middle of the creek. Jesse remained close to her. She followed the riverbed as it wound up the mountain. They needed a long-term plan to get off the mountain without being caught. There were other trails that intersected with the trail that led back into town. If they took a circuitous route, they might be able to avoid the dogs. That would take longer, though.

As she ran through the rushing stream, she was grateful for waterproof boots. The bottom of her pant legs were soaked, but her feet remained dry.

The creek curved around some rocks, cutting abruptly to the right. She got out of the water on the opposite side she'd come in on. As they hurried through the forest, her stomach growled. She kept moving until she could no longer hear the dogs.

She collapsed on a large flat rock, trying to catch her breath. "We've burned up a lot of energy. We need to eat."

Jesse took off the makeshift pack and dug into it, pulling out a handful of gummy bears. "Hold out your hand." His knuckles touched her palm as he gave her the candy.

But the carbs would provide only short-term energy. They really needed protein. They ate quickly, washing down the candy with gulps of water, then sprinted again through the trees.

Though farther away, the baying and barking of the dogs reached her ears from time to time. The echo of their persistent noise seemed to invade every crevice of the mountains. She and Jesse were by no means safe from being found.

They jogged for over an hour until they could no longer hear the dogs. Abigail stopped to assess how they could get back on an artery trail that would lead to the main trail. She redirected their steps but grew tired. She stopped and fell to the ground, using a tree trunk as a backrest. Jesse sat down beside her, their shoulders touching.

He rubbed his stomach. "My gut is gurgling."

"Mine, too." Despair came over her. From an early age, she'd been taught how to keep a cool head and solve problems when it came to being in the elements. But this was like nothing she had ever faced before. Doubt plagued the corners of her mind. Could she get them out of here alive?

Jesse leaned a little closer and patted her hand. "We'll figure this out."

His touch warmed her to the bone. She hadn't said anything. How was it that he was so tuned in to her feelings? She tilted her head and closed her eyes, saying a silent prayer for help and guidance.

When she opened her eyes, Jesse said, "Amen?"

She let out a one-syllable laugh, shaking her head. "How did you know I was praying?"

He offered her a soft smile. "It was a guess. I don't pray much anymore myself."

"Why?"

A shadow seemed to fall across his face. "It's a long story."

She studied him for a moment. For the first time, she noticed that his brown eyes had gold flecks in them. He had a tiny scar on his chin. She wanted to ask him what the story behind the scar was, because most scars came with a story. She wondered why he didn't pray... anymore. She wanted to know more about Jesse.

"We better not stay here long," she said.

Her heart fluttered a little when he nodded and nudged his shoulder against hers.

She sniffed the air. The faint smell of burning wood reached her nose. She rose to her feet. "There's a camp around here somewhere." Using her nose as a guide, she made her way through the trees.

The camp was up the mountain. Chances were, it wasn't one of the men who wanted to kill them. All the same, they needed to exercise caution. Sometime before she'd started working at Big Sky Outfitters, her boss and his now wife had encountered men living up in these mountains planning a bank robbery and other crimes to finance spreading their extreme anti-government beliefs. There might still be some stragglers at this high elevation. Men who were paranoid and prone to violence, choosing to live alone because they couldn't operate in society.

She prayed that wasn't the case. Hopefully, they were just coming upon hikers who liked to camp on the most remote parts of the mountains.

Maybe the light they'd seen coming down the mountain toward the river last night was connected to this camp. That would make more sense than the searchers having gotten so far off the mark in looking for them.

She followed the smell of the fire, choosing her steps carefully so she didn't make any noise. She caught sight of a wisp of smoke rising above the trees. Jesse had pulled his gun from his waistband. He stepped where she stepped.

As they drew nearer, the crackling of the fire reached her ears. She edged a little closer, choosing a tree with a thick trunk to hide behind. Though there were signs that the camp was active, she saw no one other than a raccoon that was gnawing on what looked like a bone. A lean-to that blended with the trees had been formed out of branches and leaves and mud. A metal pot that hung on a small sawhorse-like structure cooked over the fire.

Her stomach growled as the aroma of some sort of soup cooking tickled her nostrils. The occupant of the camp could not have gone far if he'd left his food to cook.

Still holding his gun, Jesse leaned close to her. "Man, I'm starving."

Her mouth watered at the aroma of the soup. "We

can't just take the food. We don't know what kind of person we're dealing with here."

"I know. Stealing is wrong," Jesse said. "My stomach is telling me otherwise, though. Maybe we could eat and leave something as payment."

A further survey of the camp revealed canned goods stacked just inside the lean-to. Whoever lived here must go into town for supplies once in a while or have someone bring them to him.

A breeze caressed Abigail's skin. A tinkling sound reached her ears. The sun reflected off a multifaceted object hanging from a tree. Whoever lived here had fashioned a wind chime from pieces of metal and shiny objects. Seeing it touched something in Abigail's heart. Even in the harshest conditions, people wanted things of beauty to look at. Life could not just be about survival.

A guttural voice sounded behind them. "I think the two of you better turn around real slow."

Abigail swung around to stare into the barrel of a shotgun pointed right at Jesse's heart.

Jesse was unable to tell if the man pointing the shotgun at him was thirty or fifty. Being out in the elements had made his skin leathery. He had a layer of grit on his face that probably wouldn't ever wash off, and his hair, though pulled back in a ponytail, was wild. His beard was also untrimmed and fell to the middle of his chest.

"Drop your gun," said the hermit. His cold blue eyes seemed to pierce right through Jesse.

Jesse obliged. He had to find a way to get his gun back, but now was not the time.

The man pointed the shotgun toward the fire. "Now go on over there, where Lulubell is having her lunch."

Lulubell must be the raccoon. As they approached the fire, the raccoon looked up from the scrap of fatty meat and bone she held in her dexterous paws, but did not run away.

"There's some chairs behind you," the man said as he picked up Jesse's handgun.

Jesse turned a half circle to where he saw a dilapidated lawn chair and a stump. He scooted the chair closer to the fire and offered it to Abigail, keeping one eye on the hermit while he rolled the stump closer to the fire.

The hermit leaned his shotgun against a tree and dropped the backpack he had on the ground. The pack hit the dirt with a thud. Judging from the bulk of it, it was quite full. Of what, Jesse could only guess. Either the man had gone out foraging, or the pack contained supplies he had with him all the time.

Jesse was still not able to get a clear read on the mental stability of the man. Once one of the hermit's hands was free, since he held Jesse's handgun in the other, he rubbed his knuckles on the top of his head repeatedly and did an odd shuffle when he walked—they were mannerisms that suggested mental illness. Then again, a man who spent all his time alone might develop some socially awkward behavior and might be nervous when he did encounter people.

Abigail cleared her throat. "Your soup smells good."

With the handgun still trained on them, the man narrowed his eyes. "Cooks all day to get the flavor just right." Jesse thought he saw a little bit of light come into the man's dull eyes.

"We're real hungry." Her voice held a nervous edge to it. "I'd be willing to trade something for a bowl of that soup."

The man tilted his head slightly and lowered the gun an inch or so. "Whatcha got?"

Abigail never took her eyes off the man. "Show him what we have, Jesse."

Jesse removed the makeshift backpack, pulling out the candy and the knife, and then he emptied the contents of his pockets.

The man licked his lips at the sight of the gummy bears. And then he pointed to Jesse's metro card. "What's that?"

Jesse held it up. The holographic image caught the light. "It's a metro card."

"It's pretty," said the hermit. He walked over to the backpack and unbuckled it, retrieving a leather pouch. "I'll take it and a handful of that candy." He tossed the pouch toward them. "Put the card in there. There are containers inside for soup and the candy." He lifted the gun a little higher, pointing it at Jesse. "You stay put. The girl gets the stuff. No sudden moves."

Abigail rooted through the contents of the lean-to while Jesse placed the card in the pouch, which contained smooth rocks and pieces of metal. She ladled soup for both of them after scooping several handfuls of gummy bears into a container.

With the hermit still watching them, they settled on their chairs. Jesse's spoon had been carved out of wood. The soup, which contained vegetables and some kind of meat, tasted wonderful.

The hermit pointed toward the bowie knife. "I want that, too, but that's a separate trade."

Jesse scraped the last little bit of soup out of the bottom of his bowl, which had been carved from wood, as well.

The hermit sat on the opposite side of the fire. He crossed his legs and rested the gun in the crook of his elbow.

"Your soup is so good." Abigail rubbed her belly and slurped several more spoonfuls.

Though the man's wild beard made it hard to discern his expression, Jesse thought he saw just the faintest of smiles. Abigail seemed to be breaking down his suspicion with her flattery.

"You can have another bowl if you like…on the house," said the hermit.

"Thank you so much." Abigail got up and ladled out more of the hearty soup. She sat back down. "Can my friend have some more?"

The hermit shifted his weight and tilted his head, staring at Jesse. "I'll have to think about that."

Abigail had managed to build some trust with the man, but he still wasn't so sure about Jesse.

The hermit rose to his feet, shuffled across the camp and picked up another log to throw on the fire.

Abigail ate her second bowl of soup at a slower pace than the first. "I'm from Idaho, but my folks used to come out here sometimes to take us camping. I remember when I was a little girl hearing a story about a man who was in a car wreck with his wife. The man, who was driving, survived. The woman didn't. That man disappeared. No one knows what happened to him. The gossip was that he ran up to live in these mountains. Did you ever hear that story?" Abigail had spoken slowly. Compassion saturated each word.

The hermit's eyes clouded with tears. He rose to his feet, running his knuckles over the top of his greasy hair. "I don't know nothing about that."

Abigail had figured out who the man was. Sometimes it wasn't mental illness or paranoia that drove a man to live alone; it was guilt. When he heard the story, Jesse could feel his own heart squeezing tight.

Years ago, he and Melissa had gotten married just out of high school. He had loved her since the seventh grade. Before they could celebrate their first wedding anniversary, Melissa was diagnosed with cancer. She died days after their second anniversary. Though it had been ten years, the pain of the loss, his inability to save the woman he loved, was still as raw as ever.

Jesse saw the hermit with fresh eyes now. They had a great deal in common. Because loving meant risking loss and unbearable pain, he had decided to put his energy into his work and never think about marriage again.

Abigail's spoon scraped the bowl as she finished the last bit of soup. "Jesse, are you okay? You seem kind of faraway."

The fire crackled and the hermit paced. Jesse studied the older man for a moment.

"Just thinking about something that happened a long time ago," he said, surprised by the emotion that rose up in his voice. He cleared his throat. "It's nothing."

In an effort to not fall into the black hole of pain over Melissa, Jesse averted his gaze over to the pack the man had been hauling. Some of the contents had come out when the man had searched for his pouch. Jesse recognized a brick of heroin from the plane, along with some pieces of metal. One of the bricks was broken open, the fine white powder spilling on the ground. Jesse felt a surge of hope. Inside the broken brick was the hard drive he'd been searching for.

In the distance, the baying of the search dogs rose up.

Jesse shot to his feet. "I'm not sure you want to keep that." He tilted his head toward the contents of the backpack. "Men might come for it."

"And they might be willing to trade something for it." The hermit squared his shoulders. "I can handle myself."

The barking of the dogs intensified, indicating they had picked up on a strong scent. Lulubell scurried into the trees. Abigail rose to her feet as well, panic etched across her features.

"I'll trade you the knife for that black thing there." Jesse pointed.

"Deal." The hermit seemed to understand that the dogs meant trouble and that they needed to hurry. He darted over to the backpack and tossed the black box toward Jesse. "You brought those men to my door. Get out of here."

Jesse picked up the knife and handed it to the hermit. There was no time to try to negotiate for the gun. "You might want to hide out for a bit. It's us they're after. We'll lead them away from your camp. But they won't stop at violence to try to get information out of you."

"Don't worry about me." The hermit seemed to understand. He tossed the pack into the lean-to and picked up both guns, shoved the knife into his belt and disappeared into the trees where the raccoon had gone.

It sounded as though the dogs were within a hundred feet of the camp.

"We better get out of here." Abigail bolted toward the edge of the camp, opposite of where the hermit had gone. Jesse shoved the remainder of the gummy bears into the makeshift backpack. He placed the hard drive in the pocket of his coat and hurried after Abigail.

As they pressed on, the hounds' yelping would intensify and then dim and die out altogether. Their footsteps pounded out a rhythm as they sprinted across the hard-packed dirt. The trees were far apart. Abigail chose a path that led them downward. Though he trusted that she knew where she was going, their path seemed a bit random.

As they ran, and the sound of the dogs faded, the hermit's story played at the corners of his mind. The man must have been deeply in love with his wife, had seen it as his job to protect her. He didn't know the circumstances of the car accident, but the man clearly blamed himself for it, and it had driven him into solitude. Though he lived and worked with people all around him, Jesse had chosen a solitary life, too.

Abigail stumbled. Jesse reached out to catch her before she fell.

She grabbed his arm and locked him in her gaze as she caught her breath. "Thank you."

He thought again of the hermit. What did it do to a man whose choices led to the death of a woman he loved? It was a heavy burden to love someone and lose them. The guilt that he could have done something more to save Melissa plagued him always.

His heart pounded against his rib cage as he sucked in air. He squeezed her elbow. "Let's go."

The dogs grew closer, relentless in their pursuit of their targets.

SIX

Abigail was grateful for the full belly and renewed energy. Though she avoided the trail because it would be too easy to track them, she guided them down the mountain. They walked and jogged throughout the morning into the late afternoon. When they'd gone for at least an hour without hearing the dogs, she stopped to rest at the edge of an open area, finding a log to sit down on.

Jesse sat beside her. "Where are we exactly?"

She tilted her head toward the sky. They still had four or five hours of daylight. "If we keep going straight through the night, we're probably about twelve hours from the trailhead."

He pulled the water bottle from the backpack and offered her a drink. "Then that's what we should do."

She took several gulps of water and then handed him the bottle. "I can take us sort of parallel to the trail. It's a little more treacherous but we'll be less likely to be spotted."

"That guy back there, living by himself. You knew who he was." He drank from the water bottle.

"The accident happened when I was little, but it was

big news around the Northwest. There were all kinds of rumors and stories. That he had been drinking. That the driver they collided with had been drinking. Who knows what the truth was."

"He must have loved his wife, felt responsible." Jesse closed the spout on the water bottle and put it back in the pack.

His voice was tinged with emotion that she hadn't heard before. "Something about him got to you, huh?"

"Sad, really. Living up there all alone," he said.

"That man died a long time ago. He just forgot to stop breathing." She studied him for a moment.

Jesse's features intensified, and the shadows on his cheekbones becoming more defined. He cleared his throat as though he were thinking deeply about something. "I never thought of it that way."

She wondered what was going through his mind. Why the encounter with the isolated stranger had caused such a shift for him.

Her early suspicions of him had been tainted by her own betrayal by Brent. And she'd been on her guard about wanting to show him she could do her job as well as any man.

One side of his mouth curved up in a smile. "What are you thinking?"

She shook her head, feeling a connection to him and a sudden vulnerability. She shut down the emotion as quickly as it had invaded her awareness. She jumped to her feet. "I was thinking we should get moving." Yes, he was a human being who probably had his own struggles and a story to tell, but she still didn't know what to think about him. Had he kept her alive because he needed her expertise to get out of these mountains?

Or was he who he said he was, a DEA agent who'd been framed? The jury was still out. For now, they needed to focus on getting back to Fort Madison and to her predictable life, though she wasn't sure what that life would look like without Brent and the plans they'd made together.

Jesse rose to his feet, as well.

She stepped away from the trees. From this vantage point, she could see the river snaking through the mountains. Though not visible from here, Fort Madison was just beyond the far mountain range. They had a long trek ahead of them.

They ran at a steady pace without stopping until the sky turned charcoal and then black. Darkness slowed their pace.

They walked side by side and chose their path more carefully, winding around trees and bushes and across rockier, more open terrain. From time to time, they heard the dogs baying. The barking made her heart beat a little more intensely. Because the sound echoed off the mountains, it was hard to discern where the dogs were exactly.

She got caught up in the rhythm of their footsteps and took advantage of the chance to find out more about Jesse. "You never answered my question. Did you always want to be a DEA agent?"

They walked for several more feet before he said anything. He ducked to avoid a low-hanging tree branch. An owl hooted somewhere in the distance. "I just sort of drifted into it and found out I was good at it. Did a tour in Afghanistan, was a cop for a while. I really can't talk about my work, Abigail."

So he wasn't about to give her any details about his life. "What can you talk about?"

"I thought I was supposed to be the extrovert?" His voice held just a note of teasing.

"Guess the silence was starting to bother me, too."

They walked on for hours as the sky grew even darker. The steep mountains turned to more rolling hills. When she looked all around her, there were no flashlights shining in the distance. That didn't mean they could let their guard down, though.

She stopped short and pointed off in the distance at the twinkling lights of Fort Madison so far away it would be easy to miss them unless you knew to look for them. "Not much of a city."

"But it's a welcome sight," Jesse said. "Now all we have to do is walk toward the lights, right?"

His comment sent a little wave of fear through her. What would he do if he didn't need her expertise anymore? "We still have a long way to hike. We'll go down into a valley in a little bit. Then you won't be able to see the lights anymore."

"I'm glad I'm with someone who knows the way," said Jesse.

They stopped to rest and eat handfuls of candy. Jesse remained vigilant, pacing in an arc to look all around them. "I don't see any signs of the thugs. That kind of worries me. What are they up to?"

Her chest squeezed tight at the question. She jumped to her feet. "The best thing for us to do is to keep moving."

As they drew closer to civilization, the unspoken suspicion about Jesse sat like a rock in her stomach.

When they wandered down into the valley, the

sound of a helicopter reached her ears. She could see the tiny flashing light far in the distance. The chopper didn't come anywhere near them. The lights disappeared behind the mountain they had just come down.

"That could be anybody, right?" Jesse's voice held a note of tension as they stood together in the darkness.

She trudged ahead. "Yeah, people hire choppers all the time." Tension knotted through her chest. "Night flights are a little unusual, though."

"There wasn't one available for hire when I looked into it. You never would have been dragged into this if I'd been able to go that route."

Though she could not see his expression in the dark, his tone sounded genuinely apologetic. "Hopefully, all of this will just be a memory for me soon."

Jesse walked a little faster as they rose up out of the valley and the lights of Fort Madison became visible again. Their path intersected with the trail.

"This looks familiar," said Jesse.

"Yes, the trail leads right into town." Which meant he didn't need her anymore. She tensed, waiting for his response.

"Probably be smarter not to be out in the open, right?"

She pointed. "We can zigzag through the trees that run parallel to the trail."

"Let's go, then." He patted her shoulder. "I can't thank you enough for all your help."

If he was who he said he was, a lawman who had been wronged, she would be back at home within hours. She stared at him for a long moment, unable to discern his features in the predawn light. "Let's get moving."

She darted toward the trees and trotted along the soft ground, slowed only by the lack of light.

As the sun came up, the forest thinned. She could see the outskirts of Fort Madison, some scattered cabins and barns still far away but discernable. Though the town was visible now, they still had hours of hiking ahead of them. She ran even faster. A weight seemed to lift off her as they drew closer to town. "My place is closer than the Big Sky Outfitters office. My car is there. I jog into the office most days. You can make calls from there, or I can take you where you need to go."

He stopped for a second. His forehead creased. "Yes, I guess I need to figure out my next move." He patted his pocket, where he'd put the hard drive.

They hiked for several more hours as the sun moved across the sky.

Her home, which was a thirty-foot camper trailer, was on a piece of land just outside town. She nearly cried when they came up over a hill and its silvery exterior glistened in the noon light.

"That's where you live?"

"Yes, I'm really into the tiny-house concept and traveling light. The outdoors are my living room," she said. Also, she had thought she and Brent would be buying a house together once they were married.

She felt a heaviness as they got closer to her home. What kind of life was she coming back to here, anyway? If she stayed and worked in Fort Madison, she'd run into Brent sooner or later.

They jogged the remaining distance. She got her key from underneath the trailer, where the trim was curved enough to hold an object, and unlocked the door. "I just need to get my car keys. You can come inside. I can make us some food."

She opened her trailer. Outdoor gear, backpacks, tents, sleeping bags and cross-country skis were scattered throughout the tiny space.

Jesse stepped inside. "Looks like you're prepared for almost anything."

The comment felt like a barb, though she knew he hadn't intended it that way. Because she'd grown up with older brothers, she had learned to compete with them on equal footing. The memory of Brent's parting words to her echoed in her head.

Honestly, Abigail, you're almost too capable of doing everything for yourself. Why do you even need me?

Brent's words still hurt.

"Have a seat." While Jesse settled in, she opened the refrigerator. She pulled some chili out of the freezer and popped it in the microwave, letting it heat through while she sliced some cheese, then got crackers from the cupboard. She brought the cheese and crackers to the table and said, "I make my chili kind of spicy. I hope that's okay."

He offered her a warm smile. "I love spicy."

His smile made her heart skip a beat. There hadn't been much reason to smile up until now. Once the chili was heated through, she dished it up and placed a steaming bowl in front of Jesse beside the plate of sliced cheese and crackers. She sat down opposite him and picked up her spoon. "So, what are you going to do now?"

Jesse's features hardened. "I need to look at the contents of the hard drive first." He let out a heavy breath.

"Then I have to find someone I can trust with the information, someone who will believe me."

He seemed distressed.

"And that won't be easy to do, huh?"

He brought the spoon up to his mouth. "Good chili."

He still wasn't going to talk about his work. What did it matter to her? In another hour, he would be on his way to parts unknown. She watched him eat the chili.

"Delicious," he said. "You're a good cook."

"Not really. But I have a couple of specialties I do really well."

He scraped the bottom of the bowl with his spoon. "Well, I could live on chili like this. Not too wimpy, just the right amount of kick to it."

His compliment made her feel like she was glowing from the inside. It was nice to have her cooking appreciated. "Would you like another bowl?"

"Sure. Fill 'er up." He pushed the bowl across the table and licked his lips.

She set a steaming bowl in front of him and then sat down to finish the rest of her first serving.

He raised his spoon. "To good food and good company." His voice took on a warm tone as he looked her right in the eyes. "And to a job well done, Abigail."

When he looked at her that way, her heart fluttered a little. "I know you are who you say you are. I'm sorry I didn't believe you at first." If he had wanted to do her harm, he would have by now.

He put his spoon on the table. "I understand why you thought what you did. I'm sure I looked like just another one of the bad guys."

She realized then that saying goodbye would be harder than she'd thought it would be. A bond had formed between them. You don't spend a few days running for your life with someone and not feel a connection to them. "I hope everything turns out okay for you."

They finished eating and she grabbed her car keys off the hook by the door. Jesse stepped outside first. She shuffled around the camper, looking for her purse.

She swung open the door to a view of Jesse standing with his hands in the air. Her heart pounded faster as she shifted in the doorway to see two of the thugs from the mountain, Pretty Boy and Eddy, holding their guns on Jesse. The chopper must have gone up there to get them.

Pretty Boy turned his gun on Abigail. "Get out here and stand by your partner. We're missing some product. What did you do with it?"

He must be talking about the drugs the hermit had taken. She wasn't about to put that lonely old man in danger.

"We didn't take your drugs," said Jesse.

"We'll see about that." Pretty Boy tilted his head toward Eddy, who yanked Abigail out of the trailer and then stepped inside.

She could hear Eddy moving around in her trailer, searching.

She hurried to stand beside Jesse. Of course, they'd figured out where she lived.

Eddy poked his head out. "Nothing in here."

Pretty Boy stalked toward them. "You must have hidden it somewhere on the mountain. We can make you talk." Before she could even fully absorb what was happening, he lifted his gun and landed a blow to the side of her head.

* * *

Jesse came to, thinking that he was on a boat in bad weather. He opened his eyes. As he was regaining consciousness, the jittery swaying motion of the van they were in made him think they were at sea in a storm. Now he saw his surroundings for what they really were. He and Abigail had been knocked unconscious and tossed into the back of some kind of service van. There was a back door and no windows. Both sides of the van had shelving that at one time must have contained tools of some kind. Now they looked mostly bare.

A toolbox vibrated across the floor as the van bumped down the road. A water bottle rolled toward him. He picked it up, unscrewed the top and smelled the clear liquid inside. No odor. He took a tentative sip. Water. The men who had kidnapped them had wanted to keep them alive—for now, anyway.

Beside him, Abigail was still unconscious.

He groaned. The last thing he'd wanted was for her to be mixed up in this all over again.

Abigail stirred. "My head hurts."

He patted her shoulder. "Sit up slowly."

She blinked, touched her head and then sat up. "What happened?"

"It appears that we are going for a bit of a road trip. I have no idea where we are." He could only guess at how long they'd been unconscious. Several hours at least.

His last memory was of lunging at the man who had knocked out Abigail, and then his own world had gone dark.

"They didn't kill us outright because they want to find out where those drugs are, right?"

He had to hand it to Abigail. She was sharp at figuring things out. He suspected the road trip was about taking them to someone whose methods were more *persuasive* in getting information out of people. But he kept that theory to himself.

"If those other guys find the old man, they'll know we don't have the drugs."

Though the old man seemed pretty savvy at surviving, he hoped the thugs didn't hurt him and would just trade the drugs for whatever the hermit wanted.

Abigail pulled her knees up to her chest.

"I'm really sorry. You did your job. This should have been over for you back at your trailer," he said.

Abigail met his apology with silence.

He didn't blame her for being upset.

The van rolled to a stop. He heard voices and other cars. He inched toward the back doors and rattled the handle. Locked, of course.

Abigail tilted her head. "We must be at a gas station or something."

Jesse slid open the drawers of the toolbox, desperately looking for something that might pry open the door. He found a rusty wrench.

Abigail had jumped to her feet and was running her hands along the shelving.

The door of the van swung open; a bag was tossed in.

Jesse leaped across the expanse of the van toward the door just as he heard the lock click back into place. Both of them stared at the bag, which had nothing written on it. A grease mark had formed at the bottom.

"It looks like dinner or…breakfast? I'm not sure how long we've been in here, but my stomach is growling, so it's got to be at least five or six hours since we had that chili."

Jesse shrugged. "The bag is probably not going to explode, right?"

"Right." Abigail sat back down on the floor and reached for the bag. She pulled out an item wrapped in paper and opened it up to reveal a burger. She handed it to Jesse and then lifted the second one out for herself. The final container was filled with french fries.

Jesse grabbed the water bottle and held up a french fry. "Here's to good food and great service."

Grease dripped from the bottom of the bun as Abigail took a big bite. "Yes, we'll have to make sure to leave a big tip."

He appreciated that she was so willing to play along in what was truly a dismal situation.

He offered her a drink from the water bottle. She took several gulps.

The meal was greasy but satisfying. He leaned against the far wall of the van as it rolled down the road, swaying from side to side when it gained speed, probably to pass other cars.

Abigail finished her last bite of burger.

"I left you some fries," he said.

She picked up the carton and scooted over to sit by him. She shoved the fries toward him. "I can't eat all these."

He took a fry and chewed. As they grew colder, the fries became less appetizing. Abigail set them to one side, drew her knees up to her chest and tilted her head. Minutes ticked by with neither of them saying anything.

Outside, he detected the hum of other cars whizzing

by. The van slowed down at one point, maybe due to traffic or because they were going through a town. He had no way of knowing for sure.

"You think our hosts would have at least thrown in a deck of cards," he said, trying to keep his tone light. Might as well have a conversation. Silence allowed too much opportunity for worry and speculation. He had to keep his head in this situation.

She leaned a little closer to him. "Jesse, what are we going to do?"

The fear in her voice touched something deep inside him. He longed to make her feel safe, but he couldn't lie.

He picked up the wrench he'd found. "We're going to look for an opportunity to escape. They have to stop sooner or later, and they probably have plans to pull us out of here."

"And do what with us?"

"Let's not go there," he said.

"They think we stashed those drugs somewhere. I'm sure not going to put that old man in danger." Her voice had become more frantic.

He gave her hand a quick squeeze. "We need to focus on waiting for the right moment and being ready when it comes. Did you find anything we could use on those shelves?"

"Just some old rags." She sounded distraught.

Guilt washed through him. This was not her fight. "We'll figure this out." And yet, she hadn't turned on him or blamed him.

Again, the silence fell around them. After maybe an hour, she lay down on her side and rested facing him. He pulled off his jacket, took out the hard drive, put it in his zippered pants pocket and folded the jacket. "You can use my coat for a pillow."

"Thank you." She lifted her head and he slid it underneath her.

He remained awake and vigilant. For the most part, the van moved at a consistent pace. They must have been on a road or highway without much other traffic.

Abigail stirred in her sleep. He'd gotten used to seeing her with her hat pulled down over part of her face. In an understated way, she was an attractive woman. Though she wore no makeup, she had a sort of natural beauty and inner glow.

Her eyes fluttered open. "You're staring at me."

"Sorry. There were no good shows on the television," he said.

She laughed. "Yeah, it's kind of a sensory-deprivation tank in here." She sat up.

"I was just thinking I'm so sorry for ripping you out of your life in Fort Madison. You probably have family and maybe a boyfriend."

"My family is in Idaho." She frowned. "Had a boyfriend, past tense. A fiancé actually." Her voice was filled with anguish. She tilted her head. Sadness saturated her words. "I don't want to talk about it."

He wasn't sure why he'd even broached the subject. He supposed he was curious about who she was beyond what he'd seen of her working as a guide.

"What about you? Do you have family? A girlfriend?"

"I have an aloe vera plant named George. That's about it. George doesn't mind that I'm gone for long periods of time."

"No family?"

"A sister I talk to on holidays. I usually go see her and her kids once a year."

"Mom and Dad?"

He wasn't used to talking about himself this much. The question struck a nerve. "Dad was a pilot. I guess that's where I first got the flying bug. He and Mom got caught in a storm. It was a small plane."

"I'm sorry." A quiet hush fell around them. It wasn't an uncomfortable silence. It felt more like a respectful response for what he had just told her. "How old were you when that happened?"

"Just turned eighteen. Long time ago." And after that, Melissa. The pain was just right beneath the surface. He hadn't really talked to anyone about this. It surprised him how easy it was to open up to her. He wondered, too, if he was a lot like the hermit—dead but still breathing.

The van slowed. The tires made a different sound. They were no longer on pavement. Gravel crunched beneath the tires and the van came to a stop.

Jesse took in a breath and wrapped his fingers around the wrench. He moved so he was crouching by the van doors. This was it. Something was about to happen.

SEVEN

Abigail's heart beat faster as she hurried across the van floor and settled on the opposite side of the doors. When the doors opened, they'd be ready.

She could hear music playing in the cab of the van, something jazzy and turned down to a low volume. Once in a while a voice rose up with one-or two-word sentences. Then the music shut off. Were the men waiting for something or someone?

At least five minutes passed. Abigail repositioned herself before her legs cramped.

More tires crunched underneath the gravel. Another car must have pulled into where the van was parked. A different kind of music was playing from the other car, something with a driving, pounding beat, music that was meant to intimidate. The van shook from the intensity of the doors being slammed shut.

The music continued to play. Voices rose above it. Some sort of argument was taking place. Men shouted swear words.

The music stopped.

Abigail heard a sort of zinging sound. And then the rat-a-tat of guns being fired. More shouting. Footsteps crunched on gravel and moved closer to them.

She pressed her hand against the van door as her heart raced and every muscle tensed. More gunfire. Bullets tore through the van, letting in round slivers of light.

"Get down." Jesse reached out and tugged on the top part of her shoulder. She was flat on her stomach with her hands on her head as the gunfire continued. Paralyzed by fear, she remained motionless.

As abruptly as it had started, the shooting ceased. Still lying flat, she lifted her head a few inches. She could see holes in the van walls where the bullets had gone through—four of them.

Footsteps crunched on gravel, growing closer. "Check the back. See if the merchandise is there." The volume of man's voice indicated he was outside the van. The voice was not Pretty Boy's or Eddy's.

"Now's our chance," said Jesse. He raised the wrench.

Trying to shake off the shock of having been caught in the middle of a gun battle, Abigail resumed her position on the opposite side of the doors. She gained courage from the look of determination on Jesse's face as he raised the wrench.

Some sort of latch or lever on the van was being twisted around, and then one of the doors swung open. Jesse leaped on top of the man who had opened the door. She jumped out of the van after him. The two men rolled around on the ground. Jesse had dropped the wrench in the struggle and she scrambled toward it. Her hands wrapped around the cold metal of the handle just as someone came up behind her. She whirled around, swinging the wrench. A tall man she had never seen before stepped out of range and pulled out a gun, which he aimed at her.

Abigail heard the resounding slap of flesh against flesh as Jesse and the other man exchanged blows and rolled around on the ground.

The tall man shouted something in Spanish at the other man, which made him stop fighting with Jesse. A bit ruffled from the fight, the short man stepped away from Jesse. The tall man pointed his gun at Abigail and Jesse, indicating they needed to stand to one side. The short man peered inside the van and shook his head.

The two men exchanged words in Spanish and shook their heads. The tall one got behind the wheel of the car they had come in. The short man said something to Jesse in Spanish and then shot the tires out on the van before running over to the car and getting in.

Both of them stood watching as the car pulled out on the road, growing smaller and smaller in the waning early-evening light.

Abigail let out a heavy breath. Her heart was still pounding from all the excitement. "What was that about?"

"Those guys thought they were intercepting a drug shipment. They must have been rival dealers who got bad info that these guys were hauling drugs."

"What did that man say to you?"

"He said he didn't want to complicate his life by killing us, and dealing in human cargo was not his thing," said Jesse.

She pointed at the deflated tires. "But he didn't want us following them, either."

"You stay here. I want to see what the condition of the two men who were driving the van is." He hurried around to the front end of the van, out of her view, returning several minutes later. He shook his head. "Both are dead. The guns have been taken off of them."

Abigail stared up and down the long, lonely stretch of road as her breath caught in her throat. So Pretty Boy and Eddy were dead. She knew they were not good men, but they probably had people in their lives who loved them all the same. Someone would hurt over them being gone.

"Where are we?" It was only a two-lane rural road. As far as the eye could see, it was all rolling hills—no fences, no houses, not even a cow or a barn.

"What does it look like to you?"

She shrugged. "Kind of like the badlands of eastern Montana, but I don't have a lot to go off of. We could be in Wyoming or even farther south. All of the western US has parts that are really remote. All I know is that we are not in downtown Los Angeles or Seattle."

Jesse nodded. "It was morning when they grabbed us at your trailer." He tilted his head. "Must only have a few hours of daylight left now."

She nodded. None of that information made it any clearer as to where they were. When she studied the road in either direction, she couldn't even see a sign that indicated what the next town or city was.

"Wait here." Jesse moved around to the cab of the van and opened up the doors, probably looking for anything they might be able to use. He tossed a coat in her direction. "I imagine it will get colder as the night wears on."

She grabbed the coat. "So we walk?" She knew the minute she spoke that it was a dumb question. They sure weren't going to fly out of here.

Jesse retrieved his jacket from the back of the van

and joined her by the edge of the road. "Sooner or later, we'll run into something, or someone will come along." He touched her back lightly and pointed. "Those men headed north on this road. That means they were headed toward some place. That's our best bet for running into civilization."

She tried not to look at the two dead bodies as she and Jesse made their way toward the road. "Those guys were taking us somewhere. What happens when they don't show up with us?"

Jesse let out a heavy breath. "I imagine whoever was expecting us will come looking for us."

That reality sent a wave of fear through her. When would this all end? As the sun descended lower in the sky, she focused on the tapping of their footfalls, trying not to let her imagination get the best of her.

It would be a while before whomever they were being delivered to came out looking for them and found the two dead men. This road would be the first place they'd come searching.

Jesse shoved his hands in his pockets and walked beside her.

"So, do you suppose your aloe vera plant is missing you about now?"

Jesse laughed.

"I should have been back by now from guiding you in. My boss and his wife are out of town, but some of my friends will start to wonder when I don't show up for church stuff…and choir practice." Although people probably wouldn't expect her to show up at choir practice with Brent's new girlfriend there. Really, she didn't even like the idea of going back to Fort Madison and having to face all that pain.

"No," he said, a note of sadness coming into his voice. "No one is wondering where I am."

"Someone might figure out I'm missing." She choked on her words. "But they won't even know where to look. They'll be searching the mountains and trails by Fort Madison."

Jesse wrapped his arm around her back and gave her shoulder a quick squeeze before letting go. "We're going to figure this out."

"I feel like we should pray," she said, not sure how he would react. She felt like she was at the end of her rope. Prayer seemed like the only thing that would help them now.

"Sure, you can pray."

"You don't pray anymore?"

"No, I do. I did." He stared off into the distance. "I still pray when I get myself into a tight spot. It's just that I was married years ago and she—she died. After that and losing my parents, my faith kind of went dormant, I guess."

She was honored that he had shared something so deeply private with her. Faith could be a fragile thing. Her loss was nothing compared to what he must have been through. "I understand how prayer could be hard after all that."

They walked, not saying much at all for at least an hour, still not seeing any sign of civilization.

Stars twinkled as the sky turned from gray to black. The wind blew, creating a rushing sound over the grassy fields that bordered the road. She zipped up the extra coat Jesse had given her. It was a fleece-lined jean jacket that had an odd fruity odor, but she was grateful for the extra warmth as the temperature dropped.

"I see a light over there." Jesse tugged at her elbow and pointed.

A single light bobbed across the distant hills. It was too dark and too far away to discern anything else. "That might be one person camping or out looking for a lost dog. They could be gone by the time we get over there."

"And there might be a cabin there or something. If we stay on the road, we risk an encounter with the men who are going to come looking for the dead guys," Jesse said. "And so far, we have yet to encounter another human being or even a sign of another human."

Clearly, they were on some back road that was not used much. Abigail fought off the despair that threatened to overtake her. She'd been lost before. She'd been uncertain of which way to go before.

She breathed in a quick, silent prayer. "Okay."

Under the cover of darkness, they veered off the road and hiked toward where they'd seen the light. They walked up and down the rolling hills, across a dry creek bed and through a fledgling patch of evergreens. The only signs that humans had ever been in this part of the world were a rusty soda can and a plastic bag that could have blown from somewhere else.

The land here was much flatter, with only sparse vegetation, unlike the high mountains outside Fort Madison.

They came to a hill that looked down into a valley. Though the moon provided some light, everything was mostly covered in shadows. As they hiked into the valley and back up the other side, the tinkling sound of a creek was a welcome break from the monotony of the landscape.

They stopped at the creek and took a drink by cupping their hands and filling them with cool water. They had forgotten to take the water bottle out of the back of the van. The burger and fries they'd been given by their captors had worn off long ago.

Abigail stood up. She thought she heard the barking of a dog far in the distance, but it might have been just wishful thinking.

A much more distinctive sound came from behind her—the back-and-forth ratcheting of a shotgun as the cartridge slid into the chamber.

A male voice filled with fear and anger pelted her back. "The two of you better just hold it right there. Put your hands up where I can see them."

Jesse's leg muscles tensed—he was ready for fight or flight, whatever the occasion called for now that a shotgun was pointed at his back. Not again. Hadn't they just been through this with the hermit?

Jesse let out a heavy exhale to clear his mind. The first option was always to negotiate yourself out of the violent threat. "We're not here to hurt you. We're lost. If you would just let me turn around and speak to you." He needed to know what he was dealing with.

"Stay right where you are, both of you." The man sounded more afraid than bent on violence.

The distant bleating of sheep and the sound of a dog barking reached him. Was this man a sheepherder?

"We're not armed. We don't want to rob you or anything. We're lost—we're trying to find our way back to…" He had no idea what state they were even in. If they explained why, of course it would sound nefarious and far-fetched.

"Nobody comes out this far," said the man. "Unless they're up to something."

Abigail cleared her throat. "Please, at least let us put our hands down."

After a long pause, the man replied, "All right, and turn around slowly."

Both of them dropped their arms and turned to face the man, who held a shotgun on them. Though his face was covered in shadow and he sported a hefty beard, Jesse guessed the man was in his late twenties or early thirties.

"You're a sheepherder? Out here by yourself for long periods of time?" Abigail's were words filled with compassion. She must have understood something about why the man was so paranoid.

"I'm not alone." The man whistled. A moment later, a border collie came bounding over the hill and sat at attention at the man's feet. "Cosette keeps me company."

Great. Another hermit.

"We need to get to the nearest town," said Jesse. "Where would that be?"

The man cocked his head to one side. "You don't know? Did your car break down or what? Your story has all kinds of holes in it. I can't take you into town. I can't leave the sheep."

Jesse could feel himself losing patience. "If you could just point us in the right direction. Tell us where we are?"

The border collie emitted a low growl, apparently not happy about the rising tension.

The sheepherder adjusted the shotgun, so the barrel pointed right at Jesse's chest. "Are you on drugs or something? What have you been doing that you don't even know where you are?"

Jesse clenched his teeth. "Look, buddy, no one gives good answers with a gun pointed at them."

"I know our story sounds a little crazy," Abigail said softly.

The man lowered the gun an inch or so. "More than a little crazy."

"I understand that you can't leave the sheep." She glanced down at the dog. "Cosette. That's a pretty name."

The man's squared shoulders relaxed a little. "Cozy for short."

"After the character in *Les Misérables*?"

"Yeah." The man let the gun fall to his side.

"One of my favorites, too," said Abigail. "What is your name?"

"Edward."

"Edward. I'm Abigail, and this is my friend Jesse."

Abigail had forged a connection with the man and calmed him down. He had to commend Abigail on her negotiation skills, which had never been his strong suit. He was a man of action, not words. Just like with the hermit, having her around had come in handy.

The man addressed Abigail. "Sorry for the full-on assault. I haven't heard another human voice in months. It just seems like the only reason for someone to come out here is because they're up to no good. Guess I'm wound a little tight."

Jesse wondered what Edward was referencing, about people being up to no good.

"I assure you, we just need to be pointed in the right direction," Abigail said.

Edward stepped a little closer toward Abigail. "Like I said, I haven't had any company since my employee dropped off supplies. You must be hungry. Why don't you come back to the camp?"

Jesse was starting to feel like he was invisible.

"That sounds like a plan, Edward," said Abigail.

Edward whistled and Cozy took off running, disappearing over the hill from where she'd come. "Follow the border collie. Camp is just up this way."

Edward had a knowledge of literature, and he seemed well-spoken. Jesse wondered what had led him to such a solitary life.

They hiked over the hill. In the valley below, a flock of sheep grazed while Cozy kept watch on the rim of the hill.

The sheep wagon was a camper that looked like it had been built in the fifties and restored. Edward had a cookstove set up on a table. He disappeared inside the camper.

"I wonder if I'm even going to get fed." Jesse gave Abigail a friendly punch on the shoulder.

"What do you mean?"

"He's only got eyes for you."

"I imagine this is a very lonely life out here." Abigail crossed her arms over her chest. "Obviously, nothing can come of it. We're just passing through."

Edward returned, holding several cans of food. He offered Abigail a big smile. "Sorry, don't have much in the way of fresh food."

Seeing Edward smile like that at Abigail caused a

twinge of an unfamiliar emotion to rise up in Jesse. What was that feeling? Jealousy?

He glanced over at Abigail. Her hair had come loose from the braid and was framing her face in soft waves. She was pretty, but what he liked was the complexity of who she was as a person. His first impression of her had been that she was all hard edges, but now she seemed softer, capable of a deep compassion. Maybe it was just because of what they had been through together, but he felt himself drawn to her.

Edward opened the cans, lit the cookstove and dumped the contents of the cans into the pan that rested on the burner. After the meal had heated for a while, he left again and returned with plates and utensils.

"I only have two plates," said Edward.

Jesse leaned close to Abigail and said under his breath, "See, I told you I wasn't going to get fed."

Abigail elbowed him in the stomach and gave him a raised-eyebrow reprimand. "Jesse and I can share a plate."

Edward offered Abigail his only chair while the two men sat on the ground and ate the beans that had been mixed with tomatoes.

Jesse took a couple of bites and then handed the plate to Abigail. "What did you mean when you said that most people you encounter are out here for nefarious purposes?"

"We're about ninety miles from the Bakken oil fields in North Dakota. Lot of drugs and people being trafficked through there."

Though he'd never worked in the area, Jesse was familiar with the extent of the drug problem in the Bakken. A high concentration of men working long hard hours, not many families or women and confined living quarters made it a ripe area for all sorts of criminal activity. Eddy and Pretty Boy must have been taking Abigail and Jesse there.

"I can see why you were so suspicious of us." Abigail handed the plate back to Jesse.

"The company is nice." Again with the smiles at Abigail. "I'm used to being around people. I grew up on the East Coast. Flunked out of college, made a lot of bad choices. Thought if I came out here, I could get my head cleared up, figure out my life, maybe do some writing."

Edward sure was volunteering a lot of personal information. "And how has that worked out for you?"

Edward seemed almost shocked at Jesse's question, like he'd forgotten he was present. Jesse himself was surprised that his voice had a little bit of an edge to it.

"That was three years ago. I guess I still haven't figured my life out."

They finished their meal and Jesse burst to his feet. "We should get moving." He handed Edward the empty plate. "I don't suppose you have any way to communicate with the outside world."

Edward shook his head. "No cell towers out here. I like the quiet."

"If you'll point us in the right direction, we need to get to the nearest town." Jesse wasn't sure what they would do after that.

"The main highway is to the northeast, about three miles." Edward pointed. "You should hit a small town called Stubenville."

Jesse's mind lit up. Now he knew where they were. A retired agent named Dale lived about an hour outside Stubenville. Dale might be able to help him figure out how to make the case for his innocence, see for sure what was on the hard drive and find a way to send Abigail home safely.

"Wait just a minute. I have something for you." Edward disappeared inside the camper and returned a moment later, holding two granola bars. "It might be a while before someone picks you up and…" He held up a flashlight. "You might need this." He handed the bars and flashlight to Abigail.

"Thanks, Edward. I hope everything turns out okay for you," she said.

They turned and headed up the hill. She handed Jesse the flashlight, which he clicked on. It illuminated a swath of land in front of them. After they had walked for several minutes in silence, she spoke up. "You were a little rude back there. Why?"

"I don't know. Edward was fawning over you a little too much."

But he did know why. He was starting to have feelings for Abigail. He hadn't realized it until another man had shown interest in her. They were not feelings he could ever act on. They were from different worlds. As soon as they got back to civilization, he needed to put Abigail back on a bus to Fort Madison.

All the same, he had to at least admit to himself that he admired, even liked her.

EIGHT

Though she couldn't put her finger on it, Abigail sensed that something had shifted between her and Jesse. "Edward wasn't my type."

"What is your type?"

Brent had been her boyfriend for three years, and she had known him since grade school. They'd been engaged for over a year. There had been boys in high school who had been more friends than anything, nothing serious. "I guess I don't know anymore. Don't know if I ever knew."

"What do you mean?"

Talking about Brent was painful. She'd only shared her heartache with her mom and God. But Jesse had shared something much more traumatic about his life. "Guess I'm just kind of naive. I moved to Fort Madison because my fiancé got a job there. I thought we'd get married and raise our kids there. I never questioned that until a while ago, the guy I was engaged to decided he wanted to be with someone else."

"That's tough. Really, Abigail, I'm sorry for all that pain," he said.

"Yeah, I got this idea in my head that my life was going to turn out a certain way," she said.

"Everyone thinks that. That life has a certain trajectory. High school, college, marriage, kids, retirement. No one factors in the loss and the derailment."

Jesse's profound words sank in deep as they walked on through the darkness, until they could hear the sound of an occasional car going by on the road up ahead.

"Will it be safe to be close to the main road? Won't they be looking for us?"

"Probably, but it's nighttime. It's a stretch of road to cover and there's no way we'll catch a ride into Stuben-ville if we aren't on that road."

Jesse's reasoning was sound. All the same, fear formed a knot at the base of her neck as they got closer to the road. Once they reached pavement, they walked on the shoulder.

"We'll be all right," he said.

He must have picked up on her anxiety, which surprised her. She thought she was pretty good at hiding it. Was he starting to be tuned in to her feelings and moods? The notion scared her a little. If he cared about her feelings, he probably cared about her in a deeper way than just feeling responsible for her safety.

"This is a rural community, probably lots of farms around here. Most farm people will stop if they see us walking," she said. "I just don't know how many people are going to be out at night." She talked to get her racing thoughts off the hamster wheel in her head. So what if Jesse was tuned in to her feelings? Nothing was going to come of it.

"That's good. All we need is one car to come along headed toward Stubenville."

Their shoulders bumped now and then as they walked side by side. Their footsteps made a sort of squishy, crunching sound on the loose gravel at the edge of the road.

They passed a field where cows grazed and rested. There were no lights anywhere on the landscape. No sign of a farmhouse. She crossed her arms over her chest as the night grew colder.

Then she heard the car in the distance. When she looked over her shoulder, the golden headlights were two tiny dots that disappeared as the car descended the hill.

"What if it's one of those men looking for us?"

"It's a chance we gotta take. Or we have a long walk ahead of us in the dark." He leaned a little closer to her. "We'll both keep our radar up. Talk to the guy for a few minutes before we get in the car. If either of us gets a bad feeling, we'll step away and bolt."

The car grew louder, and the headlights became visible again.

The plan was fraught with danger. "Should we have some sort of signal?"

"Just squeeze my elbow," he said. "And I'll do the same for you if I sense any red flags."

As the car drew even closer, Abigail's heart pounded a little faster.

Holding the flashlight, Jesse waved his arms in the air.

The car whizzed past.

Abigail experienced a dark moment when it looked

like the car wasn't even going to stop. The driver hit the brakes with such intensity, the car slid sideways.

They both looked at each other and then ran up to the car. Jesse stood by the driver's-side window and Abigail positioned herself behind him. She peered over her shoulder at the side of the road. If the driver was armed, they could bolt for the ditch and then head into the shelter of the cluster of trees.

The driver's window came down. Though her face was covered in shadow, the driver looked to be a middle-aged woman.

"Did you folks break down?"

"Yes, something like that," Jesse said.

From inside the car, she heard the sound of two girls arguing. Abigail breathed a sigh of relief. Chances were this mom was not someone connected to the drug trade.

"Quiet, girls." Once the fighting between the two kids stopped, the woman gripped the steering wheel and stared through the windshield. "Huh, I didn't see any broken-down cars back there." Suspicion clouded the woman's words.

"Please, if we could just get a ride into town," he said.

Abigail stepped a little closer to the car so the woman could see her. "It's dark. It would be easy to miss seeing the car."

"That's true," said the woman. She glanced at Jesse and then at Abigail. She shrugged. "You'll have to ride in the back with one of my crabby daughters. It's been a long day for us."

"Thank you. We appreciate it." Abigail put her hand forward so the woman could shake it. "I'm Abigail and this is Jesse."

"Pleased to meet you," said the woman.

Once they were in the car, the woman pulled out onto the road. "My name is Sandra. But everyone calls me Sis. These are my daughters, Arielle and Dawn."

The older daughter sat in the front seat. She looked to be in her teens. Arielle gave the two passengers a nod and then put earbuds in her ears and faced forward. Jesse and Abigail sat on either side of Dawn, who held a doll in her lap. The younger daughter was maybe seven or eight years old.

Sis glanced at them in the rearview mirror, probably still wondering if she had made the right choice. "Like I said, it's been a long day for us. My girls competed in a gymnastics tournament up in Dickenson."

Dawn lifted her doll in the air and then hugged it tight. "We didn't win."

"Arielle got fourth place on the balance beam," said Sis.

Abigail stared out at the area bordering the road. They whizzed past a historical marker. She saw lights in the distance that must be farms.

Dawn chatted away about the tournament, her lunch, the boy who was mean to her at school and anything else that popped into her head, and then she broke into song.

When there was a lull in Dawn's monologue, Sis piped up. "Dawn will talk your ear off if you let her. Arielle is my introvert."

They rounded a curve and Sis slowed down. A sign on the edge of the road said Welcome to Stubenville, Population 500.

They weren't going to find much in the way of amenities. Jesse had probably assumed the town was going to be much bigger.

"Where can I drop you folks off at?" Sis asked as she slowed down.

Doubt filled Jesse's voice. "Is there a place we might be able to make a phone call?"

"Not at this hour," Sis said. "You folks look like you could use a shower and some rest. I can drop you off at the Widow Keller's house. She runs an informal bed-and-breakfast," Sis said. "Don't worry about waking her. She's a night owl. Works on her weaving until the wee hours."

"If that's our only option," said Jesse.

Sis eventually pulled up in front of a house.

Abigail and Jesse thanked her. Abigail gave Dawn a poke in the belly. "Thanks for entertaining us, kiddo." The little girl reminded Abigail of her niece, Celeste, her oldest brother's daughter.

"No problem," Dawn chirped, lifting her doll in the air and making it dance.

Jesse and Abigail got out of the car and Sis pulled away from the curb. Dawn waved at them from the back seat. Abigail waved back before turning her attention to the house.

Even in the dark, it looked like something out of a watercolor painting. The porch light was on. Though it was still early spring, tulips and other flowers and greenery bloomed in the garden. Ivy wound around the columns before connecting with the extended roof. The porch swing looked comfortable and inviting.

Under different circumstances, staying here would be a fun adventure. A heaviness invaded Abigail's heart. This wasn't a fun adventure.

"All I have to pay with is a credit card. I'm sure DEA is looking for me to pop up so they have a trace on my card. That means we can't stay here long. Get a quick shower and some sleep. My friend Dale lives about an hour from here. He might be able to help us." Jesse knocked on the door.

A woman with wild white hair that looked like a cloud opened the door. *This must be the Widow Keller.* Jesse explained their situation and apologized for the late hour.

"No problem. I was up, anyway." She ushered them in, Jesse paid for the rooms and the widow pointed up the stairs. "Third and fourth doors on the right. It's a shared bath, but right now you're my only guests. Breakfast is at seven."

"We probably won't be here that long," said Jesse.

"Oh," said the widow as her glance bounced from Jesse to Abigail.

"We just need to get cleaned up and rest a little." Abigail could feel her cheeks getting warm. Did the widow think she and Jesse were a couple?

"Don't need to explain nothing to me. There should be fresh towels in the bath. I could loan you some of my clothes while I toss yours in the wash." She studied Jesse for a moment. "You look like you're about my husband's size. Won't take but an hour to run your clothes through the wash. No extra charge."

Abigail stared down at her muddy clothes. "That would be great."

"I'll leave the clothes outside your doors once they're washed and dried." The widow disappeared down the hallway. "I'll get the fresh ones up to you right away."

They made their way up the stairs. "Why don't you take your shower first?" said Jesse. "When the widow brings the clothes up, I'll set them outside the bathroom door."

Abigail checked several doors before finding the bathroom. Jesse disappeared into one of the rooms they had just paid for.

The bathroom had a deep claw-foot bathtub. A good soak seemed enticing, but she had a feeling time was of the essence. She turned the knobs on the bath and adjusted the temperature. Steam filled up the bathroom almost right away. As the windows steamed up, she pulled back the curtains and stared at the street down below. Light shining from a streetlamp revealed that a car, with a man sitting behind the wheel, was parked across the street.

Her heart beat a little faster. Maybe the man was a local, but in a town this small, it wouldn't be hard to figure out where they were staying. Why would someone sit in their car at night unless they were watching and waiting? The people looking for them could have sent someone to watch the place as soon as they realized they'd escaped.

Jesse was glad to see that there was a phone in his room. The room itself was cozy, with a quilt on the bed and a painting of landscapes on the wall. He picked up the phone and dialed his friend Dale's number.

He touched the hard drive in his pants pocket. Dale, who had computer expertise, would be able to install the drive so he could see exactly what was on it before deciding the best tactic for presenting it to DEA.

Dale picked up the phone after several rings. He

sounded out of breath. "Sorry, I was outside. What can I do for you?"

"Dale, this is Jesse Santorum." He and Dale had run operations out of the Southwest, until a bullet to the back put Dale on the disabled list. The man was in chronic pain and walked with a limp.

"Jesse, good to hear from you."

Even though Dale had been forced into retirement, he was still in touch with other active agents. Jesse had to assume Dale might know about the cloud of suspicion that hung over him.

"Have you heard?"

"Yeah, but I knew it wasn't true. I know you," said Dale.

Jesse felt as though a rope that had been wound around his torso had been loosened. Instead of believing the poison Lee had spread in the DEA, Dale knew Jesse's character well enough to know he would never be on the wrong side of the law. "I'm in a bit of a bind, and I'm not far from your neck of the woods."

Jesse gave the short version of all that had happened. Dale promised that he could be in Stubenville in a little over an hour. Jesse said that he and Abigail would be watching for him.

Jesse hung up. He heard a knock on the door and the Widow Keller's voice. "Clothes are just outside the door. You can keep them. Just stuff I don't use anymore. Toss your dirty ones in the hallway."

When Jesse opened the door, the widow was already at the top of the stairs headed down.

"Thanks." Jesse set the blouse and slacks outside the bathroom and picked up the dirty clothes Abigail had tossed outside the door. He could hear the shower running and Abigail singing what sounded like a hymn. No use trying to talk to her above that noise. She'd know to look for the clean clothes.

He took the clothes that were left for him and slumped down in a chair in his room. His eyelids felt heavy. His head bobbed back and then forward. A moment later, he was in a deep sleep...

His eyes shot open.

Abigail stood in front of him looking fresh and clean in a silky-looking royal blue blouse and gray dress pants. Her hair was still wet from the shower.

Seeing her made him smile. "You look nice."

She twirled from side to side. "Thanks."

He glanced around, looking for a clock but not seeing one. He ran his hands through his thick hair. "How long was I out for?"

She shrugged. "I don't know. Maybe half an hour."

"My friend Dale will be here in a little bit. I better get that shower." He jumped up.

"Yes, we should hurry." Her expression had changed. Two deep furrows formed between her eyebrows.

"Something wrong?"

"There's a car parked across the street with a man in it. You can see him from the bathroom window."

That wasn't a surprise, but Jesse tensed up all the same. "Dale will get here as fast as he can." He wished he could do something to ease the fear he saw etched on Abigail's face. He stepped toward her and squeezed her shoulder. "Once I have assurance that you'll be safe, I'll find a way to get you back home."

She slumped down in the chair. "There's not much for me to go back home to...in Fort Madison, anyway." Her eyes were rimmed with tears.

He gathered her into his arms as a desire to protect, to reassure her, surged through him. "We'll get through this. I'm so sorry I got you mixed up in all of this." He stroked the back of her head. "You've handled yourself just fine, Abigail. You're a strong woman."

She rested her head against his chest. "I don't feel very strong right now." She pulled back to look him in the eyes.

He touched her cheek with his thumb. "You are." In that moment, with her looking at him with so much trust in her eyes, he wanted to kiss her. He studied each feature on her face: her slim nose, soft eyes with lush lashes and her cheeks flushed with a rosy glow. Her eyes grew wider and rounder as her lips parted.

He pulled away. It would be wrong to kiss her. "Yeah, you have been stellar. Any other person would have fallen apart. You're cool under fire, Abigail. You'd make a good agent. You ever think about that?"

The words that spilled out of his mouth caught him off guard. Why was he saying such a thing? It sounded like he was trying to find ways to keep being with her when this was all over. Was his connection to her that deep already?

She stepped back, as well. She shook her head and then stared at the floor. The moment of heated intensity between them had been broken. "Guess I never thought about doing anything other than the family business."

He squeezed her shoulder one more time. "I'm going to shower." He stepped out into the hallway, feeling a familiar ache in his chest. The chasm of pain over losing Melissa flooded through him. To love was to risk loss, and he knew he couldn't do that ever again.

He checked the bathroom window before getting in

the shower. He saw the car with the driver sitting behind the wheel. He showered and stepped out, wrapping a towel around his waist. When he looked out the window again, the car was gone. That concerned him even more. The window to the bathroom faced a side street. He wondered if the car had moved to the front of the house. He threw his dirty clothes outside the door, taking the hard drive out of his pants pocket. He hadn't put his coat out to be washed. He could put the hard drive back in there.

It could be that whoever was sitting in that car wasn't connected to the drug trade, but he doubted it.

Jesse changed into the overalls and plaid shirt the widow had provided. A sense of urgency told him that maybe it wouldn't be a good idea to hang around here longer than they had to. He glanced at himself in the mirror. Great. He looked like Farmer Brown out to check his crops.

When he stepped into the hallway, his dirty clothes had been picked up. He found Abigail asleep in her room. She looked peaceful, with her hands crossed over her chest and the quilt only half covering her, as if she'd pulled it over herself just as she was falling asleep.

His shower hadn't taken that long. He had maybe another twenty minutes or so before Dale would be here. He left Abigail to get some much-needed rest and hurried downstairs. He stood to the side of the big front window, surveying the street. No sign of the car that had been parked on the side street.

"You gettin' ready to leave so soon?" The widow had come up behind him.

He turned to face her. She was a kind woman. He

sure didn't want to put her in any danger. "I have a friend coming to pick us up."

"Be a little while before your clothes are dry," she said.

"Don't worry about it. The clothes you gave us are fine."

She put her hands in the pockets of her apron. "At least let me make a hot cup of tea for you and your friend."

He liked that she didn't ask questions about their strange behavior. Maybe being the only place to stay for miles had taught her to be discreet.

"That would be nice." Jesse settled in a chair that was off to the side, so he had a view of the window without being visible from the street.

The widow brought in a tray with a teapot and two cups.

"This is really wonderful. Thank you." He'd been expecting a tea bag in a mug warmed in the microwave.

"If you're going to have tea, you might as well brew it proper." The widow padded down the hallway, back into a room at the end of the hallway that must be where she did her weaving. Like the hermit and sheepherder, she, too, seemed to lead a solitary life.

Abigail came down the stairs. She held her waterproof jacket. She hadn't put that in the wash.

"Did you get rested?"

He felt an awkwardness between them that hadn't been there before. Had she wanted to kiss him as much as he'd wanted to kiss her? Or was this whole thing one-sided?

"I examined the insides of my eyelids, as my grandpa

used to say." She noticed the tray with the pot and tea-cups. "Wow, what's all this?"

"The widow made us tea. Help yourself." He looked at the clock on the living room wall. "I imagine it'll be a few more minutes before Dale gets here." He slipped into his coat that contained the hard drive.

Abigail poured a cup of the steaming brew, dropped in a sugar cube and sat on the couch.

Jesse stood up and peered out the window again by standing to one side. No new cars had moved into place. "The car that you saw from the bathroom window is gone."

She took a sip of tea. "Maybe it was nothing, then."

He picked up on the tension in her voice. They both knew that someone was looking for them in the area surrounding where the shootout had taken place. It wasn't like there were a hundred small towns they could have gone to.

"I poured you some tea," Abigail said. "Sit down. There's nothing we can do until your friend comes."

She was right. He could pace until there was a hole in the floor and fret all day and night. They would deal with what they had to deal with when and if it happened. For the next few minutes—the time it took to drink a cup of tea—he could catch his breath. He sat down on the couch beside her.

She took a sip of tea. "It's really good."

He plopped in a sugar cube, stirred it with the dainty spoon and brought the steaming cup to his lips. He tasted a mixture of orange and cinnamon. He took several more sips.

Jesse heard footsteps behind him. He had only a second to register that the footfalls were too heavy to be the widow's before he turned to face the barrel of a gun and a grinning face.

Standing beside him, Abigail dropped the teacup and released an audible breath that sounded like it got choked off in the middle. The echo of the shattering porcelain of the teacup filled the air around him.

NINE

The man sneered, still holding the gun on them. "If the two of you come nice and quiet, nothing will happen to the old lady."

Abigail's heart raced. She gripped Jesse's arm below the elbow. Touching him made her feel less afraid. She sure didn't want anything to happen to the Widow Keller.

"We'll go," said Jesse. "But you have to keep your word about the woman."

"Good, then hurry on out the back door and keep your hands up where I can see them."

Abigail noticed Jesse turning his eyes but not his head toward the front window. Probably checking to see if his friend had made it.

The thug pointed with the gun. He had a scar on his right cheek. His eyes were watery and dark. "Second door on the right. Go out through the kitchen. Don't try anything. I'm right behind you."

Jesse nodded, indicating that Abigail should go ahead of him. They raced past a closed door, where loud instrumental music blared from behind it. Abigail detected the clacking sound of a weaver's loom. The widow wouldn't hear them leaving above all that noise.

They raced through the kitchen. When Abigail stepped outside, another man was waiting for them, leaning against the car they had seen earlier. He held a gun, as well. The two men must have been watching the house through the windows, figuring out how many people were inside.

Jesse glanced around, probably trying to find an escape route. The back alley was dark. They were shielded from view on the street by the neighbor's garage. It was unlikely anyone would be outside at this hour, anyway.

"Get in the back and lie down," said the man with the scar. "Get in now." The guy was clearly nervous and in a hurry to leave before they were spotted.

The car was a sort of caravan with two rows of seats and a back area for hauling larger items—the kind moms used to transport kids and soccer equipment. The kind of car nobody would think was being used for a kidnapping.

Scarface slid open the side door and gestured for Abigail and Jesse to get in.

"Keep your heads down," he said.

Both of them lay on the floor of the van. The two men climbed into the front seats. The van pulled forward and turned. Through the window, she caught flashes of trees and houses bathed in the light from streetlamps. The car gained speed as they got to the edge of the little town.

She turned so she was lying on her side, facing Jesse. She hoped her expression conveyed that she was wondering what they should do. Scarface, who sat in the passenger seat, kept a gun on them.

Jesse shook his head, meaning he didn't have a plan

yet. He leaned close to her, so he could whisper in her ear. "They've got to stop sooner or later. That will be our chance."

The heat from his breath lingered on her ear.

"No talking," said the man with the gun in the passenger seat.

The car rumbled down the road.

She prayed the stop would happen before they got to wherever they were being taken. They were being kept alive for some reason. Was it possible the drugs the hermit had taken hadn't been found yet?

In the front seats, the two men were talking. "What is that guy's problem?" said the thug who was driving.

Abigail lifted her head to see what was going on.

Scarface waved his fist in the air. "Yeah, buddy. It's a whole big road here. Why do you got to be right on our tail?" He turned his head to peer out the back window. "Slow down. Maybe he'll pass us."

Abigail lay back down before Scarface could notice her.

The van slowed. She could hear the noise of a car speeding past them. The caravan rolled down the road at a steady pace. Lights flashed in the window. When she raised her head, Abigail saw that they had passed a gas station.

Scarface turned around and waved the gun at her. "Hey, lie down flat."

Were they going to stop at all?

She quelled her fear with a deep breath and a quick prayer.

Jesse reached over and covered her hand with his, as if to reassure her. The warmth of his touch sank into the marrow and she could feel herself calming down.

"Pull over. I need to take a leak," said Scarface.

"Boss said no stopping," said the driver.

Abigail wondered whom they were referencing when they mentioned *the boss*.

"Two minutes. I drank too many energy drinks back there while I was watching the place," said Scarface.

The driver groaned but slowed and pulled over. "Hurry up."

"Okay, Rodney," said Scarface.

Rodney turned in his seat and studied them for a moment before offering them a grin that sent chills down Abigail's spine. "You two look so nice and cozy back there." He lifted his gun, jabbed it in the air and pointed it at them. "No sudden moves." Rodney laughed as he turned around to stare through the windshield. He hit the steering wheel with his palm. "What's taking that guy so long?"

Rodney turned up the radio, so it was blaring.

Once she was sure the driver was not watching them, she lifted her head. With the exception of some bushes where Scarface must have gone, the landscape was flat all around and there was no sign of any dwelling.

If they tried to escape out the back, they'd be shot before they could get to any kind of cover. The gas station they had passed was miles down the road. Rodney was constantly checking his rearview mirror and turning to look at them.

She eased back down and shook her head.

Jesse shrugged his shoulders as if to say he wasn't sure what to do. Rodney turned down the music. He craned his neck one way and then the other, searching. "This is taking too long." He inched the caravan forward and then rolled down the passenger-side window so he could lean across the seat and shout. "Hey, Larry, come on. We got to get moving!" So Scarface's name was Larry.

Jesse leaped to his feet and placed his arms around Rodney's neck. He yelled at Abigail, "Go!"

Jesse had taken advantage of the moment of distraction.

Heart racing, she struggled to lift the handle on the side door. She could hear the two men fighting. What if Rodney got to his gun and shot Jesse? Larry, the man with a scar, would come back soon enough. She jumped out of the van as she heard the noise of blows being exchanged.

Her feet hit the ground. The sound of the struggle ended. Jesse was close behind her.

The long stretch of open flat road lay to the north and south. The only cover was the bushes, where the other man must have gone. They couldn't go that way.

With Jesse right beside her, she took off at a dead run.

Gunshots boomed behind them. When she glanced over her shoulder, Larry had come out of the bushes and was taking aim at them.

The second gunshot was so loud she felt like her eardrums had been punctured. Jesse veered toward the side of the road. Smart move. Though there was no place to take cover, getting away from the road and running into the darkness would make them harder to hit.

She saw headlights in the distance looming toward them. Another vehicle.

Please, God, let this be someone who is willing to stop.

Larry continued to run toward them, stopping to fire off another round.

She stuttered in her steps, unwilling to give in to the terror that gripped her. Jesse spurted ahead of her, running parallel to the road as the headlights of the oncoming car drew near.

She heard the sound of the van starting up. Rodney must have come to. They'd have no chance at all once he got the van turned around. They had to get off the road or be run down.

The oncoming four-wheel drive braked on the shoulder some thirty feet away. His stop was so sudden that his tires spit gravel. The driver rolled down his window and stuck his head out, waving at them.

"That's Dale." Jesse ran faster.

Behind them, the van had been turned around and the driver rolled out onto the road, gaining speed as Larry, still on foot, closed the distance between them.

Dale pulled back out on the road and sped toward them. He stopped in the middle of the road. Jesse fumbled with the back door.

Another shot was fired.

Jesse swung open the door, stepped to one side so Abigail could get in first and then fell in himself while Dale shifted into Reverse, pressed the gas, cranked the steering wheel and spun around his car.

Abigail stared out the back window. The driver had stopped long enough for the passenger to hop into the van before speeding toward Dale's four-wheel drive. The delay bought them precious seconds.

"Let's see if we can lose these guys." Dale glanced in the rearview mirror.

Jesse finally succeeded in closing the back door. He pressed his back against the seat and stared at the ceiling.

"Abigail, this is my friend Dale," Jesse said, out of breath from running.

"Pleased to meet you." Dale never took his eyes off the road. "Looks like we got a job on our hands here, Jesse." Dale's voice was infused with affection. The two men must have some sort of history together. Dale increased his speed and then turned off the paved road onto a dirt one. "Nothing I can't handle."

"Pleased to meet you, too." Abigail was still recovering from the adrenaline rush of getting away from the guys in the van.

The dirt road got bumpier. The van stayed close behind them.

Dale leaned forward. "Get your seat belts on. This is going to get way worse before it gets better."

The four-wheel drive bounced and swayed on the rough road.

Looking into Jesse's eyes calmed her. The vehicle jerked wildly, and both of them jolted around as they fumbled to secure the seat belts.

"Keep 'er steady there, Dale." Jesse's tone was light-hearted, almost joking.

"I'm doing my best, friend," said Dale.

She wasn't sure how the two men could joke around with the van still bearing down on them and the condition of the road getting worse, but she would take the levity over the white-knuckle terror that she was fighting not to give in to.

Just then, Dale's four-wheel drive hit a bump.

Dale checked his rearview mirror. "Now that you two are buckled up, things are going to get really interesting."

Abigail glanced through the rear window. The van had closed the distance between them.

Dale sped up and turned off the road toward a cluster of trees. "Don't worry," said Dale. "There is a road here…sort of." Dale laughed.

Abigail was starting to wonder if she was in a vehicle with a crazy man. She shot Jesse a raised eyebrow and shook her head.

"Dale gets a thrill out of four-wheelin', is all," Jesse said. His voice gave away how exciting it was for him, too. Some men thrived on danger.

"It's even more fun when you're being chased. Remember that time in Colombia?"

"Yeah, I remember. That Jeep was so old and rusted out, you could look through the floor at the scenery." Jesse turned slightly toward Abigail. "Dale and I used to run operations together."

"So I gathered." The camaraderie between the two men was neat to witness.

Dale continued to aim toward the trees. As they got closer, she saw no sign of a road.

Dale drove through the trees and out onto ground that was rockier. His four-wheel drive was able to crawl over boulders. The headlights of the van grew farther away and then disappeared altogether. Finally, he pulled out onto what looked like a country road. She was grateful that they'd stopped jerking around as Dale increased his speed and took them up a winding road, where the trees were more abundant.

The path they were on smoothed out. They weren't being jostled from side to side as much. She couldn't see the van at all now.

Abigail closed her eyes and took in a deep breath. They were safe…for now.

Dale brought his four-wheel drive to a stop outside a cabin that was partially hidden from view by evergreens. Though he had heard about it from other agents, Jesse had never been to Dale's secluded retirement home. He pushed open his own door and hurried around to Abigail's side. Once again, she'd handled herself like a champion.

Jesse held the door for Abigail while she slid out and looked around. Dale was already headed up the trail toward the cabin.

Dale yelled over his shoulder, "Both of you can grab a couple of logs on your way in. I'll get a fire started."

Abigail glanced around. "This looks really primitive…and far away from everything."

Jesse rested his hand on her shoulder. "I'm sure Dale has made the place very livable."

Abigail made her way up the trail, where flat rocks had been pressed into the dirt to create a path.

Once they were on the cabin's porch, Jesse said, "Hold your hands out in front of you. I'll load you up with logs."

Abigail obliged and Jesse placed several logs in her C-shaped arms. "Let me know when it's heavy enough for you."

"I'm starting to see a theme here." Abigail turned slightly toward the cabin door.

"What do you mean?"

"Dale is another isolated loner. Like the hermit and Edward and even that widow."

"Some people just choose to be alone for whatever reason." Dale hadn't always lived alone. A painful divorce shortly before he retired had left the man disillusioned. "Dale has two grown sons who come out here all the time. He's in touch with lots of agents still in the field. Sometimes pain drives your life in a particular direction." He understood that more than anyone.

"I know. After Brent, I thought about going up in the mountains just living by myself, but you have to go on, right? You have to find some way to heal." She looked off in the distance. "I have to figure out what my life is going to look like without him and the plans we made together."

"Right." Jesse picked up several logs until his own arms were full. As he watched Abigail disappear inside the cabin, it occurred to him that it was possible to be living in a city and still be living in isolation. It was what he had done since Melissa's death.

He checked the surrounding woods for any signs of movement and listened for a moment. Confident that they had not been followed, he stepped inside. The cabin was one large room with a loft. One corner was dedicated to computers and computer parts, and another contained a refrigerator and stove. On the other side of the room, Dale had already started a fire in the fireplace. Jesse dumped his firewood and plopped down on a worn leather couch that faced the fire.

He pulled the hard drive he'd been hauling around out of his pocket. "Can we get this installed and see what's on it?" Jesse still didn't have a clear plan as to whom he could trust with the information on the drive.

It occurred to him that he might get it into the hands of one of the other agents who knew him, and then it could be passed up the line to the supervisors who thought he was the turncoat.

Dale threw another log on the fire. "Hold your horses now. We got time and I don't often get company."

"What about the guys in the van?"

"We'll keep watch for them. But that van they were driving won't handle as well on these roads as my vehicle." said Dale.

Abigail turned toward the kitchen area. "I could make some tea."

"That sounds like a great idea," said Dale.

The fire crackled as flames shot up and grew larger.

Dale sat opposite Jesse in an overstuffed chair that looked like something Dale might have picked up out of a dumpster or off the curb. It was made of some sort of orange velvet material. A stack of books sat beside it, so Dale must use it as his reading chair.

Dale leaned forward and held out his hand. "Let me see what you got there."

Jesse handed him the hard drive.

Dale turned it over in his hands. "Oh, yeah, this is all just standard stuff. Shouldn't be too much trouble at all."

The kettle whistled, and a moment later, Abigail brought them each a cup of tea and then returned to get one for herself. She sat down on the couch a few feet from Jesse. After several sips of tea, Jesse could feel himself relaxing. It was still dark outside. The sun would be coming up shortly.

Dale asked Abigail several questions about where she was from and what she did for a living.

"And how did you get tangled up with this guy?" Dale sat back in his chair.

Abigail gazed over at Jesse. "That's a long story."

He thought he saw affection in her eyes. Of course, after all they had been through, they felt a bond toward each other. But was he sensing even deeper feelings?

"Once I'm sure she's not going to be a target, I need to see she gets home safely," said Jesse.

Abigail circled the rim of the mug with her finger and stared into her tea. "Yes, all of this has been very exciting, but I suppose I need to go back…home."

He picked up on the pain in her voice.

Dale and Jesse talked and joked some about some of the investigations they had worked together on, and then Dale retreated to his worktable with the hard drive. "There's sandwich stuff in the fridge if you two are hungry," Dale called from across the room.

Jesse covered Abigail's hand with his. "Let me get it. You got the tea."

Abigail jumped to her feet. "I'll help you. It's not like I have something else to do."

Jesse pulled cold cuts, cheese and condiments from the refrigerator while Abigail searched the cupboards for bread.

They made the sandwiches and sat back down in front of the fire.

After he took several bites, Jesse watched the fire and contemplated the next steps he needed to take. "Abigail, I may have to travel to another state to get this information to someone who can help me. I'm concerned that if you go back to Fort Madison, you will still be a target."

Abigail straightened her spine. "I was thinking I should just go back to Idaho, where my family is. There's nothing left for me in Fort Madison other than to get my stuff and offer my employer an explanation. I can wait on getting my stuff."

"That might be safer," Jesse said.

"You don't sound so sure."

The cartel could find out easily enough where her family lived. Maybe she would be safer if she stayed here with Dale until he could clear his name and get her some protection. He wasn't sure what to do. All he knew was that the thought of being separated from her made him uneasy…and sad.

Dale pushed his rolling chair back from his worktable. "All right, folks, I think I got this thing installed and ready to run."

Jesse took in a breath. This was it. The moment of truth. Everything he'd been fighting for since he'd walked into the office of Big Sky Outfitters.

A million questions bombarded his brain as he walked across the wood floor toward the wall of computers. Would what was on the hard drive be enough to exonerate him? Would he be able to get it to someone who could help clear his name?

TEN

As they walked across the floor, Abigail felt as though she and Jesse were once again coming to the end of their need to stay together. A heaviness like a lead blanket weighed on her shoulders. The revelation that there was nothing for her in Fort Madison left a big hole inside her. Sure, she could go back to her family in Idaho. She could go back to working as a guide where she'd grown up. But was that what she wanted?

The laptop screen in front of Dale glowed, and then icons that indicated files came on the screen.

Jesse rested his hand on the back of Dale's chair and leaned closer to the screen. "So it looks like the first three are audio files." He pointed at one of the icons. "That must be the file that contains the undoctored photos. I'm not sure what this last file is that only has numbers for a title. Open up the photo file and let me see what's there."

"I'll let you have a look," said Dale, rising from his chair. "I'm going to grab a sandwich for myself."

After Jesse took over Dale's seat, Abigail edged closer, peering over Jesse's shoulder as he scrolled through photographs. The only thing the images had in common was a man with a buzz cut. The pictures showed him entering an airport holding a briefcase, sitting at a table with men who had tattoos on their necks and arms, standing outside a bar with a Spanish name. And sitting at a restaurant with men in business suits.

"Is that Lee? The man who set you up?"

Jesse nodded. "Yes, that's him. The doctored photos the DEA got had me doing all this stuff. Part of me just doesn't want to believe Lee would do such a thing."

Jesse clicked on the file that only had numbers for a title. A video of Lee came on-screen as he adjusted the camera and sat back. Lee's shoulders drooped, and he had dark circles under his eyes. Though it was dimly lit, it was clear the recording had been done inside the airplane that had been landed in the mountains outside Fort Madison.

"If you have found this file, it means I'm dead. Nobody knows I kept the original files but me. I was told to destroy them. I never meant for this to go as far as it did. I didn't want to make Agent Santorum take the fall. He's a good guy. Emily had medical bills we couldn't pay, and this was a way to make some cash on the side."

Jesse drummed on the table with his fingers. His jaw was set tight. What he was hearing was upsetting him. Abigail spoke in a soft voice. "Who was Emily?"

Jesse ran his hands through his hair. "His daughter. She had some sort of chronic illness."

Lee continued to talk on the screen. "When I tried to get out, I couldn't. Taking this plane was my insurance. A way to get the upper hand. No one knows where it is but me."

All the color drained from Jesse's face as he hit the pause button on the video. "It sounds like someone else was calling the shots on this whole working-with-the-cartel thing, and Lee was just a go-between."

Dale stood behind them holding his sandwich. "Another agent maybe?"

Jesse rubbed his chin. "Lee seemed afraid in Mexico, even before we got in that firefight. Maybe the dirty agent was there with us." Jesse's voice took on a faraway quality. He stared at the wall as though he was rerunning the events of that night. "Maybe he was going to tell me who it was…and he just ran out of time."

Jesse hit the play button on the video. Lee rested his head in his hands for a moment before looking at the camera again. His eyes were glazed with weariness and defeat. "Agent Frisk has been working with the drug dealers, feeding them information, helping them move product, giving them warnings for over a year now. He's the one who had me frame Jesse."

The screen went black.

Jesse sat back in the chair. "Agent Frisk was there the night Lee died." Jesse closed his eyes and massaged the area between his eyebrows. "When I think about the way things played out, Lee might not have been shot by the dealers. It might have been Frisk who shot him."

"Maybe Frisk figured out Lee was getting cold feet."

"Maybe." Jesse's jawline hardened. He bolted up from the chair. Turning his back toward Abigail and Dale, he took several steps, placed his hands on his hips and shook his head. The stiffness through his shoulders indicated how upset he was.

A tense quiet overtook the room. Abigail's heart

lurched. Jesse was dealing with so much right now. She wasn't sure what to say.

The window Abigail stood by shattered. Broken glass came at her like a thousand tiny knifes. Instinctually, Abigail fell to the floor and crawled toward the shelter of the computer worktable. Her heart raced as the adrenaline kicked in.

Dale scrambled across the floor on all fours. "Looks like they found us."

Jesse dived for cover by the couch.

Dale opened a table by the couch, pulled out a handgun and slid it toward Jesse. He crawled around toward a gun rack over the fireplace and retrieved a rifle.

Abigail braced for more gunshots. Shards of glass in various sizes were strewed across the floor.

"Abigail, get the laptop." Jesse pointed at the worktable.

Even as her heart pounded wildly, a curious calm washed over her. They needed to save that hard drive. She reached up and felt around for the edge of the laptop, then pulled it down toward her.

Dale made his way toward the shattered window. "If you can get to that screwdriver and pull the hard drive, that would be good."

Crouching beneath the height of the window, she moved across the floor toward where a screwdriver had rolled off the table. She returned to the safety that the underside of the worktable provided. She shut off the laptop and then flipped it over.

Dale peered above the rim of the broken window while Jesse checked out the window that faced the front of the cabin.

"See anything?" Jesse crouched beneath the window with his gun drawn.

Dale shook his head. "You?"

Jesse lifted his head again above the rim of the window. "Some movement in the trees. They're repositioning. Can't tell how many. Don't see a vehicle. They must have parked a ways away."

As she loosened the screws on the bottom of the laptop, her fingers remained steady despite her rapid pulse. It was as if some instinct had taken over. She'd felt this before when encountering animals in the wild. It was as if her body overrode whatever fear her mind was battling. Her legs knew whether the smart thing to do was to run or stand still. She felt the same thing now, even though Dale's cabin was under siege.

She opened the laptop and pulled out the hard drive, placing it in her pocket. They were in this fight together. Jesse was a good man. She wanted to help him clear his name. "Dale, you got a gun for me?"

Dale had worked his way over to the only other window by the kitchen area. "You know how to use it?"

"Yes, she does," said Jesse. Admiration colored his words as he gazed at her.

Dale pointed to a bookcase on Jesse's side of the room. "Behind *The History of Rome*."

Abigail got to the bookcase just as another shot was fired through the broken window. The bullet ricocheted off something solid, making a pinging noise. Dale returned fire, then rested his rifle on the rim of the broken window and looked through his scope. He shot two rounds before dipping below the window frame.

"Can you see them out there?" Jesse worked his way to Dale.

"I didn't see anyone, but I can tell you where the shot came from," said Dale.

Abigail pulled the heavy volume off the bookshelf, where a handgun with a short barrel was hidden. She flipped open the cylinder. The gun was a revolver with six bullets. "What do you think they're trying to do?"

"Flush us out into the open," said Jesse. "Who knows, there might just be one guy out there."

"Tell you what," said Dale. "How about I hold them or him off while you two get to my vehicle? I have another car stored deeper in the forest."

Judging from all the guns he had hidden and the second car, Dale seemed to have all sorts of contingency plans for survival and escape. Maybe agents always worried that people they had put in jail might come after them when they got out. And maybe they just learned to always have a backup plan.

"Are you sure about that?" Jesse glanced in Abigail's direction and then looked back at Dale. "That's a big risk."

"Won't be my first time in a firefight," said Dale. "I kind of miss it sometimes. Toss me your gun. I can make it sound like there are ten of us in here. You and Abigail take the little snub-nosed pistol. The keys for the four-wheel drive are in that bowl on the table by the door."

"Will do." Jesse nodded at his friend. "Thanks for everything, Dale." He hurried across the floor toward Abigail, who had already retrieved the keys from the bowl.

Behind her, Dale started to fire shots, first from the rifle and then from the handgun. The shots came so fast they almost seemed to overlap. Jesse grabbed

Abigail's hand and squeezed it before reaching for the door handle.

Taking in a breath and drawing strength from Jesse holding her hand, Abigail braced herself, ready to step out into what might be a hail of gunfire.

"Be as quiet as possible," Jesse whispered. He pushed the door open so there was a narrow slit for him and Abigail to slip through. He went first, regretting that he had to let go of Abigail's hand.

Their feet made soft padding noises as they moved across the porch. Jesse surveyed the surrounding trees for movement or the flash of a gunshot. From inside the house, they could hear the rapid exchange of fire between Dale and whoever was at the back of the house. The gunfire would cease for several seconds and then resume. Dale must have dug up more bullets at some point.

Jesse took in a deep breath. "Let's make a run for it."

They sprinted down the steps toward Dale's four-wheel drive.

The silence made him that much more vigilant. He slipped behind the steering wheel, and Abigail handed him the keys. He turned the key in the ignition.

The gunfire on the far side of the house stopped.

Jesse shifted into Reverse and turned around. "Stay down. We don't know what kind of numbers we're dealing with here." He assumed it was only the two men who had taken them from the bed-and-breakfast, but it was dangerous to assume.

Abigail put her head on the seat.

A gunshot came at them from behind. In his rear-view mirror, Jesse watched a man shooting from the side of the house, barely visible in the early-morning light.

He hit the gas and headed toward the winding trail. When he checked the rearview mirror one more time, he saw that Dale had come around the back of the shooter and overtaken him. The shooter looked like the one called Rodney. Dale would be okay and would probably get Rodney turned in to the sheriff to deal with after he questioned him. The thug might have useful information.

Jesse sped down the winding road. The glint of metal caught his eye up ahead. The thugs' van was parked to one side of the road, facing downhill for a quick escape. They must have seen the smoke from the cabin fire and known that it was just around the bend. When he drove past, there was no one behind the wheel. He saw no movement in the surrounding area, either. Both men must have gone up to the cabin.

Jesse stopped, but left the vehicle running. "Just a second. Let me make sure that other guy doesn't get off the mountain." He took the gun and walked toward the parked van, prepared to blow out the tires.

Just as he drew the gun up and placed his finger on the trigger, the engine of Dale's four-wheel drive revved up. At first, he thought Abigail had slipped over into the driver's seat to move the car for whatever reason, but then he saw the thug called Larry behind the wheel, driving away with Abigail. He must have been hiding in the trees or going to the bathroom again.

Jesse swung open the driver's-side door of the van and hopped in. He was grateful to see the keys had been tossed into the console. His heart squeezed tight as he fired up the van and pulled out, prepared to chase Larry and Abigail.

He watched the taillights of Dale's vehicle disappear around a corner. It was moving so fast it seemed to catch air as it turned. The van handled poorly on the rough roads. He fought off that feeling of helplessness—the same feeling he'd had when Melissa had first been diagnosed with cancer.

Abigail wasn't going to die. Not on his watch.

He said a quick prayer for Abigail's safety and pressed down on the gas.

ELEVEN

All the air left Abigail's lungs as her whole body tensed.

The driver, Larry, spoke through gritted teeth. "Don't try anything, lady." He drove one-handed and held his gun close to his stomach, pointed at her.

She glanced through the back window but saw only the empty winding road behind her as they rounded a curve.

"Don't you want to wait for your friend?"

"He wasn't my friend. I know what happened to him. That guy in the cabin has him. That's why I high-tailed it back down to the van before he took me out, too. Running into you makes my life that much easier."

The man seemed extremely agitated. He kept read-justing the grip of the gun in his hand.

Was there some way she could get the upper hand psychologically? She was used to dealing with wild animals. They had predictable patterns of behavior. "It doesn't matter what happened to your partner? What was his name? Rodney?"

The man kept his eyes on the road, but his whole body stiffened. "If I don't bring you two in, I'm in big trouble. That's all I know."

The words sank in just as she turned slightly to see Jesse following in the van. So the plan must be to use her as bait to lure Jesse to wherever he needed to be taken. Of course, Jesse would come after them to try to get her free.

Her hand touched the hard drive in her pocket. She hadn't had a chance to give it back to Jesse.

The driver made his way down the winding road and out onto a two-lane highway. The terrain became flat again, allowing her to see for miles. In the distance, she saw bundles of light scattered all over the landscape with one large concentration of lights. That had to be the Bakken oil fields and whatever boomtown was close to it.

Larry continued to talk. "There's a phone in my shirt pocket. Take it out. Dial the number for Ernie and tell him I'm headed toward the Tasco truck stop. We're about ten minutes away." The driver shot her a look. "And don't try anything."

She pulled out the phone, wondering if by making this phone call, she was signing her and Jesse's death warrants. She scrolled through the list of phone numbers until she found the one that said Ernie and pressed the icon to dial.

"Yes." The voice on the other end of the line came across harsh and demanding.

Abigail cleared her throat. "I'm supposed to tell you that we're headed toward the Tasco truck stop. We'll be there in ten minutes."

"Tell him target one is in the van and that I have target two in a rust-colored four-wheel drive," said Larry. "Tell him Rodney is out of the game."

It seemed a bit cavalier to say someone was out

of the game when they had been captured by Dale and would probably be turned over to the law. But she gripped the phone and repeated what Larry told her.

"Too bad about Rodney. That might come back to bite us down the line if he squawks." The voice on the phone grunted. "I can send someone to the truck stop about the same time you get there." Ernie disconnected. She doubted that was the man's real name. When she'd scrolled through the contacts, she'd noticed other names from children's programs listed. They probably all had code names on the phones.

She put down the phone and repeated what the voice had told her.

Larry seemed to calm down a little. His shoulders weren't as stiff. "Good, this is all going to turn out okay."

Abigail didn't feel any less afraid. Maybe things would turn out okay for Larry, but what about them?

She saw the lights of the truck stop up ahead. Jesse continued to follow them in the van. The truck stop was humming with activity. Larry hit his blinker and pulled off. He rolled through the truck stop, past the gas pumps and the structure that housed a café and casino. He headed toward a corner of the property that was away from all the activity.

Abigail glanced over her shoulder but didn't see any other headlights. Where had Jesse gone? Maybe he realized this was a trap and was trying to come up with a sneakier plan to get her free. She knew Jesse well enough by now to know that he wouldn't give up without a fight.

The driver brought the car to a stop and turned off

all the lights. He lifted the gun, pointing it at her head. "Don't even twitch a muscle."

Abigail sat still, but looked around Dale's car and outside by moving her eyes but not her neck.

Larry shifted in his seat. "What's taking them so long?"

Out of the corner of her eye, she saw the headlights of the van as it parked some distance away and Jesse got out, sneaking into the bushes. She shifted forward slightly to block Larry's view.

"I said don't move."

"Sorry, I'm just very uncomfortable," she said.

In her periphery vision, she watched as another car pulled up to the van. Two men got out and ran toward where Jesse was hiding. Her breath caught. Those men were after Jesse.

"Something wrong?" Larry rubbed the scar on his face.

"No, I just…" She knew she had to get away to help Jesse. She turned suddenly and punched Larry hard in the neck. Stunned, he wheezed for breath and loosened his grip on the gun. She pushed the door open and leaped out, landing hard on the gravel. She pulled herself to her feet and took off running. The car that pulled up by the van was driving away—probably with Jesse inside.

Jesse was lying in the back seat of a car with a hood over his head. The car started rolling but never gained speed. They must still be in the truck-stop parking lot. The ambush had caught him off guard. He'd been focused on his own surprise assault on the car where Abigail was.

Of course, he knew it might be a setup to get to him. Why else would the guy park and wait? But he had done a circuitous route through the truck-stop parking lot to make sure he wasn't followed.

The car stopped. Hands gripped and lifted him. Still unable to see, he struggled to break free, flailing his arms. Despite not being able to see, he landed one solid punch before a Taser made him writhe and recoil, then bend forward at the waist. He felt nauseous from the Taser blast.

He heard a door swing open, and then a voice commanded, "Get up those stairs. Two of them."

He was pushed forward and then someone put hands on his shoulders and directed him down onto a chair. The room smelled musty, like old shoes.

He stood to put up a fight, reaching to take the hood off his head.

He heard the slide of a gun whiz back and forth as a bullet slipped into the chamber. "Don't even try," said a voice.

He sat back down. Someone grabbed his hands and tied them so his wrists were bound in front of him. The hood was yanked off his head. He blinked, waiting for his eyes to adjust to the dimness of the room.

When he'd driven into the truck-stop parking lot, he'd noticed four or five run-down trailers on the far end of the multiacre property. His best guess was that he was being held in one of those trailers. The trailers were probably cheap sleeping quarters for the workers headed toward the Bakken oil fields. Though this one clearly had not been used for a long time. The wind blew through it, causing the metal to rattle. A rusty sink attached to the wall dripped water. He thought he saw a mattress in a dark corner.

He was seated on a lumpy recliner. Across from him sat a man in the shadows on a dining chair. The man with the gun stood off to one side.

The man in the shadows got up and walked toward him. Jesse recognized him as the dark-haired man from the mountain.

He leaned very close to Jesse and grinned, revealing a gold-capped tooth. He pulled back and paced. "Agent Santorum. We have a few questions to ask you, but first, stand up and let my associate search you."

The second man handed the gun to the dark-haired man and then patted Jesse down.

"There's nothing on him," said the associate.

The dark-haired man handed the gun back to his associate. "Have a seat, Agent Santorum."

Jesse hesitated. The associate poked the gun in his direction. Jesse sat back down.

The dark-haired man crossed his arms over his chest. "It seems we ran into a very strange old man up in those mountains."

"You didn't hurt him, did you?"

The dark-haired man let out a huff of air. "Relax, your little hermit pal is fine. Besides, who is he going to talk to and who's going to believe him? Turns out he was quite the negotiator in terms of us getting our product back."

Jesse had a feeling he knew where the story was leading. He wasn't about to give anything away.

"With some persuading, he mentioned that you showed a keen interest in what he called a little black box, which sounds a great deal like a hard drive. What was on that hard drive and where did you put it?"

So this was why he and Abigail had not been killed outright. They hadn't been searched by the men who found them at Abigail's trailer. Somewhere between that time and now, the other men must have run into the hermit on the mountain. The men who took them at the bed-and-breakfast had been in a rush. At first, they had been kept alive to give up where the missing product had gone. Even if these men didn't know exactly what was on the hard drive, they knew it was important and that they needed to get the hard drive back before it fell into the wrong hands. "I don't know what you're talking about."

The man with the gun leaned over and hit Jesse hard across the jaw. Jesse sat up straight, still stinging from the blow. He tasted blood in his mouth. Raising his head, he narrowed his eyes at the dark-haired man. "I still don't know what you're talking about." He'd been tortured before. He wasn't about to say that Abigail had the hard drive.

He wondered, too, if Agent Frisk was calling the shots behind all of this. If so, he seemed to have access to a lot of manpower.

The dark-haired man studied him for a long moment before nodding at his associate, who proceeded to hit Jesse in the face and stomach. Jesse doubled over as his stomach churned and his eyes watered from the blow to the face.

A long tense moment passed before the dark-haired man spoke. "Still not talking. We'll see how you feel about that after a little bit." The dark-haired man scooted his chair across the floor, making a high-pitched screeching noise.

Both men lunged for Jesse. Jesse twisted, trying to fight free. The associate pulled out a hypodermic and plunged it into Jesse's arm. He could feel the poison traveling through his veins instantly. His mind fogged and his body grew weak as one of the men stood on the chair and the other restrained Jesse.

Now he saw what they were going to do. A beam ran all the way across the ceiling of the trailer. Together the two men strung him up, so he was hanging with his arms above him and standing on tiptoe.

He was familiar with this interrogation technique. The physical and emotional strain was intended to break him down. They'd return in a few hours and promise him food and release in exchange for answers about the hard drive. He wasn't about to give in.

The drug he'd been given was clearly designed to leave him in a weakened state. His muscles became leaden, and maybe the drug would even knock him out. He didn't know. He was having a hard time thinking clearly. His vision blurred, and he felt like he was watching the two men through a window smeared with petroleum jelly as they left the trailer. The door closed with a screech.

Jesse squeezed his eyes shut and opened them several times, trying to make his mind work. His arm muscles strained from being stretched above him. He was able to turn in a half circle one way and then the other. Nothing that might help him escape was within reach.

His eyelids were so heavy, and his brain felt as though it had been stuffed with cotton.

His mind wandered to Abigail. Had they captured

her, too? Once they found the hard drive, they would dispose of her. The thought of any harm coming to Abigail helped him find his strength and resolve. He had to get out of here. Somehow. Some way.

Again, he turned in a half circle one way and then the other. He saw the gleam of metal along the wall. Some kind of tool maybe.

How was he going to get out of here and find Abigail?

TWELVE

Abigail ran toward the bright lights of the truck stop. It would be only a matter of seconds before Larry got his bearings and came after her. She'd seen where the car that held Jesse had turned, disappearing behind some trailers that looked like they were no longer used on the edge of the property opposite where Larry had taken her.

She knew she had to get to Jesse to help him, but right now she needed to go toward the safety of people, where Larry could not come after her. She was no good to Jesse if she got caught, too.

She willed her legs to move faster. When she looked over her shoulder, Larry had turned the four-wheel drive around and was driving toward her. Outside the truck stop, there were several cars parked but no people.

She ran faster even as she felt the four-wheel drive bearing down on her.

She could see the bright lights of the café, where several people sat in booths and a waitress scurried across the floor with a tray. None of them looked up or noticed her.

It felt like the car was right behind her.

A man with a potbelly wearing a baseball hat stepped out of the casino and paced the sidewalk. He looked directly at her. Something in his expression changed when he looked at her.

She glanced over her shoulder.

Larry was still headed toward the truck stop.

Her feet touched the edge of the sidewalk.

The man in the baseball hat turned toward her. His gaze went to where Larry rolled toward the sidewalk and then back to her. "Hey there, little lady. Looks like you're in some kind of trouble."

She wasn't sure if the man in the baseball hat was any safer than the one who had just tried to run her down, but she sure was glad he'd stepped outside when he did.

She pressed her palm against her chest where her heart was raging from exertion. "I'll be all right, thank you."

She hurried inside the café and took a booth that gave her a view of the edge of the property, where Jesse was probably being kept. The waitress came over to her and put down a menu.

"Can I get you anything to drink for a start?"

Disoriented, Abigail stared up at the older woman, who had a kind face. She maybe had a few dollars in her jacket pocket. "Can I just get a cup of coffee?"

"Sure, honey, no problem."

Larry eased forward in the four-wheel drive, parking right by the window where she was sitting. Even through the glass, she could see the menacing look on his face. If she left the café, he would come after her.

The waitress brought her a beige coffee cup.

"Have you decided what you want to eat?"

Abigail stared at the steam rising out of the mug. Her heart still hadn't slowed down. What was she going to do? How could she get to Jesse? What if they had plans to move him or kill him?

Her throat tightened. What if they had killed him already?

The waitress turned, took two steps away from her table and then whirled back around. "Are you okay? You seem...afraid."

Abigail gazed at the older woman. Her name tag said Mary. "I am afraid. You see that man parked in that car out there? He's stalking me. If I leave the café, he'll come after me."

Mary took a moment to answer. She placed a fist on her hip. "You poor thing. That's not right. I'm sure it will be no problem for me to give highway patrol a buzz, and they can question or hold him or whatever they do to make sure you can leave. And don't worry about that coffee. I'll cover it."

Abigail turned her head to look out the window. Off in the distance, she could see where Jesse had parked the van. "Thank you. I just want to get to my car and drive away without him following me."

"I don't know how all that works, but I'm sure I can call the highway patrol and let them know what's going on. Since this is the only truck stop for miles, they usually get here pretty quick."

She watched Mary walk away and disappear behind the swinging doors that led to the kitchen.

Her fingers were trembling as she opened the sugar packet and poured it into the coffee. She sipped the hot beverage.

Her gaze went from Larry in the car to the trailers to the long stretch of property that led out to the highway.

Her coffee was nearly gone when the highway patrol car pulled into the huge lot. She saw the shocked look on Larry's face as it rolled through the parking lot toward him. Larry started Dale's four-wheel drive and backed out of his space, pulling away and gaining speed with the highway patrol on his bumper.

Now was her chance. She hurried out of the café and jogged toward the van. She was out of breath by the time she made it across the huge lot. Her fingers touched the door handle and she clicked it open. Her spirits lifted. Jesse had left the keys in the ignition. She hopped into the driver's seat and rolled across the parking lot.

The place where the trailers were was in the far corner of the truck stop, an area that was not paved, just gravel. The bright lights of the café and gas pumps did not reach to this dark corner. She parked a short way away and then hurried toward the trailers. There were four trailers in all. She pressed her back against the first one, which had a door that hung crookedly. She rolled along the metal side of the trailer to peek inside— empty except for some broken furniture. Crouching, she hurried to the second trailer. Voices drifted out of an opening where a door used to be. It sounded like two men were playing cards and joking.

She made her way to the area between the second and third trailers, where the car that had taken Jesse was parked. She sprinted to the far side of the third trailer and swung the door open. Her breath caught when she saw Jesse strung up from the rafters. His head wobbled on his neck. He looked at her with glazed eyes. "Hey." Even in his drugged state, his face lit up when he saw her. "You found me."

"'Course I found you. We're in this together, right?" Her heart lurched. What kind of pain had he endured?

"Got to hand it to you, Abigail. I'm impressed with your skills."

She pulled her knife from her pocket and pushed the chair toward him. "We're going to get you down from here." She sawed back and forth on the rope until it broke. Jesse's arms fell to his side and his knees buckled, though he remained on his feet.

She reached toward him to steady him.

"I can make it," he said, pulling away from her. He tried to stand on his own but swayed.

She caught him. "We don't have much time."

"They want the hard drive. I'm glad you had it. Otherwise they would have killed me and taken it."

She didn't even want to think about Jesse dying. "We better get moving." She helped him down the stairs. "The van is parked a little ways away. I didn't want them to hear it." She still had her arm around his back, her hand resting on her shoulder. They stepped outside.

They were within five yards of the van when she heard the thugs' car start up. She took the few steps to the van, still supporting Jesse. She swung open the passenger-side door. With some effort, Jesse pulled himself up into the seat while she got behind the steering wheel.

The thugs' car was headed straight toward them.

When she turned the key in the ignition, the van sputtered and then started. "We're almost out of gas."

Jesse laughed. "We're at a gas station." He was still a little out of it from the drugs.

She pressed the accelerator and headed toward the lights of the truck stop, knowing they would be safe once they were around people.

The thugs' bumper hit the back of the van, jarring her in the seat.

Steeling herself, she gripped the steering wheel and drove toward one of the gas pumps.

Jesse pulled his credit card from his pocket. "Pay with this."

While she pumped the gas, the thugs stopped their car and got out. One of them leaned against the hood and crossed his arms while the other stood with his hands on his hips so the top of his gun was visible beneath his coat. She recognized the dark-haired man from the mountain.

Despite being a little unsure on his feet, Jesse got out of the van and stood beside her. He rested a supportive palm on her shoulder.

She glanced over at the two thugs as she struggled to get a deep breath because of the panic she felt. "How are we going to get out of here? They'll follow us for sure."

Both directions were miles and miles of rural roads, with only tiny towns dotting the landscape. There might not even be that much.

"I need time for this drug to wear off, and we need to find a safe hiding place for that hard drive. They got their drugs back. That's why they didn't kill us outright. If they find the hard drive on us, we're dead."

His words sent a new wave of fear through her. She finished pumping the gas. The man in Dale's four-wheel drive, Larry, had parked away from the truck stop. The highway patrol must have not been able to detain him as long as it took to question him.

"Jesse, what do we do?"

"Let's go inside the truck stop and sit until we can figure something out," Jesse said. "I need this brain fog to go away before we try anything."

With the men still watching them, Abigail got behind the wheel and pulled the van closer to the truck stop. She felt the weight of the hard drive against her stomach in her pocket.

The thing that could prove Jesse's innocence was also the thing that would get them killed.

Once they were parked close to the truck stop, Jesse got out of the van and waited on the sidewalk for Abigail. It still felt like his brain was scrambled eggs. They walked into the truck stop together. He chose a table in the middle of the room, one that would not be completely visible from outside.

A waitress who looked like she couldn't be more than eighteen came over to them. "What can I get you folks?" Her name tag said Taylor.

"Is a waitress named Mary still around?" Abigail scooted forward in her chair.

"Mary went off shift about ten minutes ago," said Taylor.

"I'll have a coffee." Jesse glanced at the menu, choosing an item at random. "And the breakfast burrito looks good."

"I'll have the same," said Abigail.

Once the waitress left to go put in their order, Jesse's gaze rested on Abigail. "Who's Mary?"

"Just a waitress who was helpful. She called the highway patrol for me. Maybe we could do that again."

"Maybe, but we need a phone." He wasn't sure about getting the locals involved. He'd used a credit card to pay for the gas and the bed-and-breakfast. DEA would be able to track him and might have alerted the locals that he was wanted. If he was in a jail cell, it would be that much harder to prove his innocence, and Abigail would be in danger. "I think we're better off figuring this out on our own."

"Thank you for coming for me and getting me out of there. That was brave." He couldn't hide the admiration and even affection that he felt for her in that moment.

"Like I said, we're in this together, right?"

He liked the softness in her eyes when she gazed at him.

"Another agent couldn't have done better than you did, Abigail."

Color rose up in her cheeks. The rosiness made her look even prettier. "I know you would do the same for me." She stared at the table for a moment.

His heart fluttered. Jesse cleared his throat, breaking the intense moment of attraction that had formed between them.

The two men who had held him captive came into the café. They took a table that gave them a full view of where Jesse and Abigail sat.

Abigail stared at the table. "We're trapped here. What do we do now?"

The waitress set down their coffees. "Cream and sugar are right by the napkins there. Your order should be here shortly." She walked away.

Jesse waited until she was out of earshot to answer.

"I'll think of something." He poured cream and sugar into his coffee.

Abigail tilted her head toward one of the big windows. "Our van is being watched by the guy who took Dale's four-wheel drive."

They were trapped. Every move they made would be known. Nothing would happen to him or Abigail as long as they stayed where there were witnesses, but they couldn't stay here forever. He had to think of some way for them to escape.

They sat through the coffee and the meal with the two men watching them. Jesse could feel the weight of their stares as he dipped his last bite of burrito. His head had cleared enough for him to start to generate a plan. The café connected with a shop that sold things truck drivers might need.

"For starters, we're going go over to that store and get a pay-as-you-go phone," he said.

"Oh, good, I was afraid we were going to have to order more food." Abigail wiped her mouth and tossed her napkin on the table.

They stood up. He could feel the gaze of the two men on his back as he went to the counter to pay his bill. They entered the shop and walked toward the sign that indicated where the phones were. When he looked over his shoulder, the dark-haired man had left the table and was moving toward the shop.

They selected a phone and walked up to the counter. The thug meandered through the shop, positioning himself so he could keep an eye on them.

Jesse stared through the window at all the semi-trucks, some parked, some fueling up and some getting ready to pull out. They had to do something unexpected.

He squeezed Abigail's elbow as she turned away from the counter where they had paid the clerk. Outside, across the lot, a trucker crawled into the cab of his truck, clearly getting ready to pull out.

He leaned close to her ear and whispered, "Run for it."

He took the lead, sprinting toward the door that led outside. The truck's wheels had already started to rotate.

The thug from the shop raced after them. He grabbed the hem of Abigail's jacket. Before Jesse could react, Abigail whirled around, kicking the man in the shin hard enough to make him let go.

Though moving at a snail's pace, the truck was rolling through the parking lot. Abigail leaped up on the running board and swung the door open. "Can I have a ride?"

The truck driver gave a one-word answer Jesse couldn't decipher.

She crawled in. Jesse raced alongside the truck, jumped up on the running board and climbed in.

"My friend is coming with us," she said. "Hope you don't mind."

The truck driver, an older man with white hair and a bushy white beard, looked stunned but kept driving. "What are you two kids up to?" Suspicion colored his words. "Are you running from something? I got a sidearm right down here if you think you're going to try anything."

Jesse stared out the window. Larry, in Dale's four-wheel drive, had pulled up to get the dark-haired man, who had followed them out of the shop.

"We're not kids. We're with the DEA and we're on a case." He included Abigail because it had begun to feel like they were partners in this whole thing, even though she wasn't really an agent.

The truck driver pulled out onto the road, gaining speed. "Can I see your credentials?"

"I'm undercover. I don't have them with me." Jesse realized how phony his story must sound. If the guy stopped and made them get out, they'd be picked up by the thugs.

"Please believe us. We're not out to harm you in any way," Abigail said.

The truck driver gave them a nervous glance and then stared straight ahead at the road for a long moment before he spoke up. "Well, ain't that a fine kettle of fish. No doubt, you're working on slowing the drug traffic in and out of the Bakken. That place is a hole. I deliver up there. That's where I'm headed right now."

Jesse checked the side-view mirror. The two cars were following behind them.

"I don't suppose you're stopping anywhere along the way." Jesse stared at the phone, which was still in its packaging. If he could get in touch with Dale, he might be able to come and help them.

The truck driver shifted gears. "I usually pull over for a few minutes to stretch my legs. Got a schedule to keep, you know. My name is Tony, by the way."

The man seemed to be warming up to them. "I'm Jesse and this is Abigail."

"So you two are with the law?"

"I am," said Jesse.

Tony's forehead crinkled. "She's with you because…?"

"It's a long story." Jesse glanced over at Abigail. "She's been a tremendous help to me." Jesse reached over and patted Abigail's leg. "She's a very capable woman."

She offered him a warm smile, which sent a charge of electricity through him. She really was quite wonderful.

While Abigail and Tony made small talk about things they had in common, Jesse took the pay-as-you-go phone out of the packaging and activated it. He stared at it. "No signal."

They passed a sign that indicated a rest stop was twenty miles up the road.

"I'll be pulling over there just for a few minutes," said Tony.

A vague plan had started to form in Jesse's mind. He was certain the men would follow the semitruck into the rest stop. He prayed there were enough people parked at the rest stop so the men would not be able to abduct them as long as they stayed out in the open. But what then? Could they try to get to one of the vehicles and escape that way, or should they stay with the truck driver? Tony seemed like a decent man. He sure didn't want to put him in any danger.

Tony slowed his rig and hit his blinker, veering toward the exit ramp that led to the rest stop.

Jesse took in a deep breath and prayed for a clear escape route.

THIRTEEN

Abigail wondered what Jesse was thinking as Tony brought his big truck to a stop. Jesse had been staring at the phone for several minutes.

"I'm only here for five minutes," said Tony. "Long enough to use the little boys' room and stretch my legs."

"I think we won't need to ride with you any farther," said Jesse. "Your help has been much appreciated."

Tony pushed open the door. "All right, then. I wish you all the best in the world in catching the bad guys." Tony hopped down.

Abigail gripped Jesse's arm. "What are we going to do?"

Jesse opened the door.

Abigail tensed as Larry in Dale's four-wheel drive pulled into the huge parking lot. A man was also in the passenger seat.

"I'm not sure yet." He glanced around. "There are people around here. We're safe as long as we stay out in the open." He lifted the phone. "Looks like I can get a signal here. I need to get in touch with Dale."

The rest stop wasn't exactly teeming with activity. There was a motor home parked in a far corner. An older woman walked a tiny dog on a leash around the motor home. Another semitruck was pulled over at the edge of the parking area. No sign of the driver. He must be sleeping. The only other car contained a family with three kids, two running around, a boy and a girl not more than seven or eight years old. Another older child sat in the back seat of the car, his head bent as if he was reading something. Two people who must be the parents sat on a bench, looking at their phones.

The rest stop was not visible from the road due to a line of tall evergreens.

Before they had even gotten down from the truck, the car that contained one of the two men who had held Jesse captive pulled into the parking area on the opposite end of the lot from the four-wheel drive. The men had positioned their cars so that they were on either side of Tony's semitruck.

The dark-haired man got out of the four-wheel drive and paced the sidewalk by the bathrooms.

Once again, their every move would be watched. Would this be a test of wills to see who blinked first?

With Jesse walking beside her, the two of them headed toward the sidewalk, keeping their distance from the thugs. Jesse slipped his hand into Abigail's and led her toward the now-empty bench. The mom and dad had put their phones away and gotten up, and were calling to the two children running around to get back to the car. Tony came out of the bathroom, waved at them and then got up into his rig. He pulled back out onto the road.

Jesse started to dial Dale's number. He glanced at the thug on the sidewalk. "I don't know how long it is safe to stay here." He held the phone to his ear while it rang on the other end.

"What if we tried to get the car that only has one guy in it and make a run for it?"

Jesse shook his head. "Those other guys would be on us so quick."

"Even with these people around."

"I don't know. It might work." Jesse drew his attention back to the phone. "Hey, Dale."

Though she could only hear one side of the conversation, Abigail gathered the gist of the exchange. Dale had been doing lots of research and making calls. The thug Dale had overtaken at the cabin wasn't talking, though he had a record a mile long. Agent Frisk was working operations in the Bakken and had been doing so on and off for over two years. Jesse's name had been so sullied that it would be hard to find an agent high up in the chain of command who didn't think he was guilty. Jesse described the truck stop where they were.

He clicked off the phone. "He's going to get here as fast as he can."

The old lady who had been walking her dog disappeared inside the motor home. The mom and dad had gathered up their wandering children, gotten into their car and were backing out, headed toward the road.

A tense hush seemed to fall over the entire parking lot. She watched the taillights of the car that contained the family disappear behind the trees that blocked the view of the road.

Larry, the thug in the four-wheel drive, got out of the car and edged toward them. The third man got out of his car, as well.

Abigail glanced at the semitruck and then the motor home, which had its curtains drawn. She prayed that another car would pull into the rest stop or that the people in the motor home would come back out.

Jesse whispered, barely moving his mouth. "Back away. We can't run toward the road. They'll cut us off."

"Maybe we can get to the motor home," she said. She didn't like the idea of putting the old woman in any danger.

Together they both burst to their feet just as the men made a run for them. Their path to the motor home was cut-off.

"Let's try to circle back around," said Jesse.

They hurried to the back of the rest stop, which had a small pond with ducks swimming in it. Jesse ran toward the trees that surrounded the water.

Abigail glanced over her shoulder. The men emerged from either side of the building. They wouldn't be able to get back to the parking.

They ran for ten minutes. The men stayed close at their heels.

A single gunshot reverberated behind them. They ran out into an open field. Two of the men, Larry and the dark-haired man, chased after them. The soil in the field had been turned over for planting. Their shoes sank down in the soft dirt. Jesse raced toward a corner of the field, where a piece of farm equipment stood.

One of the men fired off another shot. The bullet came so close to hitting her that her eardrum felt like it had been hit with a tiny mallet. Reflexively, she drew her hand up to her ear.

Jesse sprinted toward the enclosed tractor that sat in the corner of the field. He jumped up and swung the door open. "Get in."

The men were about forty yards away.

Abigail climbed into the cab of the tractor with Jesse right behind her. He gripped the steering wheel and stared at the control panel, and then at what was probably a gearshift. "How do you operate this thing? We'll just take it to the edge of the field, so the farmer can still find it. It'll provide cover and give us a head start."

The men were getting closer. One of them had stopped to raise his gun again.

Abigail looked at the dials on the tractor and saw a key. She turned it and the tractor roared to life. "Looks like you have a clutch and a brake down there."

A bullet pinged off the metal of the tractor cab as it jerked into motion.

Abigail slipped lower in the seat. Through the back window of the tractor, she could see the men still running toward them.

Jesse increased the speed of the tractor. "This isn't exactly NASCAR."

They were maybe going fifteen miles an hour. Though the men continued to run after them, they slowed as the distance between them increased.

She lifted her head and craned her neck. The landscape was completely flat. The men were still making their way across the field, though they had become small figures in the distance.

The tractor bumped along. There wasn't really any road around here.

"Take my phone and let Dale know what's happened." Jesse recited the number for Abigail. "The other guy must have waited back at the rest stop. I don't want Dale to run into an ambush."

Dale picked up on the first ring. "I'm on my way."

Abigail told him the situation, explaining they had

run at least a mile behind the rest stop, with no roads or landmarks in sight.

Dale paused for a moment. "I can't find you unless you can get up to a road or some landmark that would show up on GPS."

She stared out at the barren land. There was not so much as a farmhouse in sight, let alone a road they could identify. "We'll let you know as soon as we're in a place where you can come to us."

"Let me look at a map on my phone and see if I can tell you where the closest road would be in relation to the rest stop and the direction you ran," said Dale. "I'll call you back."

"Okay." She clicked off. Their phone was a cheap model that wouldn't pull up any maps. Would an area as remote as this even be mapped?

They came to the edge of the field.

The tractor motor made a grinding noise as the flat land turned into rolling hills with tall, thick, wild grass.

"We better get out," Jesse said. "The farmer needs to be able to find his tractor when he comes looking for it."

They climbed out of the cab. In all directions, they saw rolling hills. She saw no fences. No power lines. The tractor was the last sign that they were anywhere near people. The farms and ranches in this part of the world might be thousands of acres.

Jesse clamped a hand on Abigail's shoulder. "You're the one who knows how to navigate in the wilderness."

Maybe so, but she was used to reading mountainous terrain. She looked around, trying to get her bearings. From the rest stop, they had run west. "I say we head in the general direction of where that main highway is that leads into the Bakken, but do a wide circle around where that field was so we don't risk running into those men."

"Lead the way."

Minutes after they started walking, raindrops pelted her skin. In the distance, she saw what looked like a cabin or a barn, weathered gray by time and leaning to one side. They ran across the grassy field toward the shelter of a building that had probably not been inhabited for a hundred years.

As they drew closer to the building, she saw that it had once been a homestead. What might have been a wooden trough was off to one side, and there was a pile of logs and gray boards behind the house, which was maybe some sort of outbuilding. The drizzle of rain turned into a downpour as they slipped inside.

Though it was overcast, some light shone through the holes in the roof, and rain dripped from the rafters. She chose a corner of the room that didn't seem to be leaking.

Jesse remained standing, staring at his cell phone. "I can't get a signal."

Abigail slipped down the wall to the floorboards that seemed relatively stable. Though it didn't surprise her, not having a cell phone signal made her feel even more hopeless. Dale couldn't reach them to say what he had found on his maps.

She peered out the opening where there used to be a door. Though the rain reduced visibility, she couldn't see the men anywhere. Chances were, they would have sought shelter from the rain, as well. Maybe they would even hike back to the rest stop, but she knew better than to count on that.

Feeling a sense of despair, Abigail took in a breath and closed her eyes. "So what do we do now?"

Abigail sounded weary. He didn't blame her. He was battling a loss of hope himself. They might as well be stuck back up on that mountain, for all the good the cell phone did them. He sat down beside her, close enough that their shoulders were touching.

He closed his eyes and listened to the soothing sound of the rain.

Her hand rested on top of his. "Maybe the first thing we should do is pray."

Her hand was smooth as silk against his rough fingers. "Yes, I'd like that." Seeing her faith in the face of such adversity had restored some of his.

She closed her eyes and prayed, asking God for guidance. A tender silence fell between them, with only the whispering whooshing of the rain coming down.

She squeezed his hand. "Amen. I'm glad you decided to pray with me."

He opened his eyes and turned toward her. Her lips curled up in a faint smile. She leaned toward him. Though the sky was grey and cloud covered, there seemed to be light coming from her. He recognized the glow of affection in her features. His chest felt like it was being squeezed in a vise. Could he open his heart to her? After Melissa's death, he had felt as though his heart had turned to stone. Never again did he want to experience the helplessness of loving someone and not being able to save them.

"Thank you for all you've done for me, Abigail. You're amazing."

She pulled her knees up toward her chest. "Not too bad for a small-town girl, huh?"

He loved sitting beside her. Even in such trying circumstances, being with her nourished him. "Not too bad at all."

She kicked at the floorboards. "What if we hid the hard drive here? They would never think to come look here. We could come back for it when you're ready to make your case."

"I like the way you think, but could we even find this place again? I was hoping we could pass it to Dale for safekeeping." He stared at his phone again.

"Then we should head out. Those men are either slowed or stopped by the rain," she said. "We'll get to a spot where we can get a signal sooner or later."

He listened to the downpour outside and the dribbling off the roof. "Abigail, you've got a lot of spunk and nerves of steel."

"It would give us the head start we need. Besides, what's a little rain?" she said. "I've guided people to safety in freak snowstorms."

He gazed at her and nodded. "Okay." He jumped to his feet and held a hand out for her. Her fingers clasped his and he pulled her to her feet. They stood for a moment facing each other, their noses nearly touching. The electric charge of attraction pulsed all around him, enveloping him like a warm blanket.

"We should get moving," she said. Her turning away seemed to cut off the intensity of the moment.

They rushed out into the downpour. Because the terrain was so flat, he could see the rain coming from the sky in solid gray sheets for miles. There were pockets where no rain was falling.

Abigail walked with a determined step. "We should head due south. That way we'll be moving parallel to that field. When we think we've gotten past it, we can turn east, which should put us out on the road."

"I'm glad you're the navigator," he said.

As they walked side by side, he found himself sneaking glances at her. Then his hand slipped into hers. She held on tight as if to confirm that she had the same feelings.

Through the murkiness of the downpour, he could see another figure moving toward them. A man alone in dark clothes. It could be a farmer, or it could be one of the thugs still searching for them.

As they walked, the faraway figure turned and headed in their direction, closing the distance between them. Though they were at least a mile apart, it was clear now that he was headed toward them, and it probably wasn't a farmer coming for a friendly chat. The blurred figure changed his stalking pace into a jog.

Though there were clusters of trees, there was really no place to conceal themselves. They quickened their pace, their feet squishing in the mud when they came to a different field, where the soil had also been plowed for planting. The man edged steadily toward them until he was close enough they could see it was the dark-haired man.

As his clothes got wetter, a chill permeated Jesse's skin and settled into his bones. Abigail still had her waterproof jacket, though her pants looked soaked. They hurried across the flat terrain. He had to let go of her hand so they could run faster.

"I think we can go ahead and make a turn toward where the road should be." She was out of breath as she spoke, glancing over her shoulder at their pursuer. "There's no way to shake him, is there?"

Jesse kept jogging as he talked. "We've just got to keep moving faster than he does."

The figure was still coming toward them, showing an impressive amount of stamina. If they could just stay far enough ahead so the man couldn't get a shot with a pistol, they might be able to make it to the road alive and call Dale.

His muscles felt fatigued as they jogged across an open area with tall, lumpy grass weighed down by wind and rain. Abigail slowed, as well.

She stopped, bending over to rest her hands above her knees. "I just need to catch my breath."

The thug kept coming toward them, never slowing down, never tiring. Jesse tugged on her sleeve. "Abigail, we've got to keep moving."

She took in a ragged breath and nodded. Their run had slowed to a jog, though they kept moving despite being soaked to the bone, despite the fatigue that was overtaking both of them.

Jesse willed himself to keep moving. Across the wide, flat plain, he saw the road up ahead. The gray of the paving was so distorted by the rain that it almost looked like a mirage.

Seeing the road gave him the incentive to keep moving. Maybe a car would go by and they could catch a ride. When he glanced over his shoulder, the thug had stopped. He was close enough that Jesse could make out that he had pulled out his phone and was making a call.

Jesse's brief moment of thinking they could make it to safety was shattered.

Now that the thug had a clear location on them that he could communicate to the others, it meant even more men would be coming after them.

FOURTEEN

Abigail's lungs were sore from breathing so intensely. As she forced herself to keep moving, her leg muscles felt leaden. Her clothes must weigh an extra five pounds from all the water they'd absorbed. The road was closer, but getting to it had been a sort of false hope. The thug was only jogging toward them. Now that he'd made his phone call and had ushered even more manpower down on them, he didn't have to catch them, only keep an eye on them, which was easy enough to do when the flat land stretched for miles.

She recalled how the dark-haired man had brought the dogs into the mountains via helicopter to track them. Clearly, whoever was behind this, probably the Agent Frisk the dead man had mentioned in the video, had all kinds of resources beyond just the three men who had chased them from the rest stop.

Jesse stopped and pulled out his phone. "If he had a signal, then we have one, too." He pressed the keypad as he walked. "Keep running, Abigail. I'll catch up."

She jogged ahead. The road was within twenty yards, though there was no sign of a car coming in either direction. Maybe that was a good thing. It meant the thugs weren't close by—but it also meant there was no one who might give them temporary refuge in the form of a ride.

As her feet pounded the ground, she glanced over her shoulder. The dark-haired man was looming dangerously close to Jesse as he jogged and talked on the phone. Would Dale even be able to get to them in time?

She ran faster. A gunshot sounded behind her. All the air left her lungs. She craned her neck. Jesse was lying on the ground with the thug bearing down on him, his gun raised. Time seemed to stand still. She slowed and turned. She couldn't leave Jesse. If they both died here, so be it. She picked up a rock and ran toward Jesse. It was no match for a gun, but it was all she had.

Jesse bolted up from the ground and ran toward her. Relief spread through her like a burst of sunshine on a cloudy day. He hadn't been hit. He'd avoided the bullet by dropping to the ground.

Jesse gestured that she needed to keep running. She turned back around and headed toward the road. She stumbled when another shot was fired, but when she craned her neck, she saw Jesse sprinting toward her.

The thug who had to stop to fire off the shots was some distance behind him. Jesse caught up with her just as her feet touched the pavement of the road.

"Dale has been looking for us on the road." Jesse never slowed in his run. Because he was out of breath from running, his words came slowly. "We need to find a mile marker, so he knows where we are. Keep running."

The long straight road stretched before them. Maybe a mile away, the road rounded up over a hill and dropped out of sight. Up ahead, she saw the little green metal sign that would tell them where they were. The thug remained at their heels. They'd be slowed down when Jesse made the to call Dale again. Her only prayer was that Dale could get to them before the thugs did.

The green metal sign indicated they were at mile marker fifty-seven. She was pretty sure they were headed in the direction of the rest stop, though she had no idea how far away they were from it. She hadn't paid attention to the mile markers when they'd ridden with Tony.

Jesse kept running. "That guy is too close for me to slow down to make the call to Dale."

She still held the rock she'd picked up. Not much of a weapon. Though they weren't armed, there were two of them and only one thug. Was there a way to ambush him before he had a chance to aim the gun at them? There were clusters of trees not far from the road, but the thug would be able to see them running toward them for cover.

"What if we slow down?" Her feet pounded the concrete of the road.

"What?"

"So he thinks he can hit us. Then he'll use up his bullets."

"Good idea. But I'll do it. You stay ahead of me." Jesse's run turned into a jog.

Abigail slowed but increased the distance between herself and Jesse. There was no time to argue with him over who should be the target.

How many shots had the man fired so far? Three, maybe?

The tactic was a dangerous one. What if the dark-haired man wounded Jesse?

Two more shots were fired. Each time, Abigail's

heart stopped. She kept running but looked over her shoulder. Jesse was still behind her, still moving.

She prayed that they would both get out of this alive. *Oh, God, please help us.*

Without warning, the downpour turned to hail the size of quarters. She put her arms up to shield herself from the pelting. The storm was so intense she couldn't see more than a few feet in front of her.

Jesse was by her side, grasping her elbow and leading her off the road toward the shelter of the trees. Her skin stung from the hail hitting her. He pulled her beneath the trees, which provided only partial shelter.

When she peered out, she couldn't see where the thug was because of the intensity of the downpour.

"You all right?" Jesse wrapped his arms around her shoulder and drew her close.

"I feel like I've gone ten rounds with a prizefighter." It was nice to have Jesse's protective arm around her.

The storm sounded like a million pieces of bubble wrap being broken at the same time. Visibility was so reduced, she couldn't even see the road.

"Yeah, I'm pretty beat-up, also." Jesse leaned forward, looking all around. "That guy must have run for cover, too. I don't see him anywhere."

He squeezed her shoulder. She peered up at him, looking into his deep brown eyes. The moment was only a brief reprieve, but she relished it all the same. They'd be on the run again as soon as the storm let up. Even though their situation was tenuous and escape from harm felt like a long shot, she realized there was no other place she'd rather be than here with Jesse.

She peered out again. The clusters of trees were

barely discernable through the onslaught of hail. "I wonder where he went."

Jesse stood beside her, their shoulders touching. He shook his head and pointed at a dark patch across the road through the thick sheets of hail. "That would have been the closest place for him to run."

The intensity of the hail hitting the ground changed as the downpour let up a little. Headlights glared through the haze of the storm up the road.

Jesse pulled out his phone and clicked the screen. "I'm texting the mile marker number." He clicked the screen and then brought it close to his face to read Dale's response. "Dale says he's close."

They waited while the hail continued to spill out of the sky. In the distance, the murky glow of headlights appeared on the road.

Jesse held up the phone, turning the flashlight on and off. The vehicle slowed and flashed its headlights.

"That's the signal. It's him." Jesse burst out from the shelter of the trees.

Even as the driving hail stung her skin, her spirits lifted. They ran toward the headlights as the vehicle slowed and pulled over, though Dale kept the headlights on.

A gunshot cracked the air around them. Abigail startled into alertness. The falling hail distorted noise so much, she wasn't sure where the shot had even come from.

Jesse grabbed her hand and guided her toward the soft-focus headlights of Dale's vehicle.

On the other side of the road, she saw a dark, moving blob. That had to be the dark-haired man with the gun.

In the distance, she spotted another set of headlights coming toward Dale's vehicle.

Dale's SUV was in motion once again, heading toward them even as the other car closed the distance between them.

Another shot was fired, though it seemed to fizzle as soon as it left the gun. The dark blob became more distinct.

The other set of headlights was within yards of Dale's car. The body of the blue SUV Dale drove materialized out of the storm. The car slowed to maybe five miles an hour.

Her hand reached for a door handle and she fell into the back seat. Jesse had yanked open the passenger-side door in the front.

She was soaked, and it felt like she'd been beaten with a thousand tiny sticks. All the same, the worn muddy interior of Dale's back seat brought more relief than a soft bed or a hot bath.

"Boy, are we glad to see you," said Jesse.

The car behind them hit Dale's rear bumper with intense force, sending a new wave of terror shooting through Abigail's body.

Jesse's body flung forward toward the dashboard. His chest hit something solid, and then, as if he was being lifted by the back of his coat, his back banged against the seat. He was fumbling for the seat belt when a second jolt hit the back bumper again, though this one wasn't as jarring. Dale pressed the gas and gained some speed.

Dale's windshield wipers worked furiously to clear the hail and provide some visibility. Jesse stared through the windshield. At best, he could see only a murky impression of the road. Over and over, the center yellow line popped into view for a fraction of a second.

The hail hitting the metal of the SUV made it feel like the body of the car would split into a thousand pieces. The intensity of the assault surrounded them.

Jesse craned his neck to glance at Abigail and then out the back window. The headlights of the other car were two out-of-focus circles. The other car slowed down and then stopped, probably to pick up the dark-haired man. Jesse rested his gaze on Abigail, who had a stunned expression on her face as she buckled herself in. "You all right?"

She nodded. "Just a little shook up." And then she smiled, reached forward and covered his hand with hers where it rested on the back of the seat. "But glad to be here in Dale's car with you."

The words *with you* echoed in his head as the warmth of her touch soaked through his skin.

Yeah, he thought, *I really know how to show a lady a good time.* When all this was over, maybe he could take her out for a nice dinner as a thank-you. He felt a tightening in his chest as he spotted the headlights of the other car still behind them…if all of this was ever going to be over.

"What do we do now?" Abigail leaned back in the seat.

Dale hunched over the steering wheel, his neck strained so his face was closer to the windshield. "First, we lose these guys."

With the reduced visibility, the SUV topped out at sixty. Even that was a scary speed to be traveling. The noise of the tires rolling over payment broke up.

"Whoa, we're on the shoulder." Dale jerked the steering wheel. "Sorry about that."

The other car gained on them. The headlights looked to be about ten feet behind them.

Dale sped up. Without warning, a tree filled the whole of the windshield. They'd gone off the road. Dale swerved again. This time the vehicle fishtailed.

Every muscle in Jesse's body tensed as he gripped the dashboard.

Dale slowed down.

Though Jesse could not be sure, it appeared that the road curved off at a slight angle. The headlights of the other vehicle filled the cab of theirs.

Abigail's frightened voice pierced his awareness. "They're right behind us."

Dale pressed the gas. Tension tainted with terror filled his words. "Not to worry. We've been in tough situations like this before, right?"

Jesse swallowed. His mouth had gone completely dry. "Sure, nothing we can't handle." Dale was a cool cucumber. For him to show any sign of fear was not good.

The other car collided with their bumper, jarring Jesse in his seat. His heart pounded wildly.

Dale pressed the gas.

They were trapped. If they went too fast, they risked losing control of the SUV. If they slowed to a safe speed, the other car would be able to run them off the road.

He felt another bump, this time on the side of Dale's vehicle toward the back. Their back end swung out. Dale gripped the steering wheel; his knuckles were white, his eyes drawn into narrow slits and the veins popping up in his neck.

"There's a gun in the glove compartment," said Dale. "Maybe you can try to take it out."

Jesse reached toward the glove compartment.

"I think I could get a better shot at them from the back seat." Abigail's words seemed to come from a faraway place. "Hand it to me."

Jesse felt himself leaning forward toward the glove compartment while the rush of the storm and the incessant tapping of the hail on the car surrounded him. He opened the glove box and reached for the gun.

Everything after that happened in slow motion. Jesse felt like he was experiencing it while numb or underwater. As Dale's SUV caught air and turned at an odd angle, he wasn't sure if it was because they had been hit again or because Dale had gone off the road.

The SUV landed and bumped along, then twisted. They were floating through the air again. The vehicle was halfway upside down. Abigail screamed. And then the hood of the vehicle scraped across rough terrain for what felt like miles before they came to a stop.

Metal continued to shake and vibrate. Jesse opened his mouth to say something but no words came out. He was upside down, his head pressing against the roof of the SUV, the seat belt cutting into his chest and stomach.

He looked over at Dale. His eyes were closed. His face had gone white as rice and a trickle of blood ran past his temple.

Jesse was coherent enough to know that shock was setting in. He had to fight it. He reached toward Dale and shook his shoulder. Dale was unresponsive.

It was a challenge to get out even a single word, but he managed to utter Abigail's name. The cacophony of the hail beating against the SUV and the rush of the storm around him seemed to be turned up to an even higher volume. Abigail did not answer.

His heart squeezed tight. He struggled to take in a breath. Once again, he had the sensation of drowning, drifting deeper and deeper underwater. He was coherent enough to realize his body was going into shock.

Not today. He wasn't going to lose Abigail today or any day.

He fought to shake himself free of the numbness that threatened to envelop him.

Then he heard Abigail's sweet, soft voice. She uttered a word he couldn't quite make out. But she was alive. His mind cleared as though he had broken through the surface of the water and was gasping for air.

He wasn't sure if he said, "I'm going to get you out," or if he just thought it. But he found himself reaching to unbuckle his seat belt. He rolled around. His shoulders and back rested against the roof of the vehicle. Dale still hadn't moved.

If he thought about losing his friend, the numbness of shock would take over again.

I'll get you out, too.

He turned and reached for the door handle. He had to push all his weight against it as it scraped the ground. There was enough of an opening for him to crawl out on his belly. He pulled himself through with his hands, clawing the muddy ground. Hail stabbed at his skin.

Without getting to his feet, he dragged himself to the back of the SUV, where Abigail was. The hood was bent and compressed. He wouldn't be able to get the door open. The window glass was still in place but broken.

He poked his head back into the open front door. "Abigail, I can't get the door open. I'm going to have to break the window and pull you through that way."

Only the sound of the storm answered back. He wondered how extensive her injuries were.

He pressed his lips together and then took in a breath. "Can you hear me?"

"Yes" was the faint reply. "I think I can scoot toward the other side of the car while you break the window."

Relief spread through him. "Good."

By sitting on his behind, he was able to kick the glass out of the back window. He found a rock, broke the remainder of the glass out and then tried to brush most of the shards out of the way with the same rock. He poked his head in.

She looked like a scared animal crouching in a dark corner.

"Be careful coming through. There's still some sharp pieces in the frame and glass on the ground." He scraped some more of the glass out of the way with the rock. "Okay, crawl on through."

The hail, which had turned to rain again, slashed against his cheek and trickled down the back of his neck. He didn't hear any movement inside the cab of the SUV. He poked his head in and reached his hand toward Abigail, who had gotten down on all fours, prepared to crawl toward the window. He could barely make out her features in the darkness of the crushed vehicle.

"Sorry, I'm…just a little shook up." Her voice faltered.

"Understandable." He didn't want to rush her, but he

was pretty sure the thugs in the car that had run them off the road were searching for them. He reached a hand out toward her. "I got you." He half pulled, half guided her through the narrow opening.

Once she was out, he helped her to her feet. All around him all he could see was rain and the impression of objects like trees, rocks and grass. Everything was out of focus but stationary. No moving objects were coming toward them.

The crash had so disoriented him he wasn't even sure which way the road was. "Let's go get Dale out." He navigated around to the driver's side of the SUV.

Abigail pressed close behind him.

He dreaded dragging Dale out and discovering he was not alive. But when he got to the driver's side, the door had been pushed open. He peered inside. Dale was not there anymore. The back of the seat was high enough to shield the view of the front seat. The door had been opened so quietly that he hadn't heard it above the storm and his focus on Abigail. His first thought was that the thugs had gotten to Dale.

Abigail gripped his arm.

Before they had time to react, a man with a gun emerged from the gray sheets of the storm. Jesse recognized him as the man referred to as an associate, the man who had tortured him.

The man pointed the gun at them and lifted his chin. "I think you folks better come with me."

FIFTEEN

Abigail stared down the barrel of the gun as her pulse drummed in her ears. Without thinking about it, she reached for Jesse's hand. She could see the wheels turning inside his head. He was trying to come up with a plan of escape.

The man with the gun turned slightly and pointed. "About-face and start marching that way."

Though she could not see more than a few feet in front of her, Abigail pivoted and took several steps. A plan formed in her mind. She squeezed Jesse's hand, hoping he would understand.

She stumbled. "My leg hurts." And then she fell, hoping it looked believable.

Panic filled the voice of the man with the gun. "Get up, now!"

While the associate was focused on Abigail, Jesse jumped him, reaching for the gun. The two men wrestled, falling to the muddy ground. The man still held on to the gun. Jesse maneuvered himself to be on top of him, where he landed a blow across the man's face. The man fired a shot, but it went off to the side, low to the ground.

Abigail reached for the gun, trying to yank it out of the man's hand while Jesse restrained him. She grabbed the gun and turned it on the man.

An arm wrapped around Abigail's neck, so her chin jammed into the second thug's elbow. Then she felt the cold barrel of a gun against her temple.

The voice behind her was sinister. "I think you better drop that gun right now, little lady."

Jesse got off the man he'd wrestled to the ground and held up his hands. "Do what he says, Abigail." He glanced off to the side before resting his gaze on her.

She wondered if there was a third man behind the one who held her in a neck lock.

Abigail let the gun fall to the ground, and the man who had found them grabbed it and scrambled to his feet.

The thug who held the gun to her head spoke to the other man. "You know what to do with him."

The associate pointed the gun at Jesse. "Start walking."

Abigail watched as the rain swallowed up both men. She felt an intense panic at being separated from him. "Where are you taking him?"

The man who held the gun to her head pressed his mouth close to her ear. "Somewhere you two can't get any bright ideas together. Now, turn around and start walking."

When she turned around, she saw that a third man had been standing behind them—the dark-haired man who had been after them since they'd run through the mountains.

The dark-haired man crossed his arms. "Well, look what we have here."

The other man, who she remembered was Larry, let go of her but poked the gun in the middle of her back.

They walked for a hundred feet or so. Because of the downpour, she didn't so much see the road as it materialized beneath her feet. They led her toward Dale's four-wheel drive.

Larry searched her. His hand touched the hard drive in her pocket. Before they even pulled it out, she felt an overwhelming sense of defeat.

Defeat sank in around her. This was it. They would probably shoot her now.

Larry handed the hard drive over to the dark-haired man, who pulled out his phone, turned away and started talking in a hushed tone. She couldn't hear the conversation, but she thought she heard mention of Jesse's name. She feared that the order had been given to shoot both her and Jesse. What bothered her most of all was that she and Jesse would not die together. They would have no parting words, no chance even for a kiss. She would never get the chance to tell Jesse how much she cared about him.

The dark-haired man turned back to stare at Abigail. He seemed to end his conversation when he said, "Okay, you're the boss." Once he clicked off the phone, he reached up with his gun and hit Abigail in the side of the head with it.

She swayed and then collapsed…

She regained consciousness long enough to realize she was lying on the back seat of a car. As her awareness faded, her last thought was of Jesse. What had become of him? Was he alive? She wasn't sure why, now that they had the hard drive, she hadn't been shot outright. Maybe they were taking her some place her body wouldn't be found.

What had happened to Dale? Had they gotten to him, too?

The car rumbled down the road as the blackness surrounded her again.

When she came to, she found herself in a room that looked like it had been the pantry of an industrial kitchen at one time. There were no windows. The shelves still had spilled flour on them. A few bulk-size cans with faded, dirty and torn labels remained on the shelves, and rice was scattered across the floor.

She rose unsteadily on her feet. She had no memory of how she'd gotten here. She walked toward the door and shook the handle. Of course, it was locked. Though the room was probably ten feet square, the walls felt like they were closing in on her. Her breathing became shallow. She was trapped in here.

She moved toward the shelves that contained the bulk cans. One was for stewed tomatoes; the other looked like it was some kind of beans. She didn't see a can opener anywhere, only a piece of twisted metal that maybe had been part of an industrial mixer at one time.

She stood for a long moment, listening. Outside the walls of this room, she heard an odd whirring noise. The rhythm remained the same, like a huge fan.

Was she being left here to die, to starve to death? That way the men who had been after her and Jesse for so long wouldn't risk being tracked down for murder.

Abigail slumped down on the floor as a sense of despair seeped into her bones and muscles. Had she and Jesse come this far only to have it end this way?

She refused to let herself cry. She was a strong and capable woman—qualities that Brent had resented but that Jesse seemed to celebrate. Her heart fluttered when she thought of Jesse. But the sparkle faded quickly. She deeply regretted not telling him how she felt about him. And now, it appeared that it was too late.

She tilted her head and let out a prayer-filled breath. What was she even praying for? That God would show her a way out of this room? That she would get a chance to tell Jesse that she loved him? She couldn't even put words to the desperation she felt.

She opened her eyes after her wordless prayer. Something near the ceiling caught her eye. She stepped toward the corner of the room, where a camera was mounted. The installment of the camera must have been recent; it was the only thing in the room not covered in dust.

She was being watched. Oddly, the presence of the camera renewed her hope. They were keeping her alive for some reason.

The rope that bound Jesse's hands cut into his wrists. He'd been sitting on the hard, wooden chair for at least a half hour with no one coming to check on him. He'd been brought here with a hood over his head, after being hauled in the back of a car for at least two hours. Right before he'd been put in this room, they'd torn the hood off his head.

Two questions raged through his mind. What had become of Abigail, and why were they keeping him alive? They must have found the hard drive in her jacket pocket. He refused to consider that she might be dead. Shot and dragged into the brush on some rural stretch of road. He could not give in to that kind of despair.

He also wondered what had happened to Dale. Had his friend crawled away and died, been killed or escaped?

He wiggled in the chair. His bottom was sore from sitting. He rose to his feet and walked around. The room looked like it had been some sort of control room for watching something. There were banks of instruments, along with several monitors.

There were two doors on opposite walls. When he checked, both of them were locked.

The room had a line of small windows that allowed light in, but they were too high up for him to see out of. With his foot, he scooted the chair toward the windows. Though his balance was off because his hands were tied behind his back, he managed to stand on the chair and then raise himself on tiptoe.

He saw a series of metal buildings, maybe barracks of some sort. In the distance, a single drilling rig still turned. Several others were inert. He must be in the Bakken. This place now looked abandoned but had probably been a boomtown at the height of the oil activity. He saw several cars, one of them Dale's four-wheel drive the thugs had taken. He caught a flash of a man walking around the buildings holding a rifle, and another man was sitting on top of a car hood holding a handgun. The place was being guarded, but the men didn't seem to be on high alert.

A key turned in a lock and the door swung open. He nearly fell off the chair when he turned to see who it was.

"Ah, Agent Santorum. I see you have made yourself at home."

The man standing before him was Agent Frisk. Frisk, a man in his forties, had wavy hair that reached his shoulders and a five o'clock shadow. He wore workman's clothes, coveralls and a flannel shirt. The impression Jesse had of his appearance was that Agent Frisk was playing a part. When he wasn't undercover, Frisk was clean-shaven and his hair was cropped close to his head. Jesse didn't know that much about Agent Frisk. He'd only worked a couple of operations with him, the last being the one in Mexico where Lee Bronson had died. Agent Frisk had always seemed efficient but aloof.

Jesse stepped off the chair.

Agent Frisk closed the door behind him. The keys were on a ring, which he placed on one of the dusty counters. The handle of a gun stuck out from one of his coverall pockets. Agent Frisk gestured theatrically. "Please, have a seat."

Jesse remained standing. Even though his hands were tied, he needed to look for an opportunity to overtake Agent Frisk, but he couldn't do that sitting down.

Agent Frisk squared his shoulders. Though his voice remained level, his eyes narrowed and his jawline turned to granite. "I said have a seat, Agent Santorum." His hand fluttered over his gun.

"You're not going to use that. You kept me alive for some reason."

"You always were a smart man." Agent Frisk let his hand fall to his side. "I assure you that could be a very temporary situation."

Jesse still didn't sit down.

Agent Frisk paced. "I suppose you want to know why I didn't have you killed once we got the hard drive off your partner."

Jesse felt as though he'd been punched in the stomach twice. They had the hard drive. All of this had been for nothing, and now it might have cost him Abigail. Sweet, funny Abigail. "What have you done with her?"

Agent Frisk made a tsk-tsking noise and held out his palm toward Jesse. "All in good time." He turned to face Jesse. "I really think you're going to want to be sitting down for this."

The words held an intense coldness to them. Jesse sat down, partly because his knees were weak over the news he feared he was about to get concerning Abigail, and partly because he thought it might make Agent Frisk be less guarded. Maybe if Frisk didn't think he was going to be overtaken at any second, Jesse could wait for an opportunity to escape.

Frisk paced, stretching the moment out, increasing the tension in the room.

Jesse felt as though he was pulling up each word from the ends of his toes. "What. Have. You. Done. With. Abigail?"

"Patience. This story takes a while to tell."

Jesse clenched his jaw, enraged at the way Frisk was toying with him, taking sick pleasure at Jesse's anguish.

Frisk stopped pacing. He leaned against the counter. "What was on that hard drive could have put me away and probably exonerated you."

"I take it you destroyed the hard drive."

Frisk lifted his chin. The look of triumph on his face told Jesse everything he needed to know. "Lee Bronson was a good little soldier…up until the end, when he grew a conscience."

"He wanted out. He was just trying to pay the medical bills for his kid." Jesse shook his head.

"It was pure coincidence that you were at the operation the night he died."

"You shot him," said Jesse.

"Who's to say?" Frisk glanced at his fingernails and then grinned. "Gunfire was coming from everywhere."

A chill seeped into Jesse's skin and traveled to his bones. He shivered. He knew he was looking into the face of pure evil. Frisk was a man so consumed with the need for power and wealth, he would stop at nothing to get it and keep it.

Frisk folded his arms over his chest. "Anyway, Lee did a good job of making it look like you were the tainted DEA agent. So it got me to thinking. Things are drying up here in the Bakken. Less oil being pumped, fewer customers." Frisk turned and looked directly at Jesse. His light blue eyes were unsettling. "I want out, and I want out clean. The groundwork is already laid for you being dirty. Why not have you confess to running product in the Bakken?"

Jesse couldn't get a deep breath. His lungs felt like they were in a vise, being twisted tighter and tighter. "I never ran an operation in the Bakken."

Frisk pushed himself off the counter and took several steps toward Jesse. "You don't have to have lived here to have set up the supply line for the drugs."

"I would never confess to such a thing," Jesse said.

Frisk leaned over so his nose was almost touching Jesse's. "Oh, I think you will." He straightened up and walked back toward the counter where the dusty monitors were. "This is quite a neat setup here. When they were pumping tons of oil out of the ground, they needed a way to monitor the equipment and the workers."

He leaned forward and clicked on one of the monitors. Frisk's body blocked Jesse's view of the screen. "It just took a little rewiring and setting up a camera for what I'm about to show you." He stepped to one side so Jesse had a view of the monitor.

Jesse's heart seized up when he saw Abigail crouched on the floor in a windowless room.

Frisk pulled a phone out of his shirt pocket. "I need you to enter the room where target two is being held." There was a moment of silence before Frisk responded. "Yes, you know the plan."

Jesse watched in horror as the door where Abigail was being kept swung open and a man with a gun entered, grabbed Abigail by the back of her collar and yanked her to her feet. The thug turned her so she was looking directly at the camera and placed the gun on her temple.

Frisk reached over and turned off the monitor.

"So you see, Agent Santorum, you will confess, and I will tape your confession and send it on over to DEA."

Frisk walked over to an object covered in a tarp. He tore off the cover, revealing a camera. "I think we're all ready to begin filming."

Jesse's stomach tightened into a hard knot as he struggled to keep a clear head. The thought of losing Abigail tore him to pieces.

SIXTEEN

With the gun pointed at her head, all Abigail could think about was getting away. Why, now, did they want to make sure she was seen on camera with her life being threatened? Who was watching on the other side?

The thug pulled the gun away from her head.

"You're not going to kill me?" Her heart was still pounding wildly as she turned to face the man who had held a gun to her head. The thug was someone she had not seen before. A young man with red hair. He was maybe twenty years old, a kid, really. She took a step toward him.

He held the gun up. "Back off."

"I'm sorry, I just want to know why they're keeping me here. What was that little theater game all about? I thought you were going to kill me."

"I'm just following orders." The man's hand was trembling as he held the gun on her.

He was afraid. She might be able to overtake him, but there was a huge risk that doing that would send ten men down on her if she was being watched on camera.

Her voice filled with compassion. "I'm sure you're just following orders."

The man edged toward the door, still pointing the gun at her. The door behind him was probably still unlocked.

She glanced up at the camera, where a red light glowed above the lens. This might be her only possibility for escape. She whirled around, grabbed the man at the wrist and drove the hand that held the gun upward. The martial arts lessons she'd been dragged to by her brothers kicked in.

The man was stronger than she had expected. He held on to the gun. She punched him in the stomach. When he doubled over, she clasped her hands together and hit his back. He groaned in pain. The gun flew across the floor.

The man straightened, his face red with anger. She had miscalculated because of the man's age. He was just as violent as the others.

She turned and lunged toward where the gun had slid across the floor. The man grabbed her jacket and yanked her backward. He swung her around with such force, she fell to the floor. Again, she crawled toward the gun. Her fingers were within inches of clasping the handle when she was dragged back across the floor on her stomach.

The man was out of breath. "You make this way too hard, lady." His cowboy boots pounded the concrete floor. He reached down and picked up the gun.

There was no one between her and the door. She scrambled to her feet and reached for the handle. She pushed down on it and the door opened. Light flooded in from the windows in the other room, which was some sort of cafeteria, now dusty and abandoned.

The man pulled her back by grabbing her hair. He

got between her and the door, pointed the gun at her and pressed the door shut with his back. He looked ruffled and upset. His cheeks were crimson, and his freckles were even more prominent. "Get back." He waved the gun. "Step back toward that corner and keep your hands up where I can see them."

She gulped in air, put up her hands and stepped toward a far corner of the room.

The man reached behind him for the door handle, still watching her. "I gotta hand it to you, lady. You put up a good fight."

He disappeared behind the door. Even as she raced across the floor, she could hear the key turning in the lock. She shook the handle and kicked the door. She'd been so close to freedom.

Abigail ran her fingers through her hair and tried to calm herself with a deep breath, but she was unable to fight off the reality that she was completely and utterly defeated—and trapped.

Jesse stared at the camera. No way was he going to confess to something he hadn't done, and no way was he going to let anything happen to Abigail. He suspected that once he confessed, both he and Abigail would be killed, anyway.

Frisk leaned over the camera and clicked on a button. He straightened his back and pointed. "You can sit on that chair right over there."

The sheer arrogance of the man infuriated Jesse.

Frisk's hand fluttered over his gun. The message of the gesture was clear—Jesse had better do what he was told.

Jesse sat down. Agent Frisk stalked over to him. He

pulled a knife from his pocket and cut Jesse free. "We don't want it to look like you were under duress." Frisk pulled his gun and pointed it at Jesse. "That doesn't mean you can try anything."

Jesse massaged his wrists where his hands had been bound. A plan began to come together in his head. The keys were behind him by the monitor. He could get to them before Frisk did, but he probably couldn't get out of the room before Frisk shot him. He threw up his hands and shook his head. "I guess you win."

The ploy was designed to make Frisk let down his guard a little. If he thought Jesse was still fighting, he'd remain vigilant. Shoulders slumped, Jesse moved as though he was going to sit in the chair. Then he turned suddenly and dived toward Frisk. Jesse barreled into him, knocking him to the ground, and got on top of him. Jesse reached for Frisk's gun.

Frisk landed a blow across Jesse's jaw that made his teeth hurt and his eyes water. If Frisk pulled his gun, he'd have the upper hand. Still stunned from the hit he'd taken, Jesse lifted his arm to strike Frisk's head.

Frisk managed to angle away before Jesse's fist made contact with Frisk's head. Again Jesse reached for the gun. His fingers wrapped around the barrel. He pulled it out of Frisk's pocket. Frisk lunged for Jesse, grabbing the hand that held the gun.

As the two men struggled for possession of the gun, it went off. The bullet hit the ceiling, causing dust to rain on them.

The two men wrestled, falling to the floor and rolling around. Jesse's back rammed against the legs of the counters. He rolled to one side just as Agent Frisk came at him. Frisk had dropped the gun somewhere.

Jesse's eyes scanned the floor as a surge of adrenaline renewed his strength. He jumped to his feet and went after Frisk, landing a blow to his face and then his stomach. He kicked the backs of Frisk's knees, which caused him to tumble to the dusty floor. Jesse hit Frisk on the back of the head, knowing that would knock him out. Frisk collapsed to the floor on his stomach.

Jesse's heart pounded against his rib cage as he whirled around and grabbed the ring of keys Frisk had set on the counter. Once again, he searched for the gun but didn't see it. Frisk's phone was in the pocket that faced the floor. He couldn't waste any more time. Frisk would regain consciousness in a few minutes.

The door was unlocked. He stepped outside into the evening light.

He scanned the area around him that consisted of one functioning drilling rig and several inert ones, along with some metal buildings and trailers. He turned back to face the door and stared at the ring of five keys. The second one he tried fitted the lock. Frisk had a phone on him and could call for help, but they'd have to break him out unless someone else had a key. Jesse reasoned that it would buy him a few valuable minutes.

Now to find Abigail.

He hurried along the outside of the corrugated metal building that contained the monitoring equipment.

He ran toward the next building. A man with a gun walked by, headed toward the parking lot. Jesse hurried around the side of the building to keep from being spotted. A large shed blocked his view of much of the facilities. The room where Abigail was being kept had no windows.

He sprinted to the other side of the shed. The buildings that he could see were all trailers with windows. As he ran, he had a view of the parking lot. There were three cars and a truck parked there. One man was still perched on the hood of a car, holding a gun.

He darted around the trailers, crouching and pressing close to the siding in case there were men inside who could spot him and sound the alert. Once he was around the trailers, he saw a large rectangular building. Part of it had windows, and he could see the remnants of a cafeteria inside. But the far end of the building was windowless. He ran toward the cafeteria.

When he looked over his shoulder, he saw at least four men running toward where Frisk was trapped. So the alarm had been raised. That meant he had only a few minutes before they came looking for him.

He hurried into the cafeteria, past the dusty tables and serving areas. He ran through what must have been an industrial kitchen at one time, though it looked like all the appliances had been salvaged or stolen. He homed in on a door at the far side of the kitchen.

He pounded the door with his fist. "Abigail, are you in there?"

Seconds ticked by. No answer. His heart sank.

Then he heard a faint voice. "I'm here, Jesse."

He let out a breath as his spirit soared. She was okay. "I'm going to get you out." He stared down at the keys, eliminating the one that had locked Frisk in the control room. The first one he tried didn't budge the lock. "Hang in there."

"What else can I do?"

He appreciated her wry sense of humor in the face of such danger. The second key he shoved into the hole didn't budge, either. His heart raced. The men were probably already searching the property, headed in this direction. He pushed the third key in the hole and it turned. He swung the door open.

Abigail fell into his arms. He felt a sense of relief as joy surged through him. He kissed her hair and her forehead. "You have no idea how glad I am to see you."

She tilted her head. She gazed at him as though looking right through him to some deeper place. "I think I do, 'cause I feel it, too."

Her eyes were wide and welcoming, her lips slightly parted. For a moment, time stood still. He pressed his lips on hers.

He kissed her as a sense of melting and being on fire at the same time washed over him. He deepened the kiss, holding her close. He pulled back, still reeling from the power of the kiss. "You have no idea how much I want more of that. But they're coming for us."

She reached up and rested her hand on his cheek. "I understand. Let's get out of here."

He took her hand and led her into the cafeteria. Through the windows, he saw two men headed in their direction.

"There's a side door over there," she said.

They hurried outside. The door slammed behind them just as a gunshot sliced through the wood of the door. They raced toward a defunct oil rig, slipping behind it for cover.

Jesse stared out at the vast flat landscape with rolling hills in the distance. If they ran that way, they would probably be caught. "We need to get to that parking lot and grab one of those cars." Jesse took in a breath as his heart raged.

Abigail nodded. "You know the lay of the land. Lead the way."

A gunshot pinged off the metal of the rig. Without a word, both of them hit the ground and crawled toward the next thing that would provide cover—a dry drainage ditch.

The dimming light of evening provided them with a degree of cover as they inched their way along. Still, the two men had seen them in the cafeteria and behind the drilling rig. It would be just a matter of time before they searched the drainage ditch.

Up ahead, Jesse could make out a twisted pile of metal that created a sort of overhang they could hide under if they both curled into a tight ball. The men who were searching for them had not had time to grab flashlights, though they might have phones that had one. So far, they hadn't used it.

Abigail rolled into the tight space first, and then he slipped in beside her. In order to fit, they both had to lie on their sides. Jesse squeezed in close to Abigail, facing her. Their noses were nearly touching. He scooted his legs in so they wouldn't be visible.

Above them he could hear the men shouting at each other, their voices growing louder and then fading. When the voices sounded like the men were quite far away, Abigail reached up and rested her palm on Jesse's cheek. The silent show of affection and support warmed him all the way to the marrow of his bones.

The voices grew louder. He was so close to Abigail he could feel her body tense with fear.

The men were directly above them.

"They must have run off," said one of them.

"Out toward that field, do you think?"

The first man took a moment to answer. "They're just going to run into a big pile of nothing and a bunch of coyotes if they go out that way."

The second man laughed. "Yeah, but they don't know that."

"Better get back to the boss man and figure out how we'll mount up a search."

Jesse listened to the sound of the retreating footsteps.

The night fell silent.

Abigail lifted her head, indicating she thought they should move.

Jesse shook his head. Best to wait and listen.

She leaned close so she could whisper in his ear, "My legs are cramping."

His hand rested on her shoulder. Being this close to her reminded him of the power of the kiss they'd shared. The intensity of the moment still had him reeling. Yet the kiss had been impulsive, at a moment of intense danger. Had he kissed her because he loved her, or was it driven by fear because he thought he might lose her?

Even though they remained physically close in the tight quarters, he could feel himself retreating emotionally. He knew from experience that loving someone came at a high cost and an extreme risk of pain. Was he ready for that?

He rolled away from her. "I think the coast is clear." Jesse crawled out from beneath the tight space and got to his feet.

Abigail stood up beside him.

A light flashed suddenly in his eyes. "Fooled you," said the voice of the thug holding a gun on them.

SEVENTEEN

Abigail's heart revved into overdrive as she shielded her eyes from the intense light.

She could only discern the man's silhouette, but it was clear that he had a gun aimed at her.

Each word the man uttered seemed to be dripping with violence. "I knew it was just a matter of time before you got uncomfortable down there. I wasn't about to go crawling around in that mess. Guy could get all cut up from the metal that's been tossed in there," he said. "Now, both of you put your arms in the air and crawl out of that ditch." The man aimed his flashlight, indicating the path they were supposed to take.

Now she saw all the metal and debris that had been dumped in the dry riverbed that they could have been cut on. Abigail stepped in front of Jesse.

The man with the gun backed up as they got closer to him. He stumbled on something and flailed his arms to keep from falling. The gun flew off in the darkness somewhere. Jesse, who wasn't even to the bank of the riverbed, lunged toward the man. The two of them got into a fistfight.

Jesse could handle himself.

She searched for the gun. It was hard to see anything in the dark. She dropped to the ground and felt around with her hands in the area where she thought the gun had landed. Nothing.

When she looked over at the two men, Jesse was on top of the other man, punching him.

In the little bit of moonlight, she saw something shiny in the grass and crawled toward it. It was the thug's phone. It must have flown out of his hand when Jesse tackled him. He'd been using the flashlight on it.

The two men continued to wrestle. The thug crawled on top of Jesse, hitting him in the face and chest. Abigail switched on the flashlight on the phone and directed it into the thug's eyes. He drew a protective hand up to his face, which allowed Jesse to punch him in the stomach. The man drew his knees up to his chest. Jesse got out from under him and hit the thug several more times.

The other man grew still. Jesse leaped to his feet. "He'll be out for a little while." He ran toward her. "Come on, we don't have much time."

"Are we going back to get one of the cars?"

"They must have sent other guys in other directions looking for us. There can't be that many men still around." He grabbed her hand and they ran.

His touch brought the memory of the kiss they had just shared like a flood washing over her. They were two people from two very different worlds. Probably nothing could come of it. The lights of the barracks came into view. There was no time to think about what the kiss meant.

They ran past the nonfunctioning drilling rig and the cafeteria, not seeing anyone. Jesse slowed down

and took cover behind the first structure they encountered, a cargo container that was probably used for storage. Both of them angled around the side of it to have
a view of the rest of the camp. From where they were,
she could not see the parking lot.

One man holding a rifle stalked through the barracks. They both pressed against the cold metal of the
container as the man marched past them, preoccupied
with speaking into his phone.

They hurried toward the next building, a storage
shed. She followed Jesse around to the side of the building. Both of them crouched low. Only two cars remained in the parking lot. That meant the others were
out looking for them.

Heart racing, Abigail glanced around. So far, they'd
only seen one armed man. The thug who had ambushed
them at the drainage ditch would be waking up within
minutes and running back here to sound the alarm. She
was glad she'd taken the thug's phone. It bought them
some time. There was no way to calculate how many
men were still here, but at least they weren't dealing
with an army.

Jesse pressed his back against the building. "You
have that guy's phone."

"Yes." She held it up.

"See if Frisk's name is on there," Jesse said.

She looked down and scrolled through the list. "It
isn't here. They all have code names." She remembered seeing the names on Larry's phone when he'd
kidnapped her down the road from Dale's cabin. "I
think Frisk's code name is Ernie and that's how he's
listed. Frisk is the one behind all of this, right? Are

you thinking taking him into custody might help clear your name?"

"If we get out of here, he'll be out of the country by the time I can get the DEA to listen to me," Jesse said. "This might be my only chance. You could get to one of those cars and get out of here safely. I'll take care of this."

"We're in this together, Jesse. I'm not going to leave you." Abigail reached over and squeezed his hand.

Both she and Dale had seen the contents of the hard drive. That might help his case, too. If Dale was alive.

He leaned close to her. "I know there are a lot of maybes to this plan."

She stared out at the parking lot. She noticed a man standing in shadows at the edge of the lot. It was probably his job to watch the parking lot. Even just getting away in one of those cars held huge risk. Staying together was their best chance for escape.

She took in a deep breath. "I say we try to lure Frisk out."

Jesse's heart swelled with affection. "You have no idea what this means to me." He held out his hand. "Give me the phone. I think I can imitate the voice of that guy who jumped us back at the drainage ditch."

She placed the phone in his hand. "How exactly are we going to get the jump on Frisk?"

"I'll get him to give up his location by saying I have target two—that's you—in custody."

She nodded. "Okay."

"Hopefully he'll tell us his location. I'll bring you to him. You stand in front of me so his view of me is blocked. When I touch your back, get out of the way and I'll jump him."

"Got it," she said.

Her courage amazed him. "I'm so going to take you out for a nice meal when this is all over with," Jesse said.

"That would be great, Jesse. Just to do something ordinary."

He thought he detected a hint of sadness in her voice. Maybe she was wondering if the kiss was a mistake, just like he had. If they weren't working to stay alive, was there even enough of a bond to keep them together?

Jesse clicked on Ernie's number.

"Tell me you have good news." The voice on the other end of the line was Agent Frisk.

Jesse cleared his throat. "We have target two." The important thing was that his voice not sound like his own and that he keep his words to a minimum to avoid suspicion.

"And target one?" Frisk's voice was filled with accusation.

"He's still at large."

"Bring her here. I'm in the control room. Maybe we can use her to lure him out. I don't think he'll leave without her. He's in love with her."

Frisk's last words echoed in his brain. When Jesse had seen Abigail on that camera, Frisk must have picked up on Jesse's feelings even before he had. He was a trained agent. It was his job to be able to read people. Yet he was unsure of his own heart.

"Craig, are you still there?" Frisk sounded impatient.

Jesse glanced over at Abigail. "Yes, I'll bring her

in." Still in a state of shock, he clicked off the phone, then reached for her as fear washed over him. "I don't know what I was thinking. You don't have to do this."

"Let's end this once and for all." She stood to her feet. "I'm choosing to do this, Jesse."

There was no arguing with her.

They hurried through the barracks, darting from building to building, aware that if they were spotted someone might sound the alarm to Frisk.

They moved toward the door on the square metal building where Frisk was.

Abigail slipped in front of Jesse, and he stood directly behind her. She opened the door so Frisk would see her.

Jesse could not see him, could only hear his raspy voice. "Well, look at you."

Abigail must have managed to play the part of the frightened captive.

"You won't trick Jesse into coming for me. He's long gone. The authorities will be here any minute," she said.

Jesse stared at Abigail's long blond braid. *Way to go, Abigail.* He had to hand it to her. She played the part well. Her comment not only fed Frisk's fear, but would also continue the ruse that Jesse was not standing right behind her.

"Good work, Craig," said Frisk. "I'll take it from here."

Abigail dived to the floor. Jesse lunged toward Frisk, whose eyes had gone round with surprise. He reached for his gun. Jesse distracted him with a left hook to the jaw that seemed to stun him into momentary paralysis. Frisk's hand hovered over his gun but he didn't grasp it.

Abigail crawled across the floor, grabbed a piece of metal and hit the backs of Frisk's knees with it. He collapsed to the ground. He dived toward Abigail, wrapping one arm around her neck and then pulling his gun, pointing it at her head.

"She'll die if that's what you want," said Agent Frisk.

All the air left Jesse's lungs as he struggled to get a deep breath. His gaze rested on Abigail, who panted for air, but her eyes were not filled with fear. He saw resolve there as she nodded. Somehow, they would find a way to get the upper hand.

Jesse put his hands in the air. "Okay, just back off of her."

Frisk shoved the gun toward Abigail. "Drop that piece of metal."

Abigail let her weapon fall to the floor.

Still on his knees, Frisk waved his gun. "Both of you, go over there and sit down."

Jesse moved toward the corner on the opposite side of where the door was. Abigail crawled in that direction, as well.

Even though he had the gun, Frisk was in a defensive position. Once he stood up, he would be harder to overpower.

Frisk winced as he struggled to get to his feet. Abigail must have hurt him when she hit him. In the seconds Frisk tried to stand, he and Abigail lunged toward him together as if on cue. Abigail picked up the piece of metal again.

Jesse reached toward Frisk's hand that held the gun.

They struggled. Abigail landed another shot to Frisk's legs. The man collapsed to his knees. Jesse yanked the gun away from him.

He pointed the gun at Agent Frisk. "On your feet, hands in the air."

Abigail searched the control room, recovering a piece of wire. "Hands in front so I can tie them up."

Frisk complied with a sneer on his face. "My men will come for you. You'll never get out of here."

Jesse searched Frisk's pockets, finding a ring that contained car keys. "Come on, we don't have much time."

With Frisk in tow, they hurried out to the parking lot.

Abigail helped Frisk into the back seat and then slipped into the front passenger seat. Jesse gave her the gun to hold on Frisk while he rifled through the keys until he found the one that fitted.

"See, I told you they'd come for me." Frisk tilted his head toward the barracks, where two shadowy figures made their way toward the parking lot.

Heart racing, Jesse shifted into Reverse. Another man ran toward them from the edge of the parking lot. He must have been patrolling the area. The thug raised a pistol and took aim.

Frisk laughed. "I told you so."

Jesse pressed the gas and cranked the steering wheel. The other two men had reached the edge of the lot and were running toward the other car.

In his rearview mirror, Jesse saw the thug who had been patrolling the lot raise his gun. "Get down."

The back windshield shattered.

Jesse sped toward the edge of the parking lot. "You all right?"

Abigail's voice remained steadfast. "Yes, we're both good."

As he pulled out onto a dirt road, the other car was right on their tail. He had no idea where they were going or how far it was to civilization.

He pressed the gas, going as fast as he dared on the dirt road. They were still a long way from safety.

EIGHTEEN

Abigail kept the gun pointed at Frisk. His eyes became narrow slits as he stared straight ahead, his jaw set tight.

A breeze floated in from where the back window had been broken.

The other car was so close its headlights made her shield her eyes.

Jesse kept his focus on the road while he spoke. "Abigail, you still have that phone."

"Yes." She pulled it out of her pocket.

"Try calling Dale." Jesse recited the number to her.

She clicked in the numbers as Jesse spoke them. The phone rang once. Twice.

"No one is going to help you," said Agent Frisk.

"You be quiet."

The phone rang a third time. Then she heard a voice, faint and warbled. "Dale, is that you?"

She heard her name but not much else. It had to be Dale. He was alive.

A reply came. She could only decipher a few words. But it was clearly Dale's voice. It sounded like he was standing inside a fan.

She heard only one phrase clearly. "Stay on the line."

"Okay, I'll keep talking."

"He must be working with someone who can figure out where we are by bouncing the signal off the cell phone towers," said Jesse.

Abigail continued to talk about all that had happened to them, though she could not discern much of what Dale said in response.

Jesse came to a crossroads, taking a sharp left turn. When she glanced out the windshield, she saw lights in the distance. Maybe it was a small town.

The other car stuck to their bumper. Another shot was fired. It pinged off the outside of their car.

Abigail's heart raced. A little shaken, she kept talking into the phone but kept the gun pointed at Frisk.

Just as Jesse turned onto a paved road, the other car came up beside them.

One of the men had crawled into the back seat of the other car. He rolled down the window and pointed a pistol at them. Abigail slipped down in the seat. Jesse swerved. Their car rolled out onto the grass beside the road, bumping along.

Once he was back on pavement, Jesse did a sharp turn, headed in the other direction. Up ahead, Abigail saw no lights, just a vast, dark emptiness.

A voice came to her across the phone, clearer than before. "Abigail, are you still there?"

"Yes, Dale, I'm still here, but I have no idea where we are."

The reply was garbled and then the line went dead.

Abigail glanced out the broken back window. Changing direction had put some distance between them and the other car, but it looked like they were going back to the middle of nowhere.

The other car had gotten turned around and was headed toward them, traveling at a high speed.

She didn't need to tell Jesse the pursuers were gaining on them. She saw his nervous glance in the rearview mirror.

Her heartbeat drummed in her ears as her whole body tensed.

Jesse pulled onto a shoulder on the road and turned around again so they would be going toward the light of civilization. The other car swerved into their lane, headed straight toward them in a deadly game of chicken. The other car drew even closer, still not getting into the other lane.

"Are they crazy?" she said as her throat went tight with terror. A head-on crash would not serve anyone.

Abigail held her breath.

The other car sped toward them.

Jesse cranked the wheel to avoid a crash, bumping along the rough terrain that surrounded the road. The other car rolled off the road and came to a stop.

Jesse slammed on the gas.

Agent Frisk glanced behind him as the thug's car grew farther away. He hit the bottom of her hand so the gun flew out of her grasp. She glanced at the gun, which had landed in the front seat. He wrapped his bound hands around Abigail's neck and pressed his arms against her throat. "Let me out or she dies."

Abigail fought to break free, clawing at Frisk's hands as she gasped for air. Black spots filled her vision.

"Let her go." Jesse reached over, pounding and scratching at Frisk's arms.

The car swerved and fishtailed. Jesse slowed in an effort to regain control of the car. The grip around her neck loosened just as the car flipped. She had the sensation of being airborne before sliding along on hard ground. The car came to a standstill.

She fumbled around for the seat belt latch but couldn't find it. She was upside down and trapped in the car. She felt light-headed, dizzy. Jesse said something to her. She responded automatically, though she hadn't totally comprehended his words.

She heard doors creaking open. Men shouting. A strange whirring sound she could not identify filled the air. When she looked over to the driver's seat, Jesse was gone.

Jesse crawled out of the car. Frisk was trying to make a run for it. He wouldn't be able to run very fast with his hands bound in front of him. He'd told Abigail where he was going, but had she been coherent enough to comprehend?

Down the road, the thugs' car got closer. Jesse watched as Frisk made his way toward the road and the ride that would allow him to escape justice.

Overhead in the distance, Jesse saw the flashing lights and whirring blades of a helicopter. Had one of Frisk's cohorts been able to bring in more manpower just like they had done on the mountain?

Jesse darted toward Frisk as he drew closer to the thugs' car. Jesse's legs pumped hard. He closed the distance between him and the other agent. He leaped through the air, bringing Frisk to the ground.

The thugs' car slowed as it approached. Gunshots filled the air around Jesse.

"You will not live to see another day," Frisk said through gritted teeth as he was lying on his stomach with Jesse on top of him.

Gunshots directed at the car came from the helicopter, which hovered just above the ground.

Jesse pressed his hand on Agent Frisk's neck to keep him from getting away.

A hand cupped his shoulder. "I got this." Jesse was overjoyed to hear Dale's voice. "Go take care of Abigail."

Jesse ran back toward the overturned car. He hurried around to the passenger side, yanked open the door and reached inside. He unclicked Abigail from her seat belt and dragged her out.

He held her in his arms, touching her face and her hair. "Abigail?" He drew her limp body close to his chest.

"I'm okay." Though her voice was weak, the sound of it made joy wash through him.

She gripped his collar and gazed up at him.

Beautiful, brave Abigail. He touched her face. "We made it. Everything is going to be okay."

He hoped he was right about that, that his name would be cleared and he could go back to doing what he loved. What would happen between him and Abigail, however, was still uncertain.

NINETEEN

Abigail's stomach tensed as she surveyed the tables in the restaurant. It had been almost a week since she'd returned to Fort Madison after giving her testimony about what she had seen Frisk say and do, and what she'd seen on the destroyed hard drive.

She'd made the decision to move back to Idaho. There was nothing left for her here in Fort Madison.

Jesse stood up and waved at her from a corner booth.

His text to her had been quick and to the point. I'm back in Fort Madison and would like to take you out to dinner as a thank-you for all you did for me.

Seeing him made her heart leap.

She'd thought that once they were no longer together, once they didn't have to depend on each other to stay alive, the intense feelings she had for him would subside. But time and distance had done nothing to erase her affection for him.

He stood up and pointed at the other side of the booth for her to sit.

She sat down. He smiled at her.

"Are you back to being an agent?"

"It looks that way. Frisk didn't confess. But some

of his cohorts rolled on him. The testimonies you and Dale gave helped a lot. They're working on searching the plane for evidence. That's why I'm back here."

So he hadn't just come back to Fort Madison to take her out to dinner. She struggled to hide her disappointment. Maybe she had been entertaining fantasies that he didn't share.

"Good, so your life is back to what it used to be. And the aloe vera plant. How is he doing?"

Jesse laughed. She liked the little crinkles around his eyes when he smiled. "George was glad to see me, as always."

Abigail laced her fingers together and rested her hands on the table. Sharing small talk with Jesse made her aware of the chasm inside her. "Thank you for keeping your promise and taking me out to dinner." She wanted there to be more between them than small talk. She looked into his eyes, searching. Did he want that, too?

"It's the least I could do for you, Abigail. Considering all you went through for me," he said.

"It was scary at times. But I kind of like the adventure of it all."

"Seriously, you should think about becoming an agent."

"I never would have thought my life would go in that direction…until I met you." The longing she felt was like a wave crashing over her. Being with him now made her realize that she loved him. She wanted to be with him.

"I'm glad to hear you say that." He reached down on the seat of the booth and placed an odd-looking package on the table. It was a six-inch cube wrapped in a fast-food wrapper and held together with electrician's tape. "It's for you. I had to MacGyver the wrapping together with what I had in my car. I thought you would appreciate that."

She laughed. "Very clever." She reached for the package. When she got the wrapping off, she stared at a box that had at one time been for the bulb in a car headlight. "Okay?"

"Open it." His voice lilted with a note of excitement. "Remember when I met you, my initial impression of you was all wrong because of what Brent had done to you. Just 'cause the wrapping isn't classy doesn't mean what's inside will be trash."

She rested her hand on top of the box. "And my first impression of you was totally off, too. You are an honest man, a good man." She met his gaze. The warmth in his eyes made her heart race.

She opened the box.

Jesse cleared his throat. "I don't know where our lives will end up. I'd love it if you became an agent and we worked together. But I would be completely open to rethinking my life and living somewhere where you could be a guide."

Inside the large box was a smaller box. She pulled it out.

"The only thing that matters to me, Abigail, is that I'm with you."

She opened the box, which contained an engagement ring.

"Oh, Jesse." Joy flooded every cell of her body. "Yes, I will."

"You didn't let me ask the question." He reached over and covered her hand with his.

"The answer is still yes."

He laughed and leaned across the table, gesturing for her to come closer. She leaned in. He touched his hand to her cheek and pressed his lips on hers, sending a charge of electricity through her.

When she'd walked into the restaurant, her world had seemed upside down and empty. Now, with Jesse, it was right side up and full of possibility. She looked forward to a lifetime with the man she loved.

* * * * *

Kellie VanHorn is an award-winning author of inspirational romance and romantic suspense. She has college degrees in biology and nautical archaeology, but her sense of adventure is most satisfied by a great story. When not writing, Kellie can be found homeschooling her four children, camping, baking and gardening. She lives with her family in west Michigan.

Books by Kellie VanHorn

Love Inspired Suspense

Fatal Flashback

Visit the Author Profile page
at Harlequin.com for more titles.

FATAL FLASHBACK

Kellie VanHorn

O God, thou art my God; early will I seek thee:
my soul thirsteth for thee, my flesh longeth for thee
in a dry and thirsty land, where no water is.
—*Psalms* 63:1

For my family

Acknowledgments

My heartfelt gratitude goes to all who've helped make this book possible: my fantastic critique partner, Michelle Keener, for her thoughtful feedback; Kerry Johnson, for her critique of the beginning; Margie Reid, who shared her words of wisdom on an early version.

Thanks to my wonderful editor, Dina Davis, and the rest of the Love Inspired Suspense team for bringing this story to life.

To my parents, Gary and Denise Parker, and my brother Matt—thank you for letting me read during all those family dinners.

To my husband, Jason—thank you for your boundless encouragement. I couldn't have done it without you. To our kids, Isaiah, Nate, Ella and Luke— thank you for enduring long typing sessions in which you had to get your own snacks.

Last of all, thanks to my Savior, who gifted me with the desire to share my faith through stories.

ONE

Cold water roared through her clothes, swirling over her head and through her hair, dragging her back into consciousness. Instinctively she struggled for the surface and as soon as her head cleared the water, she coughed and gasped in a few precious breaths, wiping at her stinging eyes.

In the fading daylight the banks of the narrow river filled the horizon, impossibly high to her right but leveling out on the left. Sparse brush and skinny cottonwood trees lined the sandy river's edge.

Not a soul in sight.

Something sharp—a submerged log, maybe—jammed into her ribs. She cried out in pain but was rewarded with a mouthful of dark river water. Coughing it out, she turned against the current and kicked for the bank.

She crawled out onto the sand, tiny rocks biting into her palms, and pushed through the reeds growing at the water's edge. Collapsing onto a clear patch of ground, she struggled to catch her breath. What on earth had happened? Where was she?

The back of her head throbbed like she'd smashed it

into a rock. Worse, though, was the way her brain felt like cotton fluff, disoriented and unfocused.

She squinted into the last fading rays of light, one cheek pressed down on the cool sand. As the initial blackness receded, her senses clicked slowly into place. The tall reeds stood like sentinels between her and the flat, glossy stretch of dark river water, barely visible in the dying sunlight. She shivered as a light breeze drifted over her drenched clothes.

Sitting up slowly, she pressed a hand to the throbbing place on the back of her head. When she pulled it away, a red, sticky film coated her fingers.

Her heart jumped in her chest. If only this horrible groggy feeling would go away, she could figure out where she was. What to do now.

Some distance to her right, the river disappeared into a deep canyon with jagged cliff walls rising on both sides. From the way the current ran, she must've fallen in back there, before the cliffs became impassably steep.

That way was west—the last bit of sun was still visible dipping down behind the rim of the canyon, sending streaks of pink and orange through the distant clouds.

In the other direction, to the east, the landscape flattened out and groves of cottonwood trees grew along the riverbank. No sign of civilization for as far as she could see.

How did she end up here, in the middle of nowhere?

"Ashley," she said softly, more to reassure herself than anything else. "My name is Ashley. Thompson?"

She rolled the last name around on her tongue. Sounded right.

Somewhere through the haze in her brain, she remembered that something terrible had happened—something related to why she was here, wherever *here* was. But she couldn't remember for the life of her what it was—only that it hurt, so badly her stomach clenched into a tight, aching knot.

She pressed her hands to her temples, her forehead, her eyes, trying to calm her pounding heart. Panicking wouldn't solve anything or help her remember.

Something hard dug into her hip as she sat with her legs to one side. Fumbling in her pocket, her hand closed around the smooth, cold and heavy object, then dropped it onto the sand.

A gun.

She slid backward, staring at the dark weapon lying there like a rattlesnake ready to bite.

Law enforcement. That had to be it. She stared down at her clothing, as if her soggy black pants and white blouse could explain everything. Even though it'd been in her pocket, she had a holster. The gun had to be hers. Legally, she hoped.

And the clothes seemed familiar enough. At least they fit. She struggled to remember anything—her last meal or her last ride in a car or her last day at work—but there was nothing. Just a vast, blank space in her mind, as if someone had siphoned away her entire identity beyond her first name. How was it possible she had no idea where she was or how she had gotten there?

And what on earth was she supposed to do now?

Her lips parted to utter a prayer, but she checked herself almost instantly because, along with that certainty about her name and the sense that something terrible had happened, came the knowledge she wasn't on speaking terms with God.

She shivered. Night was coming and she had no idea where to go. The thought of wandering around looking for help in the dark was horribly unappealing.

She crawled back toward the gun and picked it up, tentatively at first, but as her hand closed around it, a familiar sense of security washed over her. She clung to that tiny bit of comfort and clasped her knees to her chest, staring out across the desert. Hoping against reason that help would come.

Logan Everett walked across the parking lot to his Jeep. The meeting with the river ranger and the border patrol agents had taken longer than he'd expected, and the sun had begun its final descent behind the Mesa de Anguila to the west.

He could still get in a good chunk of the drive back to Panther Junction before the onset of total darkness, but he had a nagging feeling something was wrong.

That black sedan that had turned around in front of the general store—he had seen it from the window during their meeting—had headed down toward Santa Elena Canyon a good hour ago, and it hadn't returned. Granted, it was hard to tell from his vantage point inside the Castolon ranger office, but it had looked like the driver, a woman, was alone.

Now that it was almost dark, she shouldn't still be there. She couldn't drive that sedan on the dirt road up to Big Bend National Park's west entrance at Terlingua and, as far as pavement went, the canyon was the end of the line.

Logan exhaled a long breath that matched his never-ending day. Well, it wouldn't hurt to check. He had learned that the hard way. He trusted his instincts—

they hadn't failed him yet—and if it turned out she was fine, or not there anymore, at least he'd be able to sleep tonight knowing he'd made sure.

An image flashed into his mind—a man's body in a ranger uniform, half a mile off the trail. Vultures circling above in the 110-degree heat. More than circling.

Logan shuddered. No, he was not going to think about Sam. Not now.

Please, Lord, he prayed, *keep this woman safe*.

The Santa Elena Canyon parking lot lay in deep shadow by the time he pulled in. The lot was empty except for the black car, its driver conspicuously absent. Logan parked and got out, pulling a flashlight from the Jeep's glove compartment.

He walked toward the trailhead, scanning his light across the sand for footprints. There were plenty, since the canyon trail was one of the most popular in the park. He frowned. It was also short enough that the woman should have returned by now.

He stopped when the arcing sweep of his light caught a set of footprints off to one side, leading toward the river. Annoying hikers. It was like they couldn't read the signs plastered all over the place.

Stay on the trails. Not only did it preserve the environment, there were enough ways to get injured without needing to wander off looking for more trouble.

Picking his way carefully, Logan followed the tracks until they ended at the river. Here the sand was wet and the marks were much clearer. Too large for a woman. The same single pair of tracks circled back to the parking lot.

Nothing. As he turned to leave, his flashlight glinted

off something lying in the brush a short distance downstream.

He snatched it off the damp sand. A woman's silver wristwatch. His breath caught in his chest. Judging by its near flawless condition, it hadn't been there long.

Hastening his pace, he walked downstream along the bank, sweeping the light ahead. He hadn't gone far when he froze. Movement—there, to the left. A woman. And she was clearly alive, because she was lying on her stomach, arms out in front of her, pointing a handgun at his chest.

He slowly lifted both hands, the law-enforcement side of him sizing her up within seconds—midtwenties, maybe five feet, eight inches in height, thin yet muscular build. She had the same long, dark hair of the driver he had seen earlier.

Only now it was wet and hung in clumps around her pale face and her sandy, soaked shirt clung to her shoulders and arms.

"Whoa, it's okay. I'm here to help you. You don't need the gun." He angled the flashlight to one side and inched toward her, hands up. "Put the gun down, okay? There's no reason for anyone to get hurt."

"Who are you?" Her voice was high-pitched and trembling.

"Logan Everett. I'm a law-enforcement ranger." He pointed at the brown arrowhead badge on his shirt. "National Park Service."

The woman sat up, keeping the gun steady. Clearly she was no stranger to handling weapons.

Law enforcement?

Or criminal? Crime was rare in Big Bend, but it *did* happen.

"Don't come any closer." Her brown eyes grew wide, the whites glistening in the fading light.

Logan stopped, crouching down ten feet away from her and holding the silver wristwatch out for her to inspect. "Is this your watch?"

"I… I don't know," she stammered. "Stay back."

There was a definite edge of panic in her voice. Something had happened to her and she was still terrified.

"Hey—" he reached toward her "—we're on the same side. How did you get out here?" The wary, frightened look in her large, dark eyes reminded him of a cornered animal.

Her forehead wrinkled and her eyes slipped out of focus as she shook her head. "I… I fell into the river."

He nodded reassuringly, even as he tried to calculate how she could have fallen in. He couldn't see her feet clearly from his present position, but he didn't think it was likely the tracks by the river had been hers. Odd.

When she didn't say anything else, he asked, "From the trail?"

"I…" She bit her lip, brows furrowed, and lowered the gun slightly. He straightened and inched forward, taking advantage of her distraction. "I don't remember."

Her eyes were still out of focus and her hands shook as she held the gun.

"Are you injured?"

She took one hand off the gun, reaching for the back of her head. When she pulled her hand away, red smeared her fingertips. She stared at the blood, the gun drooping in her other hand.

That explained it—well, at least her obvious confusion. Poor woman. She probably had a concussion.

He stepped forward, holding his hands up, inching closer and closer. Like approaching an injured mountain lion, only without the tranquilizer darts.

When he was a few feet away he dropped down onto his knees. He was directly in front of her by the time she looked at him again and, before she could react, Logan had the gun out of her hand and safely tucked into his waistband.

The woman stared at him, her expression torn between fear and confusion.

"There." He offered her a grin. "Now that you're not going to kill me, maybe I can help you."

He peered at the back of her head. Her long, brown hair was matted into a knot by the blood and there was a large bump. Had she fallen? Or was it foul play?

"Where am I?" She turned wide, dark eyes up to him.

"You must've taken quite a blow to the head. This is Big Bend National Park, in west Texas. And we're right outside Santa Elena Canyon on the Rio Grande."

"Texas?"

"Yes, ma'am."

She winced as she pulled back onto her knees.

"Easy." Logan held out his hand. She glanced up at him warily. "You might have other injuries."

She rubbed a hand slowly over her lower ribs. "I hit something in the water," she mumbled.

"We need to get you checked out. Do you think you can walk?"

When she nodded, he gently helped her to her feet. She swayed unsteadily for a moment, clinging to his arm.

"Do you remember your name?" He picked a path for them around the low brush back toward the trailhead parking lot.

"Ashley." She gripped his arm a little tighter as she stumbled over something in the growing darkness, and Logan swung his light to the ground. Despite her little dunk in the Rio Grande, a light scent of something sweet, like berries, emanated from her hair.

"What's the last thing you remember, Ashley?"

"I… I remember…" She grew thoughtful for a moment, chewing on her lip. When she spoke again, her voice held a note of hope. "Taking a cab. Yes, that was it."

"I think we can rule out that being today. So, you have no idea why you're here in Big Bend?"

She shook her head but a brief flicker of some emotion passed over her face. Grief? Or anger? He wasn't sure, but clearly something lurked under the surface and she didn't want to share or couldn't remember.

Either way, pretty women dressed in tailored slacks didn't turn up in the Rio Grande for no reason.

When they reached the parking lot, Ashley stared blankly at the two vehicles in the lot—the rental car Logan suspected was hers and his NPS Jeep.

"Recognize it?"

She dug into one of her pockets. "No. But I do have a set of keys that survived the river. I may as well try them."

The river had wrecked the electric key fob, but she was able to open the driver's door using the key. As she searched the interior for personal items, he called in the plates to a park dispatcher.

A quick search confirmed it was a rental, from an

Enterprise in El Paso, Texas—she must've flown in to the airport there.

"The name?" he asked the dispatcher.

The radio crackled. "Watson. Ashley Watson."

Ashley climbed back out of the car, holding the black blazer that completed her suit—absolutely the wrong clothing for the desert—as well as a small handbag.

"Ms. Watson?" Logan gestured at the purse. "Did you find some identification?"

She frowned, rubbing her forehead with a knuckle as she stared at the closed purse.

"Everything okay?"

"Sure." Her expression cleared but the air of confusion still lingered—must be from the head injury. She fumbled with the purse's zipper and dug out a wallet, staring at the driver's license inside for a long moment before handing it to him. Her forehead creased again.

Logan took the license from her clammy fingers. *Ashley Watson.* Issued in the District of Columbia. His brows pulled together. "No idea what brings you to Texas, Ms. Watson? You're a long way from home."

She leaned against the car. Her face was pale but she held his gaze. "No, but it'll come back to me. Otherwise, I know where to go home. Now, if you want to point me in the right direction to a medical facility, I can drive myself. I'm sure you have other places to be."

Was she trying to get rid of him? Did she remember more than she was letting on?

"Really?" He raised an eyebrow. "You think I'd let you drive in your condition?"

"I'm feeling better. Besides—" she nodded toward

his Jeep "—you probably have a cold pack in there for my head, right?"

"For starters, the road to the nearest medical facility is that way." He pointed across the parking lot toward a nearly invisible dirt road leading into the desert to the north. "And second, you'll be coming with me to park headquarters in Panther Junction after we go to the clinic."

"Why?" Somehow she managed to look both helplessly lost and irritated at the same time.

"Because it's illegal to carry a firearm in this park without a permit unless you're in law enforcement."

"So, what? You're going to arrest me after I almost drowned?" Sparks flared in her brown eyes.

"No." Logan sucked in a slow breath, searching for the tattered shreds of his patience. "I'm going to bring you in for questioning. Unless you've got a Texas-approved license to carry somewhere in there, too."

She inhaled sharply, eyes widening. *Nervous?* But why? "I'm sure there's a good reason for the gun." She dug inside her blazer pocket, her brow furrowing when her fingers came away empty. "I have a holster."

"Maybe. But we'll let the chief ranger decide."

She closed and locked her car door and then took the arm he offered, cold fingers clutching his elbow, and he escorted her to the Jeep.

He helped her into the passenger seat and handed her a thick gauze pad from a first-aid kit. "Press this to the wound, and here's an ice pack for the swelling."

Ashley took the gauze, wincing as she touched it to the injury. A wave of pity washed through him. The ride to Terlingua over that washboard dirt road was going to hurt.

She sat silently in the passenger seat, a hand pressed to her eyes, as he did his best to steer around the lumpiest sections of the road.

They'd been driving for maybe thirty minutes when headlights appeared in the rearview mirror, two tiny orbs bouncing in the distance.

Ashley craned her head over her shoulder. "Somebody else uses this road?"

"Yeah…once in a while." He frowned. The lights were growing bigger much faster than they should be. Usually only Terlingua locals and lost tourists used this road, and neither was foolish enough to go that fast.

Only a few minutes passed before the other vehicle was nearly on their tail, its headlights glaring off the dashboard and mirrors so brightly he had to squint. A truck, judging by the height of the lights.

Better to let them pass than get into an accident out here. He slowed the Jeep, driving closer to the side to allow the truck space to pass. "Impatient driver. Going to break an axle at this rate."

Impatient *and* reckless—couldn't they see this was an NPS vehicle? He'd be sure to get the plate number and call it in.

But the truck didn't pass. Instead it veered to the right with them and accelerated.

"What…?" Logan muttered. "Hold on!"

The driver was going to ram them.

TWO

Ashley scrabbled to find the handle inside the door as Logan jerked the steering wheel to the left. The Jeep swerved, its tires slipping on the loose dirt. Behind them, the truck eased off the gas long enough to follow them into the center of the road.

Could it be whoever had attacked her at the river coming back to finish the job? She shivered, clutching the door handle hard enough her fingers hurt.

The truck shot forward again, bumping the rear of the Jeep as Logan accelerated. Not hard enough to release the air bags, but enough to whip her forward and lock her seat belt. She grimaced as her head smacked back into the seat.

Logan's jaw clenched as he cranked the steering wheel to the left, trying to move the Jeep out of the way. He yanked a handheld radio out from its holder and tossed it onto her lap. "Call the dispatcher."

She fumbled for the call button, holding the radio to her mouth, but it slipped out of her fingers as the Jeep jostled and bounced over the rough edge of the road.

"Hold on," Logan said again as he slammed down the gas pedal.

Headlights filled the cabin as the truck pummeled into their bumper again. Logan grunted as he struggled to keep control of the steering wheel and Ashley clung to her seat as the Jeep careened toward cactuses and brush growing on the side of the road.

They rolled to a stop in a sea of prickly pears and spiky grasses. She let out a little sigh of relief as the truck swerved past them.

Until it stopped fifty feet ahead. Both doors opened. Whoever was getting out wasn't coming to lend them a hand.

Logan gestured at the Jeep's floorboard as he drew his gun. "Get down."

She swallowed, sliding a hand toward her seat belt to unbuckle it, but at that moment more headlights appeared in the distance. This time, from the opposite direction.

Ahead of them, the truck's doors slammed shut and its engine roared back to life. A second later it barreled away toward Terlingua in a cloud of dirt stained red by its taillights.

Logan flipped on the interior cab light. "You okay?" His brows pulled together in concern.

She took a couple of deep breaths, trying to slow her pounding heart, and nodded. "But I didn't get the plates." She retrieved the radio from her feet and handed it to him.

"It's okay," he said after calling in the incident. "Still a few miles to Terlingua. Maybe local police can get there in time."

He coaxed the Jeep out of the loose sand and back onto the packed road. When they passed the oncoming car a few minutes later, Logan flagged down the driver, but the man, a Terlingua resident, hadn't caught the truck's plates, either.

The vast Texas sky was full of stars by the time they reached the medical clinic. Ashley's head was swimming. A memory had come back as they'd jostled along on the road—the bumps had reminded her of tractor rides and apple-picking with her parents and brother. More childhood memories had seeped in after that one, filling her with relief.

Then that truck had showed up to ram them.

After what had just happened, it was a good thing Logan wanted to take her back to park headquarters. Plus, she hadn't found anything in her car other than a suit jacket and her purse. Big Bend National Park was remote—it seemed unlikely she would travel all the way out here without any luggage. But where was she staying?

And, more pressing, who was after her?

After a nurse took her to a private room, she rummaged through her handbag to see what else it contained besides the wallet. There wasn't much. A tube of lipstick. Hand sanitizer. A couple of pens. She pulled out the wallet and stared at the driver's license.

Washington, DC. Was that where she lived? The city name felt right. Comfortable.

But the license hadn't been issued to Ashley Thompson… Why? Were all her hunches and instincts wrong? She shivered, tucking the license back into its slot and pulling out the piece of paper sticking out of the next one.

A photograph.

She stared for several long minutes at the picture. It was a man, maybe college-aged, with short, dark hair and hazel eyes. A relative? Maybe her brother? The photo was well worn around the edges, as if she had handled it and carried it with her for some time.

Why did looking at him make her stomach clench into a tight knot?

Logan was pacing back and forth in the lobby when the clinic's only doctor escorted her back out. The ranger's dark green eyes locked onto her as she stepped into the room, and Ashley's breath unaccountably hitched. She hadn't seen him clearly before, what with the setting sun and her throbbing head, but in this lighting, it was obvious the man was in his element as a park ranger. Clean-shaven, tanned, sandy-brown hair. Just over six feet tall, she guessed, and at peak fitness. Every movement came with easy confidence.

She turned away from his speculative gaze. Maybe he didn't believe her about the memory loss. Maybe he thought she was trying to cover something up.

Thankfully he turned to the doctor, giving Ashley the chance to get her thoughts back under better regulation before she had to speak.

"How is she?" Logan asked.

"Her skull's intact and the wound itself should heal up nicely. Based on the symptoms she's described, I'd say she's sustained a level two, possibly level three, concussion. The good news is the CT scan is clean— no internal hemorrhaging. She needs to take it easy for several days until her symptoms are gone, and more specifically, she'll need to be monitored closely for the next twenty-four hours."

Several days? Ashley resisted the urge to frown. She had no idea why she was in Texas—how, exactly, was she supposed to lie around and relax?

Logan nodded, eyeing her thoughtfully. "And her memory loss?"

"Retrograde amnesia—limited to events prior to the injury. But given her lucidity now and her other test results, I'd say the prognosis for a full recovery is good. I expect she'll start getting her memories back anytime now, the older ones first. Childhood through adolescence typically come back first, followed by more recent events. You may be able to help the recovery with exposure to memory triggers. But," he said to Ashley, "whatever happened right before the trauma might not come back at all if your brain lost it from short-term memory."

She nodded. "Well, hopefully that won't be the case. I'd like to know what happened to me."

"Of course. At least you've found yourself in good hands with Ranger Everett."

Ashley thanked him and followed Logan outside, hoping he hadn't noticed the heat creeping into her cheeks at the doctor's comment. Especially since he couldn't be the only attractive man she'd ever been around in her life.

"How are you feeling?" he asked.

She climbed up into the passenger seat, avoiding the hand he offered. "Better. My head isn't pounding anymore and things aren't quite so fuzzy."

"Do you remember anything about coming to Big Bend?"

She shook her head. "It's like there's a blank spot in my mind and, beyond that, a lot of vague impressions rather than certainties."

"That's to be expected, I guess." He steered the Jeep toward the main road into the park. "It'll take us an hour to get back to Panther Junction. Try to get some rest and we'll find a place for you to sleep once we're finished."

Sleep seemed out of the question, but Ashley was glad for an excuse to stop talking. He hadn't asked her any more personal questions, but she could almost hear them on the tip of his tongue. *What else did you find in the purse? Why did you come to Texas? What secrets are you keeping?*

Thinking about it made her brain hurt. Logan hadn't said anything more about what had happened to her, either, but given the incident with the truck, it seemed obvious someone was after her. Probably the same someone who had hit her in the head. But who? And why? There had to be some reason she was carrying a gun. Hopefully her memories would come back before whoever it was returned to finish the job.

Ashley was out cold by the time Logan pulled into park headquarters in Panther Junction. She didn't even stir as he turned off the engine. He sat watching her for a moment under one of the few motion-activated lights in the parking lot.

Something about her seemed familiar... Maybe her mannerisms. Or the shape of her eyes. Or the way she spoke. He couldn't quite put his finger on it, or how he could possibly have met her before.

How had she ended up in the Rio Grande Wild and Scenic River? Wearing a business suit, no less. She had been barefoot all night, so he could only guess she'd lost her shoes in the river. Judging by the outfit, he assumed they would have been heels, the worst possible choice for a trip to the desert.

And the gun. Why the gun? The way Ashley had pulled it out and trained it on him was evidence enough she knew about weapons. Those actions came from physical memory, created by years of experience.

What worried him most was that incident with the truck. Her head injury and the fall into the river *could* have been an accident. The unidentified set of tracks along the river's edge might have been coincidence. But the truck? No doubts there. The driver had intended to run them off the road. If that other vehicle hadn't scared them off, he hated to think what might've happened. And since Terlingua police hadn't been able to find anything, there were no suspects to question.

What kind of trouble was Ashley in?

Even though Big Bend shared several hundred miles of border with Mexico, its vast, empty deserts and rugged mountains prevented far more criminal activity than the rangers could. More visitors got into trouble from dehydration than anything else. In fact, Logan couldn't even remember the last attempted homicide.

He frowned. The answers appeared to be locked away in that woman's mind, inaccessible. Maybe the chief ranger and the park superintendent would have better success.

"Ashley—" he nudged her shoulder "—we're here."

She sat up, rubbing her eyes, and then stumbled blearily beside him to the park office, waiting as he unlocked the door. By now it was after ten o'clock at night and the place was dark and empty inside. Logan flipped on a light and left Ashley in a chair near the receptionist's desk while he telephoned Chief Ranger Ed Chambers and Superintendent Dick Barclay.

Housing for the staff assigned to Panther Junction was a short walk from headquarters, so they only waited a few minutes before the others arrived.

Ed Chambers stepped in first. Tall, with graying hair and a face lined from years working outside, the chief looked like a quintessential career ranger. And he was exceptionally good at what he did—Logan could only hope that one day his career record would be half as accomplished as Ed's. Until then, he was grateful to have his mentorship, friendship and guidance.

The superintendent, on the other hand, stuck out like a sore thumb. He had only been stationed at Big Bend for the past six months and Logan expected him to throw in the towel any day now. But Dr. Barclay—as he insisted on being called—still kept showing up every day to make Logan's life a little more difficult.

"Dr. Barclay. Ed," Logan greeted them. "Here's the woman I told you about."

To Logan's surprise the superintendent strode over to Ashley and extended his hand. "Ms. Watson, I'm so sorry to hear you were involved in an accident."

Ashley blinked up at him like a pale-faced snowy owl. "You…you've met me?" she stammered.

Barclay turned surprised eyes on Logan, as if all the confusion was his fault. "Excuse us, Ms. Watson. We'll be right back."

Logan and Ed followed him across the room, where the superintendent dropped his voice to a whisper. "Everett, what happened to her?"

He shrugged. "Head trauma, concussion, memory loss. We're not sure of the full extent." He went on to explain how he had found her beside the river. "I brought her here because she was armed without a permit. And obviously I couldn't drop her off at a motel somewhere."

Ed clapped him on the shoulder, a glint in his eyes. "You did the right thing, bringing her here."

Logan couldn't shake the feeling that Ed was laughing at his expense. He pressed his lips together, waiting for the punchline. "What? What is it?"

"She's a new ranger, Everett," Barclay snapped. "She arrived from El Paso this afternoon."

"A new r-ranger?" he spluttered. "Why didn't anyone tell me?"

"Unique case. This hire didn't go through the normal channels—ordered by someone at the Department of the Interior. You don't need to know all the details."

"So, what about the gun?" He looked from Ed to Barclay. "No permit. She wasn't in uniform—"

"It's not important." Barclay cut him off with a shake of his head. He held out his hand expectantly toward Logan, who pulled Ashley's gun from his belt and gave it to the superintendent. "I'll talk to her about it. Everett, see to it she gets some rest and, when she's recovered, you can begin her training."

A pit opened in his stomach. "But surely I'm not the right one for that job. What about Rogers or Evanston?"

"You're the only one for the job right now, because you're the one she knows. Now quit arguing."

"Of course, sir." He bit his tongue as the superintendent walked back to Ashley.

Why him? He turned to Ed for help. Of all people, Ed knew what he'd gone through. How he wasn't ready to train anyone yet, not after the way he had failed the last ranger he'd trained. It had only been three months.

And Sam Thompson had been a natural outdoorsman in top physical condition. He had absorbed everything Logan had taught him like a sponge taking in water. Or so Logan had thought until the day the search-and-rescue team had found what was left of Sam's body baking in the June sun, a half mile off the Dodson Trail. Cause of death?

Dehydration.

So much for being a good instructor.

The worst part? That place in his gut, where intuition lived, had told him something wasn't right, that Sam was taking too long on his patrol. It was Sam's first time on the high Chisos trails alone, and Logan had almost called in a search team that afternoon when it grew late.

But he had talked himself out of it. *Sam is a good ranger. He can take care of himself. He'll be back anytime now.*

By the time the SAR team was mobilized the next day, it was too late.

Somehow, Sam had gotten lost and ended up down Juniper Canyon and onto the Outer Rim in the open desert. Death by dehydration had probably come within a matter of hours. The fine line between life and death was even thinner when summer arrived in the desert.

Ed clapped him on the shoulder in his annoyingly brisk and cheerful way. "It's time to get back out there, Logan. You're good at this job and you've been blaming yourself way too long. Sam's death wasn't your fault."

"Ed…" He ran a hand through his hair. "If I couldn't keep him alive, with all his experience, how am I going to protect *her*?" He gestured to Ashley, her disheveled business suit glaringly out of place in the bright lights of headquarters.

"Protect her?" Ed's brows pinched together. "She's a law-enforcement ranger. You don't have to protect her."

Wrong word. Why had he said that? Probably because she looked so vulnerable, helpless even, sitting over there talking to the superintendent.

"I'm sorry, I didn't mean 'protect.' Of course she can take care of herself. I meant… It's the desert here and…" His voice trailed away as he struggled to decide exactly what he did mean.

"It's okay, Logan. I think I understand." Ed's expression was far too perceptive.

"Stop looking at me like that." Logan tugged at his suddenly uncomfortable shirt collar. "Whatever you're thinking, it isn't true."

"I'm thinking you'd better show her to her quarters. And I'm thinking maybe you're finally ready to forget Erin Doyle."

"I let her go a long time ago."

Ed's smirk showed he wasn't convinced. "Right." He clapped Logan on the shoulder again. "Let me know if you need anything."

THREE

Ashley's head clouded over again as she waited for Logan to finish talking to the chief ranger. She wanted to get into bed, sleep for the next fifty years and wake up when everything was back to normal. Whatever "normal" was.

Ms. Watson, the superintendent had called her. It matched her driver's license, but not that vague impression she'd had earlier that her last name was Thompson. Was she keeping her real last name a secret for some reason?

But how on earth did she get a job here as a ranger without her real name? And why would she even want to work here in the first place? She couldn't remember any details about her old job, or *life* for that matter, but she was pretty sure it didn't have anything to do with roughing it out in the desert.

She rubbed absently at one of her arms, realizing her sleeve was still full of sand. Her clothes were dry now, but her hair was a tangled mess and nothing sounded better than a hot shower and a bed.

Logan glanced at her from across the room, his expression a mixture of confusion and concern. Finally the chief ranger clapped him on the shoulder and the flicker of emotion was replaced by a smile as he approached.

"I guess I should call you Ranger Watson now."

"Apparently so." She ignored the way her stomach curdled. The whole thing felt like a lie and she hated hiding the truth, whatever the truth was. Especially when she had no idea why. But the superintendent had asked to talk to her when she was ready to return to duty. Maybe he had some answers. "It's okay if you want to keep calling me Ashley instead."

He smiled. "Ashley, it is. And please call me Logan. Only people who don't like me use my last name."

"I doubt there's anyone who doesn't like you." She would have to add warm, considerate and easygoing to her mental description of him.

"You might be surprised." He held out his hand to help her up. "Come on, I'll walk you home."

She hesitated for a fraction of a second but, deciding it would be better not to embarrass him, took his hand. The sudden warmth of his skin on hers sent an electric jolt through her stomach and she swayed ever so slightly.

"Steady?" He still held her hand.

Her cheeks burned. "Yes." She pulled away the second he let go.

"Sure you don't want to take my arm?"

She swallowed. "No, thank you. I'll be fine." She had to be fine, because she wasn't going to let herself keep clinging to him, not when he affected her so unreasonably.

Logan opened the door and she followed him out into the dark, starlit night. They walked around to the back of the building and along a path toward a cluster of homes.

"It's all government housing," Logan said. "I'm sure you've heard all this before, but residence in the park is mandatory for rangers. Apparently you already checked in at Panther Junction earlier today and you were given a housing assignment."

Something Ashley had no recollection of... Yet another memory lost in the black swirl of her mind. To fend off the panic, she asked, "Do all the rangers live here?"

"No. There are residences at Castolon and Rio Grande Village, too, down by the river."

She followed him into a section of single homes at the west end of the complex. The Chisos Mountains loomed like jagged black teeth over the rooftops. Warm light issued from a few of the houses they passed, but the rest of the street was dark. "Aren't there any streetlights?"

"No. The park is trying to eliminate light pollution, and this street is being renovated." He waved at the dark houses beyond hers. "Those are mostly empty— that's why they're so dark."

"Sounds cozy."

"Don't worry, you'll get neighbors soon enough."

She fished the key ring out of her pocket, happy to find she had a key that turned in the lock. Finding the light switch inside the door, she flipped it and stepped over the threshold. Nothing looked familiar, but at least the collection of luggage was promising. Maybe she'd find some clues as to why she was there.

"Recognize anything?" Logan leaned against the

inside of the door frame, arms folded casually across his chest, watching her with those pensive green eyes.

She shook her head.

"Well, I'll leave you to get settled. You should have some groceries in the fridge, compliments of Sandy, the receptionist. Sure you don't need anything else right now?"

"No."

"Then I'll be back to check on you in an hour. Doctor's orders."

She grimaced. "Guess sleep isn't on the schedule for tonight."

"Not with a head injury." His lips curved into a crooked smile.

He turned to leave, but Ashley called after him. "Logan?"

"Yeah?"

"Thank you." Her toes curled in embarrassment. Apparently being rescued wasn't a typical experience. "For helping me tonight."

He grinned. The light from the front porch danced in his eyes. "It was my pleasure."

Logan walked down the dark street toward his own home, trying to quell the smile that kept popping onto his face.

Business. This was all about business. Part of his job was helping anyone in distress, and just because that someone was living in Panther Junction, and he had to train her, was no reason to keep thinking about her. Beyond having to check on her every hour, of course—doctor's orders.

In fact, their work relationship was an excellent

reason *not* to think about her, whatever Ed Chambers might say to the contrary. Seven years out here had taught him a number of painful lessons and one of them was never to fall for a fellow ranger. Because sooner or later they all left when they got the chance.

He could almost hear Erin's voice ringing in his head, as if she were still standing there arguing with him, even after all these years. She had been so beautiful, with her blond hair and green eyes a few shades lighter than his own. *A perfect match*, his family had said.

But she had hated living in Big Bend. Eight hundred thousand acres of desert, mountains and river—some of the most beautiful, remote country in the lower 48—and she had *hated* it. The place he never wanted to leave, because it had gotten into his blood, into his very soul.

He'd been ready to propose, sure that Erin was the one and convinced she would stay here for his sake—no, for their sake, at least until they could talk about asking for a reassignment. But love wasn't enough. *He* wasn't enough.

She had left, without ever looking back.

That was five years ago and no woman had caught his attention since. Probably a self-defense mechanism. Apparently it had decided to fail today. That was both unfortunate and unacceptable, because something about Ashley—maybe it was the suit, or her pale skin, or the fact she had no idea why she was here—screamed, *I don't belong in the desert*.

Keeping her alive until she could be reassigned was going to be enough trouble. He didn't need to add personal feelings. And the last thing he wanted, after the long years waiting for God to heal his broken heart after Erin, was to risk anything like it again. No, the newest ranger would be his trainee and his colleague, and nothing more.

He returned dutifully to her house an hour later, glad to find her condition appeared stable. Pupils weren't abnormally dilated, responses all coherent. Four repeat visits over the course of the night showed similar promise of no regression. She greeted him with a groggy smile each time before stumbling back to the sofa where she'd decided to crash for the night. By 7:00 a.m. he advised her to go to sleep in her bed. He'd come back and check on her later in the day, after getting some work done in the office.

He nearly collided with someone on his way into headquarters. Will Sykes, one of the newer rangers, who had started just prior to Sam Thompson. "Will, a little distracted this morning?"

"What?" The dark-haired younger man glanced up, his thoughts obviously elsewhere. He was probably heading out to one of the campgrounds on patrol. "Oh, sorry. I guess so."

Logan moved aside to let him out the door, but Will stopped, lowering his voice enough that Sandy Barnes at her receptionist desk wouldn't overhear. "Hey, I heard you pulled somebody out of the Rio Grande last night. What happened?"

Word certainly got around fast in this park. "Actually, I found her on the riverbank. We're not sure how it happened."

"Good thing you showed up." His Adam's apple bobbed and he tapped his thumb against his clipboard. "Was she all right?"

"Bit of memory loss, but she'll be okay. You'll meet her soon—turns out she's the newest ranger." Logan glanced at his watch. Only fifteen minutes until his first meeting of the day. "Listen, Sykes, I—"

The clipboard clattered to the ground and Will stooped to retrieve it.

"—need to get going."

"Of course." Will's face had gone uncharacteristically pale.

Must be thinking about Sam, too. They'd been friends and Sam's death had affected Will almost as much as Logan. Ashley was their first new law-enforcement ranger since the accident. It wasn't a surprise Will would be shaken up.

Logan squeezed the younger man's shoulder, trying to mimic Ed's natural gift of encouragement. "Nobody can replace him, but it'll be good to have someone new on the team."

"Yeah." Will left through the front door, waving on his way out.

A file for Ashley Watson lay on Logan's desk, as Ed had promised. It didn't contain anything exceptional. Twenty-seven years old, hometown of New Haven, Connecticut—that might explain why picturing her in the desert seemed like such a stretch. She had passed NPS training school with flying colors. Before going into law enforcement, she had worked for the Department of the Interior in Washington, DC—a desk job—but maybe those connections had got her the position out here.

Nothing to explain why she'd been down at the canyon yesterday, in a suit, with a gun. A gun she handled so well it looked like years of instinct, he might add—not just six months of park service training.

No word had come back on the truck, either. Whoever had attacked them had managed to vanish into the desert. Barclay had looked concerned but could only tell him to file a report. What else could they do? Nobody could explain how the newest ranger had become a target in a park where violent attacks by anything other than mountain lions were almost unheard of.

Maybe Logan would have to make his afternoon visit to her a bit longer, see if he could ask any questions that might jog her memory. Purely for the sake of investigation, of course.

By the time Ashley woke up, the sun was shooting fiery streaks onto her covers as it seared in through the cracks in the blinds. *Thank You, God, for air-conditioning.* Wait—she wasn't speaking to God.

Why was that, exactly? The only answer was that same feeling of oppressive loss she'd experienced last night. But her head didn't hurt and—

She sat up, her mind racing. She *remembered.*

Her parents—Ned and Rita. Her brother's name was Sam. Fumbling for her wallet, she dug out the picture again. Warmth flooded her chest as the memories filled her mind.

Sam and her at a theme park as kids—he'd been nearly two heads shorter than Ashley back then... Snowball fights—they'd grown up in Connecticut. Sandcastles at the beach... Sibling squabbles...

She grinned. Such good times.

But her heart twinged as she looked at his picture. Something had happened. But what? Sam was still in school, wasn't he? Or maybe he'd graduated before she'd moved to Washington.

When she'd gotten her dream job.

Ah, the irony of it all. She clapped a hand over her mouth, nearly giggling.

The call had come in the middle of dinner with her parents.

Congratulations, you've passed the background check. Your basic field training course starts in three weeks. Welcome to Quantico.

That was why she had the gun. She was an FBI special agent.

And she'd managed to finagle an assignment to the coveted Washington field office. Years of work and effort finally paying off.

Yet none of it explained why she was here. And did the fake name mean it was an undercover assignment? Had she ever even gone undercover before?

Maybe her luggage held more clues.

She found a pair of yoga pants and a cotton T-shirt in one of her bags. After dressing, she pulled her long hair into a loose ponytail. She'd been so exhausted last night, what with all the wake-up calls, that she'd stumbled through a quick shower and fallen asleep on the couch without much thought. But now, looking in the mirror, she traced the lines of her face in the glass.

It was the face she had seen for a lifetime, familiar and yet not. Older. Because Ashley knew there was still a gaping blank spot—more like a chasm—behind that face. Places in her mind where the memories were gone, or maybe squished by swelling. Everything past the age of about twenty-six was blurry, faded into nothingness as she tried to recall anything more recent. But going by her birth date on the driver's license, she was twenty-seven.

That meant more than a year of her life was incomplete or missing.

After returning her wallet to the handbag, she walked out to the living room to dig through the luggage. The suitcase was full of clothing and toiletries—each item new, yet familiar, like muscle memory recalled the feel of each thing but her eyes were seeing them for the first time.

The other bag, a small satchel, was far more interesting. It held a laptop, a cell phone and an item that at first glance appeared to be a man's leather wallet. Upon flipping it open, it turned out to be her badge.

Special Agent Ashley Thompson, Federal Bureau of Investigation.

That was what she had tried to pull out of her pocket to show Logan yesterday as her proof for the gun.

But she had left the badge in her luggage.

Only one reason an agent wouldn't carry her badge. She must be working undercover. As a park ranger? Why here, in Big Bend?

Did any of them know she was an agent? Not Logan, obviously.

The laptop might tell her…

After three failed attempts at the password, the computer locked her out for the next hour. So much for that idea.

Plugging in the cell phone to recharge, she rummaged in the kitchen for anything edible. She found an apple and a bagel. Making a mental note to thank the receptionist, she scrolled through the contacts in the phone. Her finger hovered over her mom's cell phone number. One push and Ashley would hear a familiar voice.

No. She closed the contacts file. Calling anyone would be a great way to blow her cover. Plus, she had no reception out here anyway.

Instead she opened the phone's gallery. She scrolled through one image after another, watching a blur of faces fly past until one caught her eye. Sam, standing beside her, his arm slung around her shoulders.

The picture was time-stamped from last fall—just over a year ago. His wide grin made her want to smile but... Ashley furrowed her brows. Why did seeing him make her stomach twist?

She set the phone down and carried the cold, uneaten bagel to the kitchen before tackling the large suitcase. No point in dwelling on what she couldn't remember. Better to focus on what she *did* know— that she was a federal agent and she was in west Texas for a reason.

A reason that might have something to do with what had happened to her last night.

Wheeling the suitcase into her bedroom, Ashley slowly unpacked all the neatly folded clothing. Beneath the clothes, shoes and toiletries, she found a layer of books. A Bible, a couple of novels and a guide to desert animals and vegetation.

She thumbed through each one, placing them, in turn, on top of the dresser. When she got to the guidebook, as she flipped through pages of snakes and spiders and scorpions, a piece of paper fluttered out onto the floor.

She picked it up, noting the darkened, worn edges— as if someone had held it with dirty hands—and opened it carefully to reveal a full page of hand-drawn markings and tiny words.

A map. It was a map! A long, twisting river ran along the lower section with labeled towns on both sides. Strings of upside-down V's looked like mountain ranges and they were labeled, too. She almost needed a magnifying glass to read the letters. Or a lamp might help. She glanced up, suddenly noticing how dark it was—she'd been so absorbed with unpacking she hadn't looked at a clock in hours.

It must be getting late. Logan would be here soon to check on her.

She took the map into the living room, pausing to feel for a light switch, but in the momentary silence she heard a sound that made her blood run cold. A low scraping noise coming from the bedroom window, like someone was running a chisel between the casement and the wood frame. And it was far too rhythmic to be an animal or the wind.

Someone was trying to break into her house.

FOUR

Ashley's breath echoed loudly in her ears, her heart hammering, as she hastily folded up the map and tucked it inside the waistband of her pants. The sound persisted—*scratch, scratch, scratch*—and she tried to slow her breathing as she glanced around the room for a weapon.

She wanted her gun, but Logan had given it to the superintendent and he wouldn't return it until she was ready for duty. There—in the kitchen—the knife block. She crept through the dark living room and around the peninsula into the kitchen, pulling out one of the long knives at the top of the block.

The casement was moving now. The intruder struggled with the window, trying to pull it up as quietly as possible. With all the lights off, the trespasser probably thought she wasn't home. Her eyes darted to the front door. If she slipped outside now, whoever it was might never know she'd been in here.

But what if someone was waiting out there, too? Whoever had hit her in the head? And if the person at the window *was* working alone, she didn't want to miss her chance to identify the intruder.

Taking one slow, deliberate breath after another, she crept to the doorway leading into the bedroom. She pressed her back against the living room wall and stole a glance around the doorjamb into the room. It was too dark to see who was outside the window, but gloved fingers worked underneath the inch-wide crack. If she had to pick, she'd guess they belonged to a man.

Her heart lurched. *Breathe. FBI agents don't panic.* They could wish for backup though, couldn't they?

Ashley's palms went slick with sweat. She tightened her grip on the knife handle as the window moved up another inch. She couldn't let him get all the way into the room or he might overpower her. But she wanted to see his face before she made a move.

Waiting was agony. Another inch and two hands appeared under the casement, now pushing together.

Almost time.

Somebody banged on the front door and Ashley was so startled she let out a cry. The hands disappeared from the window. That low, gritty brushing noise had to be retreating footsteps across the desert sand.

"Ashley?" Logan called, knocking again.

She dashed across the living room, throwing the door open. "Quick, around back. He's getting away."

Logan stared, his head cocked to one side. "What?"

She dropped the knife to the floor with a clatter and shoved past him, forgetting about her bare feet until she was already running around the back of the house. Even though the intruder might be long gone already, maybe she could still catch a glimpse of him. Anything that might give her a clue as to his identity.

"Where are you going?" he called, running after her. "You're supposed to be resting!"

Breathless, she stopped at the back corner of the building. Nobody. Nothing but an endless stretch of dirt, rocks and cactuses rolling toward the dark mass of the Chisos Mountains, barely visible against the sea of stars above.

He stopped next to her. "What's going on?"

Without a flashlight, it was pointless trying to run after the intruder. "A man was trying to break into my room, but you scared him off when you knocked."

"Are you all right?" Logan's resonant voice was full of concern.

"Yes, but I didn't get a description."

"Here." He pulled a flashlight from his pocket and flipped it on. "We can at least check for prints."

Of course he had a flashlight. Hers was sitting uselessly inside on the nightstand. Irritation sizzled through her veins but she forced herself to smile. "Glad you have a light."

"It's not very smart to wander around out here unprepared." The beam of light traveled across her feet, blindingly white against her black pants. "Or barefoot, for that matter. Don't you ever wear shoes?"

"It's not like I had time to lace up a pair of boots. And the river claimed the last pair. Let's look for footprints."

Logan held up his hand as she stepped toward the window. "No, you stay right there. You'll end up with your feet full of cactus spines, if they aren't already. Or worse, a rattlesnake bite."

Ashley opened her mouth to retort but then closed it, because now that he mentioned it, one of her feet did sting rather badly. But she wasn't about to tell him, so she watched silently as he waved the beam of light across the ground near the back of her house.

"Do you see anything?" she asked after a minute.

"Some crushed vegetation, but the dirt is bare and hard here. The window has been raised about two inches, though. We can dust for prints."

"He was wearing gloves."

"How do you know it was a man?" The beam of the flashlight obscured Logan's face.

"A hunch. The hands looked too large for a woman."

"Well, let's get you back inside." He shone the light on her feet again. "Can you walk?"

Ashley glared at him, even though he couldn't see her expression. "Of course. How do you think I got out here?"

"Oh, I saw it all. Just trying to be thoughtful."

"Well, you could at least light the path back for me."

He held out the light and Ashley picked her way carefully around to the front. Now that her body wasn't full of adrenaline anymore, her gaze snagged on the low-lying spiny plants and rocks. It was a wonder she hadn't tripped on them before. "Do you think there are rattlesnakes under any of those rocks?" she asked, trying to keep her voice even.

"Nah, not now. They come out at night to hunt, so they're more likely to be lying out in the open."

"You're just trying to scare me," she said hopefully.

"No, I'm not. But don't worry about the snakes. You're much more likely to step on a tarantula or a scorpion."

All those creepy pictures she had seen in the guidebook flooded into her mind. "I am?" She stopped, pulling up onto her tiptoes, as if that would help keep the spiders away.

"Sure. In fact, I think I see one right...there." He aimed the flashlight a little off to the left, and there, scuttling out from under a bush, was the largest, hairiest black spider she had ever seen.

Every muscle froze. Except her heart, which escaped into her throat along with a tiny scream. She'd rather face down a man breaking into her house any day. The tarantula crossed out of the beam of light, scuttling straight toward them. Whether out of self-preservation or sheer terror, Ashley flung her arm around Logan's neck and jumped.

He laughed, a rich, rolling sound, and easily caught her legs under the knees, until he was holding her against his chest. "You could've asked me to carry you."

"I... I," she stammered, her cheeks burning. "I *hate* spiders."

"Why exactly did you come to Big Bend, then?"

"That is the question, isn't it?"

The scent of pine trees and flannel emanated from his shirt, making her want to burrow into his arms for safety. She swallowed. What was wrong with her?

"I take it you haven't gotten back more of your memories yet?" Logan carried her around to the front of the house.

Why, *yes*, she had.

But until she learned why she was here and whom to trust, she had to keep things to herself. It would also help to know what her file here contained—surely the Bureau had invented some history for Ashley Watson. Whatever she told Logan had to match.

"Not really. Just some vague impressions. Maybe when I remember my laptop password, I'll figure out more." She hated lying to him, especially since he was the closest thing to a friend she had in the world right now.

They reached the front porch and the idea of letting the handsome ranger carry her across the threshold was more than she could take. She pushed against his chest and he released her gently onto her feet. "Thanks for the lift."

"Anytime. But—" he pointed down at her feet "—I don't want to see those bare feet again."

"Yes, Ranger Everett." She gave him a mock salute.

Logan stopped in the doorway, grinning at Ashley as she flipped on a light, picked up the knife she had dropped, and walked back into her house. She had a lot of nerve—he had to give her that. But he hated to think what might've happened if he hadn't come to her house when he had.

"What, exactly, were you going to do with that knife?" he asked casually.

She scowled. "Someone was breaking into my house, and you took away my gun. I needed some way to defend myself."

"You could've called for help."

"Like opened up the door and yelled?"

He shrugged. "It probably would've been enough."

"Probably?" Ashley dropped the knife into the kitchen sink and then walked—no, more like *hobbled*—into the living room. She must have stepped on something, after all.

"You can come in." She plopped onto her sofa and

waved him into the living room. "Unless you think we'll be giving our neighbors the wrong impression."

He pulled away from the door and stepped inside, shutting it behind him. "No, someone tried to break in tonight. I think that warrants my being in here for now." He sat on a chair next to the sofa. "Do you have any idea what they wanted?"

Ashley's eyebrows pulled together for a moment but then she shook her head. "I'm not sure."

She was keeping something from him, no question. Was it something she'd found today? Or remembered? And how to get it out of her? He ran a hand across his chin.

"It bothers me to think about you staying here alone," he said finally. "Maybe we should see about getting you into an apartment or staying with one of the families for tonight."

"No, I want to stay here. If he's stupid enough to come back, I want to see who it is."

He hadn't expected anything else. So much for worrying about giving the neighbors the wrong impression. Logan wasn't going to let her stay here alone. "Then I'm going to sleep on your sofa."

She leveled her dark brown eyes at him, as if weighing whether it was worth a battle. "Fine," she relented. "Suit yourself. But only for tonight, until I get my gun back."

"Agreed, on one condition."

"What?"

He pointed to her feet. "You let me check those for cactus spines."

Ashley frowned, pulling one foot up onto the opposite knee and leaning over to examine it. "I can do it myself."

Logan ran his hands through his hair. This woman was going to be a whole lot of trouble. "Is there a reason you can't accept my help?"

Maybe he was imagining things, but he could swear a pink tinge crept into those pale cheeks.

"You don't have to keep rescuing me." She stared at her foot. "I can pull my own weight."

"Ah." He waited until she looked up again. "You're afraid I'll think less of you."

She didn't say anything, but her cheeks turned a shade darker and she averted her eyes. She seemed so down-to-earth, so natural, sitting there with no makeup and her hair loosely pulled back. Unaware of how pretty she was.

"Ashley, I don't know why you're here, or how qualified or experienced you are, but I do know this—accepting help in a place like this is not a sign of weakness. The rangers here work as a team and we support each other. You and I are going to be spending a lot of time together, so you'd better get used to the idea."

She picked at her foot in silence for another minute before giving him a hesitant smile. "All right. I guess a pair of tweezers would help."

By the time she had retreated to her bedroom and Logan lay on the couch staring up at the dark ceiling, he could scarcely believe two hours had flown past. No more signs of the intruder, but he wasn't about to leave her alone.

Some mystery surrounded Ashley, lurking beneath the surface. Her file hadn't revealed anything insightful. But why would they assign her to Big Bend with no apparent experience in a similar environment? No ranger experience at all, in fact. Something wasn't adding up.

She had agreed to go with him to Santa Elena Canyon the next day, both to pick up her car and to see if anything jogged her memory. Until then, he had to find some way to fall asleep without thinking about the way Ashley had felt in his arms as he'd carried her back to the house. Even Erin, for all her inexperience as a new ranger, hadn't stirred such a strong protective instinct.

Maybe it was because five years had passed since Erin had left and Logan had changed during that time. He'd grown wiser. He'd seen more rangers come and go. He'd seen more loss and death.

Sam. That was who Ashley reminded him of. She didn't have quite the same youthful optimism and enthusiasm, but he could imagine she used to be that way. She certainly had the same energy, the same air of competence. Even some of their facial expressions were similar.

He rolled over on the couch for the twentieth time, wishing the government could afford better furniture. It made sense that Ashley would bring back all his memories of Sam—she was the first new law-enforcement ranger since his death.

But the thought of Ashley ending up with the same fate… He shuddered. He wouldn't let that happen, no matter how much she objected to his help.

It took another hour of prayer before he finally fell asleep.

FIVE

Ashley was relieved to find a note rather than a ranger in her living room the next morning. The events of last night had been awkward enough without waking up to share a cup of coffee and breakfast. She had felt horribly vulnerable in the last few days and now that her head was healing, it was time to reclaim some control over her life.

Logan's note indicated he wanted to get some things done before their drive to the canyon and that she could find him in his park office after her meeting with the superintendent.

She showered and dressed in one of the NPS uniforms in her closet; apparently they had been given to her when she'd arrived. More memories had solidified in her mind in the night, her past clicking back into place, giving her a reassuring sense of who she was and where she had come from.

But why she was here? Nothing. The previous months, except for that memory of a cab ride, were like staring at a blank wall.

She glanced at the time on the microwave. She had to meet with Dr. Barclay soon, but no harm in squeezing in another attempt at that laptop password. The last one she remembered hadn't worked yesterday. What else to try? Names of pets? Bobo the parakeet? Too short.

How about *JackyBoy*, after their chocolate lab?

Strike one.

College roommate? KristaReed.

Strike two.

She crinkled her nose. Only one chance left.

She closed her eyes, setting her fingers against the keyboard. Maybe muscle memory could pull out the password her conscious mind couldn't remember. It hovered right there, on the tips of her fingers. How about a hashtag first, for extra security?

Then… P-r-o-v— She stopped, rubbing her forehead.

Favorite Bible verse. Proverbs 3:5-6. But she would've abbreviated it. #Prov3:5-6.

Trust in the Lord with all thine heart, and lean not unto thine own understanding...

So painful to type, with the way the words seared her heart.

But it worked.

Ashley let out a little squeal of delight before sifting through the documents stored on the hard drive. Most of it seemed irrelevant, until she came across a file labeled "Big Bend." It contained several documents related to the park, including multiple maps and, better yet, several scanned pages of her own hand-written notes.

One name kept coming up over and over: Rico Jimenez. She shuddered. Somebody bad. But who was he?

She glanced again at the clock. Time to go. The superintendent was waiting. Tension crept into her shoulders as she hurriedly scanned the last few pages of notes. No doubt about it, she was here because of Jimenez. Now she had to figure out why.

Her gaze snagged on the message at the bottom of the last page, written in her own hand, as if her past self had left a warning. *Don't trust anyone.*

Anyone? Even the rangers? Logan? She shook her head, closing the laptop. Someone had tried to break into her house last night, and there were only two possible items she could think of that they might have wanted. This laptop or the map she'd found in the guidebook.

The map she would carry with her, but the laptop needed to be hidden. She left the case out in clear view but took the laptop itself and wedged it between the mattress and box spring in her bedroom, covering the gap with the sheets. It didn't seem likely anyone would try to break in during broad daylight, but better safe than sorry.

Ashley wanted to look at the map now, too, but she was out of time. Tucking it inside her shirt pocket, she walked the short distance to park headquarters.

The receptionist took her directly to the superintendent's office. Dick Barclay rose from his desk as she entered, shaking her hand.

"Good morning, Ranger Watson." He turned to the receptionist. "Sandy, please shut the door on your way out and see we're not disturbed."

Ashley took the seat opposite him. Wherever this conversation went, she'd have to be careful how much she revealed—at least until she knew whom to trust.

One thing was sure: she'd have to downplay the extent of her memory loss if she didn't want to be sent packing.

"I'm glad to see you're feeling better," Barclay said. "Have you remembered yet what happened?"

"No, but I'm hopeful it will come back when we drive down to Santa Elena this afternoon. My older memories have almost fully returned." Only a slight stretch.

Barclay nodded, eyeing her thoughtfully. "Do you remember why you're here, Agent Thompson?"

Thompson. He knew she was undercover. That meant he must know about Jimenez, too. "Of course," she answered smoothly. "To catch Rico Jimenez."

Whoever he was.

Barclay sighed, pulling off his eyeglasses and rubbing the bridge of his nose. "This operation is a fool's errand. I tried telling Morton that two months ago."

The name clicked into place. Special Agent in Charge Donald Morton, her superior at the Bureau. She wiped her sweaty palms against her pants.

"I assure you, Dr. Barclay," she said, injecting her voice with as much confidence as she could, "that I'm quite capable of doing my job. It won't take long to apprehend Jimenez and bring him to justice."

Barclay leaned forward, elbows braced on his desk. "Agent Thompson, I don't know what happened to you yesterday, but this park has an incredibly low crime rate. I'm not going to let that change on my watch."

Her brow furrowed. A threat? Clearly, he didn't want her here. She forced a smile. "We're on the same side, Dr. Barclay."

His mouth pressed into a thin line. "Let me be blunt.

There's no way Rico Jimenez or any other cartel leader is operating in this park under our noses. I didn't want you here before, and now that you've managed to injure yourself in your first twelve hours, I still don't want you here. My rangers are top-notch. We don't need FBI intervention."

She swallowed but held his gaze. "It would seem the Bureau doesn't agree. But I'll do my best to stay out of your way."

"You'll do more than that, Agent Thompson." Barclay's eyes narrowed. "You'll give me solid proof of Jimenez's activity, or else I'll call Morton and tell him about your memory loss."

"He'll send someone else."

He shrugged, one eyebrow rising over his wire-rimmed glasses. "But it won't be you." After a pause, he leaned forward in his seat. "Here's the thing. I agreed to this scheme as a favor to Morton, but I don't want any of you agents in my park. The sooner you get out of here, the better."

"Of course." She smiled, trying to exude the confidence she didn't feel. "I'll get you something soon."

"Three days." Barclay drummed his fingers on the desk. "I'll give you three days."

Not long, especially given the true extent of her memory loss. But Barclay didn't need to know that. She extended her hand. "No problem."

Barclay shook it firmly and rose. She stood, also. The interview certainly hadn't gone the way she'd hoped—putting her in the hot seat rather than revealing the crucial information she needed.

But as she turned to go, the superintendent held

out a file. "Here's everything we've got on Jimenez. I hope it helps."

Was that sarcasm? Ashley took the file, resisting the urge to start looking through it on the spot and keeping back the thousand questions bursting to get out. "Do any of the other rangers know who I am?"

He shook his head. "Only myself and Ed Chambers."

"Thank you." She reached for the doorknob.

"Oh…and, Thompson? If you cause any trouble for me…"

She nodded, letting the rest of the threat go unspoken. "I won't, sir."

Do your job quickly, quietly, and get out. His eyes said all of it loud and clear.

Logan was working at his desk when someone knocked on the door. "Come in." He didn't bother to glance up.

"Good morning." *Ashley.*

At the sound of her voice, his heart skipped. He gritted his teeth. *Never should have carried her last night…* Not that she had given him much choice.

Erin had made his heart skip, too, almost from the first moment they'd met at headquarters. She'd been so young—twenty-three—cute and bubbly, full of energy. Fresh out of college. The world had held so much promise.

Now wasn't the time to dwell on the past, or the long years of heartache and loneliness Erin had left in her wake. Ed knew, but nobody else.

Work. Training the new ranger. Doing his job—that was why he was here. Every time he requested reassignment at Big Bend, it was because of this job and this place. *Not* because he was hoping for another Erin in his life. One was enough.

"Good morning." He forced himself to keep his eyes on his work a minute longer. Anything to help maintain a safe distance. "How are you feeling? Still up for a trip to Santa Elena?"

"I am," she said.

When Logan finally let himself look up, he was rewarded with wide, staring eyes and long, dark lashes. *Irrelevant*. "How did you sleep?" He rummaged under a stack of papers to find his keys.

"Better. I remembered my laptop's password."

"Really?"

She nodded but didn't say anything else. Just casually shifted her weight from one foot to the other. Secrets lurked behind those eyes. Maybe he'd be able to get answers this afternoon.

"The superintendent gave this to me for you." He handed Ashley her holster and gun, lips tilting. "Don't point it at me again."

A grin played at the corners of her mouth. "I won't."

He led the way out to the parking lot and as they stepped into the front lobby, Will Sykes came through the door.

Logan nodded in greeting, but Will stared at Ashley, the color leaching out of his naturally dark skin. Could Don Juan be nervous about meeting the new ranger, after all? Or did she remind him of Sam, too?

Ashley obviously didn't share his anxiety. She held out her hand, smiling. "Hello, I'm Ashley Watson."

Will recovered instantly, making Logan think he'd imagined it all. In fact, the younger man lavished such a warm smile on Ashley as he shook her hand that her cheeks turned rosy pink.

He was holding her hand far too long for a polite handshake. Logan cleared his throat. "Sykes, Ranger Watson and I need to get going."

Will gave Ashley another suave grin full of excessively white teeth. "Hope I'll see you around."

A few minutes later Logan steered the Jeep out onto the main road that would take them north and west around the Chisos Mountains and then south toward Santa Elena Canyon. Ashley stared at the landscape as if seeing it for the first time. Right—it'd been dark when he'd taken her on this road before, and her memories of driving out there were gone.

"Here, I brought you this." He handed her a park map. "I thought you might want to see where we're going."

"Thank you." The paper rustled as she spread it across her lap.

"So…what have you remembered?"

She laughed. "What are you looking for? My life story or something?"

"Sure, whatever you want to tell me. Maybe talking about it will help the rest of your memories come back."

"Maybe. I think I've got back everything up until about a year or so ago. After that, it's still pretty fuzzy."

"What about your family? You remember them? And where you came from?"

"What is this, Twenty Questions?" The sound of her laughter made his heart light. "Yes, I remember my parents. Ne—" She coughed, cutting herself short, almost as if she'd done it on purpose. But she picked back up almost immediately. "Never could forget them for long. One brother, too. His name is Sam."

"Older or younger?"

"Younger." She stared out the window for a long moment but when she turned back her eyes were bright. "He loves anything outdoors. He'd love it here."

Logan grinned. "Maybe you can invite him to visit sometime."

She smiled, but some of the excitement had faded.

Why? Already contemplating her escape from Big Bend?

They made the turn to the south, where the volcanic activity of ages long past had created what looked like a lunar landscape. Ashley stared out her window.

"I take it you don't remember seeing this scenery before?" he asked.

"No. I had no idea this park was so vast."

"Mountains, desert and river all rolled into one area. You could spend a lifetime here and never be done learning about it all."

"How long have you lived here?"

"It'll be seven years this fall." Five years since Erin had left. He hadn't heard from her since. But why was he thinking about Erin again? That chapter of his life was over.

"That's a long time to live somewhere so remote. Don't you miss civilization?" Ashley eyed him skeptically.

He couldn't help laughing at her expression. "Civilization's overrated. Besides, I love it out here, and the work I do is meaningful." God's will for his life. The knowledge that God had prepared him for this work was what had kept him going when Erin walked away.

"What about your family? Don't they miss you?"

"Sure." He shrugged, taking a deep breath. No avoiding the spiritual nudge to share his faith. "But they're glad I'm following God's call for my life." He waited for the awkward silence, or worse, the ridicule he usually received when he talked about his faith.

But Ashley smiled. "You're a Christian, aren't you?"

"Since childhood. Although I haven't always walked faithfully with the Lord."

"Me, either." She was silent for a long moment. "I wish… I wish it was easier to understand God's plans."

"Sometimes things don't make sense until we look back on them later. I guess that's why so many people in the Bible were commended for walking by faith not sight." A lesson he needed to remind himself about. Maybe even his broken heart would make sense one day.

"Maybe." Her voice sounded hard now, almost bitter.

Was it because of the memory loss and her confusion over what had happened to her? Something else? Pain lingered there, but it wasn't his business.

Ashley stared back out the window. He wanted to ask her more questions, about what she had remembered, or whether she had requested this assignment at Big Bend. But the timing seemed all wrong. So instead he changed the subject, spending the next half hour teaching her about safety and survival in the desert. Barely the tip of the iceberg, but he'd keep going over it every day until he'd drilled it into her head.

They were nearing the road to the canyon, but first he turned into the parking lot at Castolon.

"Why are we pulling in here?" Ashley asked.

"We had your car towed here for safe-keeping. Rangers are stationed at Castolon, but Santa Elena is only monitored by patrols."

He parked the Jeep next to her black sedan, which had been left in the lot outside the general store, ice-cream stand and restrooms.

"Apparently it didn't work," she said grimly, "because one of the rear windows has been broken out."

Logan frowned as he watched her get out of the Jeep. First her house and now the car.

What did Ashley have that somebody wanted?

SIX

The backseat was littered with fragments of broken glass, bits of leaves and windblown sand. Ashley climbed into the driver's seat.

"Is anything missing?" Logan's face was lined with concern.

"I don't know." She opened the glove compartment and rummaged through the contents. Anything to shake this nagging sense of vulnerability. "I thought I took out all of my personal belongings when we left it behind, but maybe I missed something."

"The trunk was empty when we left it." His brows pulled together. "Maybe it was the same person who tried to break into your house."

Probably so. But this wasn't the kind of proof she was looking for to give Barclay. Although she couldn't remember getting the car, it had to be a rental set up through the Bureau using her fake name. Now she'd have to explain the damage to Special Agent Morton, who didn't even know yet about the incident in the river. A knot of frustration twisted in her stomach.

Logan pulled out a handheld radio and made a call. Ashley only half paid attention as she walked around the car, inspecting it for other signs of damage.

"One of the Castolon rangers is going to come take a look and talk to Jim at the general store to see if he's noticed anything suspicious." Logan nodded toward the west where, far off in the distance, puffy, white cotton-ball clouds floated on the horizon. "Storm's coming this way. We should get down to the canyon while we still have time. We can pick up the car on the way back. Jim will make sure the window gets taped up."

"All right." Wasn't much they could do about the car anyway. Even if they picked over the interior with a fine-toothed comb and dusted for prints, she doubted they'd find anything helpful. Like the break-in at her house, there was no way of knowing who it was or what they wanted.

"So—" he started the Jeep once she got in "—what were they after?"

"Probably whatever they were trying to find in my house." *Like that map.* Or maybe the truth about who she was? Did someone else in the park suspect she was an FBI agent?

Instead of backing out, Logan scanned her face. "Do you have any ideas? Maybe something you brought with you?"

She shrugged. "Your guess is as good as mine. My computer, maybe?"

"We're a little remote for petty theft, but maybe." He kept those green eyes pinned on her until Ashley couldn't bear it any longer.

She stared out the window at the old, stucco ice-cream stand, its log roof beams protruding from nubby textured walls. He could see right through her evasive answers—see that she was keeping secrets—and even though she barely knew him, she hated the deception. But until she knew whom to trust, she didn't have a choice.

Finally he threw the Jeep into reverse and pulled onto the road. The sun was now high enough overhead that heat radiated off the asphalt in shimmering waves, creating a mirage around every turn. According to the map, they'd pass Cottonwood Campground next and then have another six miles or so to the Santa Elena parking lot.

Probably the wrong time to pry for information, but she needed whatever she could get. Plus, the awkward silence was driving her nuts. "Can I ask you something?"

"Sure. Anything."

He sounded like he genuinely meant it. He'd been nothing but kind, helpful and concerned, and she had only repaid him with silence and secrets. Guilt twisted her insides.

She swallowed her self-condemnation. "What *are* the typical crimes we have to deal with here? If it's not petty theft and breaking and entering."

"Thankfully we're remote enough there isn't much crime, but as you might remember from your dip in the river, it's very shallow. The ease of crossing the border is the real issue. Even then, the most we usually see are a couple of Mexicans illegally crossing over to sell trinkets to tourists. We've had a few drug busts, but nothing large scale."

"What about illegal immigration? Human trafficking?"

"Not so much. Most of the cartels operate to the west of here, where the terrain is less rugged. You've probably heard of Organ Pipe Cactus National Monument in Arizona. The rangers there have constant issues with border crossings."

Ashley *had* heard of it—at least, somewhere in her memory, she knew there was a connection with ranger deaths there and something to do with her work here. Maybe later, when she had time to dig through the files on her laptop, she'd find more answers.

Logan drove the Jeep over a dry streambed and pulled into the parking lot at Santa Elena. She followed him in silence across a flat plain toward the trailhead into the canyon. The air felt slightly less oppressive here, closer to the river, and a breeze danced through the stray bits of hair falling around her face.

The Rio Grande had cut a deep canyon through a high plateau, leaving jagged cliffs on either side. Mexico was only a stone's throw away, a sheer cliff face towering hundreds of feet above the water. On the US side, a narrow path had been carved along the edge of the river, with steps rising and then dropping to the river's edge where the canyon widened. Vegetation grew here and there along the path, cactuses along the upper portion and tall grasses and brush down along the gravelly riverbank.

They had walked a short distance into the canyon when Logan stopped. "Anything look familiar?"

"Nothing other than the reeds and the river's edge, but that's because I remember it from crawling out." She stared down the trail, studying the undulations of the path and the way it hugged the cliff face at some points, veering back toward the river at others.

"Well, let's keep going." Logan glanced at the sky and then at his watch, the type that looked like it could endure a hurricane and still tell the time, temperature and direction of true north. "We don't have much more time."

"I'm not lying to you," she called after him as he started back up the trail. At least, not directly. Did withholding the truth count as lying?

"Never said you were." He kept walking without looking back, but his voice didn't carry much conviction.

"Please, Logan." Guilt and frustration compressed her chest like a heavy weight. It was bad enough having a hole in her mind, but for him to think badly of her, too… Well, his opinion mattered to her more than it should. "I can't remember what happened here."

He walked on in silence for a few more minutes, until the path had reached a height above the river from which she never could have fallen and survived. He stopped and pointed to the water. "There's no way you could've fallen in there by accident from this path."

"I know." She pressed a hand to her chest, looking over the edge of the cliff. It would be a long, steep, cactus-filled tumble to the river from this height.

"Ashley, why were you even out here? On your first day, why would you have driven to this canyon?"

She shook her head miserably. "I have no idea."

He placed both hands on her shoulders, pinning her with his steady gaze. "I want to believe you. But how can I help you when you won't tell me anything?"

She opened her mouth to object but realized she had nothing to say to him. Again.

His eyes, now a deep green in the shade of the canyon wall, scanned her face, as if he were trying to read her soul. "You've remembered more than you're telling me."

She swallowed, seized with the sudden urge to break free of his scrutiny and escape. "I *don't* remember asking for your help."

He raised an eyebrow. "You didn't seem to mind last night, when you leaped into my arms."

Of all the nerve. Her cheeks flamed instantly and this time she twisted free from his hands, still warm and heavy on her shoulders. "Your job, Ranger Everett, is to train me as a Big Bend ranger. Not pry into my personal life."

"Fine." He stepped past her, back in the direction they had come. "In that case, we're done here, because I don't want to be trapped with you on this side of the streambed when the rain comes."

This day hadn't gone anything like Logan planned, and the way Ashley was withholding information rubbed him the wrong way. After all his years in law enforcement, he'd learned to read people well enough to know when they were keeping secrets.

Sure, she had every right to hold back details about her personal life, but her reasons for being here were park business. His business. And her stubborn refusal to talk to him about it—to trust him—was just frustrating.

He stalked along the trail without looking back. It had been a fool's errand anyway—something he'd suspected before they'd even taken the trail. But he'd hoped she would remember something or open up about what she already knew—anything to give him some clues.

The clouds rolled closer, intermittently blotting out the sun, and the scent of impending rain danced in the air. They were running out of time to get across the streambed before it flooded. He picked up the pace but slowed again when they reached the most dangerous part of the trail, where the canyon narrowed and the path clung tenaciously to the cliff face above a long, rocky fall to the river below.

Suddenly a sharp, deafening crack split the air and a spray of rocks pelted the side of his face. He jerked around, his eyes meeting Ashley's stunned brown ones.

"What…?" she asked.

Too close for thunder. Too brief for a rockslide.

The crack came again, along with another burst of rocks between them, but this time he heard the telltale whizzing sound, too.

"Down!" he yelled, jumping toward Ashley and all but tackling her to the dirt path as another bullet zinged over their heads. "Someone's shooting at us!"

Dirt and rocks bit into his hands as he pushed himself up. Based on the angle of the bullet into the canyon, the sniper was shooting from the Mexican side.

Ashley scrambled onto her knees, pulling her gun and firing off a random shot across the river. Another crack, along with the glint of sunshine off metal at the top of the opposite cliff. Dirt sprayed near her head. That one was way too close.

"We're sitting ducks up here. We've got to get down." Logan shoved her ahead and pulled out his gun, firing in the direction of the gunman and hoping they weren't creating an international incident.

Ashley was sure-footed and nimble as she raced ahead of him, dodging rocks and spiny plants cluttering the edges of the narrow path. Despite the business suit and his earlier assumptions, she was obviously in top physical condition.

Another loud clap reached his ears as they sprinted

across the sand toward the parking lot. Thankfully the Jeep was the only vehicle in the lot. At least they didn't have to worry about protecting tourists, too.

"What kind of range does that weapon have?" she called.

"That wasn't a gunshot," he said as they reached the Jeep. "That one was thunder." He grabbed for his door handle but jerked back as a split-second later the Jeep's windshield shattered.

"And that was a bullet." Ashley dove for the pavement behind the Jeep.

He crouched beside her as another bullet ricocheted off the vehicle's hood. "There have to be two shooters. The one in the canyon couldn't clear the angle to reach us here."

"Unless he's running like we are," she panted, eyes sparking. "I thought you said there weren't many border incidents here."

"There weren't, until you arrived."

"What do we do now?"

As if in response, lightning flared bright, followed by a boom so loud it made the ground vibrate. To the west, the dark clouds loomed ever closer, even though the sky was still a breathtaking blue in the east.

"We're running out of time before the streambed floods."

"The one we drove over?" Ashley stared across the parking lot at the large yellow sign that warned tourists not to cross in flood conditions. "How much rain do you think we're going to get?"

"Doesn't take much. A couple of inches in a sudden downpour is enough to flood the streambed and arroyos."

She nodded, but her eyes had grown wide. So, a sniper didn't scare her, but the power of nature apparently did.

"Hey." He reached across the space between them and squeezed her cold hand. "God's in control here, remember? Whatever happens."

Ashley exhaled. "You get the Jeep started. I'll cover you."

She disappeared around the side of the vehicle, firing shots back across the river. Logan fumbled for the keys, waited a second longer and then dashed around the driver's side, throwing open the door and ducking behind it as a bullet lodged into the metal body of the Jeep.

He slipped the key into the ignition and turned it, keeping his head low as he climbed into the seat. The engine cranked to life and Ashley jumped in beside him. He threw the vehicle into Reverse, backing across the lot to escape the gunner's range.

He tossed her the radio as he put the Jeep in Drive, heading for the road and the streambed. "Call this in, okay?"

She pressed the talk button and made the report as the first drops of rain fell. Without windows, it would be a matter of minutes before they were soaked.

Ashley finished the call and stuffed the radio under the seat. "Marfa border control is sending a helicopter to look for the gunmen."

"It'll be too late." Logan shook his head. But what else could they do?

Rain spattered on the vehicle's metal hood, kicked up dust on the road and filled the air with a hot, wet smell.

He pulled the Jeep onto the main road as another loud crack rent the air. He and Ashley both ducked, but the shot hit somewhere in the back of the Jeep. Another clap sounded right behind them and this time the Jeep lilted ominously toward the passenger side as the rear tire blew. Logan slammed his foot on the gas anyway. They just needed to get out of the shooter's range…

More shots, but finally they were falling short, striking the road and rebounding off the asphalt. Vicious shrieking sounds of grinding metal came from the back of the Jeep, so Logan eased off the gas and let the vehicle roll to a stop.

In the streambed.

He clenched his teeth together. It couldn't be helped.

"Are we out of range yet?" Ashley asked as a bright flash of lightning lit the dark sky. A loud clap of thunder followed close behind, but no more gunshots.

"Think so. But this vehicle isn't going any farther." He climbed out of the Jeep and checked the rear tire. Completely deflated, its warped rim resting on the road. Hopefully the axle wasn't so bent it couldn't be driven. "Tire's blown," he called over the pounding rain.

Ashley stepped up beside him, rain droplets streaking down her pale face and dripping off her eyelashes as she blinked at the yellow warning sign fifty feet away.

He squeezed her arm then turned away to the Jeep's tailgate. Time to see how fast he could change a tire.

SEVEN

Ashley clutched her gun tightly, although it wasn't going to help against a flood. Instinct demanded she run, but that was panic talking. Because then what would they do? Run all the way back to Castolon?

"We've gotta try." Logan dug in the back of the Jeep for a toolbox. "Somebody over there is trying to kill us, and if he decides to cross the river and get closer, his aim is going to get a whole lot better."

He was right, of course. "What do you want me to do?" Her voice was hoarse from yelling over the din of the storm.

Taking out a wrench, he detached the spare tire from the rear gate. "Cover me. And watch the streambed. It only takes twelve inches of water to wash away a car."

"That's not very comforting." She crouched beside the Jeep as Logan wedged a jack under the rear axle.

Water trickled past them, running in narrow channels through the hard, dusty ground, forming puddles in low places and soaking through the knees of her pants. Lightning filled the darkening sky. It was followed by a clap of thunder so loud, she jumped in surprise.

How many inches of water did it take to sweep a person away?

Logan was halfway under the Jeep now, pulling off the old tire. No gunshots, no sign of the shooter. But at that moment, the heavens opened and buckets of water poured down so hard it obscured their visibility.

In a matter of seconds water swirled around her boots, carrying sticks and leaves and candy wrappers from miles upstream. How many inches were there now? Three? Her hands shook. A shooter was predictable, to a degree, and things that could be predicted could be controlled. But not this…not the fury of nature unleashed on the earth.

Only God could control that and He didn't appear interested.

She watched in mute horror as the water seeped in through the lace holes and around the tongue of her boots, soaking her socks. Surprisingly cold given the hot day. How much longer could they wait?

Logan pulled out from under the Jeep, yanking her arm as he stood. "We have to get out of here!" he yelled over the noise of the storm. "Now!"

"What about the Jeep?"

"No time. Go!"

He snatched her hand, tugging her as he ran toward the far side of the streambed. The water swirled around their ankles and kept rising fast.

The current ripped past her feet, so strong for so little water. It couldn't be more than four inches deep.

"Come on!" Logan yanked on her arm.

Her feet vanished beneath the dark, muddy stream. And the rain, pouring down in dog-size drops, made it hard to even see which direction they were running. *Stay perpendicular to the current*. She clung to the thought as if it were a lifeline.

Logan gripped her hand so hard it hurt. The dark water whirled above her ankles now, a vicious torrent threatening to sweep them away at the first misstep. Like a far deadlier version of the river she had been in a few days ago.

Only, this time, she might not be so fortunate.

"Almost there," Logan huffed.

Finally the water became shallower, making their steps easier. They reached the far side and clambered onto the bank. Ashley staggered forward a few extra paces to give the rushing stream a wide berth. Then Logan released his death grip on her hand and they both flung themselves to the muddy ground.

She lay on her side, heaving in several deep breaths as the rain continued to pour down. When she had finally recovered enough to sit, she stared at the Jeep, where they had been kneeling on the ground only moments before.

The muddy water had reached the doors and was flowing into the cab. She hugged her arms around her chest, painfully aware of her own helplessness as the now roaring current tore loose items from the Jeep and carried them away. Seconds later the Jeep itself rocked as a torrential flow of water rushed through the once-dry creek bed. Suddenly, as if pushed by a large, invisible hand, the vehicle overturned and was gone, carried by the ripping current toward the Rio Grande.

Ashley stared at the place the Jeep had stood, open-mouthed, hands trembling. She had never seen nature's fury like this before. It was as if the hand of God had reached down and touched the earth in front of her eyes. If they had stayed there a few seconds longer... The thought sent a chill down her back until, combined with her wet clothes, she shivered from head to toe.

* * *

She was shaking uncontrollably. It was a gut reaction. Before Logan could stop himself, he pulled Ashley into his arms, as if he could will away the cold and the fear by holding her close. Her breath whispered warm against his arm, the cold wet of her cheek slowly giving way to heat. Her dark hair had come loose and fell like a heavy, wet blanket down her back.

At least no one was taking shots at them anymore. But given the downpour, and the flooding, there was no way they would ever find the shooters.

No, there was only one source for answers in that regard. He gazed down at Ashley, her forehead so pale against her dark hair. Maybe now she would be willing to open up. To let him help.

Too soon Ashley pushed against him, her hand on his chest. He hated to let go. She felt too warm, too safe. But theirs was a working relationship and he couldn't afford the tangle of emotions in his chest. Not after Erin.

Logan dropped his hands and Ashley pulled away, her wide eyes filled with confusion and lingering fear that, despite his resolve, he longed to soothe away.

Instead he summoned all his effort and looked back across the streambed. The rain had stopped and the sun was forcing its way through the dark clouds in glittering brilliant streaks. The rushing water next to them slowed and began to recede now that its source had moved east.

"I'm sorry," he ground out, "that I didn't get us out of there sooner."

"It's not your fault." Ashley reached for him, her cold hand resting lightly on his arm. Although her hands still trembled slightly, the color had returned to her cheeks. "We had to try. At least no one can follow us across the creek at the moment."

Logan ran his hands through his hair, sending out a spray of water, trying to clear his head. "The radio's halfway to the Gulf of Mexico by now. We'll have to walk." They were going to get thirsty, but at least the day carried a hint of cooler fall temperatures, instead of the torturing three-digit heat they'd had all summer. He glanced at Ashley, worry gnawing at his insides. "You shouldn't be exerting yourself like this while you're still healing."

She shrugged, her dark eyes calm. "Headquarters got my call. They'll send somebody. But walking sounds better than sitting around here without any shade. And, honestly, I feel pretty good except for the memory loss."

He nodded, pressing his lips together. "Well, I'm not happy about it, but you've got a point."

They started up the road toward Castolon. It felt good to stretch his stiff muscles as he walked, keeping the pace easy for Ashley. The sun was gaining strength again and slowly drying out their clothes and hair.

She strolled silently beside him, staring at the road ahead.

He kept stealing glances to make sure she was all right, until finally she gave him a crooked grin. "Logan, I'm okay. Obviously, I only remember bits and pieces about the last year, but I must've exercised regularly. I feel *fine*."

He frowned, watching the remains of the puffy gray clouds as they disappeared to the east. "It's not just the exertion I'm worried about. First you turn up in the river with a head injury, then your house and your car are broken into, and now someone is shooting at us.

Whatever is going on here, *you* are at the center of it. Do you have any idea why?"

Yes, she did. It took a major effort to swallow the word before it popped out. The effect this man had on her was almost more frustrating than her lost memories. Ashley wanted nothing more than to tell him everything and crawl into the safety of his arms.

Her heart wanted to trust him implicitly, but logic dictated that was foolish. She hardly knew him. And her own words before coming here were to trust no one. That *had* to include Logan.

But he was waiting for her to say something and she owed it to him after putting his life in jeopardy. Though she didn't know who'd been shooting at them, she had no doubt the incident was linked to Jimenez. Did that mean her cover was blown? Before she'd even had the chance to remember everything?

Regardless, she wasn't about to admit defeat yet.

She couldn't tell Logan she was with the FBI or searching for Rico Jimenez, but maybe she could tell him about the map. Maybe he could even help her figure out why it was important.

She sucked in a deep breath, letting it out slowly. "I think I might know what they want."

He raised an eyebrow. "What?"

She unbuttoned the flap on her shirt pocket, pulling out the now rather damp piece of paper she had carried with her all day. Gingerly she unfolded the map, smoothing the rumpled corners.

Logan leaned closer, looking over her shoulder, and every nerve flared to life at his nearness. *Not* what she was supposed to be thinking about.

"I think it's a map, but I haven't had time to study it yet."

He ran his hand over his chin. "Where did you find it?"

"Tucked into a guidebook I brought with me." She glanced up at him, right into those green eyes that made her think of pine trees and snowcapped mountains and cozy ski lodges. Her breath stuck in her throat. Good-looking, kindhearted and selfless. A wonder he wasn't married yet. *Focus. Not important details.* "What do you think it is?"

"Honestly, it looks like Big Bend. This—" he pointed at different features as he spoke "—is the Rio Grande. And here are the Chisos Mountains. Elephant Tusk. Mariscal Mountain. The hot springs. Boquillas Canyon. Whoever made this knew the area well."

"And this is Mexico?" She pointed to the area south of the river.

He nodded. "There are a couple of small villages out here—Santa Elena, San Vicente, Boquillas. But most of this area is a nature preserve protected by the Mexican government. The nearest big city is Ojinaga, across the border from El Paso."

"Look, it's dated. Right here—1567." She pointed at the tiny numbers written near the text.

Logan's brow wrinkled. "The paper seems old, but not *that* old."

"It could be a copy, couldn't it?" Ashley squinted at the tiny letters. "This writing… Is it Spanish?"

"Looks like it. I have a dictionary in my office. And you don't have any idea where you got it from?"

Something about the map—maybe the way the paper felt in her hand—tugged at her memory. "I remember…" She paused, trying to seize the vague impressions in her mind. "I remember opening an envelope. The map was inside. Something about it made me feel…sad."

She tried to picture that moment in her mind. If only she could remember when it had happened and the return address on the envelope. But wait—the envelope hadn't been marked with a return address, had it?

It had only borne her name and address, and the post office's cancellation. From…

"Panther Junction." She snapped her eyes up to his. "It was posted from Panther Junction. There's a post office, isn't there?"

He nodded. "It's the only one in the park. When did you get it in the mail?"

She thought for a moment. "It was recent. One of the last things I remember before waking up on the riverbank."

"Who would send you a map of Big Bend?"

"No idea." She shrugged helplessly. And, more important, how was this map linked to Jimenez?

"So, what's it for?"

She stared at the writing again as the hot sun scorched the top of her head. Probably time to refold the map and give up. *Wait*—a written phrase caught her eye. "Look—" she pointed above one of the mountain peaks "—there's a notation here in English. And the handwriting is different. It says 'lost mine.'"

"Sure, it's called Lost Mine Peak. Second in height behind Emory Peak."

"But look here, at this symbol—*Au*. It's written in the same handwriting."

Logan squinted at the map. "So?"

"Gold. It's the symbol for gold, from the periodic table."

"How do you know it's referring to the periodic table?"

"And here," she persisted. "'Mariscal.' It's a mine, too, right? I remember seeing it on the map you gave me."

"Hg," he murmured.

"Mercury. It was a mercury mine, wasn't it?"

He nodded. "First half of the twentieth century. It produced nearly a quarter of the country's mercury."

Ashley glanced over her shoulder, making sure the road was still empty. "Logan, what if this map shows the location of a gold mine right here in Big Bend?"

Logan stared, vaguely aware that his mouth was hanging open. *Rookie.* "Right there on Lost Mine Peak? It's just a name, Ashley. Hundreds of places in the west are named after lost mines."

"You're an expert on Big Bend, right?" Her dark eyes narrowed. "Aren't there any legends about lost mines?"

"Well, sure, but there are also legends about lost canyons full of bison, and we haven't found any of those yet, either."

She stared at him, waiting.

He tugged at his shirt collar, hot now that his clothes had dried out. "We'd better keep walking. Still have a few miles to go."

She folded the map and returned it to her shirt pocket. "Tell me one of the legends. You've got to know one. In fact, I bet you know one about Lost Mine Peak, don't you?"

"Maybe. You're not going to drop it, are you?"

"No." A grin lit up her face, making her eyes sparkle. "I'm very persistent."

He sighed. "The legend says that back in the 1500s—"

"Fifteen sixty-seven!" she said triumphantly. "That's the date on this map!"

He scowled before continuing, as if she hadn't interrupted. "The Spanish found a rich vein of gold near the top of Lost Mine Peak. They hauled life-term prisoners twenty miles across the desert from the presidio at San Vicente, blindfolded part of the way, to work the mine."

"That must've been miserable." She frowned. "What happened?"

"The Comanche, angry over the Spanish invasion of their lands, found the mine and killed all the workers, to a man. Then they filled in the entrance to hide it from anyone else who might come looking."

"And you don't think it could be true?"

"Well… I guess if I'm being objective, the Chisos Mountains are igneous rock formations, so theoretically it's possible there could be veins of gold. It just seems so…improbable."

She stared across the desert at the mountains in the north. "Apparently whoever made this map doesn't agree with you."

"And the people trying to get it from you?" He raised an eyebrow. How could he believe such a ridiculous theory? Still, there was no denying someone wanted *something* from her.

Ashley nodded.

"And you think the people after the map are the ones who threw you into the river?"

"I have no idea. But it's my best guess. Somehow

they found me in the park, realized I didn't have the map, and dumped me into the river."

When she put it like that... He swallowed, his stomach flipping. The thought of some thug attacking her, searching her and throwing her into the river like a piece of trash... It made him want to find whoever had done it and bring them to justice. Maybe after he knocked a couple of teeth out.

She was still pale, whether from the same line of thought or from the incident by the river, he didn't know. But she needed help.

Or to get out of Big Bend.

"It's not safe for you here," he said at last. "You should leave the park. Turn that map over to Ed Chambers and the superintendent and let them sort it out. I'm sure they could get you a transfer." Even if the thought of her leaving twisted uncomfortably at his heart, her safety was more important.

"I can't." She clenched her teeth.

"Why?"

She shook her head. "Don't ask, because I don't know all the reasons yet myself. I only know that I can't leave."

He ran a hand through his hair. "At least turn the map over to the superintendent. If the NPS sends rangers out searching for this mine, then maybe whoever is after the map will give up."

"Aren't you at all concerned about finding whoever it is and arresting them? We *are* in law enforcement, aren't we?"

He stopped and, before he quite knew what he was doing, gently gripped both of her arms and stared into her dark eyes. "Of course. But I'm more concerned about protecting you."

Confusion flickered across her face—warmth mingled with wariness, as if she couldn't make up her mind.

For a moment Logan didn't know what she would do, or what he wanted her to do—step into his arms or walk away. The latter would certainly be better for his sanity.

She did neither. Instead she stood like a statue, saying in a clipped voice, "I'm here to do a job. I don't need your protection."

Worse than a slap in the face. He pulled his hands back, retreating a step. With a curt nod, he walked ahead in silence.

It seemed obvious Ashley needed his help—someone had tried to shoot them, after all. So why was she pushing him away? Either she had a chip on her shoulder the size of Montana about accepting help or…he was letting things get too personal, and she could tell.

And it was obvious she didn't want any part of his unruly emotions.

Logan kicked a rock on the road as they trudged on under the hot sun. He barely knew Ashley. It had been…what, three days since they had met? Why did it feel like so much longer?

He had to get his feelings back under control, take them out of the picture. View her for what she was—a coworker who needed training. Not an attractive, mysterious, brave woman who needed his protection.

He could turn off his heart. Somehow.

EIGHT

Pressing a washcloth to her face, Ashley scrubbed away the grime, wishing she could wash away all the fear and uncertainty inside just as easily. The past three days had lasted an eternity.

After they'd walked a long way, a ranger had picked them up and given them a lift back to Castolon. From there, she and Logan had driven her car to Panther Junction. He'd kept teaching her about the park as they'd driven: its layout, wildlife, policies…anything to avoid the uncomfortable looming silence. Despite her admittedly cold words to him earlier in the day, Logan had insisted on checking her house to make sure no one had broken in, before leaving for his office.

She had to give him credit for his work ethic. Long hours, flexibility and dedication were a given with the Bureau, but the working conditions weren't typically quite this…wet. Or sandy. After all they'd been through, all she'd wanted was a shower.

And some time alone to figure things out.

After throwing on a pair of blue jeans and a black T-shirt, she retrieved her laptop and carried it out to the living room. She flipped it open, finding the file with her notes.

Two more days. She had two more days to come up with some sort of information for Dick Barclay—something to convince him not to call Morton. She had no doubt what would happen if her boss found out about the memory loss—she'd be on the next flight home.

Ashley rested her chin on her hand. It would help, obviously, if *she* knew why she was there. Why this place, and this map, mattered. Although Dick Barclay knew she was with the FBI, and here to investigate Jimenez, he didn't seem to know about the map or the gold mine—otherwise he would have mentioned them.

Unless… She tapped her chin. What if Barclay hadn't wanted to remind her about it?

No, that was ridiculous. Barclay had only been here…what? Six months? How could he know about the mine when not even Logan did?

The map was connected to this case somehow, though. Maybe it was the lead that had brought her here. Maybe the cartel was searching for the mine, too, and if she found it, she'd find Jimenez.

Or maybe she was desperate and grasping for straws. She'd be able to concentrate a whole lot better if she could stop thinking about Logan. She had hurt his feelings today, that was obvious, but it was safer this way. When she didn't know whom she could trust, or what tomorrow might bring, it was too dangerous to let him in. Just being around her had put him in physical danger.

And no matter how rational Ashley tried to be about him, her stubborn heart wasn't listening. He had held her so closely this afternoon, and the last thing her heart had wanted was for him to let go.

Even now, that same foolish part of her wanted him to knock on the door. To listen to her, help her, keep her safe.

"Absolutely not," she muttered aloud. She'd worked too long and too hard to succeed in a man's world, and she wasn't about to turn herself into a needy, withering female just because a good-looking, good-hearted man had rescued her once or twice. Or three times. She was beginning to lose count.

Ashley turned back to her notes, forcing her mind to concentrate on the screen in front of her. There were those words again—the best reason not to let Logan Everett too close. *Trust no one.*

Why? She scanned page after page and then she found it. A reference to an FBI report on Jimenez's suspected criminal activity in the Big Bend country. *Please let it be here on this computer.*

Oh, happy day, there it was. Finally something was going her way. The document claimed Jimenez had split off from a large cartel in western Mexico, starting his own operation a couple of years ago. He or his men had a long string of associated violent crimes linked to drug running and serving as coyotes for illegal immigrants.

But what would Jimenez want with Big Bend? The river was shallow here, making crossings easier, and the area was understaffed. Yet the terrain was so rugged, it would be nearly impossible to move drugs or people safely into the States on a large scale. So what *was* Jimenez doing in Big Bend?

According to the file, the Bureau had a contact in

San Vicente who'd reported on Jimenez. Small drug runs. Cartel members moving back and forth across the border... Was it related to the mine? And how was he doing it undetected?

Obviously, Logan hadn't heard anything about the cartel. Even the superintendent didn't think Jimenez was working in the area, if the file he had given her was any indication.

Ashley shivered as the answer came to her. Of course. Someone on the inside was helping him. It could be border patrol or the local authorities or someone right here with the NPS. Whoever it was, they were orchestrating Jimenez's movements to pass unnoticed.

At that thought, memories of conversations with Morton back in his DC office flooded into her mind. *That* was why she was here undercover—not only to avoid scaring off Jimenez, but because the FBI suspected it was one of the Big Bend rangers. And it was her job to figure out whom, along with pinning Jimenez.

Something else niggled at the edge of her memory. She couldn't shake the feeling that this specific assignment was personal. She'd fought to convince Morton she was the right agent. But why?

Ashley patted her jeans' pocket, where she'd tucked the map safely away. It had to have something to do with this map. What? And why had someone sent it to her? She rubbed her hands across her face, straining to dredge up any other memories that might help.

A sudden knock on the door interrupted her and Ashley's shoulders tensed. It had to be Logan. She wasn't ready to face him again yet, not now. He seemed so good, so trustworthy… The thought of him being the traitor, however unlikely, made her stomach hurt.

The knock came again and she closed her laptop. Her lights were on, so it was obvious she was home. She couldn't hide forever.

Only, it wasn't Logan. It was Will Sykes, the ranger she had met this morning.

"Hi, Will," she said. With his dark good looks and charming smile, he might've chosen a career in Hollywood instead of life in remote Big Bend.

"Ashley." He flashed a wide grin. "I heard you had some sort of crazy incident down at Santa Elena this afternoon."

"Yeah." Did every ranger know by now? "It was a little more than I bargained for on my first day of work."

"I bet." He leaned casually against the door frame, his dark eyes unreadable. "Hey, didn't you have some sort of accident there the other day, too? I heard something about Logan finding you in the river."

"Something like that. He found me along the river's edge."

Why was he asking? Curiosity?

Will's mouth opened, as if to ask another question, but then he smiled. "I'm glad he could help you. How are you recovering?"

"I'm doing pretty well. I think I'll be avoiding the canyon for a while, though."

"Too bad. It's a beautiful place." Will's dark eyes lingered on her face, his lips curving into a grin that veered toward flirtatious. Maybe he was trying to be friendly, not pry.

Those files were messing with her head. Not every ranger was secretly helping Jimenez. She just needed to find the one who was.

"Yes, it is. How long have you been a ranger here, Will?"

"A couple of years, but my family is from Texas."

"Oh?" He looked Hispanic, with his dark hair and eyes, but she didn't want to make him feel like he was under interrogation. His file had included the background check they'd run when he was hired. Nothing of interest, except for one relative south of the border. A distant cousin. "Did you grow up nearby?"

"El Paso. My father was American, my mother Mexican." He winked. "It's okay, everybody wonders. They're just not brave enough to ask."

She smiled in a vain attempt to cover up her curiosity. "Sykes isn't exactly a Hispanic name. So…" She paused. "How do you like working here?"

"It's been…good." His focus shifted for a moment, as if he were thinking about other things. Almost as quickly, he turned his attention back to Ashley. Flashing her another one of those perfect, movie-star grins, he asked, "Are you planning on sticking around? I mean, after all the bad things that have happened?"

She smiled, but her brows pulled together in confusion. Did rangers quit right away that often? "I'm planning on it for now. Don't think they'd approve a transfer quite yet."

Was he happy or not about that answer?

And the Mexican cousin… Was there a connection?

He pulled away from the door. His gaze was cryptic as he glanced back. "You won't regret it."

* * *

Logan was on the verge of falling asleep at his desk.

Time to call it a night. The shadows had grown long and he craved a shower and a meal. He locked his office door and headed out across the parking lot toward his house, debating whether he should check on Ashley.

The memory of her wet hair lingered against his arm, the warmth of her body cradled against his chest. *No. Work. Keep it about work.* Maybe all the pain of Erin was long gone, but the memory of it wasn't. Those months after she'd left had been some of the hardest of his life. So much joy followed by crushing despair. No way was he going to endure that kind of heart-break again.

He'd made it worse for himself—always aware in the back of his mind that she *might* call. Might change her mind once she realized what she'd lost. He hadn't given up hope until his mom had told him Erin was engaged. The fact she'd told his family first had only twisted the knife in his back.

Still, that was years ago now. Once he'd come to terms with reality—with God's call to singleness and dedicating his life to protecting this corner of creation—he'd been happy.

He *was* happy. Or, he had been, until Ashley showed up.

But no matter what kind of havoc she wreaked on his emotions, she still needed his help. No harm in walking past her house to make sure everything appeared safe.

The lingering afternoon heat was fading away with the last embers of daylight, the first stars peeking through the veil of deepening twilight as he strode into the neighborhood behind headquarters. As he approached Ashley's house—the only one with lights on in her section of the street—he slowed. The door was ajar, someone standing in the doorway.

It looked like… Will Sykes. Well, wasn't that considerate of him? And such a coincidence, given that Ashley was both pretty and apparently unattached. Will sure wouldn't have showed up at any other ranger's house to check on them.

Not that it should matter to me. Ashley had made it clear she wanted to take care of herself.

Will left her house and she closed the door. Logan ducked behind a car on the street to avoid being seen, even though it was ridiculous. He should go home. Forget all about it. He had found out what he'd wanted to know. She was safe.

But his feet wouldn't comply. They carried him up to Ashley's door, where he knocked firmly.

"Just a minute!" Ashley called from inside.

After a moment she opened the door, her smile fading into surprise at the sight of him instead of Will. "Hi, Logan."

He stood on her doorstep, forgetting why he was there. She was stunning, thick chocolate hair hanging past her shoulders, the ends flipped into unruly curls.

"I…" He swallowed, striving for some semblance of professionalism. "I wanted to check on you. After what happened today." He stuffed his hands into his pockets. This woman had a knack for turning him back into an awkward teenager.

Even more embarrassing, she didn't look at all awkward. If anything, she looked annoyed, with her eyebrows raised and her lips pressed together. "I'm fine,

Logan. Really." She stayed in the doorway, the door partially closed against her back. "If I need anything, I know where to find you."

An obvious dismissal. But he wasn't giving up that easily. "I'm sorry about earlier today."

"It wasn't your—"

He held up his hand. "Not the stream and the Jeep. I mean about thinking you were keeping information from me. If we're going to work together, we need to trust each other."

Her face paled. Or was it a trick of the light? "Not a big deal. Don't mention it."

"It has to be hard for you, having your memories erased and then trickling back bit by bit."

"It's been…unpleasant, to say the least." She gnawed at her lip, her gaze focused on the ground. Her smile was back in place when she looked up again. "But I'm fine. Thanks for checking."

Was that confusion flickering in her dark eyes? He casually glanced past her, noting the open laptop on the coffee table illuminated by the lamp's glow. These old houses didn't have WiFi or cell phone reception. What was she working on in there? "Have you been able to get in touch with any of your family or friends?"

Her eyes widened a bit and she sucked in a slow breath before answering. "Um, no." She waved a hand vaguely toward the living room. "Maybe I could use the internet at headquarters?"

"Of course. I should've offered sooner." He smiled, trying to ignore the questions swirling in his brain. Why hadn't she asked? Wouldn't she want to tell her family she'd made it here safely, now that she'd remembered them? "In fact, why don't we walk over there now?"

Her mouth hung open for a fraction of a second before she clamped it into a smile. "Sure. Let me grab my computer." She wiped both hands against her jeans and retreated into the living room.

Sweaty palms, a sign of discomfort. Or was she lying? If only there was a way to check her pulse...

"Hey," he called after her, "before we walk over there, let me check your eyes for concussion symptoms again. I should've done that after we got back, but I didn't think about it."

She tilted her head to one side, one eyebrow quirked.

"Yes, it's necessary," he insisted. "Doctor's orders, remember?"

"Fine." The scowl lingered on her face as she stood before him, clutching the laptop.

Now, to get her to lie again, if that's what she'd been doing.

He slipped both hands around her jaw, making sure a couple of his fingers rested over the steady thump of her pulse. All of it to better examine her eyes, of course.

Such a beautiful color. Dark like coffee, wide and trusting.

Focus. He cleared his throat, tilting her head one way and then the other to watch the movement of her eyes. "I'm sure your parents will be relieved to hear from you. Do you want to email or call?"

"Email will be fine," she murmured. Her irises were fascinating, the way they had that ring of dark around the pupil, radiating into lighter, almost golden edges. Like honey.

Such a curious mix of strength and vulnerability rolled into one woman. He rubbed a thumb gently across her jawbone. Her pulse danced erratically beneath his last two fingers.

When she swallowed, her throat bobbed beneath his touch. "Am I okay?"

Logan blinked, whipping back his hands like he'd been caressing a rattlesnake. His heart hammered like it would pound its way out of his chest. "Absolutely. Great recovery. I think you're well on your way." He practically leaped to the sidewalk. "Let's go, before it gets late."

So much for that idea.

Ashley could scarcely get her lungs to draw in adequate oxygen as she closed the front door. Good thing holding the laptop hid her trembling hands. Granted, she was still missing a year's worth of memories, but to her recollection, she'd never been that close to a man before.

Not one that attracted her like a magnet, anyway.

She'd had boys who were friends. She'd gone on a couple of dates. But she'd been so absorbed with academics in school, and then with her career, she'd never invested much effort in romance. Somehow it had always felt like an either-or choice. She knew a handful of special agents who managed to balance both full-time work and family, but most of them were men. And throwing kids into the mix? No thanks. Her work was rigorous and demanding—why try to add more to an already full plate?

She'd always prioritized focusing on things she could control. Like becoming a federal agent.

And solving this case.

But no amount of evaluating the sidewalk would remove the warm strength of Logan's hands on her skin, or the way he'd studied her face. He'd been doing his job—that was all—and she needed to do likewise.

"Job. Focus on the job," she muttered.

"What?" he asked, a half step ahead of her.

"Huh?" Her cheeks warmed. "Nothing."

Good grief. Answering his questions about her family without outright lying had been hard enough. This attraction to him was unacceptable.

On the positive side, maybe a little communication with the outside world would be helpful. As long as her protocol for contacting Morton hadn't changed in the last year, maybe she could access any shared files or messages he'd sent in the past couple of days.

Logan held the door open for her when they reached headquarters. A handful of rangers and other staff members was still there, wrapping up the day's concerns.

"You'll get your own cubicle in there—" he pointed to a room crammed with gray-fabric-covered dividers "—as soon as we can clear out a space. For tonight, it'll be easier to use my office."

"Thanks." She smiled warmly, grateful for the added privacy.

It took a few minutes to connect her laptop to the park's internet service, but then Logan left her alone. After confirming the network's security, she pulled up the encryption program on her laptop and connected to the Bureau's messaging system, which, mercifully, worked exactly as she remembered.

A quick message to Morton informed him of her

arrival and the damage to the rental car, but she was careful to downplay the incident as a random break-in. If he even suspected her cover had been blown, or that someone was after her, he'd pull her out before she could make the connections she so desperately needed.

A return email arrived almost instantly.

Contact wants to meet in San Vicente.
Thursday, 1:00 p.m. Behind the chapel.
He'll find you. Go alone.
Morton.

Alone... Ashley drummed her fingers on the desk. That meant Morton didn't suspect a double-cross and he was concerned she'd scare off their contact if she brought backup. Not to mention that whole issue of not knowing whom to trust.

Logan had mentioned San Vicente—it was one of the small towns across the border. How could she get there without drawing suspicion either from him or whoever knew she was here?

Maybe she could convince Logan to go with her and then separate herself for a few minutes. Long enough to find the chapel.

She'd have to give it some more thought, but one way or another, she'd make this meet. For the first time in days, hope bubbled in her chest. Maybe she'd finally get some of the clues she needed to figure out how everything tied together.

NINE

Logan glanced up at the clock for the tenth time as he pulled a folder out of his desk. Ashley should be arriving for work any minute. He'd walked her home after she'd sent her emails last night, but he'd kept their interaction as professional as possible and she'd seemed happy to do likewise.

No more touching.

Ever.

She appeared in his office long before he felt ready.

"Hi, Logan." She sat in the chair across the desk. She was dressed once more in her ranger uniform, her hair tucked neatly back behind her head. Her expression was one of indifferent friendliness, like he could be any old person in the office. Not someone who'd been staring into her eyes the night before. Good—that should make it easier to rebuild the wall he had to keep between them.

"Good morning," he replied. "How did you sleep?"

"Well enough. Any news on the shooters at Santa Elena?"

He shook his head, hardly surprised it would be her first question. "Border patrol couldn't find any trace of them. The downpour didn't help. We could send men across the border, but the odds of them finding anything…"

"Wouldn't be very good," she finished for him. "So much for that idea."

"With no evidence of drug running, or anyone crossing the border, we're calling it a random act of violence. Maybe even gang-related. You and I were in the wrong place at the wrong time."

"Is that what *you* think?" She raised an eyebrow, her gaze intent.

Fishing for the answer she wanted. *Tough.* He wasn't a rookie and he had to play by the rules. He shrugged. "We have nothing to go on, no evidence besides that map you won't share with anyone else, so at this point, officially, I have to agree with the chief ranger."

"And unofficially?"

"Until you can remember more, I'm not sure it matters what I think. Not much we can do, other than monitor the situation."

"There hasn't been any organized crime here we might link the shootings with?"

"Nothing beyond what we talked about yesterday. I don't know what kind of skeletons you're looking for, but we've got a pretty clean closet here. Other than a few petty crimes, the biggest dangers around here are from the landscape and the wildlife. Not people."

"Of course." She flashed a small, tight-lipped smile straight from the Mona Lisa.

Did she not believe him? Either that or, back to Logan's original suspicion: she was keeping secrets. Just like the Mona Lisa. "What?"

She shook her head and stared at the poster of native Big Bend plants on the wall behind him. From the unfocused look in her eyes, she was lost in thought.

"For your training today—" he began finally.

But she cut him off, as if she hadn't even heard him speak. "We should look for the mine."

"We should do what?" He raised his eyebrows.

Her eyes snapped to his, alert once more. "There's a reason someone sent me that map. Maybe the only way to find out why is to locate the mine."

"You do realize we were almost killed yesterday, don't you?"

"Obviously. But since you agree that yesterday's incident was a random occurrence, what's your objection?"

He ran his hand through his hair. Difficult woman. "Ashley, you clearly haven't told me everything you know. And even this map—you refuse to take it to the chief ranger. Your house and your car have both been broken into. Somebody wants something from you, and the facts aren't adding up. What are you not telling me?"

"I don't expect you to understand." She shrugged. "I've told you as much as I can. If you want me to spend the day on training exercises, fine. I can take care of this in my free time."

"Right." He couldn't hold back a snort. "As if I would let you go traipsing out into the Chisos alone after all the things that have already happened to you."

He held her gaze for a long moment, her dark eyes stubbornly refusing to yield. She lifted her chin, as if to crush any hope she might change her mind.

Nothing for it. "Fine." Why was he was agreeing to this mad scheme? "But I'm coming with you."

"Deal." Ashley's grin lit up the room.

Seeing her smile made the whole madcap plan worth it. "Where do we start?"

She spread the tattered map out on the desk between them, puzzling over the writing. "For how meticulously the map was drawn, whoever made it could've written a little bit neater."

"Rather particular about your treasure maps, aren't you?"

Her lips tipped, laughter dancing at the corner of her eyes, and she pointed at an arrow drawn from the Mexican town of San Vicente across the border toward the Chisos. There was a large chunk of Spanish text beside it. "Do you have that Spanish-English dictionary?"

He nodded, pulling it off one of the shelves behind his desk. A cascade of papers fluttered to the floor. Filling out paperwork was *not* one of his strengths. He handed Ashley the book and stooped to gather the loose forms.

"You have heard of filing cabinets, haven't you?" she asked. "Or is this park too remote?"

"Ha, ha, very funny." Logan shoved the messy stack back onto the shelf. "I may not be organized, but I have other virtues."

She flashed him another grin before turning her attention to the task of translating. He watched her work, so efficient and focused. Somehow, she managed to look as at home in her ranger uniform as she had in that fancy business suit the first day he'd met her.

After a moment she smiled again, this time without looking up. "You can quit watching me do all the work, you know."

He shrugged. "There's nothing else for me to do at the moment." Besides, it was fascinating the way that one clump of hair kept coming loose from behind her ear, no matter how many times she tucked it back.

"Here's what I've got. 'Chapel steps at dawn on Easter morning—first light touches the entrance.'" She glanced up. "Can you even see the Chisos Mountains from San Vicente?"

He pulled out a current park map, laying it beside the hand-drawn one. "Chilicotal Mountain lies between San Vicente and the Chisos, but it's a good 3,000 feet shorter, so you can still see the peaks from the river."

"Time for a day trip?" That speculative gleam in her eye suggested she wasn't going to take *no* for an answer.

"We could go—" he shrugged "—but we're about six months too early for Easter morning."

She held up a finger, shaking it as she spoke. "But what really matters is where the sun would have first hit the peak five hundred years ago, when the Spanish first found it."

Logan picked up her train of thought. "So, if we photograph the mountain peak, maybe with a little research we can extrapolate where the entrance should be?"

"Exactly."

"*If* this mine even exists."

"Of course." Her smile was obviously fake. Agreeing for the sake of keeping the peace. "How about Thursday? Since we have that staff picnic this afternoon."

When he'd told her about it earlier, she'd practically grimaced. She didn't exactly strike him as the social type. "Remembered, did you? I'm impressed."

Ashley handed him the dictionary, her face scrunching. "Yeah, about that…do I have to go?"

Ah, right. Trying to get out of it, after all. But he

could be stubborn, too. "You'll get to meet more of
the other rangers." He folded the park map. "Besides,
a little fun will be good for you."

Ashley sent a quick confirmation message to Morton and left work early under the pretense of needing
time to get ready. In reality, it would only take five
minutes to change out of her park uniform, but Logan
didn't argue. After how easy it had been to convince
him to take her to San Vicente, she could hardly complain about being dragged to a picnic.

As soon as she walked into the house, she dropped
her keys on the coffee table and pulled out her laptop.
It had occurred to her that maybe she'd find files on
some of the other rangers on her computer. Useful information prior to meeting more of them in person.

Sure enough, she had personnel files from the Department of the Interior—she had no idea how Morton
had gotten them without going through Barclay and
arousing suspicion—and perhaps, better yet, personal
information gathered through the Bureau's resources.

Her hand hovered over the computer mouse. The list
was alphabetical, containing almost a hundred files. But
one name immediately drew her attention and, unable
to resist, she clicked on the file marked *Logan Everett*. He had become her partner, so she needed to know
whether he was trustworthy. But logic couldn't shake
the guilt niggling at her conscience as she read his file.

Thirty-two years old—about what she'd guessed.
Graduated with honors from a top environmental sci-
ence program before going directly into the park service. Three years at Crater Lake—that must've been

beautiful—and now seven years here. He'd taken on the role of training new rangers about four years ago.

She moved on to his personal information, shifting in her seat and wishing she had the luxury of waiting for him to tell her all these facts when he was ready. But everything she read was, if anything, admirable. Newspaper clippings showed various things he'd done during his time with the park service: a few criminal arrests, but mostly successful search-and-rescue operations.

Exactly the sort of man you'd want on your side for an investigation. And no motive to help Rico Jimenez.

She moved on to others she'd already met: Ed Chambers, Will Sykes, the superintendent. Ed had a sick sister who needed surgery. The superintendent had recently gone through a divorce. His only daughter was in college. Will had only been with the park service for two years—Big Bend was his first assignment. His father had died a long time ago, leaving his mother to raise him and his sister alone. They still lived in a suburb of El Paso.

Reading the files was like sifting through everyone's laundry, searching for the stinky socks.

And still more than ninety files to go. Ashley shut the computer, momentarily disgusted with her job. Was this hunt a waste of her time? Maybe Jimenez was a criminal genius and didn't need anybody's help. Maybe there weren't any dirty socks to find. The thought that any of these people—so dedicated, so willing to make sacrifices to protect others—could be a traitor, made her stomach churn.

She just hoped—no, *prayed*—that that someone wasn't Logan, because sometimes it was the person you'd never suspect.

It took less than five minutes to change into the only

dress she'd brought with her and to run a comb through her hair. Then she slipped her laptop into its hiding place under the mattress and tucked the map into the camisole she wore underneath her dress.

"Hey, Ashley." Will sauntered toward her as she approached the party, carrying a drink in his hand. His crisp, white shirt matched his perfect teeth and contrasted beautifully with his dark skin and hair. "I was hoping you'd be here."

She smiled ruefully. "Logan told me I had to come."

"I'm glad he did." To her surprise, Will took her arm, leading her toward the crowded tent. As they walked, she caught a sudden scent on the breeze—something clean, like detergent or fabric softener. Strikingly familiar but gone before she could place it.

There probably weren't more than a hundred residents in Panther Junction, but it appeared that most of them had made it to this event. And now they were watching her walk arm-in-arm with Will Sykes, jumping to who-knew-what conclusions. Ashley extricated her arm under the pretense of smoothing some flyaway hairs from her face. They all knew Will—they would know he was merely being friendly.

And he proved to be a great escort. Not only did he seem to be on good terms with everyone, he made a point to introduce her. She soon lost track—elementary school teachers, interpretive rangers, postal clerks, the janitorial staff. Most of them looked about a thousand times more likely to win a quilting bee or a game of shuffleboard than to secretly help a Mexican drug lord. Still, she would check their files later.

The small talk was already wearing on her by the

time Ed Chambers clattered a wooden spoon against one of the tables. "Welcome, everyone," he called. After offering a short prayer, he invited all of them to line up and "dig in" to the heaping platters of beef brisket, potato salad and beans.

She took her loaded plate and followed Will to a table, mentally cataloguing each new person she met. And *not* looking around the crowd for Logan.

He came up to her as she threw away her trash. "Well?" A mischievous light glinted in his eyes.

"Well what?" Despite the heat creeping into her cheeks at his nearness, she held his steady gaze.

"Did you get the meat sweats?"

"Excuse me?" She did her best to look politely disgusted.

He laughed. "You know, when you eat too much meat."

"Ugh. You don't need to say anything else."

"That's my girl. I knew you would like the brisket." He put his arm around her shoulders and squeezed, unknowingly setting off an electric jolt through her insides.

What on earth was *wrong* with her? She was a federal agent, not a high-schooler.

"Ashley—" Will walked up to them "—want an escort home? Unless you need to stay longer?" The half smirk on his face as he glanced at Logan's hand on her shoulder filled her cheeks with heat.

She pulled away, swallowing her embarrassment. Logan was her trainer, after all. There was *nothing* personal.

"No, go ahead." Logan stuffed his hands into his pockets. "I'll see you in the morning."

* * *

"So, want to talk about it?" Ed Chambers asked as they walked over to park headquarters.

Logan stopped wiping at the barbecue sauce hopelessly smeared across his shirt and glanced up at his friend. "What?" he snapped, instantly regretting his tone of voice. It wasn't Ed's fault Logan had plowed into the trash can.

No, come to think of it, maybe it *was* Ed's fault. He had paired Logan and Ashley together, after all. And if Logan had been watching where he was going instead of staring at her brown hair dancing in the breeze...

Ed glanced over his shoulder, toward the tent. "Whatever, or whoever, was distracting you back there. I have a guess already."

"Maybe it's none of your business, old man." He couldn't hold back a laugh. Ed had been both a friend and spiritual mentor to him for years—there could be no keeping secrets from him.

They reached headquarters and Ed unlocked the door, pulling it open. "I'm glad to see you're finally opening yourself up to new possibilities. She's the first woman to turn your head in a long time."

"Who said it had anything to do with her?"

Ed raised his hands in mock surrender. "Just making an observation. I'll see you later."

"Hey, Ed?" Logan called as the chief ranger turned to go. "What else do you know about Ashley? Why is she here?"

A curious expression flickered on Ed's face but vanished almost immediately. He shrugged. "Providence, I guess. Why?"

Did he know more than he was saying? Logan opened his office door. "I'm concerned about her."

"That's why I picked you to train her."

After saying good-night to Ed, Logan pored over the park map on his desk. If only he could feel so confident. Personal feelings aside, he still worried about Ashley. They'd left Santa Elena Canyon alive only by the grace of God. What if someone *was* after that map? How was he going to keep her safe the next time? She was quite capable with the law-enforcement side, but she didn't know the terrain like he did. And after what had happened with Sam…

He wanted to believe what Superintendent Barclay thought—that the shooting had been a random incident. Bored teenagers daring each other. Or maybe the newest cartel member proving his loyalty by taking shots across the border.

But deep down, he didn't believe it. Of course, that left an even bigger question. How had anyone known Ashley would be there? Or were they waiting, in case she came back?

And what had happened to her that first night, when he had found her near the river?

Too many questions without any answers. And the woman herself working against him. One minute she would be in his arms, staring up at him with those eyes large enough for a man to drown in, and the next she was pushing him away. Refusing his help. Keeping her secrets.

He pursed his lips together. Ed was right—he *hadn't* felt this way about anyone since Erin.

That thought was almost more terrifying than anything else.

TEN

Ashley kept her hand tucked into her pocket to keep from glancing at her watch. The steeple of the San Vicente chapel stretched its small brown cross up to the brilliant blue sky on the far side of the marketplace, beckoning her as she wound her way between the vendors'-booths. From their position on the northwest corner, the steps should have a perfect view of the US side of the river.

The small square was a feast for the senses, packed with colors and textures and spicy, pungent smells. Along the edges of the square, sand-colored adobe buildings stood sentry, their bright awnings flapping in the breeze.

Fifteen minutes. She had fifteen minutes to stroll through this marketplace, find a way to ditch Logan at the last second and identify her contact at the chapel. Would he or she be waiting in the street behind it?

At least they were dressed like tourists. Logan carried a Nikon DSLR slung in a bag across his broad shoulders, ready to snap pictures from the chapel steps. The perfect pretense for being there, but she hoped he wouldn't scare her contact away.

She paused in front of a booth full of blankets, fingering the vibrantly woven wool. The vendor smiled, his brown face crinkling around his dark eyes. Hoping for a sale, no doubt.

"Can we shop later?" Logan stopped next to her and nudged her with his elbow. He'd stayed on her heels like a loyal dog—she laughed at the image, pretty sure he wouldn't find it quite as funny. The way he kept scanning the square, as if he assumed somebody was about to jump them at any second, was sure to chase off her contact at this rate. Logan didn't have FBI training, of course, but it'd be nice if he could be a *little* more covert about it.

One of these blankets *would* make a lovely gift for her parents…

"You know—" she smiled sweetly up at him "—my mom's birthday is coming up. She'd love one of these blankets. Why don't you go ahead?" She nodded toward the chapel. "I'll catch up in a minute."

His brows pulled together into a slight frown. "For somebody so insistent on coming down here, I don't get how you could shop at a time like this."

She shrugged. "The chapel's not going anywhere. Five minutes won't kill me."

He raised a brow, his lips pursing to one side. "Women and shopping."

A decidedly false stereotype, in Ashley's case—she'd far rather be at the shooting range—but she could hardly say that to Logan, so she shrugged again and waved him off toward the chapel. "Five minutes."

He hesitated, scanning the market again.

"I'll be fine." She looked at him pointedly.

"All right." He let out a resigned sigh, evidently deciding he wasn't going to win this argument, and ambled off toward the chapel.

One problem solved. Ashley snuck a glance at her watch. Less than ten minutes. She picked up one of the blankets, barely paying attention to the intricate black, green and white weaving, and purchased it from the vendor without haggling.

His wide grin assured her she'd probably paid more than anybody else in the market would've, but she could chalk it up to keeping up her disguise as a tourist. Stupid Americans, right?

In the distance, Logan glanced back at her and waved. She held up the blanket, pasting on a ridiculous smile of delight at her new treasure.

As soon as his back was turned, she tucked the blanket under one arm and slowly wove her way toward the chapel, doing her best to look like she was following Logan but veering a little more to the left. When he disappeared around the front of the chapel, she cut straight across the square, ducking around textile booths and stepping past carts laden with tomatoes, peppers and corn.

She'd almost reached the far side of the square when a man stepped in front of her, holding a tray of silver jewelry.

"Pretty lady," he said in broken English. "See the jewelry?" His face was wrinkled and weathered, and his smile revealed a chipped front tooth.

On the far side of his booth, an alley led behind the old chapel. The bright overhead sun cast a heavy shadow along the chapel's back wall, but nobody appeared to be waiting for her. Farther down, the alley was empty, save for laundry hanging on lines strung between the houses. Maybe her contact wasn't here yet. She still had five minutes or so.

The man pushed the tray at her. "Lovely, yes?"

"Yes." She scanned the booths around her. Nothing out of the ordinary. And, thankfully, no sign of Logan.

"Come, see more." The man set his tray down on his stand, beckoning her closer.

Might as well. She could keep a good eye on the alley from here and, in a couple of minutes, she'd cut between this booth and the neighbor selling baskets and slip into the alley to wait.

Some of the pieces were quite lovely. Beautiful craftsmanship.

"Did you make—?" she started to ask, but the man placed a rough hand on her arm and tipped his head toward the alley. Her contact?

"This way," he whispered.

Nobody seemed interested as she followed the man behind the booth, ducking with him into the dark shadows beside the crumbling adobe wall of the chapel. They both glanced up and down the alley to make sure no one lurked nearby. Empty. Above them, the chapel's large cast-iron bell gonged once to mark the hour.

"Agent Thompson?" The man kept his voice low. He gazed over her shoulder, toward the marketplace and his unattended booth.

Ashley nodded. She'd followed him into the alley. If this was a setup, the cat was already out of the proverbial bag. "What do you have for me?"

"Jimenez knows you go undercover in park."

She clenched her teeth, fighting the unease knotting her stomach. *Not* what she was hoping to hear. "How?"

He shook his head. "I do not know."

Cover blown. Should she call Morton, abandon the mission? She'd suspected as much after the break-in at her house, but with this confirmation…

No. She was here for a reason, beyond catching Jimenez, and she was determined to figure out what it was. The street was still empty. She fished out the map, which she'd stowed along with her passport inside a plastic sandwich bag in a pouch beneath her waistband. She showed it to the man, indicating the mine. "Do you know where this is?"

His eyes widened slightly. "Is where Jimenez gets gold. Pine Canyon Trail." He pointed to a long squiggly line running below the mine, and then dragged his finger down to another set of mountains closer to the border. "Drives gold out from Juniper Canyon to hide it here, until he can cross border."

She'd ask Logan the names of those mountains next chance she got. The illegal mining alone would be enough to arrest Jimenez, but knowing the way the cartel lords operated, he was bound to have other infractions. Illegal laborers. Weapons. Drugs. They'd put him away for a long time, *if* she could catch him before he got to her. "Thank you. Where is he now? At the mine?"

"Goes back and forth." The man waggled his finger between the mine and the southern mountains. "Work during day. Drive out gold at night."

It was enough. Ashley's heart soared inside her chest. With a little surveillance, they'd catch him. Maybe she'd finally figure out why this place mattered.

She folded the map, sealed it back inside its plastic bag—just in case—and tucked the pouch beneath her waistband. She touched the man's arm. "Thank you. We'll see he gets the justice he deserves."

The man nodded, his lips pressed into a thin line, eyes turning liquid. "For my Lena." He swallowed, blinked a few times, and walked past Ashley back to his booth.

She lingered in the shadows a moment longer, scanning the marketplace for Logan's tall figure, but finding no sign of him. The crowd had thinned now that it was afternoon. The heat scorched the dusty, packed earth of the square. She edged along the chapel wall, following it behind vendors' booths, as she kept an eye on the marketplace.

Something felt off—she didn't know what, but her instincts told her to stay alert.

A moment later she spied two men hurrying through the booths. One was white, the other Mexican. Both were muscular and wore cargo pants, white shirts and heavy utility belts. They ignored the goods and produce, and instead surveyed the shoppers, their dark eyes drifting periodically to the narrow alleys providing access to the square. Almost as if they were looking for someone.

The hairs stood on the back of her neck. She glanced back at the man from the jewelry booth. His stand was nearly empty as he hastily wrapped up the last of the necklaces and rings on display.

Ashley hurried along the chapel wall, trying to keep the nearby booths and their occupants between her and the two men. They still scanned the square, but they'd picked up their pace.

She rounded the front corner of the chapel, letting out a quick burst of breath at the sight of Logan standing on the chapel steps, blissfully unaware of the men on her tail. He held the camera up to his eye, taking a series of shots of the landscape across the river.

Here the terrain dropped down from the plateau, giving an unobstructed view above the rooftops of the small San Vicente homes built onto the hillside. Down near the glittering ribbon of the Rio Grande stood the old 1775 presidio, a large, square-ish adobe structure used as a fort by the Spanish. On the far side, vast desert stretched up to the roots of the Chisos, jutting like ragged teeth from the surrounding flatland.

"Logan." She tugged on his sleeve. "We need to go."

He lowered the camera, his face crinkling in annoyance. "You messed up my shot." His green eyes drifted over the blanket still tucked under her arm. "Glad you found what you wanted."

Ashley released his sleeve and took a step back, peering out into the square. Her breath caught.

The men were gone.

Logan tucked the camera into the bag dangling at his side. He'd gotten some good shots. Hard to say how helpful they'd be, though. He glanced at Ashley, wrinkling his forehead. He'd never understand women. She'd been so determined to come here, and now she couldn't stop staring at the marketplace. He hardly would've pegged her for the shop-till-you-drop type.

"They're gone," she said, the blood draining from her face.

His hand automatically dropped to his waistband before he remembered there was no gun. Mexican law only allowed select US agents to bear arms, and only with special written permission from the government. Big Bend park rangers didn't make the cut. "Who?"

"The men in the market. Come on." The words tumbled out of her mouth as she grabbed his arm, tugging him around the far side of the chapel, away from the square. The dirt road was narrow and dark, lined with tightly packed adobe homes. Ashley let go of his arm and jogged along the side, keeping close to the chapel wall.

Logan followed, glancing behind them as they went, but the alley remained empty. "What men? Where are we going?"

She paused at the back of the chapel and peered around the corner into the cross street. "Two men in the marketplace. I think they were following me."

He peered over her shoulder, the strawberry scent of her hair filling his nose. The street was empty. "Maybe we can lose them between here and the other side of town."

"We'll have to catch a ride to the border crossing." Her pretty face held an uncharacteristic grimace. "There's no way to walk back without being seen."

They'd left the park at the official border crossing at Boquillas, paying ten bucks to a teenage boy to row them across the river. The only way to cross the six or so miles from Boquillas to San Vicente was in the bed of a pickup, and they'd need the same way back. "We'll figure something out," he promised. "If we can slip out of town unnoticed, we'll be okay."

They darted across the street, keeping close to the buildings and the little bit of shadow created by the midday sun. Noise from the lingering crowd in the market carried down the alley. A low, rhythmic sound echoed below the murmur of the crowd.

Footsteps. And close.

He stopped, snatching Ashley's shirtsleeve, and they both pressed back against a dusty wall coated in chipping orange plaster.

Two men turned into the alley from behind the chapel. Both stocky and muscular, and no doubt carrying at least one illegal firearm apiece. One of them pointed at Logan and Ashley. *"¡Por ahi!"*

"Run." Logan gave her a little shove, but she was already off, sprinting down the narrow street.

He followed as they took one turn after another, dodging children playing ball and hapless burros led by scrunched old men. South around the marketplace, then west, zigzagging up and down the narrow streets, heading ever closer to the road that would lead them out of San Vicente.

She pulled up after a few minutes and Logan glanced behind them. No sign of their pursuers.

"Do you think we lost them?" She massaged a stitch in her side.

"Hope so. We're about out of real estate." He nodded toward the far end of the street, where the last little gaily painted cantina fended off the endless desert, its sign advertising cold *cervezas* creaking against a rusty frame. "Maybe we can catch a ride."

"Worth a try."

They jogged the last hundred yards to the small terrace surrounding the cantina. Benches lined both sides of its open door, covered by a bright yellow-and-orange awning to provide a welcome bit of shade. The couple of metal tables and chairs beneath the awning were empty.

Logan peered through the windows as they approached, then stuck his head inside the door, glancing both ways before giving Ashley the all-clear. A pair of old men sat at a table beneath the only ceiling fan, its rickety thumping blades scarcely making a dent in the oppressive heat.

A long, wooden counter occupied most of the small place, lined with tall metal stools. Shelves hung on the wall in the background and held an assortment of glassware and dingy framed photographs of tourists. A door at the end presumably led into the kitchen.

Ashley wiped her arm against her forehead and walked up to the bar. *"¡Hola!"* she called. When nobody answered, she glanced at Logan and shrugged. "That's about the extent of my Spanish."

His wasn't much better, but living in the park for a few years had helped. He pulled out a handful of dollar bills and smacked the counter. *"Dos agua sin gas, por favor."*

A moment later an older man came out, wiping his hands on a white apron. *"Buenos días.* Hello. Americans. So nice. You want water?"

"Yes. Two bottles." Logan slid the money across the counter as the man slapped two tepid bottles down.

Ashley cracked hers open and guzzled it.

"Impressive." Logan winked, laughing when she blushed. He turned back to the man behind the counter. "We need a ride back to Boquillas. Can you help?"

The man eyed them for a moment, then nodded. "One moment. I see." The kitchen door swung shut behind him as he disappeared.

Logan leaned against the counter and slipped his hands into his pockets. No sign of their pursuers outside. The two old men sat at their table, languidly sipping bottles of beer and gesticulating with their hands.

Ashley perched on one of the stools, every one of her muscles taut like a coil ready to spring. Her dark hair, normally slicked back straight in a ponytail, fell in frizzy clumps around her cheeks. It was strange how calm she was, considering they were unarmed and under pursuit in a foreign country.

She was a constant mystery—one moment looking entirely out of place, the next like she belonged there. Erin had been the same in many ways, though never so coolly confident. Yet he'd still been blindsided when she told him she'd always hated Big Bend.

Ashley didn't seem to hate it, but maybe today would change her mind.

The door to the kitchen swung open and the man thumped back out, waving his hand for them to follow. "This way. My nephew give you ride. Fifteen dollar."

Logan let out a sigh of relief, exchanging a quick glance with Ashley. Her lips tilted into a half smile, her shoulders relaxing a touch. Maybe they'd get out without any more trouble, after all.

He and Ashley followed the man out beneath the awning and around to the back of the cantina. A lone bench with faded blue paint stood beside a dusty vending machine that had seen better days. Farther down, the cantina's wall disappeared into shadow beneath a makeshift roof of corrugated plastic, creating a storage shed between the cantina and the next building. The rusty bumper of a truck peeked out from the shadows.

The man pointed at the bench. "You wait. He be here in few minutes."

"Gracias," Logan said.

"De nada." The man disappeared around to the front, leaving them alone in the hundred-degree heat.

Ashley wiped sweat from her forehead and pointed at the truck. "Think that's our ride?"

"Maybe." He swallowed a few sips of warm water. "If it gets us to the border, that's what matters." The intense afternoon heat tugged a yawn out of his chest.

"I wish I could've gotten a better look at them." She gnawed on her lower lip, staring north across the desert.

"Do you think they were after…" He trailed off, not wanting to mention the map out loud. Just in case.

She nodded. "Maybe the same ones who tried to break into my house."

"We'll run the descriptions through the database when we get back. Maybe it'll turn up a hit." He patted the camera bag. "At least I got the shots before we had to run."

"That's something." She paced back and forth in front of the vending machine, glancing alternately between the desert and her wristwatch. "Has it been a few minutes yet?"

The truck engine in the shed sputtered to life. Logan went rigid, stepping between Ashley and the vehicle more out of habit than anything else. But he relaxed as it eased out from under the awning, rolling toward them.

"Sí, señorita."

Logan and Ashley both spun at the voice coming from the corner of the cantina.

One of the men who'd been chasing them stood there, his gun aimed at Ashley's head.

Logan raised his hands slowly, nudging Ashley's arm when she hesitated. His mind raced through their options, coming up dismally short beyond priority number one. Not getting shot. "We don't want any trouble. Tourists."

"Right." The man smirked. "Then we have a tour all lined up for you." He was white, perhaps an inch over six feet tall, two hundred pounds, American accent. Hair color possibly light brown, but hard to say under the blue ball cap.

The truck stopped, its engine idling. The other man, Mexican, with a long, jagged scar cutting across his right cheek, sat behind the wheel. He tapped the glass behind his seat and a third man, whom Logan hadn't seen before, hopped out of the bed of the truck.

Also armed.

Ashley stiffened.

First rule of an abduction was to stay out of the vehicle. But with two guns trained on their heads, they hardly had a choice.

"Into the truck," the American ordered.

"Where are you taking us?" Ashley asked.

He angled the muzzle of his gun up over her shoulder and fired, the bullet lodging into the cantina's yellow plaster wall a few feet beyond her. Logan shot her a warning glance, his stomach clenching into knots. Her face was pale, but her knees didn't wobble. The woman had nerves of steel.

Something cold and hard pressed against the back of his skull—the other gun. He gritted his teeth.

Ashley's eyes went wide with alarm. If all they

wanted was the map, or something else she had, maybe he was disposable.

The American nodded.

Time slowed, each millisecond passing in an eternal haze of waiting for the click of the trigger, the impact of the bullet, the loss of consciousness. The moment he'd see Jesus face to face, after the blinding agony of death.

"No!" Fear laced Ashley's voice, tugging at his heart.

The impact came, but not the click. And the bullet felt heavier, blunter, more crushing than he'd expected. He crumpled to the ground, stars flaring in the blackness.

The last thing he heard was the American's voice, repeating his order to Ashley. "Get in the truck."

ELEVEN

Ashley couldn't see where they were going as the truck jostled and bounced over the uneven dirt road, but at least they were both still alive. She'd thought, for a moment there, they'd kill Logan. When the man had hit him with the butt of his gun instead, her legs had gone so weak she'd nearly collapsed.

His breathing was slow and steady, his eyes still closed, as he lay facing her on the hot metal of the truck bed. Ropes chafed at her ankles and wrists, bound behind her back, and the smell of exhaust choked her.

Logan stirred as the truck slowed to a stop.

"Logan?" she whispered.

He blinked a few times, his gaze snapping into focus when he saw her face. The back gate dropped open with a loud clang. Somebody barked rapid commands in Spanish and the man who'd ridden in the back with them, his gun always aimed at her chest, yanked on the ropes around her ankles.

She sat up, scooching herself toward the tailgate as the man pulled and stealing a quick glance at their surroundings. They were parked in the open courtyard of a large, square adobe structure—inside the presidio, she guessed. The walls were half in ruins, but a long, low building ran along the south side, close to where the truck was parked. Four or five open doorways suggested multiple rooms.

Beyond the walls, a little town—she assumed it was San Vicente—sat on a low hill a mile or two away. In the other direction lay the river, the Chisos Mountains and the United States.

Freedom.

But first they had to get out.

The men hauled her and Logan through one of the open doorways into a long room. Four high, narrow windows revealed glimpses of blue sky in the wall with the door. Heavy wood lintels stood above the door and windows, and hewed logs supported the roof. An empty niche in the back wall probably held a religious statue long ago. The only other items in the room were a single chair and a stack of decaying baskets.

"Tie them up." The order came from the man with the American accent. Working with a drug cartel to get rich. Ashley couldn't stop her nose from wrinkling in disgust. If she could figure out who he was, would that help her identify the insider with the park service?

She wanted to ask questions but decided to keep her mouth shut for the moment. They tied her to the room's lone chair and dragged Logan over to the end wall, looping his tied wrists over a hook above his head. Keeping him alive, thankfully. But why? Jimenez would never let either of them leave alive.

The answer, she knew, lay hidden inside the secret pouch, where she'd stowed the map after meeting her contact. Once they had it, she and Logan were as good as dead.

"Good." The American gestured to the man who'd driven the truck. "Manuel, report to the boss."

Jimenez. Did that mean he was here? Or were they merely calling him?

Across the room, Logan's head drooped and he groaned as he lifted it again. His shoulder blades jutted out in what had to be a terribly uncomfortable position.

Ashley's heart thrummed against her ribs. She had to get them out of here. Logan hadn't deserved to be dragged into this mess.

Focus. She needed to focus. Assess the situation, like she'd been trained. She flexed her hands behind her back. The ropes dug into her skin. No gun tucked comfortably under her waistband. Their best odds would be to get the two men out of the room. Give them a chance to figure out a plan.

The American bent in front of her, his face filling her vision. "Where is it?"

Ashley clamped her mouth shut.

"What…are you…talking about?" Logan sounded as if he was talking through a mouthful of packing peanuts. His eyes were still unfocused and dried blood was smeared across his cheek.

"Nobody asked you anything." The other man, the one who'd knocked him out, slapped him hard across the face. Ashley's stomach lurched at the sound.

Logan glared, spitting blood onto the floor. "What do you want from us?"

"The map, my friend. Where is it? Get your girlfriend to tell me and we will give you a painless death."

No less than she'd expected. They hadn't mentioned her contact, but they'd known she would be in San Vicente. Had he given her up or had it been somebody else? And if it was her contact, why give her all that information first? Was it false?

"Dunno what you're talking about," Logan mumbled.

The American ignored him, kneeling in front of Ashley, his face inches away. "Where is the map?" His fingers stopped inches away from her shirt. "Or shall I search for it myself?"

"Don't you dare touch her," Logan snarled, his tone fierce.

Ashley held the man's steely gaze, despite the fear skittering along her spine. She *hated* feeling vulnerable. Hearing about attacks on girls was one reason she'd chosen law enforcement in the first place.

His hand was very close.

She whipped her head forward, clamping her teeth down on his fingers as hard as she could. He howled, jerking back so fast he nearly pulled some of her teeth out.

His face turned splotchy red but when he finally spoke to her again, the words were calm. "Either you can tell me or we can do this the hard way."

When Ashley merely stared at him, unflinching, he nodded. "José."

The man called José drew back his fist and slammed it into Logan's unprotected stomach. A groan slipped out and his face contorted in agony.

Ashley pressed her lips together.

José struck again. And again—until the horrible muffled thump of each strike etched itself permanently into her mind.

That's why they'd kept him alive. To torture the truth out of her.

Her insides curdled with fear but she took a steadying breath. "Let him go. He doesn't know anything."

"No, no." The American contorted his mouth into a wicked grin. "You see, I don't like to hit women, so it's very convenient you brought him with you. Now, tell me where it is."

She couldn't look at Logan, not when he was paying for her silence. She shook her head.

The man didn't take his dark eyes off her face. "Again."

The impact was different this time—harder—bone on bone. When she dared a glance out of the corner of her eye, she could see blood trickling down the side of Logan's face. His eyes were steely, but how much could he take? Was the map worth Logan's life?

"I have been reasonable." The man rose to his feet. "This is your last chance. Tell me what I want to know." With a slow scraping sound, he drew a long knife from a sheath at his waist. He tapped it lazily against his outstretched palm.

That knife was coming for both of them, unless she thought of something quick.

Ashley ignored the shiver that crept up her spine. Time to take a gamble. "Why does Jimenez need it, anyway? We all know that mine is a legend."

Surprise flickered across Logan's features. And an unmistakable warning lit his eyes. *Tread carefully.*

The American laughed. "Because he likes to tie up loose ends. The last thing we need is the park service intruding into our business."

"How do you know they don't already have it?"

He didn't appear concerned as he paced back and forth in front of Ashley. "We have our ways. And once we have your copy and you both are gone, there will be no one else to stop us. Now, where is it?"

"Why should I tell you, if you're going to kill us anyway?"

Faster than she could blink, the man turned toward Logan and released the knife. Ashley's heart lurched into her throat, stopping her breath, as the knife embedded itself into the adobe wall six inches from Logan's ear.

Slowly, carefully, the man walked over and pulled the knife out of the wall, tracing the blade along Logan's cheek. "Unless you want to watch me cut him apart, piece by piece, you will tell me what I want to know."

"Ashley," Logan growled, "don't listen to him. Don't worry about me."

The man laughed, kneeling in front of Ashley again, but safely beyond the reach of her teeth. He dropped his voice low, smirking. "He's brave, isn't he? But you know better. You know I will do it. And you are a woman—too weak to watch me carve him apart."

Oh, he would pay one day—when she brought down Jimenez and his men. But the red-hot anger flaring in her gut wasn't going to help now.

So instead she sighed deeply, hanging her head. "I'm sorry, Logan. I have to tell him. I couldn't bear..." She sniffled for effect.

The man stared at her, waiting expectantly.

What would he believe? A lie mixed with truth would be easiest to swallow. And whatever she said, she needed to get both men out of the room. "A man threatened me in the marketplace today. After that, I was scared, so I hid the map. You chased us before I could go back for it."

"Where? Here, in San Vicente?"

"The side street to the right of the chapel, off the plaza," Ashley said, infusing her voice with the weakness he expected to hear. "There was a crack in the adobe wall of the house across the street from the chapel's side entrance. I stuffed it in there, as high up as I could reach."

The man's eyes narrowed as he searched her face. He turned to his companion. "José, go get it."

José mumbled something in Spanish that Ashley didn't understand.

The other man frowned impatiently. "Fine. Wait outside. I don't want you killing them before I find the map."

He grabbed a fistful of Ashley's hair to expose her neck. With a sudden flick of his wrist, the long knife was at her throat. "If I find you've lied to me, you'll regret it."

She didn't dare breathe. The cold steel pricked unforgivingly at her skin. For a split second she thought he might kill her, but he pulled the knife away, releasing her hair. She slumped, tension ebbing out of her shoulders as the men stalked out of the room.

There was nothing to do but watch as the heavy oak door slammed shut and was bolted on the far side.

Logan let out a long breath, staring across the room at Ashley. She was absolutely composed—the only hint of fear had been in the slight strain of her voice, as if it was a battle to keep it steady. That, and the flash of panic in her eyes when the man had thrown a knife at his head. The rest of it—the simpering female—had been an obvious act.

She held his gaze for a moment and then nodded. "Okay. Let's get out of here."

"How are we going to do that, exactly?" He looked up at the rope knotted around his hands, looped over the hook. Too high for him to stretch and pull himself free. The tied ankles didn't help, either. And Ashley... well, she wasn't getting out of that chair anytime soon.

A small scraping noise pulled his attention back to her. Using her feet, she was part jumping, part sliding the chair toward him.

"If I can get close enough, maybe you can use the chair to unhook your hands."

"And," he recollected, "I've got a knife in my shirt pocket."

She slid the chair another foot closer, so painfully slowly. "I thought we weren't allowed to bring weapons across the border."

"It's got a two-inch blade." He rolled his eyes. "It hardly counts as a weapon. Besides, you never know when a Swiss army knife will come in handy."

Finally, Ashley managed to slide the chair right up to his knees. Using his aching abdominal muscles, he hoisted his tied feet up onto the edge of the chair and pushed off, simultaneously lifting the rope around his wrists off the hook. His sudden weight on the chair sent both it and Ashley rocking precariously, but she didn't tip.

"That feels so much better." He rotated his shoulders to get the blood circulating again and gingerly touched his side. A couple of bruised ribs, but nothing felt broken.

"Good. Then get me out of this chair." Her dark eyes sparked. She had more guts than half the park rangers he'd worked with, and this was her first job in the field. Something inside his chest swelled.

"You're a real magnet for trouble, you know that?" He fished the knife out of his pocket and worked the blade open. "And the worst part is, you seem to like it."

"Like it?" she scoffed. "I won't like it if they come back here while you're dawdling around with that knife."

"Maybe I should leave you tied up, if you're going to complain."

She gave him a crooked smile, watching as Logan carefully maneuvered the sharp blade against the ropes binding his wrists. In a matter of minutes he had sawed through the coil and unraveled the bonds. After freeing his ankles, he worked on the ropes securing Ashley's feet and upper body to the chair.

She stood, holding out her hands so he could free her wrists. "You're pretty proficient at this. Do you get captured often?"

"No, never done it before." He gave her a wry grin. "I have you to thank for this pleasure."

He took both her hands—so soft and warm—in one of his, holding as he sawed at the rope with the knife. As the last of the binding came loose, Logan pulled it from her wrists to reveal bright red chafing marks on her skin. Anger surged in his gut and he looked up at her, searching her face.

"They didn't touch you, did they?" He'd been pretty delirious after that knock to the head. No telling what might've happened while he was out.

"No." Her cheeks flushed. "But what about you? How's your head?"

He shrugged. "It hurts."

His heart skipped as she brushed her fingertips lightly against the back of his head, gently moving his hair. Something shifted in her brown eyes, her brows raising in the center.

"You've got a big knot." Her throat bobbed. "We'd better watch for signs of concussion." She smiled wryly. "I know all about them."

"Yes, you do." Logan cleared his throat, torn between the need to comfort her and to punch the men who had hurt her. But neither would help at the moment—they still needed to escape. "First, let's get out of here."

"I noticed the roof looked pretty dilapidated from the outside—do you think we could find a place to climb out?"

"Maybe." He paced the room, assessing the ceiling. "The adobe is probably at least a foot thick. It would take a long time to carve our way out unless we find a weak spot."

She pointed to a section along the back wall where bits of adobe had broken loose. "What about there? Along the beam?"

Logan grabbed the chair and walked over to the spot. Climbing up, he scraped along the crevice with his knife. "The beam is called a *viga*, incidentally, and these—" he pointed to smaller crossbeams "— are called *latillas*."

Ashley tapped her foot impatiently. "I guess I know who to ask the next time I want a lesson on adobe construction. Now, can we get out through there or not?"

Logan shot her a quick scowl as he dug his knife into the adobe above his head. "This might work. If you can muster a little more patience, I'll try to cut us a hole. Keep an eye on that door."

Digging through the hardened mud was slow work, but a steady trickle of dust and small pieces kept falling to the floor. A large chunk of mud and straw broke free, crashing to the ground near the base of the chair.

"I think I'm through." He wiped dust away from his face using his forearm. A patch of blue sky peeked through the newly opened hole.

"What's going on in there?" Someone drew back the door latch with a heavy thud.

"Ashley," Logan whispered, "over here. I can get you out."

"Too late." She shook her head, pressing herself against the wall beside the door.

The door that was opening as José walked in, holding a gun.

TWELVE

Ashley knew she'd have a split-second advantage as José's eyes adjusted to the dark room. She waited, holding her breath, as he stepped inside, his gun arm outstretched.

She made her move as soon as he had taken a full step inside the doorway, seizing his arm and rotating the weapon backward and out of his hand. Before he could cry out, she jerked his arm around behind his back and dropped him to the floor. Pressing her knee into his back, she trained the gun on his head. "Don't move. And don't make a sound. Logan, bring me a rope."

Logan, who was staring at her openmouthed, jumped down off the chair and brought the rope, helping her to tie José's hands behind his back. "You didn't learn that in NPS training."

A statement, not a question. So much for working undercover. But now wasn't the time to talk about her real identity.

He cut off a strip of cloth from the hem of his shirt and wrapped it around José's mouth. "Better gag him, too, just to be safe."

"Your boss isn't going to be too happy," Ashley said to the bound man, cinching another rope around his ankles. She glanced up at Logan, nodding at the door. "Is it clear?"

He looked out but then slid the door shut. "Guards pacing the perimeter. And the American will be back any minute. We've got a better chance on the roof."

"All right." Ashley stood, tucking José's gun into her waistband. Forget the Mexican laws. Their lives were on the line.

She followed Logan over to the chair underneath the hole he had carved into the ceiling. He jumped up onto it and a minute later expanded the hole wide enough to allow her shoulders through.

"Ladies first." His expression allowed no room for argument. "You can help me from up there. Stay low to the roof and close to the back wall so they don't see you from below."

Ashley nodded.

"When he comes back empty-handed," Logan continued, "he's going to be after blood. I don't want you anywhere near here. If you see anyone coming, get yourself as far away from here as you can."

"I'm not leaving you behind, so stop talking and help me up. I'll wait for you on the roof."

"No, you'll run if I tell you to." Logan's gaze was unyielding. "I'm training you, remember? That makes me in charge." He reached down to help her onto the chair.

Ashley took his hand and climbed up, finding herself suddenly only inches away from him. Her knees buckled a bit and she reached out a quick hand for the back of the chair. In response, Logan wrapped a steadying arm around her waist.

Avoiding eye contact and doing her best to keep her heart rate from skyrocketing, she said a bit breathlessly, "Okay, I'm ready. Lift me up."

"Try to keep your weight on the beams. Who knows how weak the rest of the adobe is."

Placing both hands on her waist, Logan lifted until she could squeeze her arms and shoulders out through the hole. Using the *viga* to support her weight, she carefully maneuvered the rest of her body until she was fully out in the bright, hot, sunshine.

Crouching low to the roof, Ashley glanced over the presidio. She let out a quick breath. No movement. She peeked back into the hole. "The coast looks clear so far. Let's get you out."

They both started digging through the adobe, Logan with his knife, Ashley scratching with her nails until her fingertips were raw. Finally the hole looked big enough to squeeze his broad shoulders through.

"Now what?" she asked. "How do we get you out?"

"Lie down and give me your hands. I can pull myself up, but you've got to hold on tight until I reach the exposed wood."

She did as he instructed, already feeling the sweat building on her palms. No pressure. She could do this... How much did he weigh, anyway?

Logan squeezed her hands, looking up at her in his steadfast way. "You can do this. Ready?"

Fortifying herself with a deep breath, Ashley tightened her grip on his hands. "Ready."

With a sudden strain on her arms, Logan heaved himself upward, using the back of the chair as extra leverage to help him gain enough height to reach the exposed log. The force of his weight on the chair back caused it to tip, until his feet were dangling in the air. He released one of her hands to find a handhold on the beam. For a split second, she thought he might fall, but at the last moment he dug his fingers into the wood.

She helped direct his other hand to the wood and waited as he pulled his head out through the hole, a crooked grin on his dusty face.

"Thanks," he said, puffing with exertion. The tendons and muscles in his lower arms could have been carved out of rock.

"Anytime." She dipped her chin in a quick nod.

Soon his upper body was through the hole. He was swinging up his other leg when voices below made them freeze. Ashley tensed, casting him an anxious glance.

Logan held a finger to his lips and motioned to the upper wall of the presidio running parallel to the roof. She followed him over to the wall and they ran along it toward the west end of the complex.

They had only gone a short distance when they heard the oak door open below. Almost immediately, shouting broke out, followed by random gunshots into the adobe roof.

Throwing caution to the wind, they stumbled ahead as fast as they could for the far wall of the complex. A voice called out from the courtyard below. Ashley ducked lower as bullets whizzed past her head.

A second later the shooting stopped. Two men climbed up onto the roof in pursuit. She didn't recognize one of them, but the other was the American she'd sent on the fool's errand to find the map. She could see the rage etched on his face from all the way across the roof.

She and Logan reached the far wall as the pursuing men opened fire. Logan cupped his hands for her to step up and she pulled herself onto the wall. Large chunks of adobe broke loose and fell on the far side as she scrambled to maintain her balance.

Logan hoisted himself up next to her, narrowly avoiding a gunshot to the leg, and grabbed her hand. "We have to jump."

A wave of horror crashed through her insides as she surveyed the huge drop on the far side. Fifteen, twenty feet? Enough to make her head swim.

But Logan yanked on her arm, shouting, "Now!"

In an instant she catapulted into the air, her stomach finding its way up into her throat, her legs scrambling to brace for impact.

A second later they hit the sand. Ashley's legs absorbed the brunt of the blow, but momentum carried her forward until she fell facedown into the scorching sand.

Logan was already pulling on her again, urging her to run.

The men hadn't jumped, but bullets bit into the sand at her feet. Pulling José's gun from her waistband, she fired a couple of shots in their direction before sprinting toward the river and the hope of safety.

Logan raced for the river, still in a partial state of shock at the way Ashley had taken down José like it was a training exercise. Even now, as they tore across the rough terrain, her face was a mask of concentration.

He zigzagged around the scrubby desert brush, his feet sinking deep into the sand with each step. Exertion stole the oxygen from his lungs, making his legs burn. And it was even harder for Ashley, who wasn't used to the heat or the landscape.

Yet there she was, barely lagging, in better physical condition than most park rangers.

Something about her wasn't adding up.

Gunfire sounded behind them again, another reminder now was not the time to ask.

"Where...are...we...going?" Ashley's question came out between gasps for air.

Logan had already been considering the answer as they ran toward the Rio Grande. The shouting and gunshots receded and he slowed the pace as they forced their way through the thick grasses and reeds near the river's edge.

"After we cross the river," he panted, "we'll try to lose them in the trees as we make our way back to the park's main road."

She nodded. "What about water?"

"The rangers keep a cache nearby, maybe a mile away. But we don't really have a choice."

"No, we don't." She gnawed her lip. "But I'd rather risk doubling back to San Vicente than turning into dinner for the turkey vultures. The river road isn't even paved, is it?"

Logan shook his head. "No. But we do patrol it. Prayerfully we'll meet a ranger before we have to walk all the way to Rio Grande Village."

The absence of gunfire suggested they hadn't been seen yet, but it was only a matter of time before their pursuers found their tracks. Taking Ashley's hand, Logan crept into the center of the river where the water was waist deep and the current was stronger. A bullet zinged past his shoulder.

Seconds later three men scrambled down the slope toward the river, shooting wildly as they came.

"Duck!" Logan called.

Ashley dived under in the nick of time, a bullet skipping past where she had been a heartbeat before.

The three men reached the river's edge. Two of them charged into the water while the other raised his weapon and fired.

Logan lunged forward. Searing pain ripped across his upper left arm as he kicked into a dive under the murky water. Bracing the injured arm against his side, he used the other arm to swim with the current, staying under as long as possible.

Surfacing with a splutter, he scanned the surface for Ashley. Her head bobbed downstream twenty yards ahead. They had traveled far enough that their entry point, with the solitary shooter, was now out of sight.

But the other two were still in the water somewhere behind them, firing as soon as Logan surfaced. He dove under again, accelerating to catch Ashley. His arm ached so badly it was impossible to use. But she was kicking against the current to wait for him and a moment later the current swept him to her position.

"There are two of them in the river behind us," he said, swimming alongside her.

"There." Ashley pointed downstream to a cluster of bushes on the US bank.

"Perfect."

They both kicked hard, trying to gain distance on their pursuers before reaching the bushes. Ashley fired off shots upstream to distract their pursuers as she and Logan clambered onto the grainy, wet sand.

Logan flung himself underneath one of the prickly bushes, pulling Ashley down beside him. She held the gun out, at the ready, as they waited.

The leafy undergrowth obscured much of their view of the river, but they watched in silence as two heads bobbed past, facing downstream.

Logan let out a long breath. "Praise God." He rolled onto his back. His arm throbbed mercilessly, and he hated to think about how many bacteria had just washed into the wound. But at least they were alive.

"You can say that again." Ashley propped herself up onto her elbows. "Now what?"

She glanced over her shoulders, as if assessing their options. But when her gaze swept across Logan, she stopped, her dark eyes filling with alarm.

"Logan, what is it? You're white as a sheet." She stared down at the sand between them, stained red from his blood. "You've been hit."

"My shoulder." He pointed across his body. "I'll be fine. Right now, we need to get away from the river before they decide to double back." Every word was becoming harder to get out as the pain radiated from his shoulder down through his upper chest and side. He hadn't even looked at it yet, but part of him felt nauseous just thinking about it. He had never done well with personal injuries.

It was much better to think about getting away.

Ashley watched him a moment longer, her brow compressed with concern. She checked over her shoulder again. "Still clear."

She crawled out from under the bush and crouched behind it, waiting as Logan gingerly slid out.

Her eyes went wide. "Your shirtsleeve is soaked with blood."

"Don't tell me that right now." Logan gritted his teeth against a wave of nausea. He nodded toward the north. "By my reckoning, we traveled half a mile down the river. That gives us about another quarter mile until we reach a couple of backcountry sites and the water cache. Keep low and behind the bushes as much as possible."

Ashley nodded. "All right, but we're going to look at that arm as soon as we get to the water. Got it?"

"Yes, ma'am."

And then maybe he'd finally get some answers as to how she'd taken out an armed man like it was her job.

THIRTEEN

Logan set out in the direction of the water cache, crouching low and dodging from bush to bush. It'd only be a matter of time before their pursuers decided to double back. Ashley stayed right behind him, gun at the ready.

As they approached the first campsite, he scoured the tree line for the telltale color of a tent. Nothing.

Ashley stopped beside him inside the cover of the trees. "See anyone?"

He shook his head, pointing. "The water cache is up that dirt road, toward River Road East."

Cautiously he led the way along the edge of the brush toward the large metal box serving as the cache.

Ashley tugged at the lock that secured the door.

"I've got the key." He fished into his pocket, breathing a quick prayer of thanks that his key ring had survived their river excursion.

He opened the door, revealing several gallons of water. He pulled two jugs out, setting them on the ground as Ashley rummaged through the first-aid kit. After relocking the box, they found a nearby copse of cottonwood trees that would offer some degree of protection.

Finding a patch of grass shielded by overhanging brush, he collapsed onto the ground. Ashley sat nearby, opening one of the gallons and offering it to him.

He waved her off. "You first."

She took a long drink before handing it back. "Mmm, 150-degree water. Too bad I didn't think to bring a tea bag." She wiped her lips with the back of her hand.

Logan chuckled. "Hey, out in here in the desert, this is liquid gold. Don't complain."

"We probably already swallowed enough river water to die of dysentery." She frowned.

"You survived just fine the last time you went swimming in the Rio Grande." Setting down the water, he gingerly touched the aching place on his left arm with his free hand, fresh blood coming away on his fingertips.

Ashley pulled his hand back. "Let me help you." The words were gentle and soft, like her touch.

He watched her as she examined the wound. The way her wet hair fell against the curve of her cheek. Long lashes framing thoughtful eyes. The sweet, subtle scent of berries that made it hard to concentrate when she was near.

Had he ever seen anyone so beautiful? And it wasn't only physical beauty. There was something about her— her inner strength and courage, the intelligence and compassion behind those eyes—that grabbed him deep inside. Made him want to protect her, even though she clearly didn't need his help.

Before he could stop himself, he reached out to

brush a finger against her cheek. He expected her to shy away, but instead her gaze turned to his. The depths of her eyes mirrored the same turmoil of emotions tucked inside his chest. Awareness. Fear. Longing. Hope. Was there love? Could there be so quickly?

His throat closed, seized with panic, and he jerked his hand back, inadvertently sending another shudder of pain through his body at the rapid movement.

Erin. For one brief, glorious moment he'd forgotten entirely about her and the way she'd shattered his heart.

He forced a deep breath. No matter what feelings were flitting through his chest, he couldn't act on them. Ashley had her own secrets and one day she would leave the same way Erin had. Hadn't he learned his lesson the first time?

Pushing the unsettling thoughts aside, he glanced at Ashley. She'd turned her attention back to his arm, but a flicker of hurt crossed her features before she pressed her lips together into a thin line. Irritated at him? Somehow, Logan didn't think so.

A relationship wasn't something either of them could afford right now, especially when it was guaranteed to fail.

He'd have to try harder, much harder, if he was going to protect them both.

When Ashley spoke again, her tone was even. "It looks like the bullet only grazed you, but the wound is deep. Your deltoid is torn and you're still losing blood."

"Deltoid? What are you, an undercover medical doctor?" he asked, half laughing, half grimacing.

Ashley didn't laugh. "Not exactly."

"What then?"

She didn't meet his gaze. "I'm going to rip off part of your sleeve, so I can clean this."

Avoiding the question? One way or another, he was going to get the truth out of her.

When she poured water over the wound, washing away sand and debris from the river, he bit his tongue in pain. "That…really…hurts…" he said through gritted teeth.

"I know." She smiled faintly, her eyes full of compassion. "And we haven't even gotten to the isopropanol yet." She held up a small bottle from the first-aid kit.

Logan groaned.

"Here. Squeeze my hand."

It fit perfectly inside his larger one, as if she belonged there with him. He kept his focus on their hands, even as his shoulder caught fire and red flamed in front of his vision.

A moment later she pulled her hand away. "All done. I've gotten as much dirt out as I can."

"You mean I won't die of a strep infection?"

"You're going to be fine." It took a couple of minutes more for her to bind the wound with a roll of sterile gauze. Using the rest of his shirt as a sling, she secured the injured arm to his side.

"Thank you. I'm glad you paid attention during first aid."

She gave him a crooked smile. "I bet you didn't think your training job would be so easy."

"You call this easy?" He held up his hand and she pulled him to his feet.

He felt better after the rest, but not as strong as he

would've liked, especially since they might have to walk several more miles if a car didn't drive by.

Ashley stayed beside him, ready to help if he needed it. Her shoulders were tense, her face wary, as she watched the surrounding foliage for any sign of their pursuers.

After they had reached the unpaved road along the river, Logan broke the silence. "Can I ask you something?"

"Of course." Her dark brows pulled together, head tilting to one side.

"Who are you?"

Ashley swallowed, staring at her feet as she trudged up the dusty road. "I'm sorry I put you in danger." She glanced at him after a long moment.

"That wasn't what I asked." His face was pale and drawn from the injury, but his eyes were drilling a hole through her head.

No choice but to trust him now. If he was working for Jimenez, if he was the inside man, he'd just blown several perfect opportunities to kill her. And unless she left the park, she was going to keep placing his life in danger.

He deserved to know why.

"My real name is Ashley Thompson. I'm an agent for the Federal Bureau of Investigation." She glanced sharply at him, waiting for some kind of response, but he merely watched her, his gaze unreadable. "I was sent here undercover to track Rico Jimenez."

He was quiet for a long moment. "I've heard of Jimenez. He's a cartel boss. But why are you *here*? I thought he operated mainly to the west, south of Arizona."

"Not anymore. At least, not according to FBI intel."

"And those men in San Vicente, you think they're part of his cartel?"

"Yes." She gnawed at her lip. Might as well come out with all of it. "The reason I wanted to go to San Vicente wasn't for the chapel. I had to meet a contact. Jimenez must've found out and sent those men after us."

His eyes narrowed. "When did you meet with this contact? I was with you the whole time." His gaze drifted to her arm, the one no longer carrying a souvenir blanket, and he raised his brows. "Ah. The shopping. Now that makes more sense."

She nodded. "I met him behind the chapel while you were taking pictures." She filled him in briefly on what the man had said. "Jimenez is working the mine."

Logan shook his head. "No, not possible. No way he could keep something like that secret, even in a remote place like this."

She arched an eyebrow. "Oh, really? Dick Barclay gave me a file on him, and it was almost empty. But my file from the FBI contains *pages* of tips we've received of his activity through this park. He's doing it, all right, and he's doing it right under our noses."

He frowned. "But why are you here undercover? Why didn't the feds tell us?"

"I asked myself the same thing, until I pieced it together from the files on my laptop. He's got someone on the inside, Logan. How else could he be smuggling drugs and cartel members through here without being caught? That's why I couldn't say anything to you. Barclay and Ed Chambers think I'm here undercover to avoid scaring Jimenez off, but the real reason is to find the mole in the park service."

He ran his good hand through his hair, turning even paler. "That explains a few things." His green gaze was steady. "Thank you for trusting me."

"Well—" her lips tipped up "—if it was your job to get rid of me, you've failed miserably."

"The last thing I want to do is get rid of you." The gentle tone of his voice made her cheeks flush. "Does this mean you'll let me help you?"

"I've already put you in enough danger." Her chest constricted. "Besides, Barclay threatened to tell my boss about the head injury if I didn't bring him hard proof of Jimenez's activity. I've got nothing to report so far other than nearly getting both of us killed." She gestured at Logan's chest. "And losing a National Park Service camera."

"Jimenez's thugs stole it." He raised an eyebrow. "That hardly counts as losing it. Besides, we still have the map. We even know what trail to search, thanks to your contact. And we've seen the view from San Vicente. I'm sure I can dig up some photographs from the archives to help us narrow the search radius."

"You're just trying to make me feel better."

"Is it working?" The skin around his eyes crinkled as he grinned.

"Maybe." Ashley smiled back. "You're not mad at me?"

"For what?"

"Lying to you about who I am."

"No. You were doing your job. I probably would've done the same thing." He cocked his head to one side, eyeing her for a moment. "But what about the memory loss? The first day I met you? Did you remember any of this?"

She shook her head. "I figured it out when I got home to Panther Junction and found my badge. But I couldn't tell you. Even though I wanted to…" Her voice trailed away, remembering both the frustrating darkness in her mind and how much she'd wanted to trust Logan. A part of her felt very glad he knew the truth now.

His hand slipped around hers, rough and warm and comfortable, and a tangle of emotions fluttered through her chest.

"Thank you for telling me now. I want to help you." He gave her hand a squeeze and then released it, leaving her fingers cold despite the afternoon heat.

"I know." But how could he help? Realistically, Barclay would be on the phone with Morton the second he heard about what had happened today.

Logan cut into her thoughts. "Do you remember anything more about what happened to you that first day?"

"No. And I can't think of any reason why I would even be driving down there." So frustrating, these remaining bits of missing information. She frowned. "I've got this nagging feeling it has something to do with my brother. But that doesn't make any sense."

They walked in silence for a few moments. She kept glancing at Logan, at the way his brows knit together in concentration. Processing everything she'd told him.

He kicked a rock. Stared at his boots. Ran a hand through his hair. Stared at the horizon. When he finally looked at her again, he wouldn't hold her gaze. "I might have an idea." He hesitated. "You said your brother's name was Sam, right? Sam Thompson?"

"Yes." Why was Logan looking at her like that?

"Do you remember what he did? Where he worked?"

She thought for a long moment. "It's not DC. Somewhere else, far away. At first, I could only remember him being in school, but that would've been two years ago." She frowned. "Why are you asking?" And why was he using past tense?

Logan kept watching her, waiting, as if he knew the answer already and wanted her to work it out for herself.

"What?" she asked impatiently.

He pressed his lips together. "I think I knew him, Ashley. If it's the same Sam Thompson, I think he worked here."

She stared at Logan, not sure she'd heard him correctly. "But…how? How could you know him?" Something twisted inside her chest—the same feeling she had every time she looked at his photograph. Or remembered that she wasn't on speaking terms with God.

"It might not be the same man," Logan said quietly. "But we lost a ranger about three months ago. His name was Sam Thompson. He was young—early twenties. One of the most joyful people I've ever met."

"'Lost him'?" She repeated the words slowly, her brain struggling to catch up. Dead? She shook her head. "Sam's still alive. He couldn't be the same person. I know…"

Her voice dwindled away as images flung themselves into her conscious mind. A phone call and a broken drinking glass, crystal splinters scattered across the tile of her apartment floor… Her mother clutching

her father and weeping like her heart had split in two…
A closed wooden casket and a church full of people
dressed in black…

She pressed her hand to her mouth, stifling the sob
trying to choke her. Her throat burned, tears stinging
her eyes.

"I'm sorry." Logan wrapped his good arm around
her back, pulling her to his chest. "I'm so sorry. Those
aren't the good memories to get back."

"I don't…" She swallowed but the lump wouldn't go
away. Burying her face into Logan's shirt didn't help.
"I don't know what happened. How could I forget?"

He stroked her hair, his touch gentle and soothing.
"It was only three months ago, Ashley. Your brain is
still healing."

"What…what happened to him?" So hard to breathe.
As if someone had dropped a heavy rock on her chest.

"He didn't come back from patrol. We sent out a
search-and-rescue team, and…" His voice trailed away,
his eyes full of raw emotion. Whatever had happened,
he hadn't recovered from it yet.

"And?" she prompted softly.

"We…" He swallowed. "I…found the body a half
mile off the trail. He didn't have any water with him.
He'd wandered off the trail, gotten lost without proper
supplies…and…we were too late." Logan's voice
cracked.

Ashley dug her forehead back into his shirt, shaking her head. It shouldn't be true and yet… His words
struck a chord of truth deep inside her. Hadn't she felt
sick to her stomach every time she looked at pictures
of Sam?

Latent memories of him trickled into her mind. His

laughter. All the lame jokes he used to tell. His insistence on going to church every week. His love of camping and the outdoors… Suddenly she could picture him in a ranger's uniform. Maybe he *had* worked here. But—

"No," she insisted. "That couldn't have been Sam. It must have been someone else. He was an expert outdoorsman. He never would've gone out unprepared."

"Maybe it wasn't your brother. I don't know. But I do know the desert is a harsh place and even experts have underestimated it before."

"But wasn't he trained? I mean, you all wouldn't have sent him out alone if he didn't know the trails or know how much water to carry, right?"

Logan didn't meet her eyes as he answered. "No, we wouldn't have. A rookie ranger can't go on patrol alone until their trainer verifies they're ready."

"So…what, then?" Ashley asked sharply. Anger felt so much better than the misery of grief. "Someone sent him out too soon? Who trained him?"

Logan stared straight ahead down the road, a muscle twitching in his jaw.

After a long time he turned to her and Ashley's breath caught at the storm of sorrow and self-reproach in his eyes.

"I did."

FOURTEEN

"Oh, Logan." All the anger had melted out of her voice. She pulled away from his chest and laid a hand on his arm. Logan had to resist the overwhelming urge to pull away from the touch meant to comfort. He didn't deserve comfort. "It couldn't have been your fault. You're excellent at what you do."

"Would you still say that if you knew for sure it was your brother?"

She looked down at the dirt. "I have his picture at home, in Panther Junction. I'll show it to you when we get back."

If *we get back*, Logan thought. Sometimes no amount of knowing about a place was enough to guarantee survival. He and Ashley might end up meeting the same fate as Sam—dehydration and heat stroke.

He hadn't said anything to Ashley, but he was feeling worse the longer they walked. There might come a point where he would have to send her on alone, without his help—a terrifying thought. Whether the Big Bend Sam had been her brother or not, Logan didn't think he could take losing another ranger that way.

And the closer the sun got to the horizon, the more their chances of spending the night out here increased.

When he stumbled over a rock in the path, Ashley glanced up at him, a crease forming between her brows. "How much farther is it to the main road?"

"Longer than I'd like," he admitted. "Maybe two or three miles. But the hot spring site is closer, maybe a mile from here."

"Will anyone be there this time of day?"

He sighed. "Hit or miss. It's popular with tourists, but it's also right on the river. We might run into the shooters."

"I think it's a chance we'll have to take." She took his good arm in hers. "Let me help you."

They didn't talk much over the next half hour. Logan concentrated on each step, one foot in front of the other, and the steady support of the woman beside him.

The sun had become a giant orange ball dipping behind the Chisos Mountains by the time Logan caught sight of the low buildings that marked the hot spring. The natural spring of hot water, located right next to the Rio Grande, had been discovered and used by early European settlers hundreds of years ago. A small town had sprung up at one point, complete with a general store and post office. But, like most small towns in so remote an area, its lifetime had been short-lived and now only a few ramshackle, abandoned buildings remained.

The park service had built a parking lot near the old town and a trail to the hot spring itself, a few hundred yards away near the river. It was a favorite swimming hole for park visitors, but not usually this late in the day.

He hadn't expected anyone to be there, but that didn't prevent the disappointment that washed over him anyway as they walked past the hot spring and up to the trail leading to the parking lot.

"It'll be another two miles from here to the main road." He struggled to keep his voice even.

"We can do it." Ashley smiled encouragingly, but the creases lingered between her eyes.

They rounded the bend leading past the old post office. Suddenly slamming car doors broke the silence. Two engines started, one after the other. One of the vehicles pulled away immediately, but the other idled for one precious moment.

Ashley's gaze darted to his.

Logan pulled his arm away. "Run."

She raced up the slope toward the paved lot, waving her arms and yelling so loudly they'd certainly be shot if their pursuers were anywhere nearby.

But then he crested the hill behind her and saw a truck. And—*oh, thank You, Lord*—it was the dark green of the park service. But it was almost out of the parking lot.

"Stop!" Ashley yelled, waving her arms and chasing it from behind.

The truck slammed into Reverse and pulled to a stop a short distance away. The door opened.

Ed Chambers. Logan's legs went weak as relief flooded his insides. He sank to his knees and waited as Ashley and the chief ranger ran over to him.

"Ed…"

"Hey, brother." Ed knelt. "Looks like you got yourself into a bit of a tussle. I can't wait to hear the story."

Logan arched his eyebrows. "It's pretty exciting…"

"I'm sure it is. You can tell me about it on the way to the clinic. Ashley, help me get him to the truck."

Ashley slid into the center of the truck's single bench seat and helped Logan into the passenger seat. Ed climbed in behind the wheel.

The distance to Terlingua was excruciatingly long: an hour up past Panther Junction, plus another out to the west entrance.

As they drew near to Panther Junction, Ed glanced at Ashley. "I imagine you'll want to come to Terlingua, too. Otherwise, I can drop you off here."

Logan could swear red tinted Ashley's cheeks. Ed did have a knack for reading the human heart.

Graciously, Ed continued, "You might need to get looked at, too. Seems like you've had quite a day out there."

His friend had *no* idea.

Ashley and Ed had been sitting in the waiting room at the Terlingua medical center for a good hour. A nurse had examined Ashley and, after painfully removing at least a dozen cactus spines and cleaning out several cuts, she'd offered some ibuprofen and released her. Now, as they waited for Logan, Ashley shared as many details as she could. Ed already knew she was with the FBI and searching for Jimenez, but she didn't tell him about the map or her real motive for being undercover.

"So, what did they want from you?" Ed scratched his forehead.

Ashley shrugged. She hated lying to him, almost as much as she had hated lying to Logan. But she still didn't know whom she could trust, and she certainly didn't want to put anyone else in danger. "Somehow they knew we were with the park service. I think they wanted to find out how much we knew. If we were on to them or not."

Ed nodded. "This is bad news for us, for the park. If word leaks out that a cartel is operating through here, we'll lose our tourists, even after Jimenez is long gone."

"We don't have any proof yet," Ashley cautioned. The last thing she wanted was to scare Jimenez off before she and Logan found the mine. She hoped today's escape wouldn't be enough to do so.

"But you have the tips that brought you here in the first place. And your contact. Did he give you any details on where Jimenez is operating?"

Nothing she could share. Especially before she figured out who the insider was in the park service. "Nothing we can act on quite yet. I need to discuss this with my supervisor at the Bureau before we do anything."

"All right," Ed agreed. "But if we find those gunmen on this side of the Rio Grande, I'm arresting them."

"Fair enough."

"How much does Logan know about you?"

Ashley got the feeling the question pertained as much to his friend's well-being as it did to the safety of her mission. "Everything." Finally, something she didn't have to lie about. "I couldn't keep it a secret anymore."

He stared at the empty plastic chairs across the room for a moment, his expression thoughtful. But then his features relaxed into a grin. "Well, you chose wisely. I'd trust that man with my life."

"I know." She studied her hands. If only things could be different. If only she and Logan could have met under normal circumstances, not in this web of intrigue and danger.

"He's had his heart broken before." Ed's soft words pulled her out of her reverie. "He's a good man, but you have to be patient with him."

"Why are you telling me this?" She cocked her head to the side.

"Because I can see something's there, between the two of you. It's taken him a long time to get over the past."

"I…" She started to deny it but gave up. If it was so obvious Ed could see it, there wasn't any point in lying to him. Or to herself, for that matter.

Ed smiled. "He'd probably kill me if he knew I told you that."

"Told her what?" Logan stood at the entrance to the waiting room. His arm was bandaged and secured in a proper sling, and his face had some of its regular color back. A smile played on his lips, at odds with his narrowed eyes.

"That you are the most stubborn, toughest ranger I've ever had the pleasure of working with." Ed rose to his feet and clapped Logan on his good arm.

"They say I'll live. And they didn't even have to amputate." Logan shot them a lopsided grin. "Thanks to you two."

"I'm just grateful Ed was at the hot spring," Ashley said.

"God was very merciful to us." Logan shook his head.

As much as Ashley wanted to leave God out of the equation, she had to agree the timing had been downright providential. Another minute later and they would've missed Ed entirely.

"What were you doing there, anyway, Ed?" Logan asked as they headed for the exit.

He shrugged. "I had a meeting with Adam Smith to talk about opening up the old post office and general store for visitors." Glancing at Ashley, he added, "He's the chief of resource management."

Ed turned back to Logan. "I was there all afternoon. Your girl here caught me seconds before I drove off. I'm glad you weren't any later."

Ashley frowned as she thought about what could have happened. Catching Ed's reference to her, she glanced up to see Logan's eyes go wide. For one moment she imagined what it would be like to be with someone like him—respected, loved, secure. An equal, valued partner. She'd put her career first for so long, she'd never realized what she was missing.

Her heart hurt. Maybe someday.

Right now, she had a case to solve.

She cleared her throat. "It's late. We'd better get back to headquarters."

The heat of the day had faded into a cool desert night by the time they arrived at Panther Junction.

"I'll talk to the superintendent about what happened," Ed said. "You two get some rest. I don't want to see either of your faces skulking around the park tomorrow, got it? Logan, you need to give that arm a chance to heal, so I want you to take off a couple of days, at least. I'm sure the superintendent will agree with me."

"Maybe a day or two," Logan said begrudgingly. "But I don't want to be left out of the loop."

"Don't worry, I'll keep you informed." Ed waved good-night.

"He's right, you know." The first stars glittered above as Ashley and Logan strolled toward his house. "You do need time to recover." She tapped her temple. "Especially with the head injury."

"I can't let you go looking for that mine alone and, if I know you, that's exactly what you'll do while I'm lying around on my couch resting."

"I guess you know me pretty well." She grinned. "But if it makes you feel any better, I don't know where to look yet. All I've got is the trail name."

"How about if we try to track down some pictures in the archives? I'm not so incapacitated I can't at least do that."

She nodded. "All right. But sleep in tomorrow. I won't do anything stupid."

"Promise?"

"Pinky swear."

Logan held out his good hand and she hooked her little finger with his, sending a jolt of warmth up her arm. "I'm going to hold you to that."

They reached his house but Logan didn't turn toward his door. "I'm taking you home."

"You don't need to," Ashley protested, facing him. His sandy-brown hair stuck out at odd angles after the chaos of their day, and she was filled with the sudden urge to touch it. *Absolutely not.*

"I know. I want to." His eyes were gentle. Caring. But then he stared down at the sidewalk. "And I want to see your brother's picture."

Of course. *Of course.* She was letting her personal feelings get in the way of work again. Logan wanted to help her catch Jimenez and get her memories back. He had never communicated an interest in anything more—not with words, anyway—and even if he did… She wasn't interested. She couldn't be interested. The job came first.

Her front door was still locked. She exhaled slowly as she dug her key out of her pocket. Apparently whoever had tried to break in the first time hadn't gained the courage to try again. Either that or they were extremely good at replacing everything the way she had left it.

"Where is the map, anyway?" Logan sat on her sofa.

"I've been carrying it with me." She glanced down at her waist.

"I'm glad they didn't search you."

"Me, too." She stepped inside her bedroom, pulling the cloth pouch out of the place where it had rubbed against her skin all day, and brought the map and the picture of Sam back to the living room. "At least I put it in a plastic bag, so it wouldn't get wet. Learned my lesson after the Jeep incident."

She handed the picture to Logan. "I found it in my wallet. It took me too long to remember who he was."

"It's not because you didn't love him," he said softly, taking the picture from her. She could scarcely breathe as she waited for him to say something.

He stared at the snapshot for a long moment before looking up, his eyes glistening in the lamplight. "I'm so, so sorry, Ashley." His voice broke. "Sam told me he had a sister who lived in DC, but I never made the connection until I heard your real last name. He never gave us any details about you."

She bit her lip, letting out a painful laugh. "He knew

better than to divulge any of my secrets." Probably the only reason she managed to convince Morton to let her come here undercover. Nobody knew they were related.

"We had a memorial service here, so none of us traveled to the funeral."

Her eyes burned, and Ashley impatiently wiped the tears away as she took the picture back. "He wasn't very old, was he? Younger than me."

"Twenty-three." Logan pressed his lips together.

"Just out of college, then." She tried to keep the bitterness out of her voice, but there was so much of it filling her heart. It wasn't fair.

"It should never have happened." He dragged his hand over his face, through his hair. "I never should have sent him out there alone."

She dropped onto the cushion beside him. "It wasn't your fault. I know you well enough to know you wouldn't have let Sam go unless you thought he was ready. And, like I said, Sam knew his way around the outdoors." She wiped again at her cheeks. "Whatever happened wasn't your fault."

"Thank you for saying that. I still feel like I failed him. Like I should have gotten there or found him sooner. There must've been something I could've done differently."

"You're not all-powerful, Logan. You can't hold yourself to that standard." She looked down at her lap. "But Someone else is and He *could* have saved my brother. He just…didn't care." She pursed her lips, clenching her teeth before any more of the ugliness inside spilled out. Logan didn't deserve it.

"Oh, Ashley." The agony in his eyes threatened to break her angry heart into a thousand shards. "Is that what you think? That God took him away because He doesn't care?"

The bubble of unshed tears formed a solid lump in Ashley's throat. She swallowed. "What I think doesn't matter. It doesn't change the facts. Sam is gone and it doesn't make any sense."

"No, it doesn't make any sense to *us*." His warm hand rested on her knee. "Grief is a terrible, unavoidable part of this life. But it doesn't change the fact that God loves us, so much He was willing to die for us. We may never know or understand why Sam died. But God wants us to trust Him. And to let Him comfort us."

She wiped at her cheeks again. Stupid tears. If she didn't get Logan out of there soon, she'd turn into an unhinged, blubbering mess. "I'm sorry. It's obviously been a long day. I need some rest."

He pulled his hand back. "Of course. Get some sleep. I'll find you in the morning. And, Ashley? Be safe, okay? If anyone tries to get in here, you call me right away. Got it?"

She nodded. "I'll see you later, Logan."

The door latched shut with a soft click.

Gone. Sam was gone and there was nothing she could do about it. And though Logan's unwavering faith tugged at her heart, she could never trust God again, not the way Logan wanted her to.

Yet another reason she could never think of him as more than a colleague.

Ashley managed to flip the dead bolt into place and sink onto the couch before the tears she'd been holding back all night escaped.

FIFTEEN

No one tried to break in during the night, though Ashley had half expected it. She slept with the map inside her shirt and her gun under her pillow. It wasn't until almost morning that she finally fell into a deep sleep. Her first thoughts when she woke were of Sam.

Missing memories had come back in the night, spurred on by what she'd learned. She could picture Sam's excitement when he'd gotten the job out here. How she had promised to visit him, but several months had passed and she'd never done it.

Later, Sam. I'll be able to get away later. There had never been a good time.

Until now, when it was too late. Her mouth filled with the taste of bitterness again. Dwelling on the past wouldn't help.

At least she knew now why she'd fought to get this assignment. To be a little closer to her brother and to see the place he'd loved. The same way Logan loved it.

The new day was beautiful in its own way. Dewdrops on the cactus spines and thick succulents glittered like diamonds in the early morning sunlight. Ashley sucked in a lungful of the fresh, pure mountain air as she took the familiar path to headquarters.

Hopefully, Logan was still asleep. In the meantime, she needed to update Morton and find a way to stall Barclay. Three days had come and gone.

Sandy, the receptionist, smiled pleasantly as Ashley entered the air-conditioned building. "Dr. Barclay would like to see you in his office."

No surprise there. "Thanks." She forced a smile, trying to ignore the knot in her stomach.

She knocked on his door, which was already ajar, and peeked her head inside. "Dr. Barclay?"

Barclay sat behind his metal desk, eyes closed, fingers rubbing the bridge of his nose beneath his eyeglasses. He waved her inside without looking up.

She closed the door and stood, waiting, gnawing the inside of her cheek.

"Have a seat, Thompson." He watched her expectantly, waiting until she sat. Dark circles under his eyes testified to a bad night's sleep. "What happened yesterday?"

"I had to meet a contact," she began, telling him nearly verbatim the same story she'd given Ed, leaving out any details that could possibly trickle back to Jimenez and scare him off.

"Do you realize what a mess you've created? Shots fired at the border? Not to mention the property damage to one of their historical sites. How am I going to explain this to the Mexican government?"

Anger flared in her gut. "Dr. Barclay, those were Jimenez's men. Somehow they knew I'd be down there. What else were we supposed to do?"

"Avoid the situation in the first place, Agent Thompson." His eyes grew hard. "I told you to do your job and get out. Now you've created an international incident I'll have to smooth over with the local authorities."

"You gave me three days to give you proof," she insisted. "Well, here it is."

Barclay shook his head and something about his expression made her heart plunge. "Not good enough." He picked up the handset of his phone, pressing one of the buttons. "Here she is, Agent Morton."

Lead filled Ashley's stomach, but she accepted the receiver and pasted on a smile. "Sir? I've almost got the proof on Jimenez we need. Another twenty-four hours will be enough."

"And the other part of your mission?" Morton asked gruffly.

The mole. If only she had more to tell him—not that she could in front of Barclay. "No leads. Yet. But I'm close."

"Barclay will have my head," he grumbled. "But all right, Thompson. Twenty-four hours. Tell him I'm pulling you. Today's Friday. If you don't get what you need, be back here by Monday morning and we'll find another angle. Got it?"

"Yes, sir." She sighed heavily for effect. "I'll be back by Monday." She passed the receiver to Barclay, slumping in her seat.

His smile was smug. "And good riddance. Now go pack your bags and make your travel arrangements."

She stood, pressing her lips together to keep from smiling. With a salute at the door, she turned away to search for Logan.

"How long have you been down here?" Ashley appeared in the doorway to the archive room, her pretty lips quirked despite the way her forehead crinkled.

Logan shrugged. "An hour, maybe?" He hadn't exactly paid attention to the time. Sleep had been impossible once his pain meds had worn off, and he couldn't afford to spend the day doped up on whatever that was they'd prescribed for him. It made a whole lot more sense to come down to the basement of headquarters, where they stored all the archival material, and to get to work searching for the photographs they wanted.

"You were supposed to come find me." She pulled out the metal chair on the opposite side of his table and plopped down. "You were *supposed* to sleep in."

"I couldn't. You were with Barclay. Besides—" he gestured to the stack of cardboard document boxes on the table "—there's plenty to do. Might as well get started instead of squandering the day sleeping."

She scowled again. "You're going to work yourself into an early grave."

"I won't be alone." He gave her a pointed look, grinning when she rolled her eyes.

"So, what've you got?" She leaned forward over the table and scanned the open file spread out in front of him.

"Nothing yet. I started with the oldest boxes that might have photographs. We had some records from the 1920s, but nothing from San Vicente. Now I'm up to the 1950s." He thumbed through the files remaining in the top box, its label "San Vicente and Boquillas" cracking with age. "Here, try this one."

They worked in companionable silence, sifting through yellowed newspaper articles, old documents and black-and-white photographs.

"Wait a minute." Logan let out a whoosh of air. Finally, they were getting somewhere.

Ashley brushed hair out of her face and leaned across the table. "What've you got?"

He sorted through the old photographs, one after another. "The presidio. The marketplace." He held one up, grinning. "The chapel. Looks pretty much the same today." His pulse quickened.

A series of pictures followed in which the photographer had turned in a circle, capturing a panorama… "Here." He held it up triumphantly.

The Chisos range, as seen from the chapel steps, stared back at him from the photograph. A tiny "April 1957" was handwritten on the bottom right corner.

"And it's even springtime," he proclaimed, exultant.

She wiggled her fingers. "Let me see."

He stood, walked around the edge of the table, set down the photograph and swiveled the desk light closer. Together he and Ashley hunched over the picture, their shoulders touching, as he held a magnifying glass above it. The top of Lost Mine Peak was visible, along with portions of the south face stretching down into the V-shaped wedge made by Juniper Canyon.

He grinned at her like a kid on Christmas break.

Her dark eyes gleamed. So beautiful.

And so close. The air crackled between them. How easy it would be to give in to these wild feelings surging in his chest, to bridge the distance and kiss her.

Something shifted in her eyes and she averted her gaze back to the photograph.

Logan swallowed. What was *wrong* with him? Colleagues. Erin. Foolish heart. He cleared his throat and reached for a blank piece of paper. "Let's narrow this down to where the light would hit first."

After overlaying the paper on the image, he traced

the outline of the mountain and the surrounding terrain. A spur of Pummel Peak, to the east, would obscure everything but the top two thousand feet or so as the sun rose. He shaded in the remaining area, comparing it again with the photograph. "What trail did your contact say they were using?"

Ashley spread out a park map and studied it, nibbling at one of her fingertips. "He said the access was from Pine Canyon Trail, but they're driving the gold out through Juniper Canyon. To here."

"Mariscal Mountain. One of the least accessible areas of the park." Logan traced the route with his pencil. "Maybe even using the old mercury mine as a base, though that's open to any tourists brave enough to off-road out there." He tapped the pencil on the table. "Nobody's reported anything suspicious."

"Think we can find the mine?" Her eyebrows lifted, but her expression fell as she surveyed his arm wrapped in its sling. "You can't go out there."

"I absolutely can. Reconnaissance only."

Her face lit up. "Deal."

The sun was high overhead and blazing hot as Ashley hoisted her pack onto her back and started down Pine Canyon Trail after Logan. She'd insisted on carrying the camera and all the water for the hike—a full gallon, even though they'd only be out here a couple of hours.

Already her shirt clung to her back with sweat, making it hard not to think of Sam. How exhausted, how hot, how thirsty he must have been. He was probably delirious by the end. She hadn't had the stomach to ask Logan about the condition his body had been in—whether the vultures or coyotes had found it.

The trail wound upward as it left the open desert plateau and entered Pine Canyon. Inside the steep walls, pinyon pines, oaks and maples replaced the cactuses of the open desert, providing welcome relief from the sun.

Logan slowed the pace as they neared Lost Mine Peak.

Jimenez's men could be anywhere—he was bound to have guards along this path. Shooting a couple of rangers would get him noticed by the park service, but still… Ashley wouldn't put anything past him.

They followed the path around a bend. A rocky slope rose steeply on the right. To the left, a small ridge diverged from the level of the path, increasing in elevation as it ran westward. The canyon narrowed considerably ahead but appeared to open again where the ridge curved away to the south and the path disappeared into the trees.

She stopped Logan, pointing at the ridge. "What do you think?" she whispered. "Could we see well enough from up there?"

He nodded. "Should give us a good view of the south face. And provide some cover."

"Let me go first, okay?"

He frowned, but moved aside, following Ashley as she picked her way up the ridge. After another half hour, they reached a place near the end of the ridge where it widened enough to provide a decent lookout—maybe a hundred feet from where the path below disappeared into the woods.

She and Logan crouched behind the cover of some scrubby bushes as she took off the pack and pulled out the camera. They both crawled forward—awkward for

Logan with his bound arm—until they could see over the edge of the ridge. She spent several minutes snapping pictures with the digital camera, from the top of the peak to the trail below.

"See anything?" he whispered.

She shook her head. "Nothing. Hopefully, the pictures will help." She was about to suggest heading back when voices echoed off the canyon walls.

Logan stiffened beside her.

Craning her neck for a better view, she watched as three men emerged from an invisible cleft in the rock partway up the mountain face, maybe twenty feet east of where the path ended. The sun glinted off an AK-47 assault rifle slung over one of the men's backs. She zoomed in with the camera, snapping a series of shots. The one with the gun kept glancing down at the path and along the trail.

Beside her, Logan propped up a pair of binoculars with one hand. "To think that thing's been there this whole time," he whispered, "and we never knew."

"Surely this will be enough proof for Morton."

Ashley kept taking pictures until two of the men turned back inside the opening. The third, the one with the gun, picked his way down the mountainside to the trail fifty feet below. He pulled the rifle off his back and propped it up against one shoulder as he started down the trail to the east, in the direction of the trailhead.

She exchanged a glance with Logan. "Now what?"

His forehead crinkled into a frown. "They can't be patrolling this trail like that all the time. Otherwise we'd have gotten reports or seen one of them. What if he runs into a hiker?"

"We'd better go after him. Make sure the trail is

safe, in case anybody else is out here." She backed out from under the bushes, stowing the camera in her pack.

"Agreed. But no gunfire or else we'll scare them away before we can get back here with a team."

The sun was slipping behind Emory Peak as they worked their way carefully back down the ridge, keeping vigilant watch on the trail for any sign of the guard. Long shadows shrouded the wooded trail and each step over twigs and decaying leaves echoed too loudly off the silent trees.

Far off in the distance, something shrieked—a high-pitched scream, almost like that of a child. A shiver of fear skittered down Ashley's spine. She stopped, silently clutching Logan's hand.

Mountain lion. He mouthed the words.

It was getting close to dusk, wasn't it? The time predators came out. She took a couple of deep breaths, trying to slow her hammering heart. He squeezed her hand and released it, his fingers drifting toward his holster as he freed his other arm from its sling.

How much did mountain lions weigh? Enough to crush a person, she guessed. And then there were the claws. And the teeth.

This place was a long way from the streets of Washington, DC.

Breathe, she reminded herself. *Federal agents don't panic.* The canyon walls pressed in close on either side of the trees, and the darkness seemed to grow exponentially. Good thing she wasn't alone.

The path curved ahead, bending out of sight through a clump of trees. That one on the right, with the thick trunk, would be perfect for someone to hide behind, waiting.

Her fingers were on her gun before she realized it, nerves and instinct doing the decision-making. She pulled it out and released the safety, keeping it low and to the side, even though her conscious mind told her she was being paranoid.

Logan glanced back at her, shaking his head slightly. They'd agreed no gunfire. But his own fingers rested on the weapon in his holster.

The scream came again, louder this time. Exactly how long were a mountain lion's claws?

Only a few feet to go now to that bend.

A sudden flurry of motion in the bushes made Ashley swivel to the left, gun in front, as her heart leaped into her throat.

Two eyes gleamed up at her from beneath large ears in the growing twilight. A jackrabbit. Her breath came out in a ragged sort of laugh as it bolted across the path. She *was* being paranoid, but she wasn't used to dealing with criminals *and* wildlife.

Logan smirked, shaking his head at her. He walked forward again, passing the big tree without anything cataclysmic happening.

So much for all her hunches.

She let out a deep sigh as another sound from behind made her jump. From the right this time; probably the jackrabbit's cousin. She started to turn but something cold and hard jabbed into her side.

The muzzle of a gun.

"Drop it," the voice said. A man with a thick Spanish accent. Jimenez's guard.

SIXTEEN

Logan pulled his gun and spun around on the trail the moment he heard the man's voice. He inched back around the big tree until Ashley came into view. It was the same man they'd seen from the ridge, his rifle crammed into Ashley's ribs. Her jaw was clenched tight and both hands were up in the air, still clutching her gun.

"Freeze!" Logan ordered, aiming his weapon at the portion of the man's chest exposed on Ashley's right side. He was painfully aware how easily the man could shoot her before he could do anything about it. Beads of sweat formed on his forehead, but he kept his voice level. "I'm a law-enforcement ranger with the National Park Service. Put the gun down and back away from the lady. No one needs to get hurt."

The man shifted, moving further behind Ashley to use her as a shield. "Both of you, guns down. Now. Or I shoot her."

Logan gritted his teeth, trying to keep his heart from bursting out of his rib cage. Ashley's face was pale but her gaze was steely in the fading light. Silently, she mouthed the words, *Take the shot.* So much trust.

His chest filled with warmth, even though his injured arm shook from the strain of keeping his gun steady.

He raised the gun to aim at the man's head, above Ashley's right shoulder. "You know we can't do that."

A loud scream rent the air—the mountain lion—so close even Logan started. Ashley's eyes went wide, the whites visible around her dark irises.

"¡Espíritu de Chisos!" the guard gasped. He glanced around at the dark woods, letting the rifle drop from Ashley's back.

All the chance she needed. She spun, shoving the rifle up and away from her body and aiming her own weapon at his torso. He reacted almost instantly, angling the muzzle out of her reach and slamming the butt of the rifle into her face before she could fire.

Logan lunged forward as she stumbled to the side, blood streaming from her nose. He drove his good shoulder into the man's stomach, sending the assault rifle flying and both of them crashing to the ground.

"Logan, the gun!" Ashley called, her voice muffled by the blood.

The man twisted and strained to reach the rifle, but Logan pushed off his chest and stretched as his injured shoulder screamed in protest. His fingertips found the strap and he flung the weapon backward out of reach. The man twisted again, trying to knock Logan off, but he pressed his knee down hard into the man's stomach.

"You're under arrest for assault." He pointed his gun at the man's chest, releasing one hand to get the cuffs from his belt.

"Logan…" Ashley's voice trembled.

"What?" he grunted, his injured shoulder arguing as his fingers closed around the cool metal of the cuffs.

A low growl came from the woods to his left. Very close.

The man pinned beneath his knee shook, muttering what almost sounded like a prayer in Spanish. Logan followed his stare into the nearby trees.

A full-grown mountain lion, its eyes dancing like twin golden orbs, clung to one of the branches. The path lay easily within its forty-five-foot leaping ability.

Great. Logan's shoulders tensed. Maybe two dozen mountain lions lived in the eight hundred thousand acres making up this park, and one had to pick now to show up.

"Don't. Run." He emphasized each word. "Wave your arms and back away slowly."

The mountain lion growled again—more to announce its presence than to show aggression, he thought. He flipped the cuffs open, his gaze darting back and forth between the cougar and the paralyzed man beneath his knee.

Before Logan could get the cuffs around the man's wrists, he twisted, throwing Logan off balance and shoving him sideways. He crashed onto the path as the big cat snarled again. It shifted its weight on the branch, making the leaves swish and crackle.

"*¡Espíritu!*" the man cried out again, backing away from the mountain lion and Logan, his eyes wide.

"Don't run!" Logan scrambled to his feet, waving his arms. Mountain lions were shy of people, unless they felt threatened. Or were starving. This one held its ground.

Until the man took off down the path to the west in an all-out sprint.

The mountain lion coiled back on its haunches, and,

in one fluid motion, leaped onto the path ten feet away. In a heartbeat, it was gone, bolting after the fleeing man.

Logan gritted his teeth and lifted his gun toward the sky, firing three shots in quick succession. Hopefully enough to scare the big cat back into the woods. "Fool," he muttered through clenched teeth. "Never turn your back on a predator."

He'd call in the cougar sighting over the radio, and they'd have to get somebody out here to check the path for the man. Just in case.

Ashley touched his arm. "It wasn't your fault. Maybe he got away."

Her face was puffy and dark where the man had struck her, and blood crusted her nose and upper lip. He brushed a finger against her cheek. "Are you all right?"

"Fine." Her voice sounded muffled, like she was keeping in a big lump of tears. Always trying to prove herself.

"Come here." He slipped his hand around her back, tugging her into an embrace.

She buried her face in his shoulder, crying softly. After a few minutes she drew in a ragged breath. "I'm sorry."

"For what? Getting my shirt wet?" He laughed, and she laughed, too, mingled with the crying. He rubbed his hand up and down on her back, leaning his face against her hair. "I don't mind."

Far too intimate for coworkers, and yet... It felt right. In a different way than things ever had with Erin. Like they were in this thing together, not him trying to convince her to stay.

After a moment Ashley pulled back, blinking away

the last of her tears. Breathtakingly beautiful despite the rapidly swelling cheek where she'd been hit. "My dad never wanted me to join the FBI. Said it was too dangerous. I always thought he meant criminals, not mountain lions."

Ah. That explained a few things. "Is that why you always have to prove yourself?"

"Probably." She wiped at her cheeks, taking a couple of deep breaths. "Time to get these photos back?"

He nodded. "Let's go catch the bad guys."

Night had fallen by the time they returned to Ashley's house and downloaded the pictures onto her laptop. Logan stuffed his aching arm back into the sling as they flipped through the images. The shots were good—several with clear, if small, views of the men's faces. Enough that Ashley thought she'd be able to run them through the FBI's database for possible matches.

The stars were out in full force as they walked past the quiet homes to headquarters, the white band of the Milky Way draped across the sky like a gauzy strip of fabric.

The lights were off, all the windows dark, as Logan unlocked the front door and let Ashley inside. They walked down the hall until they reached Logan's office.

"Whose light is that?" She pointed farther down the hall, where a soft glow emanated from beneath one of the doors.

"It's a conference room." One without an exterior window. Huh. He rubbed his chin. "I have no idea who would be in here this late on a Friday night." He let Ashley into his office. "You email Morton, I'm going to find out who it is."

"Be careful."

The hallway was silent as Logan tiptoed toward the conference room. The door was ajar and a hushed voice issued from the crack. He stopped beside the door, listening.

"No, I didn't get your message. I've been out all afternoon."

It sounded like…the superintendent? Why would he be here so late?

No response—must be on the phone. But why wasn't he using his own office?

"How do you know it was one of mine?" Barclay snapped.

Another pause as someone answered, and a sigh that sounded almost like he was in pain.

"I remember. I'll take care of it." With a noise loud enough to make Logan jump, Barclay slammed down the receiver. A chair scraped on the floor.

Logan retreated a handful of steps and approached the door again, this time making loud footsteps. There was no way to hide that he and Ashley were there, but at least he could pretend he hadn't heard Barclay's conversation.

This time only silence came from within as he knocked against the door, pushing it open enough to peek inside.

Barclay stood, leaning against a chair. His shoulders were slumped and there were dark circles under his eyes. Apparently under a lot of stress lately.

"Dr. Barclay? I saw the light. Just wondering who was working this late."

Barclay sighed. "Of course, Ranger Everett. I had to attend to a personal matter."

In the conference room? Probably better not to ask. But the gears turned in Logan's mind.

"I think I'll head home for the night." Barclay pulled away from the chair. One of his hands was wrapped in white bandaging.

Logan gestured at the injury. "What happened?"

The superintendent shifted his weight but offered a lopsided smile. Forced? "Slammed it in the car door. I broke three fingers. Pretty careless, huh?"

Very. Or was there another explanation? Logan hated that his mind jumped immediately to the mole… but Barclay had never felt like the right fit for Big Bend.

They were getting closer to pinning Jimenez—was the broken hand a reminder of what Barclay had at stake?

"I hope it heals quickly."

Barclay walked over to the door and Logan moved aside for him as he flipped off the light and entered the hallway. "Why are *you* here so late?" He scanned Logan, his gaze lingering on the wrapped arm. "Didn't Chambers give you time off?"

"Yes, but I had a little work to catch up on." Guilt niggled at his insides at the stretched truth. Although, technically, it *was* park-related work that had him here now. "My trainee has taken up a lot of my time, so I'm getting behind on some of my regular tasks."

That was the truth. And apparently it appealed to Barclay's anger about the San Vicente incident, because he nodded. "Of course. I understand. Get some rest."

Logan stepped inside the office, his brows drawn in apparent concentration.

"Who was it?" Ashley glanced at him from over the top of her open laptop, curiosity pricking at her insides.

He sat in the chair opposite her—like a guest in his own office—and ran a hand through his hair. He waited, eyes on the door, as the echo of footsteps in the hallway receded. "Barclay."

"The superintendent?" Now that was a little unusual, wasn't it?

He nodded, pursing his lips. "And he had a few broken fingers."

"You don't suppose…?" Her mind leaped to the inevitable conclusion. He *had* been eager to get rid of her almost since the moment she'd arrived.

"Not gonna lie, the thought crossed my mind."

"Well…" She tapped a finger on her chin. "He knows who I am, which could explain how Jimenez's men knew my identity."

"And why they were breaking into your house right away." He rubbed his hand over his forehead. "But Ed Chambers knows your identity, too, doesn't he?"

"He does. But I don't think he's the guy."

Logan frowned. "What if we're letting personal feelings cloud our judgment?" He stood and began to pace. "Ed has a motive. His sister is sick, and I know they need money for her medical bills."

Ashley shook her head. "I've seen his personnel file. He's had nothing but a brilliant record of service. The case is stronger against Barclay. New to the park. Under visible stress. The file he gave me on Jimenez had almost nothing in it. And he's been against this investigation from the start."

Logan stopped pacing. "And there's the broken hand. But what's his motive?"

"Money? Maybe Ed knows more about his personal life."

"Maybe." Logan stared at the window for a moment, the inside of his office reflecting off the dark glass. "But did Barclay know we were going to San Vicente?"

She drummed her fingers on the desk. "Maybe Jimenez has men down there all the time and they recognized me from a photograph. Or they ID'd my contact and followed him."

"Then what about the map?" He sat, pointing at the yellowed paper on the desk. "Who sent it to you and how does Barclay know you have it?"

"Sam." The missing memory snapped into place with beautiful clarity and Ashley slapped her hand down on the desk, scattering Logan's papers. "Sam sent it to me."

"You're sure? He never mentioned it to me."

"Absolutely sure. I remember now. I talked to him on the phone a few weeks before his death, and he told me he might've stumbled across something big. He said he was going to send me something." She could almost picture the way Sam must have looked as he'd talked to her, the way his eyes glowed when he was excited. "At the time, I figured he was talking about a new species of cactus or something, because he could get so animated about anything."

Logan grinned. "Sounds like Sam. Probably the most enthusiastic person I've ever met."

She leaned her chin against her hand, staring across the office for a moment, deep in thought. "But the question is…where did Sam get it?"

"What if he found it, say, in someone's office?"

"And then sent it to me? Why?"

He stood again, pointing at her as he spoke. "Because *you* are a federal agent. And if he suspected a mole within the park service, he wouldn't have known whom to trust. But he knew you could do something about it."

"And whoever he took it from must have figured, or even suspected, that I had it."

"He was friends with Will Sykes. I wonder if he told Will about the map."

Ashley chewed the inside of her lip. "Maybe. How can I find out without telling him who I am?"

"You can't. But we'll think of something. What about that first day you were here? Why did you go to Santa Elena, and who knew about it?"

It always came back to that one day still missing from her mind. She blew out an exasperated sigh. "I wish I could remember. I've got almost everything back, except for those twenty-four hours. All I know is I went to sleep in my apartment in DC, and I woke up in the Rio Grande."

"Nothing in the middle? Not even a clue?"

"Believe me, I've tried." She tapped a finger against her chin, trying to catch the elusive idea fluttering through her mind. "Where did you say you…found Sam?" So hard to ask without letting her voice crack.

"Dodson Trail—the outer rim." He showed her on a park map. "About here. Why?"

"I wonder… Maybe I wanted to drive past the trail. Surely the park service must've told us where he was found. You don't suppose his death could be linked to Jimenez, do you?"

"Maybe." Logan's brow furrowed. "But he wasn't

found anywhere near the mine. As much as I want it to not be my fault."

She leveled her gaze at him, wishing there was some way to wipe the regret from his features. "It wasn't your fault, Logan. Either way."

"But how did you end up at Santa Elena if you were only driving to the trailhead?"

Ashley shrugged. "Who knows? Curiosity? A lead I was following on Jimenez?"

"Well, it doesn't matter. We can still solve this case." He resumed pacing, as if the movement helped his thoughts. It only took him three strides in each direction to cross the room. Every muscle in his upper body was taut, alert, despite the arm in the sling. She couldn't have hand-picked a better partner.

Her heart twisted. Her job here was almost done. And even though she knew *something* was happening between them, she didn't know what it meant. Or if either of them would be willing to act on it. A relationship between the two of them would be doomed from the start, wouldn't it?

Her computer chimed—a response from her boss at the FBI. "Morton got back to me."

"And?"

She scanned the message. "All three men can be positively identified as working for Jimenez. And—" she reread the last few sentences just to make sure "— he gave me the green light to arrest them."

Logan froze, his eyes sparking with energy as they flicked to meet Ashley's gaze.

She rounded the desk and flung her arms around his neck, being careful of his injured shoulder. "We did it."

He slipped his arm around her back, holding her tightly. "We sure did."

She pulled back, gazing up at him, her breath catching at the way the light shifted in his green eyes, from excitement to something more subdued. Cautious. Questioning. The ache of past hurt lingered there beneath the surface and she longed to soothe it away.

He tipped his chin lower, closer, and without giving herself time to second-guess, she stretched to press her lips to his mouth. He kissed her back, threatening to make her heart burst from sheer joy. It was like coming home, to a place she'd been missing her whole life. Finally something made sense amid the heartache and confusion and fear of the last week.

If only it could last. But their lives were in two different places, and she wasn't naïve enough to think one kiss meant forever. They were only making things harder.

Placing both hands on his cheeks, she pulled away. Swallowed. "I… I'm sorry. I have no right to—" She broke off, shaking her head. *Stupid.* He'd already had his heart broken once. "After we arrest Jimenez and the case is over, I have to—"

"It's okay, Ashley." He clasped one of her hands, pressing it to his lips. "I know. You don't have to say it. I won't kiss you again." His lips tipped into a crooked grin. "Unless you ask."

He released her hand, leaving her breathless and confused. Did he *want* her to stay in Big Bend? Would she, if he asked?

"Thanks," she mumbled, gnawing at the inside of her lip. She'd worked her whole life to get to this point in her career, never questioning the sacrifices. But now? She wasn't so sure.

Logan cleared his throat. "What about the inside man? We'll never catch him."

Back to business. Time to stuff her heart in a drawer and ignore its protests. "I know. But the Bureau or the federal prosecutor might be able to get it out of Jimenez later."

"Plea bargain?"

"Let's hope it doesn't come to that." Maybe whoever it was would slip up during the arrest.

Logan resumed his pacing, rubbing his hand against his jaw. "How do we pull this off without the mole tipping off Jimenez?"

"We'll call in an FBI team from the local office in El Paso."

"You know that's five hours away, right?"

"Yes, I know. But we have to figure out the right timing anyway. If we arrive when Jimenez isn't there, we'll scare him off." She rubbed her eyes, suddenly exhausted by all the logistics that had seemed exciting only minutes ago. "Here's what I think. Since we believe they might be transporting the gold at night, our best bet would be to reach the mine at midday. That will give Jimenez's crew time to get involved with their work, and hopefully give us the element of surprise."

"Agreed." He hesitated, adding, "How do we keep something like this secret from our rangers?"

"I'll tell the agents to meet us at the trailhead. It won't be a big team. They should be able to slip under the radar."

"What about Ed? If we bring him in on the raid, he can help with the cover-up."

Ashley nodded. It made sense. They trusted him, and he could ensure whoever was assigned to patrol the trailhead wasn't there at midday. "And it'll be good to have another person who knows this terrain."

"Barclay is going to hate this when he finds out." Logan's mouth tipped into a crooked smile as he ran a hand through his sandy-brown hair, making the ends stand out at odd angles. He looked almost boyish for a moment, but she knew a warrior's heart beat in his chest.

Even with everything that had happened, she'd never regret coming here and meeting him.

"Yeah, he will." She smiled. "Even if he's innocent."

Between Morton's advance communication and Ashley's call to the El Paso office, it didn't take long to arrange for a small team of agents to meet them at the Pine Canyon trailhead the next day.

When she hung up the phone, Logan nodded toward the door. "Come on, it's late. Let me walk you home. We can finalize plans in the morning."

They followed the familiar path to her house in silence and Ashley stopped in front of her door. His face was visible in the soft glow of the moonlight. Strong chin. Warm eyes. And his lips... Well, she didn't need to remember what they felt like.

"Thank you. For everything. I couldn't have done this without you."

He smiled, joy and sorrow mingling. His voice was low and rough when he spoke. "It's been my pleasure."

She rested her fingertips lightly on his chest. "Good night, Logan."

"Good night, Ashley."

It took a long, long time to fall asleep.

SEVENTEEN

The day dawned hot and muggy, with hazy wisps of clouds hovering on the edges of a dull blue, faded-denim sky. Ashley woke early—too early to expect Logan. But there was no way she could fall back to sleep, not with the day looming ahead.

She tried to roll some of the tension out of her shoulders, shifting restlessly on the edge of her bed. Why the sudden nerves? Maybe because she still didn't know who the traitor was. Or maybe it was because the day looked sultry and miserable, and she'd hoped for a more auspicious beginning.

Whatever the case, maybe a jog around the neighborhood would clear away the jitters. It only took a few minutes to pull on a pair of black yoga pants and a running top. She left her gun in its place under the extra pillow and the map tucked between the mattress and box spring, along with her computer. She'd just finished quaffing a large glass of water when someone knocked at the door.

"Logan, you're early—" She stopped short as she opened the door. Not Logan. "Oh, hey, Will. What's up?" Perhaps a golden opportunity to see what he knew about Sam.

He shifted his weight from one foot to the other and leaned one forearm against her doorjamb, somehow managing to look both suave and nervous at the same time. "Hey, got a minute? I'm heading out on patrol, but I wanted to talk to you. It'll be quick."

"Sure." She opened the door. As he passed by her, Ashley caught a sudden whiff of that same soap she had noticed at the staff picnic. So familiar—hauntingly familiar—but the connection dangled there on the edge of her brain, just out of reach.

"What happened to your face?" He gestured at her bruised cheek, which didn't look a whole lot better this morning. His dark eyes were full of concern. "Did that happen in San Vicente?"

"Oh, um, n-no," she stammered, grasping for a reasonable explanation that didn't involve telling the truth. "I ran into some trouble out on the trail yesterday. But I'll tell you about it some other time. Want to sit?"

"No time. I wanted to see how you were doing. It's a big adjustment, moving here, and now with all these scary things that keep happening to you…" He let the words trail away, fidgeting with a button on his cuff.

"That's so kind of you, Will." Ashley smiled, trying to set him at ease. There had to be some way to steer this conversation toward his friendship with Sam. But how? "You know, there was something I wanted to ask you. I heard a rumor about a ranger dying here recently. Is it true?" She shifted her weight back and forth, feigning nervousness. "I'm a little hesitant to ask Logan. He seems kind of secretive about it."

An outright lie. *Sorry, Logan.* She was pretty sure he'd understand.

Will ran his hand through his thick, dark hair, a gesture that reminded her of Logan. But along with the motion came that scent of fabric softener, demanding her attention. "Um, yeah. It was pretty tragic."

Ashley heard the words, saw his lips moving, but her mind suddenly filled with recognition so forceful she had to swallow back the bile rising into her esophagus.

Will was the one who had dumped her into the river.

Images flashed through her mind, one after another, filling the last blank place in her memory. She had driven down past the trail where Sam had died, and then, with nothing else to do but grieve, she had kept going all the way to the end of the road. Right to the Santa Elena Canyon parking lot, where she had inadvertently stumbled across a drug exchange.

She remembered the blow to the head, the distant sound of voices and the feel of someone stuffing her gun into her pocket. And the smell—that fabric softener—on the man's shirt as he'd lugged her limp body to the river.

Well, Sykes, one of the others had said, *you're in for it now. She looks like law enforcement. How are we going to cover up this mess?*

Don't tell my uncle.

Will had panicked. He had picked her up, carried her to the Rio Grande and thrown her in.

And he had gone out of his way to be friendly to her ever since, because he wanted to know what she remembered.

That truck that had run her and Logan off the road

on the way to Terlingua? It was probably whomever had picked up the drugs on this side of the river.

"Ashley, what's wrong?" Will's words snapped her back to the present, where they both stood inside her house. With the door shut. And Will's back leaning against it.

"Nothing." She forced a smile even though her head was spinning. She had to tell Logan—if Barclay *was* one of Jimenez's men, he wasn't alone. Will, so deceptively charming, was a mole, too. It took all her self-control to keep her hands from shaking. "Just sad. For the family. Of the ranger that died."

Her gun—it was in the bedroom, under the pillow. How long would it take to reach it? Should she try taking him down now, before he realized she had remembered the truth?

"You know…" Her voice came out a half octave too high. "I've got some things to take care of, and I'm sure you need to get going. We can talk more later."

Her stomach turned over as she waited, hoping he couldn't read the visceral terror on her face.

"Of course." Will's lips curled into a smile, but his eyes filled with something else that looked a lot like… fear.

She took a step back, letting out the breath she'd been holding as he turned for the door.

Before she could react, he lunged. Black flashed in his hand and the gun smashed into the side of her head, filling her vision with stars as her legs crumpled. The last thing she heard before she blacked out was Will's voice.

"I'm sorry, Ashley. I didn't want it to end like this. Not for you and not for Sam."

* * *

Ashley was gone. Logan pounded on her door as Ed waited with him on the front step, but nobody answered. All the hairs stood up on his arms.

He strode over to her window and peered into the living area. Empty. Tension roiled in his stomach. With a glance at Ed, he walked around the back to the bedroom window.

Nothing.

Wait! The sash was open an inch. And on the ground— footprints. At least two sets.

"Ed!"

The chief ranger dashed around to the back and examined his find. "Too big for Ashley's?"

"They're not hers," Logan managed to choke out. *Failed.* He'd failed. The world collapsed in on him as he imagined her tied up, gagged, maybe dead.

Please, Lord, not that… The prayer ripped its way out of his soul.

Ed grasped his shoulders. "We're going to find her. You and me. Okay, buddy?"

He nodded woodenly, digging cold fingertips into his hair, and walked with Ed around to the front.

The door was unlocked, no sign of a struggle inside. Except… He dropped to one knee, examining the white linoleum tiles in the entryway, where a few red splotches had almost escaped his attention. Some of the blood came away on one of his fingers. "Happened this morning."

Ed nodded grimly.

It didn't take long to search the small home. In her bedroom, Ed lifted one of the pillows to reveal Ashley's gun.

Logan pursed his lips. "She must've let whoever it was in."

"Or forgot to lock her door."

No, it had to have been the mole. Somebody she trusted enough to let inside her house. But who? Surely not Barclay, not after last night's conversation. Somebody else they'd overlooked?

Thinking about it wasn't going to get Ashley back. "We have to assume Jimenez has her and take the team in to the mine."

"Agreed."

The next two hours passed in a brutally slow haze of anxiety and preparation. Logan notified the FBI team of Ashley's capture and arranged for them to put a helicopter in the air as soon as the raid was finished. Just in case she wasn't there.

Logan and Ed were already waiting at the Pine Canyon trailhead when the team of agents arrived. Six agents, wearing FBI windbreakers over body armor, climbed out of two vehicles. Logan spread a trail map out on the hood of one of the cars and went over the details of the raid.

Fifteen minutes later Ed led two agents in first to clear the trail of guards. They only found one and, mercifully, no evidence of anyone being mauled by a mountain lion the previous night.

Once the guard was secured, Logan signaled his team. One agent stayed on the trail to cover their backs and the rest scrambled in behind Logan up the steep mountainside. His legs burned from the extra weight of his Kevlar flak jacket and gear, but he barely noticed as he prayed for Ashley's safety. She *had* to be in there.

The mine entrance, hidden in a cleft of rock behind

a cover of bushes, stayed quiet as they approached. To avoid direct observation, Logan led the team in from above, positioning them around the mine entrance. A guard sounded the alarm, opening fire.

"Stop!" Ed called out from behind the protection of a large boulder. "This is National Park Service law enforcement and the FBI. Cease fire or we'll shoot."

When the man ignored him, Ed signaled to the agent who'd claimed to be their best shot. The man nodded, braced his gun against a rock and took the guard down.

Logan dropped into the cleft from above, followed by one of the agents, who secured the fallen guard. When the others were in position, he stepped inside the mine, gun up, flashlight on.

Pale faces blinked at him from within the darkness. A few lanterns glowed in the background, casting dark shadows from the occupants on the glittering walls.

"Freeze!" he ordered, though no one had moved. Most of them held tools—a jackhammer, a shovel, an old-school pickax like something out of a Western movie.

Sudden movement to his side sent his heart into his throat, but another agent was ready. "Drop it."

The man's face, illuminated in a flashlight beam, was familiar. José, from San Vicente. He scowled but dropped his gun with a heavy clatter to the cave floor. Only one other man was armed. The rest, unfortunate souls, had been carted in solely for the purpose of manual labor.

"Amazing." Ed shone his light around the inside of the mine. Narrow veins of white and yellow quartz, most of them already partially removed, ran through the hard rock wall.

Logan traced his fingers along one of the rough veins where someone had recently been working. Tiny gold flecks glinted in the quartz. Gold in Big Bend, right there beneath his fingertips. Ashley had been right.

But she wasn't here.

They'd cuffed everyone they'd found and searched the mine, which ran back in a single tunnel that grew narrower and narrower to the point of claustrophobia before it ended. Three guards in total, plus six workers. No Jimenez and no Ashley. The other two men from San Vicente weren't there, either.

Logan stalked out the mine entrance and scrambled back down the hill to the trail, where the agents had hauled the suspects. He found José. "Where's Jimenez?"

"No hablo inglés." José shrugged.

Logan stepped closer, his face inches away. "You can either cooperate, or I can make the next few days very difficult for you."

José smirked. "You're not allowed to hurt me."

Without hesitating, Logan crushed his knuckles into the man's mouth. "Try me."

"Logan!" Ed called, eyebrows raised.

But Logan ignored him. Time was slipping away and every passing moment increased the odds of Jimenez and Ashley disappearing across the border where he would never find them again. Too many hours had passed already.

José turned to the side, spitting out a mouthful of blood. "He's not here."

"That's obvious," Logan growled. "Where is he? And the woman?"

"The federal agent?" José laughed. "Dead by now."

A knife in the stomach would've felt better, but Logan clenched his jaw and sucked in a deep breath. Maybe he was telling the truth, maybe not. In either case, José had known exactly whom he was talking about. Did that mean she'd been there?

Movement behind José caught his eye. One of the forced laborers. He raised a wavering left hand. The fingertips were filthy and ragged, and multiple scrapes covered his knuckles. Poor man.

Logan strode over to him. "Do you speak English?"

"A little." The man nodded, glancing nervously at José.

"You're free. He can't hurt you anymore," Logan assured him. "Have you seen an American woman? Brown hair?" He held up a hand. "This tall?"

When the man nodded again, Logan's breath lodged in his lungs. Ashley *had* been here.

"When?" he prompted.

"Today. Gone now. Jimenez take her." The man pointed to the west, where the trail dwindled away into a wall of thick brush. "That way. We go that way with gold, too. Trucks wait on road."

Just as Ashley's contact had told her, they were getting the gold out through Juniper Canyon. He could see now where the foliage had been damaged and cut at the trail's end, leaving a narrow, barely visible path.

"Where's he taking her?" Logan balled his fists, every nerve in his body waiting impatiently for the answer. "To Mexico?"

"No. To desert. Kill her."

No. His fingernails dug into his palms as he turned to find Ed already beside him. "I'm taking two agents into Juniper Canyon. Will's checking campsites on Glenn Spring Road. He can help search."

"I'll get that FBI chopper up over the stretch between Juniper and Mariscal." Ed squeezed Logan's shoulder, his voice steady as always. "Go get her."

Ashley's head throbbed. Again. She groaned, forcing her eyes open. The sun scorched down like an oven set to broil.

"Good, she's awake." Someone kicked her hard in the ribs. Not Will's voice, but the face was invisible against the bright yellow orb of sun overhead.

Another voice—a man's, crisp and clear but with an accent—said, "Manuel, stop kicking the federal agent. Stand her up."

Ah, one of her friends from San Vicente. Lovely. He yanked her to her feet, making her head spin like a top. A black SUV and a beat-up truck were parked nearby, off to the side of the dirt road where they now stood. Her hands were bound tightly behind her back and a rock dug into her foot.

Great. No shoes. She'd never had the chance to put them on. Logan would have a thing or two to say about that…if she ever saw him again.

She was still in her running clothes, which meant she had nothing. No gun, no cell phone, no water, no knife. No way to tell Logan what had happened, or where to find her, or that he had to arrest Will Sykes.

A man dressed in a linen shirt and khaki pants stood a few feet away. "We meet at last, Agent Thompson."

"Jimenez?" she asked, although it was hardly necessary. Despite his short stature, he wore the air of a man used to getting his way.

He nodded.

She glanced around, trying to orient herself. The Chisos towered behind her, close enough she was still on the US side. But the profile of the mountains didn't match the view from the mine and the cactuses and low brush of the open desert surrounded them. They must be somewhere in that long barren stretch between the mine and the border. "What do you want with me?"

"We've known who you are since your second day in this park. You don't think I can let you keep chasing me, do you?"

Second day? That would explain the almost immediate break-in at her home. "Will?" She faltered. How could he have known? "Did Barclay tell him?"

"The superintendent?" Jimenez laughed. "No, my nephew knew the moment he met you."

"Nephew?" She shook her head, trying to clear away the cobwebs. "He's only got one relative listed on his record, and it isn't an uncle."

"His mother is my sister." Jimenez smirked. "Naturally, I wouldn't want his record tarnished by association. Easy enough to change, with the right influence."

She scrunched her eyebrows together. So hot out here. Her mouth already felt pasty dry. "But how did he recognize—" She stopped short.

Of course. The variable she'd always known was possible but hadn't expected. "Sam showed him my picture, didn't he?" He must've been very close to Will. Maybe even wanted to set her up with him one day. She shook her head.

"Yes. It was a coincidence he had the chance to kill you on your first night. Unfortunately he didn't realize it was you until the next day, when he got a good look at your face. A shame he didn't take a closer look the first time around. But, no matter, we will finish the job soon." The cold glint in his eyes sent a shiver down Ashley's spine.

She had to stall, to give Logan time to find her. Ignoring the fear clawing at her heart, she took a steadying breath. "What about the map? How did you know I had it?"

"The logical conclusion. After my careless nephew lost his copy, your brother found the mine. When you showed up, the best explanation was that he had sent the map to you."

Sam had found the mine. Her heart broke. Why had he gone searching alone? Impulsive, overconfident, energetic Sam. "And his death…?"

"Not an accident. Very good, Agent Thompson. Shooting him would have been too obvious, so we left him to die of exposure." He shrugged. *No loss.*

Her insides burned. The man who had killed her brother stood three feet away and here she was, unable to do anything about it.

Where was God's perfect justice? *How long, oh Lord, will You wait?*

"They'll find you," she snapped, "and you'll spend a lifetime in jail for all the people you've hurt."

He laughed again. "I think not. In fact, before you join your brother, I wanted to show you something." He raised a hand toward one of the vehicles and two men got out, one with his hands behind his back.

Her stomach tightened. It was her contact from San Vicente.

"Recognize him?" Jimenez asked softly. Dangerously. "He won't be feeding tips to the FBI anymore."

He pulled a handgun from his belt as the guard forced the man to his knees on the hot, dusty road.

The man on the ground wept, tears running down his wrinkled cheeks, but he kept his back straight. *"Para mi Lena."*

Jimenez placed the barrel of the gun against the man's forehead. "This is your fault, Agent Thompson."

Ashley opened her mouth to object, or to beg—she wasn't sure which—but before any sound came out, Jimenez pulled the trigger.

Her eyes snapped shut as the man's blood splattered across her face. Bile burned in her esophagus.

It would be her turn next. She clenched her jaw, staring at Jimenez. Logan would catch him and bring him to justice. "They'll find you."

"But they won't find you," he jeered. "Not alive, anyway."

Unshed tears burned in Ashley's eyes as she waited to be forced to her knees. To feel the cold metal ring of the barrel dig into her skin.

Instead, at a nod from Jimenez, Manuel and the other man dragged her toward the truck.

"Goodbye, Agent Thompson," Jimenez called after her. "Please give my best to your brother."

Her stomach dropped. They were going to dump her in the desert, right there on Dodson Trail, like they had done with Sam. And Logan would have no idea where to look.

She didn't know which hurt more—the thought of never seeing him again or knowing he would blame himself for her death.

EIGHTEEN

Logan crouched behind a rock formation at the trail-head of Juniper Canyon, watching the two parked vehicles fifty yards away on the dirt road that led south. He and the two agents had taken the narrow, rugged path—created by Jimenez—across the ridge from Pine Canyon Trail to Juniper Canyon, and then followed the steep descent through the canyon to the base of the mountains.

Here they were in the Sierra Quemada, the burnt lands, where the only cover came in the form of rocks and barrel cactuses. Moments before, when a gunshot catapulted his heart into his throat, Logan had crept as close as he could without risking being seen. The other two agents had split to either side.

The truck engine roared to life. They couldn't afford to wait, not if Ashley was in one of those vehicles. The way the SUV was parked blocked his view of the people, but there were at least two, maybe three, sets of boots visible beneath the vehicle. And what looked like the victim of the gunshot.

He couldn't stop to consider the possibilities.

He dashed forward, keeping low to the ground, moving from barrel cactus to cactus, until he finally reached the back right bumper of the SUV. Doors slammed, and the truck sped away, kicking up a cloud of dust on the dirt road.

Voices came from the far side of the SUV, speaking rapidly in Spanish. Logan crouched low, peered beneath the vehicle and watched as a pair of hands hoisted a body.

Not Ashley. Relief threatened to make his legs go weak.

As the man with the body headed for the SUV, Logan slipped along the far side. A faint pulsing reached his ears from across the desert to the west—the helicopter.

He edged around to the front of the SUV as the latch clicked to open the rear tailgate.

The other man had stopped beside the driver's-side door.

Leading with his gun, Logan swiveled around the bumper and aimed his gun at a well-dressed man who could only be Jimenez. "National Park Service. Drop your weapon."

Jimenez's eyes widened for a second before his face contorted into a smile.

"Drop it," Logan repeated. "Or I *will* shoot."

Jimenez held up his handgun, dropping it onto the sand. "No, you won't. You Americans are all the same. So worried about protecting everyone's rights. Trials and justice and law."

"Instead of the anarchy you want?"

"It's not anarchy." He smirked. "I'm merely helping the government. Offering employment. And justice."

The other man appeared from behind the vehicle— Manuel, from San Vicente—his gun pointed at Logan. Not more than ten feet away. Hard to miss at that range.

Logan didn't flinch, even though every nerve in his body begged for self-preservation. "Drop the weapon, Manuel."

Manuel ignored him, taking a step forward.

"Last chance, Manuel," Logan said through gritted teeth. "FBI agents are in position. You're not getting out of here."

Manuel's gaze darted back and forth, his knuckles white around the gun. But Jimenez's eyes narrowed, his lips parting to give the order to fire.

Before any sound came out, the two agents stepped up behind Manuel. "Freeze."

Manuel's eyes went wide, nostrils flaring.

Logan sensed his panic, the way his finger hovered over the trigger despite the agents behind him. Instinct told him to move and he flung himself sideways, rolling across the hard dirt as bullets from Manuel's gun raked the sand where he'd been standing a split second before.

Another shot fired and Manuel crumpled to the ground.

Jimenez's face paled, but he clenched his teeth together. "I'll repay you for this."

"I don't think so." Logan climbed to his feet, pulling out his handcuffs. "Not where you're going."

While the agents secured the two suspects, Logan radioed in their position. Precious minutes had passed since the truck had driven away. Had Ashley been inside it? Or had they taken her somewhere else entirely?

Questioning Jimenez was useless.

Logan would need that chopper, a dark speck growing larger on the horizon.

Ed's voice crackled over the radio. "Sykes will be at your position in five minutes to help search."

Ashley sank to the ground beside a barrel cactus, narrowly avoiding the giant spines. Everything around her was brown, brittle, dry. Or spikey. Dead, crunchy grasses. Brown brush that wouldn't sprout leaves until the next rain. Leathery succulents hoarding their toxic alkaloid water beneath a thousand spikes.

The Chisos loomed to the north, Emory Peak visible against the bright blue sky. To the southwest lay the smaller outlying mountains. Somewhere in between ran Dodson Trail, the one tiny thread of hope she had, because at the end of its twelve-mile length lay a paved parking lot and a water cache.

The other option was to go back. They'd blindfolded her before dumping her out here, but the dirt road where she'd seen Jimenez was probably only a few miles away. No water that way, though, unless rangers were searching the area.

She turned over one of her feet, prodding gently at the red, bubbling blisters and pulling out a sharp spine. At least they'd had the decency to cut her hands free.

Sweat dripped down her back, down her neck, down over her eyebrows. Soaking even her sweat-wicking workout gear. She'd laugh if it wasn't so much effort.

Logan had taught her all about desert survival and the signs of heat stroke. Muscle cramps would start soon. Her arms and face were already red, both from her internal heat and from sun exposure. But the real danger wouldn't begin until she stopped sweating. When her body ran out of moisture reserves and her internal temperature would rise unchecked.

Ashley shuddered. Better to think about survival than death.

First rule of desert survival: don't panic. *Check.* FBI training had taught her to stay calm in any situation.

Second rule: find cover. Shade wasn't an option. She'd considered ripping off part of her shirt to make a hat of sorts but decided stretchy black fabric over one's head probably wouldn't make a big dent on things.

Third rule: conserve water. Breathing with her mouth shut was about the extent of things. Logan had cleared up the cactus misconception on the first day. Those big, old barrel cactuses weren't full of water, they were full of alkaloid toxins that would send the unwary backpacker into a downward spiral of gut-emptying vomiting and diarrhea. A few varieties, like the prickly pear, were edible, but how exactly did one get into a cactus with nothing but bare hands? A sharp rock might do the job…if it came to that.

She'd keep an eye out for any young prickly pear pads, or *nopales*, as she walked. Or a tinaja. Maybe there'd be a bit of collected water left from the rainfall earlier in the week.

Her limbs felt like lead weights as she hauled herself to her feet. Maybe it was better to sit still in the hot sun than to walk in it, but surely there was shade somewhere out here. Surely, if she pressed on a little bit longer, she'd find the trail. Maybe with hikers.

Sam had thought the same thing, hadn't he? He'd almost made it to the trail. A half mile away, Logan had said.

Was Sam's skin this red already?

Did his tongue cling to the roof of his mouth the way Ashley's did? Like a cotton ball ready to choke her.

Why did the good people have to die, while the bad guys drove away in their air-conditioned trucks with bags full of gold?

Didn't God care?

Useless anger tore at her insides. The same question had plagued her since Sam's death. Her brother had loved God. Trusted Him.

She had loved and trusted Him, too. And what had He done for them?

She stopped short as a picture forced its way into her mind, into her heart, so abruptly her breath caught.

Jesus, a crown of thorns on his head. Nails in his hands. A spear thrust into his side. Crying out as he bore the sins of the world, taking the punishment each one of them deserved. God made flesh.

God had done *that* for her and Sam.

And all she could do was complain. She sank to her knees on the hot, rocky ground, hardly able to breathe, and pressed a trembling hand to her mouth.

I'm sorry. Her esophagus burned, but no tears came. No water to spare. *I'm so, so sorry for doubting You.*

Her anger melted away like snow in the face of His love and, finally, His peace—the peace that passed all understanding—flowed into the brittle hole she had guarded for so long inside her chest.

A little tinaja filled with living water.

But whosoever drinketh of the water that I shall give him shall never thirst.

She smiled. Sam had that water. He was with Jesus now. Waiting for her.

The thought reverberated in her chest as she struggled to her feet. She'd get to see him soon, and she could tell him she finally understood about Jimenez and the map and what had happened. She could even understand why he loved this place. Vast, dangerous, wild…but free. The constraints of the city, the noise of everyday life that prevented her from really thinking and feeling—they were all gone. Out here, in air so fresh it was like no one else had ever breathed it, nothing stood between her and the things that mattered. Like knowing her Savior.

And acknowledging all those feelings she'd tried so hard to avoid. Grief for Sam. Anger at God. Love for…

Ashley tried to stop his name from forming in her mind, but she was too weary to fight anymore. The words rolled around in her head and in her heart, unwilling to be contained any longer. She was in love with Logan. It didn't make sense—she'd known him such a short time, and she'd never see him again—but there it was. She loved him.

There were so many things she would have liked to tell him.

The trail of footprints was fading away as the wind shifted. Logan jogged after them, ignoring the sweat beading on his forehead. Ignoring the way his heart hammered in his chest each time he passed another plant to look behind.

Exactly as it had been when he'd searched for Sam, only that time it had been too late. Vultures had circled overhead then; their dark shapes blotted the blue sky now. He could hardly breathe as he imagined what might be beneath them. He wasn't sure he could handle it if he found her like that. Especially not when there was so much bound up in his heart he hadn't told her. Ashley needed to know how he felt about her… How much he cared about her—no, *loved* her—despite all his efforts not to.

Please, Lord, please…

He scarcely noticed the pack rubbing against his back, holding two precious containers of water. Will was coming right behind him with the radio. They would call her location in to the chopper as soon as they found her. Airlift her to safety.

How much farther could she have gone? He and Will had followed the pickup's tracks and Ashley's prints as far into the desert as they could. When they'd had to stop driving, Logan had tumbled out to continue on foot, Will only a few minutes behind as he called in their location and gathered more supplies from the NPS truck.

The thought squirmed in the back of his mind that maybe he had missed her. Walked right on past. Ashley was strong, but nobody was strong enough to walk for miles in this heat without water. At some point, she'd have to stop, even without shade.

He called her name again, as he had done every minute for the past fifteen. Always willing her to answer, always hearing nothing but the wind and the sound of his own footsteps.

This time, though, he heard something else. He stopped, heart lodging in his throat, listening.

"Ashley!" he called again.

Rustling nearby.

He spun toward a waist-high prickly pear cactus a short distance to his left. And then he saw it. A pile of brown hair, dark against the sand. *Ashley.* He covered the space between them in a heartbeat, throwing himself to his knees beside her, his breath—no, his life— on hold as he slipped his fingers against her burning red throat to feel for a pulse.

Alive. Praise God, *she was alive.* He wasn't too late.

NINETEEN

Somewhere through her haze of utter exhaustion, Ashley felt a hand slide under the back of her head. Cold wetness ran along her bloody, chapped lips and down her chin. A little trickle made it into her mouth—sweet like sugar—and she opened her mouth wider, desperate for more.

"Easy. Just a little at a time or you'll throw it back up."

Logan. She pried her eyelids open, taking in his tanned face, defined jaw and the way his hair ruffled in the wind. Had to be her imagination. Maybe she was delirious, sucking down sand. But the strong arm under her—she didn't think her mind could come up with that, too.

"Chopper'll be here soon. Hang in there for me, okay?" The tender, aching tone to his words tore at Ashley's heart. He glanced away. "Over here, Will! I found her!"

Wait. Fear pulsed through her veins. *No, not Will.* Logan didn't know. She wanted to shake her head but her muscles wouldn't work.

Logan smiled. "It's okay. We've got you now. You're safe."

Why didn't he understand? She moved her lips but

her desiccated brick of a tongue refused to move. Logan gave her more of the precious water, stroking her hair with his hand, not knowing whom he had called over.

She groaned, struggling to lift her head. May as well be a cannonball attached to her shoulders.

"Easy." Logan glanced over his shoulder.

"Will…" she rasped.

"He'll be here in a minute." His brows drew together. "What is it?"

Too late. A man stepped into view behind Logan, his dark hair and tanned face immediately recognizable in the blinding sunlight. One hand dangled at his side, the other was behind his back.

"Did you find her?" Will's voice was choked with anxiety. "Is she alive?"

"Yeah." Logan grinned. "She'll make it, but we need to call in a medevac now."

"I was afraid of that." Will's voice was cold and sterile as he pulled his hand out from behind his back, sunlight flashing off his gun. "Hands up, Logan."

No. Ashley mouthed the word, but no sound came out. Will's eyes had a haunted, half-wild look that removed any doubt he would fire. But the small mouthfuls of water Logan had given her? They were working into her body, replenishing the shriveling cells.

She couldn't speak; she certainly couldn't stand. But maybe, just maybe, she could reach Logan's gun where it rested in the holster at his waist.

The color drained from Logan's face. His lips parted as if he wanted to say something, but he stayed silent. Slowly he raised his hands, never taking his eyes off her.

She glanced at his gun, so rapidly she wasn't sure Logan would catch the flash of her eyes. He froze, staring at her for a fraction of a second, almost as if he was deliberating whether it was worth the risk. He nodded, his mouth forming a grim line.

"It was you, wasn't it?" Logan asked Will, trying to buy them time as the strength trickled back into her limbs. "You were the one helping Jimenez smuggle drugs in and gold out."

"Yes." Will frowned. "And no one would have figured it out, if she had gone back home before she remembered everything."

"Remembered what, Will?" Logan's voice was calm, almost soothing—meant to keep him talking.

Ashley slid her hand across her stomach, toward the gun.

"I…" Will's voice cracked and he sucked in a ragged breath. When he spoke again, the words came out emotionless once more. "She showed up at an exchange—surprised us. It was dark and I didn't recognize her. Not until I'd already knocked her out. Then… I panicked."

"You threw her in the river?" Logan's tone was still calm but strained with concealed rage beneath the words.

"When she…when she showed up at work as a new ranger, I thought it was over. But she didn't recognize me, didn't remember." Will's voice trembled as the emotion leaked back into it. "But my uncle wanted—"

"Your uncle?" Logan interrupted, his eyes widening with the realization. "Jimenez?"

Will nodded miserably. "My mother's brother. She tried to hide us from him, but after my father died… I had to work for him, to protect my family. He wanted me to watch Ashley and to get back that stupid map. Sam was my friend. You have to believe me." His eyes begged them to understand. "When she remembered what happened, I had to turn her over. And now that she's still not dead... I have no choice."

"You do have a choice." Logan's voice was both authoritative and soothing. "You can still make the right decision. We can all walk out of here together."

Will shook his head, his face contorted into a grimace. "I can't spend my life in jail. No one else will take care of my mother and my sister."

"What do you think will happen if you return without us?"

His eyes grew hard. "I think they'll believe me. Before we could find Ashley, one of Jimenez's men caught us. You were shot and left for dead. I barely escaped. Of course, I'll have to drag your body a fair way from here, but I'm sure I can manage."

"Will—"

"Enough talking!" Will snapped, waving the gun at Logan. "Toss me your gun and back away from her. There's no reason for her to see this."

Will hadn't even looked at her—as if he didn't dare risk eye contact with the woman he kept trying to kill.

Ashley's arm dropped down against the hot sand, her hand mere inches from Logan's gun.

"Let me say goodbye," Logan said thickly. He leaned forward over Ashley, pressing a kiss against her forehead, and closing the gap enough that her fingers brushed the cool metal of his gun.

"Back away!" Will barked. "Now."

Logan raised his hands, flinching at the pain in his still healing shoulder, and pulled away from Ashley. His eyes locked onto hers—one last, lingering look in case everything went terribly wrong. She'd only get one chance, because as soon as Will saw the gun, he'd shoot.

Her fingers latched onto the grip, pulling the gun out of Logan's holster at the same time he moved out of her line of sight. She didn't hesitate.

The gun fired, its near deafening crack followed by a shot from Will's gun. The recoil was more than Ashley's weak arm could handle and she dropped the weapon onto the hot sand, struggling to keep her head up to see what had happened.

Will was down. Her heart broke for him, but at the same time...she praised God that he was down.

But the second shot? Will's shot...?

"Logan?" she rasped, forcing her mouth to form his name. He was on the ground, a few feet away, and her throat constricted as she scanned the sand for blood. Not now, not after all of this. She couldn't lose him on a last, cheap shot. *"Logan?"*

But then he moved and the air rushed back into Ashley's lungs as he pushed up onto his hands and knees. The heavy weight in her ribs released as he crawled over to her and her chest heaved even though no tears could come.

"Shh." He cradled her head in his lap. "I'm here. His shot missed. You did it." His green eyes were full of emotion. So many things they'd left unsaid.

"Will?" she asked weakly.

"I'll check." Logan's voice was grim, his face clouded with sorrow. "And I'll call in our location on the radio. Stay with me, okay?"

She knew what he meant—here and now, because she was so weak—but her heart blurted out the answer.

"Always."

TWENTY

The whir of the helicopter rotors was the sweetest sound Logan had ever heard. He sat with his hands pressed against the bullet wound in Will's side, watching as the chopper set down a short distance away. It had been the longest minutes of his life, sitting ten feet away from Ashley as he tried to keep Will alive. He had kept talking to her, kept reassuring her, even though she was so weak she could barely move. If she had stopped responding... He was glad he hadn't had to make that choice to let Will bleed out.

"Thank You, Lord. They're here," he said almost as much to himself as to Ashley. She waved a limp hand.

He held that hand the entire way to the hospital in Alpine as the EMT hooked up an IV to her other arm and her eyes drifted shut from exhaustion. She looked peaceful now, and safe, and his heart overflowed with gratitude to God for letting him find her in time. And for protecting them from Will.

Will. The betrayal stung, especially when he remembered how close Sam and Will had been. How much had Will known about Sam's death? Had he been involved? There would be time to ask him those questions later. He, too, was hooked up to an IV, his body stable but unconscious for now. He would have a long road to recovery, only to awaken to a lifetime of consequences.

Ed Chambers met Logan in the ER waiting room a few hours later. "How is she?" He took a seat beside Logan.

"She'll be fine. The doc wants to keep her overnight to make sure."

"And Will?"

"In intensive care, but alive." He'd already told Ed everything that happened, and even though Jimenez wouldn't talk, they'd gotten one of his men to admit that Jimenez was Will Sykes's uncle.

Ed nodded. "Good work out there. I'm glad to see you all in one piece."

"She saved my life, you know." Logan ran a hand through his hair. The horror of that moment, when Will had pulled the gun on them, might stick with him for the rest of his life. He'd been so worried about Ashley, and so relieved at finding her, he'd barely even paid attention to Will.

"I know. You've told me a few times." Ed's eyes sparkled. "I guess we'll need to hire a couple of new law-enforcement rangers now. Especially after I retire in a few months and you take over as chief ranger."

Logan raised his brows. He knew Ed would have to retire eventually, but— "A few months? You never said anything about it before."

"I've been toying with the idea for a while. It's time."

"Barclay would never pick me as your replacement." Especially if he knew Logan had suspected him of working with Jimenez. But after Ed finished laughing at his suspicions, he'd vouched for the superintendent.

Apparently the call he'd overheard had had something to do with Barclay's daughter in college.

"He will now." Ed laughed quietly. "I think you've proved yourself."

Ashley awoke to bright sunlight. She had to check the clock before she had any clue how long she'd slept. The entire night, apparently.

Beside her, Logan sat awkwardly crammed into a chair. His eyes were shut and his head lolled to one side. As she shifted in the bed, he stirred.

"Hey," he said groggily, rubbing his thumb and fore-finger over his eyes. He straightened and looked her over from head to toe and back, his eyes pausing on the IV set in her left arm. "How are you feeling?"

"Like a rehydrated raisin." She grinned.

"At least you've gotten your sense of humor back." He grew silent, studying his hands. "We contacted the FBI. I spoke with your boss, let him know what happened and that you were okay."

"Thank you," she said, suddenly acutely aware of the space between them. That gap she'd almost forgotten, filled by the wedge that was Big Bend National Park and the Federal Bureau of Investigation. So strange they could both be in law enforcement yet still be worlds apart.

Logan reached out to her, enclosing her hand in his own. The warmth radiated through her whole body.

"How long have you been here?" she asked, torn between letting his hand go now to get it over with or clinging on for dear life.

"Since we brought you in." He grinned sheepishly. "There were probably other things I should've been doing, but... I had to make sure you were okay."

She squeezed his hand. "Thank you, Logan, for everything."

"Of course. I wish I could have done the same for Sam. At least now I know it wasn't his fault, or mine. It was Jimenez. And he'll have a lifetime in jail to answer for his crimes."

She almost didn't want to ask. "And Will?"

Logan stared down at their hands, intertwining his fingers with hers. "Alive and recovering. I don't think he can avoid jail time, but at least we've learned a little bit more about why he did it. One of Rico Jimenez's men told us everything he knew. Jimenez has been threatening Elena Sykes and her family for years, ever since he found them in El Paso. Apparently after Will's father refused to join the cartel, he died under mysterious circumstances. Then Jimenez pressured Will into joining by threatening his sister."

"That's awful." Despite everything, Ashley shivered. No one deserved to be put in that position. If only he had chosen a different path—asked for help.

"That was about three years ago," Logan went on, "right before Will applied for the job here, and right after Jimenez finally got his hands on that old map to the mine."

"I take it Will verified its existence once he worked here?"

"I'd assume so. Jimenez has been running drugs through the park on the side, but his main goal was to remove the gold. He chose summer because he knew there'd be less people out in the park to discover him."

It ought to have been awkward, sitting there, fingers interlaced, discussing a case, but Ashley couldn't imagine anything more natural. They had to talk about their relationship. She had to pull away. But not yet. "Where were they taking the gold?"

"Just as we thought—down past Mariscal Mountain and across the river." Logan paused, studying her. "What happened yesterday morning, Ashley? How did they get into your house?"

"Will came to my door and I let him in. Just to talk. And then it all came back to me, how I'd seen the drug deal and he'd thrown me into the river…" She couldn't help trembling at the memory. How she'd nearly panicked when she realized the truth. Taking a deep breath, she recounted everything for Logan. "And when I woke up, they'd taken me to Jimenez."

"Of course." Understanding dawned in his eyes. "But Will wasn't the one who drove off with you—that would have been too risky. So they sent another man to meet Will at your back window, and that's why there was no sign of forced entry. Or a struggle."

"No." She frowned. "I never had a chance."

"Smart on their part—" his lips tilted "—because I've seen what you can do."

Yes, he had. She smiled, too, despite it all. Then she wiggled her bandaged feet. "I never had a chance to put on my boots."

He raised an eyebrow, giving her a mock frown. "I noticed. I was thinking about firing you. Obviously you haven't been paying attention during training."

She laughed, but right behind the joy came a pang of grief. They'd talked about the case. There would be paperwork, suspects to question, reports to file. Maybe a trial. But they would still end up in two different cities, with two separate lives, and they hadn't had that conversation yet. Probably because thinking about it made her heart feel like it was being trampled by a bison.

She sighed, soul deep, and began to retract her fingers. Logan opened his hand, letting her pull back. "Don't."

Even in the hospital bed, covered by those starchy, thick, white sheets, she was beautiful. Letting her fingers slide away from his was the hardest thing Logan had ever done. It had to be her choice, but he couldn't give her up without at least telling her the truth. After all they'd been through, he owed it to her.

"Don't," he repeated, and her hand stopped, her fingers barely touching his. "Ashley, when I thought I'd lost you…when I thought you would die the way Sam had…" Water pooled in his eyes and he blinked it away. "I couldn't bear it that I'd never told you how I feel, how I care about you. I know we haven't known each other for long, and it doesn't make sense, but… I love you. More than I ever thought possible. It's like I've been missing something my whole life and…it's you."

There, he'd said it. Fragile heart held out for her to take or destroy. A great weight lifted off his chest, even though he had no idea how she'd respond. He knew she cared about him, but how much? Enough to find a way to be together?

Ashley's brown eyes went wide, her lips parting slightly. But when her hand slipped back into his, Logan's heart beat double time.

Her words were soft and he leaned closer to hear. "I thought I was going to die out there, the same way my brother did. But even being that close to the end, I never felt alone." Her voice hitched as she spoke and, after a brief pause, she continued, "I knew God was with me, and that no matter what, I'd spend eternity with Him. And I knew you were out there, searching for me, and that you wouldn't give up."

"We made a pretty good team, didn't we?" Her words hadn't exactly been what he'd wanted to hear, but he would still let her go. It might split his heart in two, but it had to be her choice. And he would still rejoice that she had found the path back to trusting the God he loved so much.

"Logan…" A tear slipped down her cheek and Logan's chest ached at what was coming. "I…" She sniffled as another tear broke loose.

"Shh," he said, unable to resist the urge to calm her, protect her, even from emotional pain. "It's okay, you don't have to say it. I understand." Or he would, someday. He hoped. He started to pull his hand away.

Ashley held on tightly. "No, that's not it." Her voice was muffled by the tears streaming down her cheeks. "I can't imagine life without you. I'm completely, madly in love with you, Ranger Logan Everett."

Logan couldn't contain the grin that broke out on his face. He wiped her cheek with his thumb. "But only people who don't like me use my last name."

"Except me." She smiled, blinking away the tears. "I love you, all of you, last name included."

Perhaps enough to make it her own one day? Logan didn't ask, but her eyes held the promise of the future.

She pulled her hand from his and reached up to lay it on his cheek. "Now, kiss me, please."

"Does that mean you're asking?" He leaned closer, until their faces were inches apart.

"Begging."

That was all he needed to hear.

EPILOGUE

Ashley stood by a window in the Chisos Lodge, staring out as puffy white clouds drifted high above the mountaintops. She couldn't have asked for a more spectacular day. It was April and the weather was gorgeous—past the rain and cold nights of winter, but not into the triple-digit temperatures of summer yet. Even after six months, she wasn't sure she'd ever become accustomed to the beauty of this place.

It probably should have been harder to leave her job as a federal agent and move to Big Bend. But after working here as a law-enforcement ranger, she could not imagine going back to Washington. Dick Barclay and Ed Chambers had been more than happy to give her the job. Special Agent in Charge Morton, while sad to lose her, had understood.

There was a noise behind her and Ashley turned to find a breathtakingly handsome man in a tuxedo enter the room.

"Logan Everett," she objected, "you're not supposed to see the bride before the wedding."

He paused, his gaze sweeping from the flowing hemline of her gown, past the simple, flattering neckline, to the pile of glossy brown curls on her head.

"I couldn't help it." He walked up to her and Ashley's heart raced at the nearness of him. "Ranger Thompson," he said breathlessly, "you are the most beautiful woman I've ever seen."

She smiled, taking in the love and admiration shining from his eyes. "You'll have to call me Ranger Everett soon."

"I can't imagine anything I'd like better. Maybe besides kissing you." He arched an eyebrow.

Her cheeks heated and she gave his arm a playful swat. "Don't you have somewhere else to be?"

"I'm going." He took a step back, but his eyes lingered. "Just wanted to make sure you were ready."

"I've never been more ready for anything in my life."

Logan's grin lit up his eyes. "Then let's get hitched, soon-to-be Ranger Everett."

And when Ashley stepped out into the bright Texas sunlight, her arm linked through her father's, and her heart full of God's goodness, she walked down the aisle toward Logan and the hope of a bright future before them.

* * * * *

WE HOPE YOU ENJOYED
THIS BOOK FROM

LOVE INSPIRED SUSPENSE
INSPIRATIONAL ROMANCE

Courage. Danger. Faith.

Find strength and determination in stories
of faith and love in the face of danger.

6 NEW BOOKS AVAILABLE EVERY MONTH!

*A wedding party is attacked in the Alaskan wilderness.
Can a K-9 trooper and his dog keep the bridesmaid
safe from the lurking danger?*

Read on for a sneak preview of
Alaskan Rescue *by Terri Reed in the new*
Alaska K-9 Unit *series from Love Inspired Suspense.*

A groan echoed in Ariel Potter's ears. Was someone hurt? She needed to help them.

She heard another moan and decided she was the source of the noise. The world seemed to spin. What was happening?

Somewhere in her mind, she realized she was being turned over onto a hard surface. Dull pain pounded the back of her head.

"Miss? Miss?"

A hand on her shoulder brought Ariel out of the foggy state engulfing her. Opening her eyelids proved to be a struggle. Snow fell from the sky. Then a hand shielded her face from the elements.

Her gaze passed across broad shoulders to a very handsome face beneath a helmet. Dark hair peeked out from the edge of the helmet and a pair of goggles hung from her neck. Who was this man?

The pull of sleep was hard to resist. She closed her eyes.

"Stay with me," the man murmured.

His voice coaxed her to do as he instructed, and she forced her eyes open.

Where was she?

Awareness of aches and pains screamed throughout her body, bringing the world into sharp focus. She was flat on her back and her head throbbed.

Ariel started to raise a hand to touch her head, but something was holding her arm down. She tried to sit up, and when she discovered she couldn't, she lifted her head to see why. Straps had been placed across her shoulders, her torso, hips and knees to keep her in place on a rescue basket.

"Hey, now, I need you to concentrate on staying awake."

That deep, rich voice brought her focus back to the moment. Memory flooded her on a wave of terror. The horror of rolling down the side of the cliff, hitting her head, landing in a bramble bush and the fear of moving that would take her plummeting to the bottom of the mountain. She must have gone in and out of consciousness before being rescued. She gasped with realization. "Someone pushed me!"

Don't miss
Alaskan Rescue *by Terri Reed,*
available wherever Love Inspired Suspense
books and ebooks are sold.

LoveInspired.com

LOVE INSPIRED

INSPIRATIONAL ROMANCE

UPLIFTING STORIES OF FAITH, FORGIVENESS AND HOPE.

Join our social communities to connect with other readers who share your love!

Sign up for the Love Inspired newsletter at **LoveInspired.com** to be the first to find out about upcoming titles, special promotions and exclusive content.

CONNECT WITH US AT:

Facebook.com/LoveInspiredBooks

Twitter.com/LoveInspiredBks

Facebook.com/groups/HarlequinConnection

LISOCIAL2020

HARLEQUIN

Heartfelt or thrilling, passionate or uplifting—Harlequin is more than just happily-ever-after.

With twelve different series to choose from and new books available every month, you are sure to find stories that will move you, uplift you, inspire and delight you.

SIGN UP FOR THE HARLEQUIN NEWSLETTER

Be the first to hear about great new reads and exciting offers!

Harlequin.com/newsletters